Flanders Point

ALSO BY JACQUIE GORDON

Give Me One Wish

Flanders Point

Jacquie Gordon

St. Martin's Press
New York

FLANDERS POINT. Copyright © 1997 by Jacquie Gordon. All rights reserved. Printed in the United States of America. No part of this book may be used or reproduced in any manner whatsoever without written permission except in the case of brief quotations embodied in critical articles or reviews. For information, address St. Martin's Press, 175 Fifth Avenue, New York, N.Y. 10010.

Design by Ellen R. Sasahara

Grateful acknowledgment is given for permission to reprint selections from the following authors and their published works:

E. E. Cummings: "it is so long since my heart has been with yours." Copyright 1926, 1954, © 1991 by the Trustees for the E. E. Cummings Trust. Copyright © 1985 by George James Firmage. Lines from "the moon looked into my window." Copyright 1926, 1954, © 1991 by the Trustees for the E. E. Cummings Trust. Copyright © 1985 by George James Firmage. Line from "come a little further—why be afraid—" Copyright 1931, © 1959, 1991 by the Trustees for the E. E. Cummings Trust. Copyright © 1979 by George James Firmage. Excerpt from Introduction to *New Poems* (from *Collected Poems*). Copyright 1938, © 1966, 1991 by the Trustees for the E. E. Cummings Trust, from *Complete Poems: 1904–1962* by E. E. Cummings, edited by George J. Firmage. Reprinted by permission of Liveright Publishing Corporation.

T. S. Eliot: Lines from *The Waste Land* in *Collected Poems 1909–1962* by T. S. Eliot. Copyright 1939 by Harcourt Brace & Company. Copyright © 1963, 1964 by T. S. Eliot. Reprinted by permission of the publisher and Faber and Faber Ltd., London.

Allen Ginsberg: Lines from *Howl* in *Collected Poems 1947–1980*. Copyright © 1955 by Allen Ginsberg. Reprinted by permission of HarperCollins Publishers, Inc.

Geoffrey Hartman: Lines from *Criticism in the Wilderness*. Copyright © 1980 by Yale University Press. Reprinted by permissions.

Haniel Long: Lines from a poem in *Lyric America: An Anthology of American Poetry (1630–1930)*, edited by Alfred Kreymborg. Coward McCann, Inc. 1930.

Plato: Lines from *Phaedrus* in *The Collected Dialogues of Plato*, edited by Edith Hamilton and Huntington Cairns, Bollingen Series LXXI. Copyright © 1961 by Princeton University Press. © renewed 1989. Used with permission.

Library of Congress Cataloging-in-Publication Data

Gordon, Jacquie.
    Flanders Point / Jacquie Gordon.
        p.   cm.
    ISBN 0-312-15531-X
    I.   Title.
PS3557.06677F58   1997
813'.54—dc21   96-54501
                                                        CIP

First Edition: July 1997

10   9   8   7   6   5   4   3   2   1

For Jim

Contents

$\mathcal{A}cknowledgments$

I cannot rest without acknowledging the friends and teachers who supported my hesitant beginnings.

Hilary Hinzmann and Angus Cameron, my mentors, whose comments on the manuscript were as sensitive as they were supportive. Bernard Mac-Donald, emeritus professor of English at Connecticut State University, who listened to my ideas, reminded me there is Eros in teaching as well as learning, and who gently encouraged me. Heinrich von Staden, professor of Classics at Yale University, for sharing his views on reading and the importance of the classical canon to modernity. Maureen Howard, author and visiting professor at Yale, for her tough-minded challenge to avoid any temptation toward sentimentality, as well as Elizabeth Wilson, assistant professor at Yale, who understood the controversial nature of the story and urged me ever forward. My sister, Francie Jalet-Miller, an editor whose critical work on the first draft both humbled and elated me. Dr. Edward Brennan, psychiatrist, who generously shared his understanding of student-teacher relationships and the teacher's role as "occupant." My agent, Molly Friedrich, whose humorous edge and blazing energy in all of our conversations provided just the right amount of literary adrenalin when the going was hard. This first novel, for all its flaws, owes much to these friends.

And finally, my editor at St. Martin's Press, Jennifer Weis, who was stalwart in her belief in the story I had to tell.

Nor can I forget the inspiration of Abelard and Héloïse, a theologian teacher and his student who fell in love in France in the twelfth century and who paid so dearly for their passion. In particular, I salute the tragic and formidable Héloïse, who revealed her woman's heart to the ages, as no other woman ever had, in carefully worded letters to Peter Abelard, her teacher and her lover.

A tranquillizing spirit presses now
On my corporeal frame, so wide appears
The vacancy between me and those days,
Which yet have such self-presence in my heart
That sometimes when I think of them I seem
Two consciousnesses—conscious of myself,
And of some other being.

—William Wordsworth,
The Two-Part Prelude of 1799

Flanders Point

Flanders Point

Haddam Academy lay beside the marshlands of an inlet formed when the last glacier pushed southward forty thousand years ago, ripped and tore at the land's edge, sheared off mountaintops, plowed out riverbeds, and carved up the rough Connecticut coast. For thirty thousand years the land lay under its icy grip. And when the crushing ice began its epic melt back to Greenland, it left behind ragged promontories, narrow coves, tidal salt marshes, and a great gorge that the sea rushed in to fill, creating Long Island Sound.

The glacier gave bird and fish and sea to the fisherman, but it laid a curse on the farmers who worked the Connecticut land. Great boulders lay half concealed in the shallow earth, shoved under by the scraping weight of the ice. The smaller rocks could be dug out, and lacy dry walls crisscrossed the miles of surging hills. But no matter how many a farmer dug out, there were more and larger stones that could only be left in place. They rose out of the fields like surfacing gray whales.

The seventy-foot sugar maples here were peculiar. Instead of trunks lifting gracefully from a tapered base of wide, spreading roots, they poked straight up through the ground, and grew skyward like so many top-heavy flagpoles. It was girdling roots. When the trees' young roots fingered out, they were blocked by the great buried stones, so they reversed themselves and grew back to the trees and circled the base of the trunks like a girdle. They wrapped so tightly the maples were eventually strangled by their own roots. Rarely would the trees die. Nature compensates, and though they might be the first to come down in a storm, maples are hardy and they endured. But they grew oddly. One side might fail to branch out or the leaves might be meager or a leader limb might take an eccentric twist. Such were the old maples on Flanders Point, a wild and beautiful spit of land across from Haddam Academy. But as unusual as were these giant trees, the giant houses were traditional—Colonial or Tudor with the old farmers' walls and split-rail fences tracking their land.

In the fall of 1955, the solitary figure of a young woman began to appear among the twisted branches, the uncombed fields, and the windy marshes. No matter what the weather, she was likely to be out, although no one knew who she was and on such a private place as Flanders Point, no one asked.

The Interview

CHARLOTTE HAD TO struggle with the iron ring handle that opened the heavy oak door into the foyer of Haddam Academy. The door reminded her of a dungeon but once the black ring was turned, the door swung wide and easy and the hall was full of sunlight. The building was quiet and seemed deserted and Charlotte was wondering if she had the right day when she saw a small older woman wearing a flowered cotton dress and black orthopedic shoes bend over to pick something up off the floor. Charlotte assumed she was a maid. She said, "Excuse me, could you tell me where I can find Miss Haddam's office?"

The woman drew her small frame up and said, "*I* am Miss Haddam."

"Oh . . . I'm here for my interview. My name is Charlotte Delafield."

"Aren't you early, my dear?"

Frumpy dress or not, this was a patrician voice addressing her.

"I didn't want to be late."

"Well, how nice. Come with me, then." And Charlotte followed her down a white stucco hall with thick wood moldings along the ceiling and a highly polished wide plank floor. The floor creaked with every step and Miss Haddam glanced over her shoulder and said cheerfully, "Pick up your feet, don't shuffle." Once settled in a small office, she asked Charlotte, "Shall we wait for your mother?"

"I came by myself," said Charlotte, watching the woman's wispy white hair drift around her face. Miss Haddam didn't seem surprised that she was alone but Charlotte felt some change in the room, an interest as Miss Haddam raised a blue-veined hand and pushed her hair into place with stiff little gestures. Charlotte felt as if the hand were a third person in the room, as if she should address the hand instead of Miss Haddam. There was no wedding ring and Charlotte had to pull her eyes away. She focused instead on what a pretty face Miss Haddam had, even though there was one long white whisker growing under her chin.

Perhaps it was just the woman's age, perhaps it was Haddam's reputation as being a small, selective girls' school or because Charlotte hadn't expected to meet Miss Haddam, let alone be interviewed by her. Whatever it was, Charlotte found the woman impressive but incongruous. Something didn't add up. Miss Haddam spoke with pride about her school but she sounded too defiant and energetic to be inhabiting such a frail and submissive body. Her left hand pushed at her hair again and again and her skin looked like ancient parchment with four curled, frozen fingers as delicate as an eagle's claw and just as sharp. Only the wrist moved. Something must have happened to that hand, thought Charlotte, when she suddenly heard Miss Haddam ask abruptly, "And why have you come to us . . . so late?"

Charlotte said, "I know it's unusual to apply for my junior year, but even two years at a school like Haddam would prepare me better for college, hopefully one of the Seven Sisters."

Miss Haddam looked at her in silence, though not unkindly, and not moving the faded blue eyes that could still make a student squirm she said, "And what are the other reasons?"

Maybe if Charlotte had been there with her mother, that question would neither have been asked that way nor answered in quite the same way, but Charlotte was alone and said, "Well, I don't join in the football games and the cheerleading and the girls' clubs and all that kind of thing at the high school, and I care about getting A's and I ride a bike to school and no one else does. They have cars and they drive their friends, or maybe they drive their parents' cars, I'm not sure, but they think I'm odd. I don't feel odd, but I don't think I belong at such a big high school." Right after she said it Charlotte thought how trivial it sounded, and how stupid it was to be honest. She sounded like a social misfit and had just ruined her chances. Thank God she hadn't gone on. There was a long silence, which Charlotte was afraid to fill with any words, so she studied the soft brown spots on Miss Haddam's arms, wondering if they were giant freckles or what and Miss Haddam said simply, "I think you might like it here." And the interview was over. No tour of the school was offered but Charlotte didn't think Miss Haddam could manage the stone steps that wound up and around the buildings on the hill. Charlotte didn't mind. She'd just been accepted.

She picked up a brochure about the school from the hall table, and the secretary, who was almost as old as Miss Haddam but looked a little spiffier, showed her out the dungeon door. At the end of the long stone walk that led to the road, Charlotte turned around and looked back. Behind the building she'd just left, and at the bottom of a steep rocky hill lay Flanders Cove, calm and sleepy with water the glossy brown color of tarnished silver. The main gray clapboard and stone building they called Dovecote merged like camouflage into the trunks of towering old elms and there were four small white clapboard houses settled around it like four white goslings nested around a gray mother goose. She thought to herself, It's not fancy at all, in fact it's almost drab. No Georgian brick with white columns, no domes, no bell towers, no tree-lined driveways, not even any playing fields that she could see. She liked how beautiful it was in a plain, brown-wrapper kind of way. No makeup, thought Charlotte, just like old Miss Haddam and me. But the Gothic details, the small gargoyles under the corners of the roof and the ornate carved banisters on the terraces, were like something from Edgar Allan Poe. She went back and asked the secretary, "Do you mind if I walk around a little?"

The secretary said it was fine. Charlotte saw another house through the woods. This *was* grand, with four white pillars across the front. A small sign on the walk said LITTLE HOUSE. Miss Haddam lived there but the house needed painting and the windows needed washing. Charlotte thought it was a little sad and old. She walked back to the main building on a path that wound through high bush blueberries, leggy mountain laurels, junipers, and gnarled Henry lilacs. Everything was a little overgrown and scrubby like a wooded glen in *Grimms' Fairy Tales*, where a toad prince might live through the years, biding his time, waiting for his kiss. When she got back, she was startled to look up and see an old man with one arm standing on the roof watching her. Shaking off the feeling that she was Nancy Drew, she hurried up the walk to the road and to the bus stop, reading the brochure while she waited. One paragraph caught her eye.

Frequently, the whole structure of personality that a student is trying to make is collapsing under some unrecognized pressure. A change of environment, with a systematic strengthening of the weak points, may make possible a successful return to the original sense of self.

Apparently it hadn't been a mistake to admit that she was having some problems fitting in.

It's been said you can't walk away from yourself, that wherever you go, you take your troubles with you, but perhaps youth is exempt for a time because the soul hasn't set and family troubles may still be shed and though Charlotte wasn't sure about this, she was hopeful and she had to take a chance. Miss Haddam may have understood that the timing was critical when Charlotte walked into her office that day in June, so earnest and unhappy and intent on changing her life. She couldn't remember the last time a student had come alone and when she said to Charlotte that she'd like the school, she was right. Charlotte found her starting point at Haddam Academy. She believed she came into her existence there, which is not to say there was anything easy about it. And though Charlotte knew it wasn't the beginning of her story, it was where she would choose to start.

Charlotte hadn't told Miss Haddam the other reasons for transferring. Everything seemed out of place. She'd lived for the last eight years in a dreary, run-down green house on the wrong side of an affluent, upper-middle-class town, part of the "gold coast" of Connecticut, and it made her ashamed of her family and that made her ashamed of herself. But that's not the same as humble. You have to have pride to be ashamed, even if it's false pride, and Charlotte clothed herself in it. At the high school she didn't miss the irony of the way she retained a perverse ability to look down on the classmates who looked down on her, like the popular Italian girl whose father owned the bar where Charlotte's father used to go and drink. She saw the foolishness of her position, but she seemed bound to uphold it. In this she was like her father. He too looked down on the patrons of the bar, even though he was one of them. He didn't see it that way, and Charlotte would have agreed, and so would the patrons at the bar if they'd known that when he wasn't drinking too much there, he was drinking too much at the Harvard

Club. Charlotte's brother, Max, once said, "Charlotte, stop making excuses for him. A drunk is a drunk." But Charlotte made excuses for him even though Max's comments colored her thoughts a little.

It should be added that because of the social role in which she found herself in those days before Haddam Academy, that of observant outsider, she'd developed a keen aesthetic sense that saw glory in the smallest details of the local landscape. And because she held intercourse with nature, not people, her sense of beauty included no awareness of her own. For Charlotte was not the bookish, bland outline of a girl she thought she was. She was pretty. Her father sometimes said she looked fetching, but she'd always thought it was a term of consolation for the plain. For her aloof manner held people at a distance, even at Haddam—until she smiled, that is. Smiles have different quirky shapes and Charlotte's turned neither up nor down but swept across her face in wide, balanced horizontal lines that revealed, as the word implies, a new horizon. And this sudden smile could catch at the heart as if a joyful soul had suddenly emerged from its own shadow for the first time. But Charlotte had never seen this smile. There were no photographs. There was no mirror in her room at home and she wasn't given to mirror watching in any event. All this, however, was about to change.

She entered the new school that fall. She was five feet tall. She'd been the tiniest girl at Eastport High, a nerd. But by the end of her first year at Haddam, she'd grown six inches. When her parents' divorce was final, a week before her senior year began, her mother and sisters moved to Washington, DC. Charlotte refused to go. She knew where she belonged and it was at the school called Haddam. But it was not a boarding school, so living arrangements would be a problem. Margaret Chase, the new headmistress, lived on Flanders Point, and she told Charlotte's mother not to worry, she'd work something out. Mrs. Chase couldn't afford to lose a student, not even one.

The School and the Teacher

When Brian Parton was offered the job of head of the English department at Haddam in 1957, he was warned the school had fallen on hard times. Enrollment was down and the founding headmistress was eighty. He thought of saying no. Whenever someone asked Brian Parton to do something, his first impulse was to say no. Long before he was an English teacher, even as a child, he'd been a master at the self-chosen task. But because he never could say no to anyone, because the impulse to say no died on his lips, with an internal sigh he usually did what he was asked. And then he ended up glad he hadn't said no. Over the years, though passive by nature, he saw himself as a rather optimistic creature, made so from the many pleasant surprises life had given him. Maybe he'd be surprised again, and he was persuaded by the new headmistress, Margaret Chase, to take the job. She was a widowed Bryn Mawr graduate who, though she'd never been a headmistress before, had served on local school boards, and she talked about needing his help to get the school back on its feet. This was her second year at Haddam and she'd been directed by old Miss Haddam to hire new teachers. His appointment was part of that effort, and though Brian knew the English "department" at Haddam consisted of only one other teacher in the middle school, he was hopeful.

He'd taught for a year at a prosperous but stuffy boys' boarding school where he was always asked to do things he didn't like: chaperoning class trips, coaching the swim team, tutoring the reluctant, arranging detentions, monitoring evening study halls, so a small country day school for girls suited him fine. The word *progressive* in Haddam's description was encouraging, though he had yet to learn exactly what it meant, and he liked the thought of teaching girls. And best of all, because it was a day school, his evenings would be his own. He could reclaim his life and he'd have time to write. The board of trustees found him a garage apartment on a large Tudor estate on Flanders Point. There was a private beach behind the main house, which meant he could swim every day late into the fall. It was more than he'd hoped for. He settled in. But when the school began, one of the first things the headmistress asked him to do was something he didn't like. Of course he said yes.

The same day, Charlotte moved to Flanders Point, where she was to live with the Macready family, who lived near the headmistress and a mile from Brian Parton's apartment. Mrs. Macready was pregnant with her fifth child and had told Margaret Chase that she needed a mother's helper. Proceeding cautiously, Margaret went to the house to see what sort of housekeeper Mrs. Macready was and what she had in mind for help. She met the children: an eight-year-old boy, twin girls, who were four, and a two-year-old. After a few minutes of small talk, Margaret said to Mrs. Macready, "We have a senior who needs to board this year. If you have the room, this is ideal. She comes from a large family herself." So Charlotte's situation was settled.

Charlotte was still living in her family's empty house, which had just been sold. She was relieved and confident that this would work well. She'd grown up helping her mother take care of her three little sisters and she'd be close to school. It was like a miniature version of her own family. But the day she moved in she knew there was one difference. Her house had always been an appalling mess. The Macreadys' was immaculate, though oddly, the bedrooms were downstairs and the living room, dining room, and kitchen were upstairs. The house was built on the edge of the great salt marsh instead of on the water, like most of the houses on Flanders Point, but there was a striking view of the sound from the second floor, and the builders had taken advantage of it. Charlotte's room was by the garage and had prisonlike cinder-block walls and a cement floor but it was set apart from the rest of the house and she liked that. On the second night of her stay there, Mrs. Macready, who seemed a quiet, worried woman, wasn't feeling well and Mr. Macready invited

Charlotte to the living room to talk while he had a bourbon.

His first question surprised her. "Are you Catholic?"

"No, Episcopalian."

"I'll want the children to say grace before supper, I'll teach it to you, and their prayers every night. We are Catholic, of course. Elite Catholics."

Mr. Macready seemed to want a response but Charlotte wasn't going to ask what that meant. He stood up as if it might fill the silence and said, "Look at this view."

"It's very nice," she said.

"Where do you think you might go to college?"

"I'd apply to Harvard if they took women, but they don't, of course, so I'm applying to Radcliffe," she said, trying to sound casual.

"Really—Princeton beat Harvard last year."

"What do you mean?"

"Princeton football. I played varsity. We had a winning team the year I played." Charlotte didn't like all this name-dropping. "Here," he said, "have a look." He sat down and opened an album on the coffee table. There were pictures of him in his uniform with different girls in each picture. She didn't see Mrs. Macready in any of the pictures and wondered how old he was. He was busy turning pages, pointing here and there, and his warm, ripe breath was too close for comfort and reminded her of her father's breath. The sweet liquor smell she hated.

Thank God he was interested only in the pictures of himself and not her. And when he excused her, she went downstairs to spend her first nervous night—as quiet as she could be—in another family's house.

Since Charlotte had no way to get to school, the new headmistress, Margaret Chase, arranged for her to ride with the English teacher, Brian Parton. He didn't pick her up at the Macreadys', of course. She walked to a split-rail fence by a wide orchard not far from his house. Brian told Mrs. Chase he didn't mind driving a student to school since it was on his way, but this was an invasion of his privacy. The first morning, as soon as his car went around the bend, he saw her there, watching for him. And each morning after that the sight of this thin, quiet girl balanced on the split-rail fence irritated him. He wasn't sure why. He wasn't late but she made him feel that he was. She got in and flung her thick brown hair back as if she was snapping a cape for his attention. She didn't talk and he was glad. Neither did he. He wasn't nice to her and he felt guilty, but it didn't make him any nicer.

Charlotte didn't mind at first. When on that first day his blue Buick had come tearing around the bend, sliding to a stop on the sandy cove road, she was surprised. He seemed to be in a hurry. It was the same every morning. She didn't dare ask him why he drove the way he did, shifting gears with a grave solemnity that contradicted the exciting way he floored the gas pedal, but it reminded her of the way her brother Max drove, as if Mr. Parton took some pleasure in abusing his car. And she felt like laughing when they pulled up at school and he stepped out of the car, drawing himself to an imposing six feet as if now he was ready to be the proper teacher of English at the proper Haddam Academy. He'd slam the car door as if to say, "Thank God that's over." But Charlotte knew something that no one else did. That he was not entirely proper and that was exciting. She waited for that blue Buick every morning as if it might take her somewhere she had never been. Somewhere she wanted to go. And Brian Parton was set against her. In fact, he couldn't wait to get her out of his car.

Haddam Academy was across the cove from Flanders Point. It was known in the education community as the "Haddam experiment"—a progressive girls' school, poor in endowment, rich in ideals. It's doubtful that Miss Haddam had ever heard the term "capital campaign" and no effort was made to remind the parents of annual giving. Records were kept in spiral notebooks in pencil and mixed in with orders for new textbooks. Maude Potter, a senior, had been working in the office one day and seen a budget for the teacher's salaries written on the back of a manila envelope. They made eight hundred dollars a year. Tuition bills were often late in being sent, and at times a parent's failure to send a check was forgotten over the summer. The school's yearbook was called *High Tide* but the budget might have been called "ebb tide." There was no money. Haddam was pure. Haddam was all heart.

The reason the academic community didn't sneer at the idea of one woman and her experimental school was because of the colleges that accepted Haddam girls. Miss Haddam was fond of telling new teachers the story about the English mother who was looking for the best school to prepare her daughter for Radcliffe. The dean of Radcliffe, in an informal interview with the mother, had said, "If you want your daughter to learn about New England, you should send your daughter to a school in Boston. If you want her to learn about government and politics, you might consider a school in Washington, DC. But if you want your daughter to be well educated, you should send her to a school in a little town on the coast of Connecticut called Haddam. From this school, the girl will be able to get into Radcliffe." The mother had sent her daughter to Haddam and she went to Radcliffe. And the mother sent Miss Haddam a letter telling her the story.

Miss Haddam had no interest in teaching the girls how to cook, or how to look polished, well shod, made-up, furry, or fashionable. This was no finishing school. The idea that a young woman was finished when she graduated from prep school was enough to make Miss Haddam gag. The girls took shop. They learned to debate, to read music, to argue about ethics in student court. The most Miss Haddam felt she could do for her girls was teach them to think for themselves. She was not interested in conformists (except in the area of good manners), and when the new headmistress had hired Brian Parton, Miss Haddam eventually approved, though she hesitated at first to bring in another male teacher. Haddam was a woman's place and this male was young and single. When she asked him in her blunt way what he thought he had to offer the Haddam girls, he overlooked the brittle tone and said, "I won't hold out the promise of Proust before puberty. It's a love of literature I'd like to teach, and critical thinking." She liked his answer.

But the change in headmistresses and the new English teacher were not the only things new at Haddam, just the most visible. Coming in with the insistent wind from the cove was something else, an impatience, a challenge, a simmer of rebellion. It hadn't been identified by the faculty yet or noticed by anyone. Well, noticed, perhaps, but no teacher wanted to give legitimacy to the girls' new assertiveness by naming it. It was unpredictable. It was subtle. A different kind of laughter when material they were reading in English contained the slightest hint of sexuality. Wry glances if the word *virgin* came up. More girls snuck cigarettes in the woods. The push for bare legs and lipstick. An insistence from Charlotte, the editor of the yearbook, that one page be devoted to their "SUPPRESSED DESIRES" because, they complained, they had to suppress so many. There were *not* so many, but the girls' desires were growing. They demanded that boys from a neighboring prep school be cast in the school plays instead of all girls. Miss Haddam refused. The girls didn't see anything so radical about their idea and they met on the cove wall, where the tide rose and the sun hit the water like hammered silver, and they planned to boycott classes for a day, but then they lost their nerve. Charlotte heard from an underclassman that her class was known as a problem class. The upper school started each day singing Bach chorales in assembly, and ended each assembly with the words from Micah, "What doth the Lord require of thee, but to do justly, to love mercy, and to walk humbly with thy God."

The seniors were increasingly less humble.

Classes Begin

THE FIRST DAY, they'd studied him briefly in assembly, where he stood motionless in a neatly pressed light gray suit. Brian Parton looked straight ahead, though he must have been aware of the turning of heads during the singing of a Bach chorale. When the seniors walked into his class as quiet and polite as could be, there was a moment of silence and they just stood there.

"You can sit. The three books on your desks will be the texts. The double volume is American writers and poets, and the thick blue one, Victorian writers."

Maude said, "We studied the Victorians last year."

"We'll do them again. But don't worry. We won't make the usual forced march through the nineteenth and twentieth century. I'll pick and choose." He noticed three of the girls slouched back in what he suspected was un-Haddam-like posture. He said, "Let me set one rule for this class. There'll be no rules. You're five. I'm one. That's more than ideal—it's unheard of. We can have a dialogue—a seminar." He paused, feeling their mood. "If I ever seem unclear in class, interrupt me and ask what I mean. Perhaps I'll discover I don't know what I mean, but either way, I'll clarify." They glanced at one another and he wasn't sure if he was seeing smiles or smirks.

"Interrupt without raising our hand?" asked Charlotte.

"Yes, if it's me. I'd look less favorably on your interrupting each other."

"Oh, don't worry about that," said Charlotte. "Courtesy is part of the culture here."

"Oh? I'd like to hear about it."

"About what?" she asked.

"About Haddam. Every school has its own character. I've read the brochure. I've met Miss Haddam. What do *you* think of your school?"

Dana said, "It's a small, closely knit school with too many rules."

"I was told there were no rules."

Maude said, "Nothing's written down. They're understandings."

"Like what?"

"Respect for teachers," she said. "We stand up when they come into the room and don't sit until the teacher does."

"You don't need to stand up for me."

Theo said, "It's a reflex."

"I don't sit much, so you may want to."

Dana said, "You might say this is a 'school for the special case.' "

Charlotte turned to Dana. "Where'd you get that?"

"Miss Haddam, a couple years ago. We're a school for normal misfits."

"I never heard that. It sounds terrible."

"Well, normal misfits is my word."

"Oh," said Charlotte. "Maybe you should get rid of it."

"We're not supposed to limit ourselves because we're women," said Maude. "No cooking is taught here, thank goodness."

Brian raised his eyebrows. "It would seem to me learning to cook is part of survival and the dominion of all." He swiveled. "How's the school spirit?"

Cora said, "We play field hockey with other schools, but we don't get pumped up. Alumnae come back for the Christmas pageant and sing 'Lo, How a Rose e're Blooming' along with us, and they cry their eyes out. That's about it."

There was silence. "Anything else?" said Brian.

Theo said, "Haddam is egalitarian in theory but elitist in practice."

"How so?" said Brian.

"In assembly last year, Miss Haddam suggested we take summer jobs like checking out groceries in a Gristede's or being a belt turner in a Ford factory, so we'd know what it was like to live like other people. That seems to imply that *we* aren't."

"Perhaps," said Brian, appalled.

Maude, whose mother taught in the lower school, bristled. "I don't remember that talk."

"I do," said Charlotte, "because I checked out groceries last summer. I had to."

"What did you learn?" asked Brian.

"The eating habits of strangers."

"Good for you," said Brian. Charlotte was interested in this discussion. She'd never given any thought to elitism at Haddam or anywhere else. Thinking was something Charlotte had yet to learn.

Dana said, "I'd add one other thing. We all have to learn to read music. Music is the soul of Haddam."

Actually, there were two sounds Brian identified from the beginning. Music was one and laughter was the other. And the reason they stood out was because they were set so clearly against the third sound—silence. Silence was treasured, from the library to the lab. The school did have playing fields, but by design, they were a mile away from the school. One of the teachers had said to Brian the first day, "You've come to our haven, I see."

From the beginning he felt a certain otherness that he liked. And a certain worry. There were supposed to be 150 students this year. He'd counted eighty the first day and there were only five seniors. Margaret Chase had said she'd get the school back on its feet and he'd be a shot of adrenaline. Haddam didn't need adrenaline. It needed a blood transfusion, or, barring that, a miracle.

And while he settled in and observed his surroundings, he was also being observed. The seniors quickly marked how different Brian Parton was from the Latin teacher, Dr. Dierig. Dr. Dierig was taller than Brian but thin and gangly and his suits hung on him. Dr. Dierig slouched so low in his chair, he almost went horizontal, with his legs crossed, his free foot swinging, and his hands in his pants pockets. They wondered he didn't slide off the chair onto the floor. Brian Parton stood, book in hand, roaming the room. Sometimes he jiggled a piece of chalk in his hand and moved in front of them in a smooth lateral pacing like an impatient, hungry cat. When he turned around in class, they all noticed his athletic shoulders and the strong, broad back that tugged at the center seam of his jacket. The girls found Dr. Dierig cozy, affectionate, and avuncular. But *virile* was the word Theo used for Mr. Parton. Dana just called him a hunk. Brian would have been shocked. He'd always been called a brain.

Dr. Dierig was also a flirt. They knew how to charm him. No one seemed to charm Brian, but Dana claimed he was on the edge of something, some tantalizing hint of possibility, though Charlotte always said to her, "Dana, you think that about anything that wears pants." Brian was moody in class, a little tense, stating an opinion and then stating an opposing one in the next breath. No one knew his position on anything. Of course, it was a fine approach for a teacher if critical thinking was what he wanted to teach, but what Brian hadn't thought of was that by never letting the girls know what he was thinking, they wanted to know what he thought about everything, and "getting into Brian" was a new focus. And there was this other little thing: whenever he made eye contact, his color rose and he looked away. They all saw the blush. That was what did it.

Brian Parton's Car

After a week of driving to school with Brian Parton, Charlotte knew he didn't like it. Maybe he didn't like her. Neither talked, and with each day of difficult silence she wondered more about him. He was so upbeat in class, but he was a different person in the car. Prickly. Going home she took a town bus that let her off near the Flanders Point gatehouse. She was glad he didn't drive her home. At least in the morning they could pretend they were half asleep. But Charlotte was wide awake, and she thought he was too.

One rainy morning when he picked her up at the fence, Charlotte said, "You don't like driving me to school, do you?"

"I don't mind at all," he said, without looking over. Charlotte thought he looked a little annoyed.

"You don't have to lie," she said. "I don't blame you. I was thinking about it. Peter Macready comes into the kitchen in the morning and I'm sitting like a slug staring at the Rice Krispies, and I'm never ready for him. But it's *his* kitchen." Her pause was met with grim silence. "This is your car."

"I said I don't mind."

Charlotte was afraid her voice would tremble, but she said, "I know and I don't believe you, but it's okay. I don't think I've ever said thank you. So I'm saying it now. Thank you for every morning." He nodded but still didn't say anything and Charlotte felt worse. He wasn't easy to cheer up.

Brian was off balance all day. She wasn't shy. No one shy could be so brutal with the truth. In class the girls struggled with Tennyson's "Crossing the Bar," and Brian looked at Charlotte several times but she wouldn't look at him. What had he failed to do? Talk? He didn't like calling attention to himself and he didn't like to let people down. He'd just done both, it seemed. He also didn't take criticism well, especially from an eighteen-year-old girl, and it was hard not to set his heart against her. He decided to make more of an effort. She was a major irritant, but in a school so small he couldn't just flick her off . . . damn it to hell.

The next morning in a sort of apology he said, "Charlotte, my silence is an engine that runs rough in the morning, not annoyance at you."

Out of the corner of his eye, he saw her hopeful look in his direction. She was so gullible. She said, "I just thought maybe you'd rather drive by yourself. Just 'cause I like it doesn't mean you have to."

He said, "Just because I'm mute in the morning doesn't mean you have to be." And to his surprise, the silence was a little lighter. After that, Charlotte tried to talk.

She went for a walk every day after school before she gave the children supper, and made up dialogues with Mr. Parton. Only the sight of the geese beating their way into a dusky sky toward the south stopped her thoughts. Their long, undulating line, their calls, and the rhythmic sound of their wings spilling the air were more satisfying than her imaginary conversation, and she listened.

But in his car, her mind was a blank again. He'd invited her to talk and she couldn't think of anything to say. The ride was turning into ten minutes of humiliation. One afternoon she grabbed a three-by-five card and scribbled down a thought she had about Whitman. Maybe if she could memorize an opening thought, she'd be able to get started. She went upstairs to make the soft-boiled eggs for the little ones' supper. When a sudden thought about Whitman came into her head, she wrote it on a paper towel. So that was how she started. She copied two topic sentences on the three-by-five cards and memorized them.

He seemed resistant at first, he didn't smile, didn't look over at her. But then, after a few hesitant tries that made her feel like a bird flopping around with stunted wings, they talked—for at least part of the ride.

Then one day when she got in the car she said, "Was Whitman queer?"

To her surprise he let out a small laugh before turning serious. "Well, the accusations were there. He claimed six illegitimate children, but no one identified any. Why do you ask?"

"In *Song of Myself*, he seems to be talking about male love—not female love."

"I'm not sure I agree. Though there's a certain virility. Remember, Whitman was reclaiming the sensual in his poetry. That's why he was so controversial. He says himself, 'I believe in the flesh and in the appetites.' He didn't say abnormal appetites."

"He didn't exclude them, though."

"Read the 'Calamus' poems. Those are the ones critics point to as homosexual." Out of the corner of his eye he saw her open her notebook and write it down. She was always writing things down. He looked over. "But sex was a taboo subject back then. He was fired from a government job when they found out he was the notorious poet who wrote *Leaves of Grass*.

"Why?"

"He was accused of obscenity."

"Sort of an overreaction, don't you think?"

"Not for then. Words like *copulation, flesh, genitals, pulse, passion, lust* weren't the currency of the day." Brian paused a minute, wondering if he'd said too much, but Charlotte seemed to be waiting for more. Misreading her silence he went on, "If he'd have written about female sexuality, he would have been tarred and feathered." Brian thought he heard a slight intake of breath, and enjoying himself, he said, "Women in those days were not thought to have a sex life."

Charlotte was startled. This was amazing coming from him.

"He states the case himself in the poem, in the lines, 'Through me forbidden voices, voices of sexes and lusts, voices veiled and I remove the veil.' "

"You remember the exact words?" said Charlotte.

"I was reading it last night."

"So was I. Do you know the whole thing?"

"Just what strikes me."

"I was thinking of doing my poetry paper on him, but maybe I shouldn't."

"Don't worry. He's safe."

But Charlotte was shaken. She decided to be a little more careful. How could he speak of such things? But it made her feel safe that nothing fazed him.

Brian found he liked talking to Charlotte. She was like a tabula rasa, but even so she had strong opinions and he liked upsetting them. Then one morning in late October she was mute again, and he wondered what was up. The next morning again, silence. Suddenly she said, "How can you stand to go swimming in the cove in October? Isn't the water freezing?"

He looked over at her. "How do you know about that?"

"I took the Macreadys' little boy, Peter, for a walk along the sand flats. I saw you."

Brian was crisp. "I get sleepy in the afternoon. The shock of the water reminds me that now is not the time for sleep."

"How long will you do it?"

"Maybe all winter." That ought to shut her up.

He looked over and she was spellbound. The way her eyes were fastened on his face touched him. As she looked quickly away he scowled, surprised to see he'd just let the Buick drift over the center line. He swerved back hard.

When Charlotte went to the boathouse porch that day she gave her lunch to Theo and didn't join in the seniors' discussion about Brian. She watched the way the wind rippled the hems of their skirts. She didn't even hear the girls talking. There was some new energy in her bones and she thought of Walt Whitman singing the body electric. Was this what Whitman was writing about?

The fourth week of school, Brian Parton had lunch with the Latin teacher, Hans Dierig. He was the only other man on campus except for Jimmy, the one-armed handyman. They walked to Dovecote together, and the sky was silver blue, hinting of winter, and seagulls called as they talked. Brian asked Hans about Miss Haddam.

"How old is she, anyway?"

"About eighty."

"Was she ever married?"

"No. But she was the first woman graduate of MIT."

"Was she—"

"No, no, she married her school instead of a man."

"The seniors tell me the school has no rules."

"Oh, there's rules. The girls aren't allowed to wear makeup. No lipstick. No nail polish. Their knees have to be covered, lisle stockings worn during the muddy months, flat shoes only, permanents not permitted."

"I'd hardly call that progressive."

"Miss Haddam never calls the school progressive. But she doesn't approve of artifice of any kind."

"Pardon me, but it sounds like what she doesn't approve of is sex," said Brian.

Hans smiled. "That's probably true."

"Why is the senior class so small?"

"Four years ago when they were ninth graders there were rumors the school was closing—and there was a large defection. These are the diehards."

"There's something else. What do you mean when you call the seniors *mein Kleine Backfisch?*"

Dr. Dierig stroked his gray mustache. "It means teenage girl—the 'little vixens.' "

"Are they?"

"They're usually up to something. This class is very provocative."

Brian was reserved but there was nothing dull about him. He had wiry brown hair and navy blue eyes under prominent eyebrows that balanced a wide jaw. He thought he should like his face but his cheeks were too jowly, like they were storing food for the winter. They made his lips look a bit deflated. The seniors said he stored extra words in his cheeks because he knew so many his brain wouldn't hold them all. He would have preferred a lean and hungry look to the softness of his jawline, and maybe because of it he was careful about his appearance, his posture, his nails, his clothes. If he got sloppy, he'd look like an ignorant bear hunter from the north. He always polished his shoes. But his athletic build belied the aloof, private, critical, and unbending demeanor of a man of external calm and smooth bearing. He'd been a competitive swimmer. Brian was drawn to water, any water, but especially the ocean. He didn't know why. People just were, he supposed. But it was more intense with Brian. He had no wish to walk on the shore, sit on the sand, or ponder the horizon and the nature of the sea. He wanted none of it.

To be in the water, under it, exerting and immersing himself as if he had gills as well as lungs, water the colder the better, deep water a hundred feet from his bed was what he wanted. He made contact with some neglected part of himself, a diffuse ritual communion with the element that renewed him. And when he didn't swim for more than a day or two, his discomfort was real. Some negative energy pulled him off balance and his calm began to unravel.

He wasn't used to being the center of attention. Because he always thought of himself as marginal he was well versed in the response of no response, but he was secretly embarrassed to find he liked causing the stir and he was convinced the seniors' eyes were full of overt invitation they didn't mean. At first he thought it was funny and he had no sexual thoughts about them. He was twenty-eight and they were all so young. But as he got to know them, they didn't seem so young, just youngish. And driving home one day in October, he was surprised to find himself going through a kind of erotic inventory. But once he walked in the door to his apartment, erotic thoughts were forgotten. More difficult was how he cared about his students. Though staunch and unapproachable, Brian had a heart and it took some effort to conceal it.

Trying to Save the School

PROSPECTIVE PARENTS AND students were trooping through the school in record numbers that fall. The faculty was thrilled. Hans was overheard saying, "Mrs. Chase knows people all over New England, it seems," and seniors gave spirited if irreverent tours. But Margaret Chase cringed every time Miss Haddam doddered past in her chunky black shoes and trident cane. She took Hans aside.

"Look, Hans, I need you to take charge of being sure that Miss Haddam is either in her office—sitting—or at home—sitting. Seated, she's magisterial, but when she walks around campus, she looks like she'd fold up in a heap of crumbly bones if anyone so much as sneezed. Parents are going to think the school's about to fold too. We have yet to quiet *that* rumor."

"Keep her seated?" He laughed. "I hear she even sleeps standing up. How would you feel about my getting the seniors to help on this?"

"Whatever works," said Mrs. Chase. "If they're in on the effort, they'll behave and they'll make my job look easy. They're the ones who sell the school."

"Even if they have to be pulled out of class."

"If we don't do something, there will be no classes to pull them out of."

"Is it that serious?"

"I can't make payroll past December. Thirty-five students didn't return and some didn't even let us know."

"I wondered. That's a lot."

The seniors loved the aging headmistress and relished a minor deception. If Dana was called to sit with her, she played Miss Haddam oboe solos. Charlotte sorted old school pictures that only Miss Haddam knew. Theo pretended she was about to have a nervous breakdown because of her father's philandering. Cora said she needed remedial reading help (which she did as she struggled with a suspected learning disability), and Maude claimed to be writing a book on the McCarthy hearings. And though underclassmen couldn't figure out why in the middle of class they saw loose seniors floating down the stone steps on the way to Miss Haddam's while parents got the treatment, everyone was happy. Miss Haddam felt needed (though she told Hans she knew what was going on), Mrs. Chase relaxed, and the girls felt wonderfully conspiratorial. So, as the seniors saw it, two projects took precedence that fall—saving Haddam and tormenting Brian. He was so eminently tormentable, so nonreactive, yet so perpetually crimson. They left lipstick kisses on his blackboard, risqué limericks in his textbook, love poems under the windshield wiper of his Buick, wrinkled bras in his desk drawer, stockings in his raincoat pocket, anything they could think of that would embarrass him. To their annoyance, they never managed to be around when he discovered the small leavings, though Dana was endlessly creative, and they never got caught. Except once. Mrs. Chase was giving a tour one afternoon when classes were over and the girls were up at the hockey field. They'd stuffed one of their bras and fastened it to the back of his chair in the English room. Mrs. Chase walked in backward, talking as she stepped into the room, and stopped mid-sentence when she saw the parents staring at Brian's desk. She turned around and saw the mute, white shape stretched around the back of his chair, and as she smiled tightly, saw the word *surprise* written in big letters on the board. She stammered a bit before saying, "This is usually the English room but as you can see, our senior class is busy inventing reasons to be suspended." The entire class was put on probation. But no one took it seriously. This was one year no one would be expelled.

So that fall, silence was less cherished. And gray gulls flying over Dovecote looking for leftover lunch bags on the sea wall could hardly make a dive because the school, though wounded and limping, was humming with activity.

Brian was put on the faculty advisory board in November. When he asked Hans why, Hans said, "The founding principles here are *veritas* and *poēticēs*. The written arts are core, so you're central."

"But what about MIT and science?"

Hans shrugged. "It's our weakest department. But don't worry. The board never meets."

"How come?"

"We don't decide anything. Miss Haddam does."

"Not Margaret Chase?"

"Not quite yet," said Hans. "By the way, have you met Hazel Pierce?"

Brian said, "No. She's like a phantom," and Hans made no further comment. But the very next day, a faculty meeting was called. Brian was annoyed. He wanted to teach, not advise. And as if to confirm his fears, Mrs. Chase stopped by his apartment unannounced the night before the meeting. Brian was barefoot, didn't want company, and resented her dropping in unannounced. Mrs. Chase looked around and said, "I'd like your opinion on this booklet Miss Haddam wrote last year. Call me later and tell me if you think we should use it."

"What's the problem?" he said.

"It's . . . a little defensive. There were rumors about the school closing. I don't think this helps."

"Who gets it?"

"Prospective parents, but I don't give it out. It was printed just after we incorporated."

"All right, Mrs. Chase."

"Call me Margaret," she said, and left awkwardly. Brian knew he should have asked her to stay and talk but he was cooking a pot of brussel sprouts and the apartment stank. Besides, he hadn't eaten and he was hungry. He read the brochure over his brussel sprouts, wishing he had a thick lamb chop to go with them, but it was the end of the month and he was broke. He had no trouble finding problems with the brochure. The foreword said: "Haddam Academy is gratefully aware of the solidity of its reputation. Its incorporation now rises to defy rumors of the School's evaporation."

That would have to go. He wondered what unruly baggage lay behind the rumors. On another page, Miss Haddam wrote about why she'd begun her own school: "It occurred to me that I only knew the best, the cream of Boston's youth, and that it would be well to see what was being done with the other level, the dregs."

The dregs? But Miss Haddam redeemed herself in the next paragraph, talking about the "top layer" of girls at her former school, admitting that though some of every class consisted of wealthy "down and outs" the majority was the neglected middle. But her school would sound a new call to excellence, and Dana was right—the headmistress did call Haddam "The School of the Special Case," a place for bright girls who didn't fit the mold.

At the faculty meeting the issue of the brochure never came up. While Brian sat with Hans watching the women get coffee, he noticed a stunning tall woman whose presence seemed to diminish the other women. He leaned over, "Hans, is that Hazel Pierce?"

"Yes."

"How come I haven't seen her around? When I said she was a phantom, I had no idea what she looked like."

"She's very close to Miss Haddam and she has her classes in Little House. She prefers to be marginal."

"Teaching writing? Isn't she *central?*" Hans shrugged. "Is she married?"

"Sometimes."

Before Brian could counter, the meeting began. Margaret opened with "The bank has shut off our credit line. They're threatening to foreclose in January so, mmmm, well, the spring semester is in doubt." No one spoke. "I know you're not financiers, but does anyone have any ideas?"

She was greeted with numbing silence.

"This week, try to think of anyone who might, umm-mm—step in. An angel, as they say on Broadway. But be discreet. We . . . " Mrs. Chase seemed lost for words for a few seconds, "We have to cast a wide net quietly. If it gets out this time, we're dead in the water. I'll be in Boston and New York next week meeting with people I know."

"What kind of money are we talking about?" said Hans.

"In an ideal world, we need fifty thousand. But we'll accept anything." Hans looked startled. "I'm not hopeful," she added, sounding oddly hopeful, and then, "Unless there are any questions, uhh, I guess that's it."

Brian sat there with Hans. The women got up and stood around the coffeepot, turning to Hazel and murmuring. Hazel Pierce looked like no woman Brian had ever seen, like an irritated gray swan, lean, erect, almost six feet tall, with hair that appeared to have the consistency of thin silver wire, short, and swept back and up off her neck and into the air, where it held its place and gave her head a windswept majesty. Yet her profile, with a bump in the center of her straight nose, had a narrow and sharp look as of an ancient Egyptian bird. Her eyes were gray, heavy lidded, and steely. When she walked, that chiseled profile was like the prow of an ancient ship and seemed to part the air and leave a wake behind. Suddenly, she looked at him and Brian felt a chill. He gave her a nod and turned away. He decided to walk over to Little House that week and get to know her, and he wondered what such a tangle of long, lean, sinewy bones would feel like in bed and if there was any warmth behind the crystal presence.

The next day, the girls arrived at school and found ice coating the insides of the first floor windows. The burner had shut down and the pipes had frozen overnight and burst. Three young men came to repair the damage and spent two days refitting the pipes. Brian and Hans chuckled over the stir the young men created, ogling the girls, flirting with the seniors at lunch. Suddenly Brian and Hans were superfluous. It was a bit sobering and very amusing. Brian noticed with interest that the only two girls who were uncertain and watchful were Maude and Charlotte.

During the freeze there was another brief faculty meeting at Dovecote, and this time Brian noticed that Hazel smoked foul French cigarettes. He also noted her expensive English shoes and that she had legs most women would kill for. She didn't acknowledge his presence during the meeting, but afterward they talked. He was surprised at how open she was and how she managed to draw him out. As they walked back to Little House, he was taken aback to hear his own voice saying, "Hazel, how do you keep your distance from the girls? Don't you find that you get too fond of them?"

"Fond, but not too fond. After a few years a pattern develops. Remember, they're just passing through. It's a temporal project. So don't stop to engage. After a while, it's easy."

"I'm glad to hear it."

"You grow, you age, but your 'clientele' remains the same. The same age, the same temper."

"Oh? They all seem so different," said Brian.

"This year. But next year, the difference will be the same difference."

"Oh, I see what you mean. Do you like teaching?"

"Yes. I'm bossy. I like telling people what to do, being right."

Brian looked at her dubiously. "So harsh . . . "

"Not really. I just talk tough. I adore them. But rarely do they surprise me." She paused and changed the subject. "What do you think of Margaret?"

"I don't think of her."

Hazel smiled and said, "I don't mean that way."

"I know—I'm kidding," said Brian.

"Maybe you're not. She took an instant liking to you. Didn't you notice?"

Brian said sincerely, "No."

"Well, notice."

"Why? What would she want from me?"

"I heard from my ex-husband she likes younger men."

"She wouldn't wear those ugly shoes if she did."

"Suit yourself," said Hazel and disappeared into her office without so much as a glance backward.

That fall, Charlotte's scrawny hips and flat chest went through rapid changes. Suddenly she had what she'd wanted since she was twelve, and what she'd given up having—a figure. Charlotte knew what women were expected to wear. Nothing should jiggle. Derrieres were bound in rubber girdles and breasts were held tight in thick bras with heavily stitched, pointy cups. Nothing was left to nature. Charlotte had always noticed where men looked when women got on the bus, and she knew why no one ever looked at her. Now at last maybe someone would.

She studied her chest in the mirror. Too little, too late, she thought, but better than nothing. Some mornings she'd look in the mirror and say, "Morning, Boobs." And she grew fond of them. The girls at Eastport High had worn training bras in the seventh grade. Charlotte had asked her mother for one but she'd said, "I don't think breasts need any training, thank you." Charlotte didn't own one and now that she had no mother nearby, she made no effort to buy one but kept wearing her thin white undershirts.

Brian watched with interest. There had been an absence of women in his life. His mother died when he was ten, and he had no sisters and was raised by an aloof and silent father. He had an older brother, whom he could say he loved in some muted way, but after his mother died, there had been an unspoken competition for the small measure of nourishment their father was able to provide, and this was a competition that Brian never won. He'd gone to Jesuit schools with male teachers. What he knew about women he had gotten from books, and he couldn't believe the fiction. He'd been in love (he thought) only once, with a Catholic girl at college, a buoyant redhead named Bridget. He'd grown tolerant of her consuming Catholicism while at the same time managing to pressure her into intimacy. But her guilt over their lovemaking and her unreliable adherence to birth control, coupled with his, came between them. Mistaking sex for intimacy, not ready for marriage and unwilling to return to celibacy with her, his confidence was shaken when she broke it off and disappeared. Months later he had been stunned to hear she'd had an abortion. That was the rumor, at least, and he blamed himself. Their conversations had not held the same intimacy as their physical relationship. She used to say, "What are you thinking, why are you so quiet, talk to me." And he'd say, "I'm not thinking anything." He had to learn to talk to women. But that had been two years ago and since then his life had been on hold.

Brian was sulking and he didn't know it. The anger was like a convenient, hinged carapace that moved when he moved. He could eat, sleep, walk, function, but there was a blunt adherent heaviness through which his emotional needs failed to emerge. When he got up in the morning his back cracked and it reminded him of the sound a beetle would make if its shell was bent the wrong way.

At Haddam Academy, for no reason yet apparent to him, the coagulation began to break up and words reemerged. He worked over his poetry, shuffled around in adjectives and verbs and new images, a beginning, at least, like little seedlings planted in cold frames in late winter, waiting to be transplanted to warmer soil. What had not yet appeared was his need for love. This had been shut down for years. Or maybe never even called up. Any woman aiming for Brian's hidden heart at this point would find little in the way of a target. Daily he entered Dovecote and the women engaged him, though he rarely smiled. Smiling didn't come naturally to his facial muscles, not a well-worn path. But female voices and laughter entered his mind and heart, seeped into his pores like incremental doses of an invisible elixir, like a lover's repeated embrace. These girls didn't love him, but they loved life, and he was lifted. Brian was changing. It wasn't cataclysmic, nor tidal. It was small progress.

Haddam girls played field hockey after school, and when he drove home he passed them walking up the field in their short green pleated tunics. He wondered if they had as much repressed sexuality as the boys he'd taught. He wasn't a particularly observant man, but once he thought of it, he couldn't miss it. He found himself blushing in class. It was such little things. Theo, who made no effort to restrain her sensuality, stretching her long arms over her head, the sun on her hair. Or Dana, who had a certain hard edge until she leaned forward into her Robert Browning, touching her throat gently with her fingers as she read. Cora had no hard edges anywhere, but soft, sweet, and gracefully shy, she'd asked him not to call on her to read aloud, unless he let her know the day before. And Charlotte, who read with a natural cadence that reminded Brian of muffled bells, as if passion might come ringing through and betray her, and whose eyes never left him as he paced in front of the class. He liked Maude the best, a born skeptic who was itching to engage and who laughed at his comments. He liked it, and he liked them.

He began to go to the field hockey games with Hans. They sat on the top bleacher watching, talking, enjoying the late-day sun. One day Brian said, "If ducks could run, they'd run like Charlotte."

"She does have a funny run," Hans agreed, and they laughed when she tripped over her hockey stick, fell to the ground, and lay there laughing while the game turned ferocious at the goal line.

"How does she get away without wearing a bra?"

Hans turned to him. "What?"

"There's no bra on that girl," muttered Brian.

"Of course there is," said Hans, squinting in concentration. "Then, you know, I think you're right."

That afternoon, Brian felt as if the fault lines in his brain had shifted and he found himself thinking for the first time of the female bodies that surrounded him. Well, not the first time, but this time he didn't brush the thoughts aside. As he pulled into the driveway and shut the motor off, he looked at the heavens and muttered in his head, "Dear God, wouldn't mind seeing all this without the undershirts and bras, if you could work it out."

Finding the Dinghy

CHARLOTTE WAS BORN on Flanders Point and had lived there until she was eight. Then, they'd moved to the house in Eastport. As a girl, Charlotte didn't notice the neighborhood change, she only remembered that on Flanders Point there were times of pure joy and that within a few months of her father's accident, they'd had to sell the house.

Eastport was different. The houses were so close together there was a feeling of uncomfortable exposure. Not that Charlotte watched her neighbors, but some things you couldn't miss. Mr. Hammerneck tying up his tomatoes in August, tipping his head sideways so the cigarette in his teeth wouldn't get smoke in his eyes, as he sweated in his undershirt and his pants slid low on his backside. And she could still see Mrs. Falvey standing at her clothesline, hanging out her underwear inside the sheets so no one would see her pants and bras. Or Suky Flower's mother working outside the house, washing the windows with damp newspaper and her stockings rolled carelessly to just above her knees. Charlotte remembered how her father always came out in the backyard when Mrs. Flowers was up on her ladder doing the top windows, and her high reach pulled her dress above the rolled stockings. And sweet old Mrs. Holly, who kept her yard so neat, picking up the little twigs the wind brought down from her dying dogwood tree. Charlotte also remembered that none of the neighbors talked to each other much, but then, you didn't need to. You could see. And Charlotte sensed unspoken mutual disapproval between them all rather then friendliness.

But on Flanders Point there were so few houses so far apart, Charlotte never saw anyone except gardeners and women in cars on Saturday. She liked the rough, sprawling isolation, but there was also something a little wild and risky. Anything could happen; no one would know. A man could shoot his wife and the sound would go unheard. Or you could get lost in the woods or the marsh and they'd have to call in dogs to find you. And at night the point was so dark the stars arched to higher visibility and the Milky Way was clearly visible like a broad stroke of stardust. Before long Charlotte learned she was more likely to see a great blue heron on the beach than a person, but she also preferred it that way.

One windy Saturday morning, she got up early and went out. A storm front was moving in. Racks of disheveled clouds hurried east and with each erratic disappearance of the sun the air darkened as if it were alive. The wind whipped her hair as if to remind her, "You're part of this world. You belong and we'll blow right down your throat if you ever forget it." She jumped off the wall into the salt marsh and heard the *ki-ki*-ing mud hens rush about like so many noisy ghosts. They summered in the salt marsh, shy birds, heard but never seen. Mr. Macready told her she could flush one out if she dragged a knotted rope through the reeds, but Charlotte thought that was a mean thing to do. What if the rope pulled one of their nests apart?

She was picking her way through barnacled rocks, peering at tidal pools, when she saw an odd gray shape hidden in the cordgrass. She walked over. An old dinghy with a rotting gunnel lay right side up. It reminded her of the *Little Dipper*, the dinghy she'd had when they'd lived on the Point. Max had taken his penknife one day and carved seven little gouges on the bow of the boat in the pattern of the Little Dipper. She tucked her hair in under her collar and ran her fingers along the bow under the gunnel. There was a little groove worn soft in the wood. Her fingers quickened as she found six more gouges. A whisper murmured in her head and her teeth opened and the cove wind pushed down her throat and stirred old things inside. Her old boat. It couldn't be. Impossible. Was this another of her mother's careless leavings? Another mess? A nervous thing tiptoed up her throat and her mouth moistened. She looked under the boat. The grass was still fresh, so it hadn't been there long. Where had it come from? What tide had brought it?

Oh, Fate, she thought, you cheat. How dare you. Leave me alone. I walk by the meadow where I used to climb the apple trees, with my eyes straight ahead. From the crescent beach where I learned to swim with Max, I turn my back, and now I find the past washed up like wreckage. She stood up and her wet eyes didn't see, but her heart had eyes, and as if there was a distant call she turned to the horizon where the sea was black and ripped with whitecaps. The wind worked her hair loose as she let the cold hit her. *Let the damn thing lie here. It's nothing to me.*

But that night, she called her brother. Max was a sophomore at the state college, two towns from Eastport. He was living with a family, too.

"Hi, Max."

"Hi, Charlotte."

She'd forgotten how soft his voice was. "How are you doing?"

"Okay, I guess," said Max.

"Just okay?" she said. There was silence on his end. "I guess you can't talk."

"No."

"Max?"

"What?"

"Remember the *Little Dipper*? The dinghy we had at the beach club?"

"Yeah, I must have dumped you out of it a hundred times."

"Well, I found it this morning in the salt marsh."

"Are you sure?"

"Yes."

There was some silence. "Ten years. That's pretty amazing," he said.

"I know. I thought maybe you could drive over on Sunday. I want to show you."

"All right."

"You'll come?"

"Sure. What time?"

"Is ten okay?"

"Okay," he said.

"Good, I'll see you then. Bye, Max," said Charlotte.

She was surprised he'd agreed. Max always said no to any idea of Charlotte's. He used to push her out of his room and tell her to get lost. Now it was yes and she felt a quiet turning in her heart.

Max used to act like he didn't care if Charlotte lived or died. She knew it was a pose. She took his knuckle punches, his cool disdain, wet towels snapping at her legs, thumbs bent down to her wrist. Whatever he dished out she could take. And he taught her a lot. About the stars, about people, about cars, about records, about sex. And he'd been her voice of authority in high school. Charlotte got the better grades, but they both knew Max was the smart one. He built his own hi-fi as soon as they came on the market. He just couldn't keep his hands off anything electrical and it used to kill her that their father was such a know-it-all and never noticed what Max could do—gentle, watchful Max.

She was a tiny, flat-chested twerp but Max—Max was the tall, quiet outsider with the amused green eyes that knew a secret. He understood the culture of the school. He thought people had no use for him because he wasn't athletic but Charlotte saw the way the girls' eyes followed him in the lunch room, in the bleachers. The high school was hateful to Charlotte when Max left. What friends he and Charlotte had been. What secrets they'd shared. The secret in the bathroom was the best. She was twelve when that happened. It was when her mother had tried renting out a room.

Max noticed the crack in the horizontal molding on the bathroom door around Eastertime. The house was old with raised panel doors and plaster walls. Little cracks had opened in the panels, and one at eye level was large enough to see through. Since their father's accident, they'd had to take on boarders, and the former master bedroom was now rented to an odd young couple. They had the bathroom with the crack in the door. The woman was blond and emaciated looking. She had large, tubular breasts and she was always eating raw vegetables and leaving the carrot tops, broccoli stems, and radish leaves on the kitchen and pantry counters. Max found her rabbitlike and she had big ears. The man was thin, too, and blond and had acne. He didn't say much, nodded slightly when he passed through the front hall, and Max and Charlotte thought he looked like a man who would do it only when he wanted a child. The husband was an accountant. The wife was nothing.

The hall was quiet. The bathroom was large and the toilet, sink, and bathtub were in a cluster at the far end, and Max had begun spying on them through the crack in the bathroom door. It was like watching a movie and some rather gross and odd practices went on behind that door, and though he was thirteen and he'd figured out what they were doing, still he wasn't sure. One day Max brought Charlotte down to the bathroom and showed her the crack in the door, and while Charlotte kept a lookout, Max took his penknife and sliced gently along the split in the wood, widening the crack enough so that he could see better, but not enough so the couple would notice.

And Max did something else. He went into the couple's bathroom and unscrewed the bulb over the sink. It was sixty watts. He took it down to the basement, unscrewed the hundred-watt bulb that dangled from a cord, switched them, and put the hundred-watt bulb in the couple's bathroom. He resumed his spying.

What the couple was doing was this. The man would sit on the toilet reading a magazine. He had no clothes on. The wife would be naked too, and Max loved that she faced the door when she did her part. She would bend over her husband intently, examine his back and squeeze things, and then wipe his back with toilet paper and drop the paper into the toilet behind the man. Max had noticed with interest that when she bent over him, her breasts hung so long and thin they almost looked like cucumbers hanging from a vine. Max told Charlotte what the couple was doing.

Charlotte said, "Ugh, that's vile beyond words." But she wanted to see, so one night they both crept down the hall and watched. Because Charlotte was shorter than Max she had to strain to look in without touching the door and she got tired quickly and left, so she hadn't seen the other thing the couple did. Max decided he was going to show this to Charlotte too. It was much better.

The other thing was this. The woman turned on the water in the bathtub. This was the old-style, free-standing tub before tubs were tiled in. It stood on eagle-claw feet. The husband rubbed her back as she adjusted the spigot until she had the temperature she wanted. Then the man got in the tub as the water started to fill. The woman got in, in front of him, and leaned back against him between his legs, and she put her legs up over the front of the tub, her feet dangling over from the edge. It looked like she was letting the warm water run between her legs.

The husband soaped his wife's drooping breasts, their shape changing as he rubbed and soaped. They didn't look like cucumbers now. And while the wife lay back the water ran between her legs. After a few minutes Max noticed she raised her hips to meet the running water and the man soaped her breasts harder. Max was aware of his penis getting hard when he watched this. Sometimes the wife reached around behind her as if she was holding the man and Max wondered if she was doing what he thought she was doing, as the man closed his eyes and seemed to like it. Max spied on them every night even though they didn't do it every night. He would have, if it were his wife. They did it on Tuesdays and Fridays.

Max didn't tell Charlotte about this other thing, but Tuesday he brought her down to watch. Charlotte put her eyes to the crack. After a minute Max tapped her on the shoulder and she waved him away. She watched and watched. Then she turned to Max and signaled that they should go back to their rooms and she said, "It's an odd way to take a bath; why are her knees over the edge of the tub?"

Max shrugged. "I don't know. Let's try it."

"What?"

"Well, you promised when you were twelve you'd show me yours if I showed you mine."

"Well, I'm just *barely* twelve." It was so long ago Charlotte thought Max had forgotten. He was tall and his voice had changed. He was different.

"Twelve is twelve."

"Oh, okay." She sighed. There was a big smile on Max's face.

So the next night when their mother was not home from her second job and their father was drinking alone at the dining room table, they went into their bathroom and locked the door.

Max and Charlotte got undressed. Charlotte looked at Max's penis, smiled slightly, and said, "That's very amusing." But she also thought it was appealing, which she didn't say. Three separate, neat parts. A perfect grouping, a logical center. Something she would not forget, and she felt a new nervousness. Max crouched down and stared at Charlotte for a minute. She looked at the ceiling and pretended she was somewhere else. She was glad the light in their bathroom was dim. Then Max said, "Could you move your legs apart? I can't see anything."

"I most certainly will not. *That's it.* Let's do the tub thing."

So she turned on the water and Max got in the tub, and Charlotte climbed in front of him and lay back against her brother.

Max looked down at Charlotte's chest. "It would be more fun if you had tits."

"Just soap me and shut up," she said. This was a sore point—some of Charlotte's friends were already wearing bras. She draped her legs over the front of the tub but they were too short to hook over the top so she rested her calves on the porcelain rim with her feet sticking up in the air on either side of the faucet, and she slid her hips forward to meet the water. It was the closest she could come to the wife's position, and the water ran between her legs.

She looked back at Max. "Start soaping, slave," she said. She thought this would be more embarrassing but it was almost cozy. But suddenly she felt something and it wasn't just the water. Some new sensation, warm and licking, began to creep up the inside walls of her body. It probed and reached like a wave rippling up to her stomach and down her thighs. It was the most wonderful thing she'd ever felt. Charlotte knew immediately what the wife was doing and she had to try hard to keep her body from the motion it wanted to make. And there was an arched rise and twist in her muscles and a deep, soft fall that made her close her eyes and gasp.

"What?" said Max.

"Nothing," breathed Charlotte. This was none of Max's business. "The water got too hot." She pretended to adjust the spigot. It was hard to breathe normally at the moment. Max took her other hand from the tub edge and pulled it back toward him awkwardly. She pulled her hand away.

"Max, what are you *doing*?"

"You haven't done the woman's part."

"What woman's part?"

Max was embarrassed. Hadn't she seen it? "She puts her hand behind her and holds her husband."

"I didn't see her do that."

"She did, though. I saw her."

"Well, I didn't—so forget it."

Max started soaping her again. Charlotte pushed herself forward and said, "You can stop soaping. This is enough." She was also noticing something hard against her back and she guessed what it was and pulled the plug. It was interesting what happened with boys. She wanted to look at her brother but she didn't—even though she knew he wanted her to. Without a word, she stood up and rinsed herself quickly. She got out of the tub and dried herself off, sensing her brother's eyes on her, waiting for some revelation. She ignored him, put on her plaid flannel bathrobe, and turned where he sat forlorn in the empty tub, his dark hair damp around his ears, his green eyes watching her face, his shoulders hunched over and his legs still open from holding her. He didn't look like the clever boy who could knuckle-punch her arm so it never left a bruise.

"You're going to catch cold like that," she said.

Suddenly he stood up straight, and standing in the tub, he faced her, full front. Startled, she met his eyes and saw something in them sweet and hopeful she'd never seen before, and it didn't seem to go with the other thing she could see without looking, as her field of vision revealed why he'd stood and faced her. She turned away, hating the reticence that held her back.

They didn't talk about what they'd done. But she had the feeling she hadn't fooled Max. In the next few weeks, not a day went by that she didn't expect to hear the words, "Could we do it again?" But he said nothing. She was relieved, but she was disappointed too. The image of her brother sitting in the tub alone stayed with her. She wished now that when he had taken off his clothes he'd said, "Touch me. It's okay." She would have. Just for a second. Or when he did take her hand she wished she hadn't pulled away. If he ever wanted to do it again, she would. But he seemed to forget the whole thing and was back to hurling gobs of spit at her as she passed his room. Charlotte had always loved Max but she loved him more after that. It wasn't just because it was always he who taught her things, and it wasn't that he showed more patience with his four noisy little sisters than her father ever did. It wasn't even because she'd now seen his erection. Such a private thing. It was something else about how tender he could be, how hidden, and how he had let go of his false bravado and stood before her naked, proud like a man but still needing something even while accepting without question that it would not be given. She'd thought her brother had it all figured out. It wasn't so.

When Charlotte was thirteen, her mother gave her a book called *How Shall I Tell My Child*, as if it were about death and dying or something. Charlotte read it with interest. She laughed at the part admonishing parents never to scold their children, never to suggest that their hands would fall off if they did it. That it was nothing to be ashamed of and quite normal. Charlotte laughed because she was never ashamed. Not guilty, even for a minute. She felt lucky that she had stumbled upon it at such an early age, and she knew she had Max to thank. She wondered if Max had gotten to read the book. There were things about women that Max should know. Charlotte doubted that her mother would have given this to Max. She decided to leave the book on his bed, and she put it under his pillow so he'd know who put it there. This was private.

Max and Charlotte and the Dinghy

WHEN MAX DROVE up on Sunday, Charlotte looked out the window. Max waited at the door, his hands in his corduroy pockets, his wool plaid jacket unzipped, crew cut newly grown out. He slouched as he always had. Max never stood at his full six feet. Her father used to snarl at him, "Stand up straight." Max wouldn't. Charlotte thought he stood with a humble grace that fit his reticent nature. She heard the front door open and hurried down. Mrs. Macready was unusually friendly to Max. Grown women liked Max. He'd always been her mother's favorite, too. Charlotte didn't mind. Maybe it made up a little for their father, who used to go days without even speaking to Max.

Max and Charlotte looked at each other shyly but they didn't hug. They never had. She thought of all the insults he'd thrown her way, and all the gobs of spit that never missed. She wanted to pick up his hands and see if they still smelled like minerals or press her nose to his neck. Her brother used to smell of carbon from grinding the mirrors for his telescopes, and she used to think of him as earth and stonedust. The elements. They'd been wrestling on his bed once, and she'd noticed his ears and neck had this wonderful other smell, other than carbon. It could have been the smell of the moon, or Jupiter, or Mars, or something otherworldly. Max had much to do with escapes—his ham radio, his telescope, his long disappearances in the summer. Charlotte always thought if the light-years were solid beams of light, Max would ride them away and never come back. Max was science fiction, dreaming of worlds beyond.

They walked across the field to the retaining wall on the edge of the marsh, and Charlotte climbed up. She wanted to talk but she couldn't think of a thing to say. Her own brother. What a cripple she was.

"What are the Macreadys like?" he asked.

"Okay. Three little girls and a boy who's eight. The father likes his liquor. The mother's nice."

"Sounds like our family," said Max.

"Much nicer. What about yours?"

"Jerks . . . except for the daughter."

"There's a daughter?"

He nodded. "She's my age." Charlotte looked up with interest. His expression had changed.

"Pretty?" she asked.

"Yup. She makes it bearable. Everybody's always yelling. They don't have the silent fights we used to have in our house. They fight in Italian. The mother is fat. She screams. She throws things. But, boy, can she cook."

The tide was out. Charlotte jumped off the stone wall onto the dry rocks on the water's edge and said, "The dinghy's over here."

Max stepped to the bow and ran his fingers over the gouges. He straightened as his head ducked sideways, and his hands went back in his pockets. Charlotte had forgotten how he always moved his head that way, ducking as if he were avoiding a blow.

"What the hell," he wondered softly.

"It's weird, isn't it?" said Charlotte. "Left over from another life."

"Yeah, some life." He rocked it thoughtfully with his foot and they both sat on the wall. There was only the sound of the water moving in the rocks and reeds.

"Do you still use your telescope?" asked Charlotte.

"Yes. It's useful for things other than looking at stars."

"What?"

"Getting girls."

"By looking at the stars, you mean?"

"Yup. You can only look when it's dark, and they usually get cold. I'm good at warming them up."

Charlotte laughed. "I bet you are."

"Anyone interesting in your life, Charlotte?" He looked at her with a sidelong glance and her heart opened to him.

"My English teacher, Brian Parton."

"Why not pick someone where something can happen?"

She shrugged. "Maybe I don't want anything to happen." Max studied Charlotte and said with quiet disapproval, "Dreams aren't going to do it for you, Charlotte."

A mud hen sputtered in the reeds and that set the terns calling. Max looked around. "What a view. Is that your school across the cove?"

Charlotte nodded. He seemed to invite her closer. "Max, do men think constantly about sex?"

"God, Charlotte." He ducked his head but she saw a little smile appear as he glanced over at her and stood up. "What a question."

"You're the only man I can trust." How could girls resist him, she wondered. "Well, *do* they?"

He glanced over. "Constantly . . . and instantly."

"Instantly?"

He heaved an impatient sigh. "When a guy sees a girl that interests him, he thinks of sex. What would she look like with her clothes off, could I get them off, and what would she be like in bed? Something along those lines."

"Thanks," said Charlotte, trying not to smile.

"So now you know the private, universal reflections of men—men *my* age, anyway."

"That's what one of the girls at school told me. I didn't believe her."

"What's her name? Could you arrange a date for me with this girl?" They both laughed.

"Her name is Dana Scully."

Max sat back down next to her and turned rocks over with his shoe. "So, do women?" he said slyly.

"What?"

"You know."

Charlotte squirmed. "The answer is frequently, but not the other."

Max mulled it over. "Let's go for a drive around the point."

"Fine with me." And they drove around, stopping several times to stare at their old house on the hill. During one loop Charlotte pointed to the Tudor garage at the Armbrusters' and said, "That's where my English teacher lives."

"That's interesting."

"What's interesting about it? He may as well be a thousand miles away."

"He *is* a thousand miles away. Forget about him. I'll try and think of someone to fix you up with."

"You will not."

"Yeah. You're right. I won't." But Charlotte didn't mind.

Radcliffe Essay

BRIAN HAD SAID in class one day—one of his seemingly marginal comments delivered in an offhand way—"Dare to break the rules, for goodness's sake. See where it takes you." But he doubted anyone had heard him.

"Mr. Parton, would you read my college essay before I send it?" Charlotte asked.

"Did you take it to Mrs. Reed?"

"Guidance counselors have no imagination and she's no help. All she cares about is a five-paragraph essay and punctuation."

"Well, that's a good start."

"Would you take a look at it?"

"Stop by class after tomorrow." She handed him the two neatly written pages.

The next day, Charlotte went into the English room after school and stood by his desk.

"Sit down," said Brian. "Is this for Radcliffe?" She nodded happily. "Charlotte, what makes you think you can write a finished essay with no capital letters? They won't even read it this way."

Charlotte's smile faded. "Well, E. E. Cummings does it. You said once rules were made to be broken."

"Not on a college essay." He sat back and threw his pencil on her essay. "Have you *read* E. E. Cummings?"

Charlotte looked at the floor. He seemed angry. She could feel something shake in her heart. "No."

"Then what do you know?"

"Theo showed me one of his poems."

"Charlotte, your nerve does you no credit. It comes from ignorance. Forget about E. E. Cummings. All this will show them is that you're a defiant little rebel who can't follow instructions."

Charlotte whispered, her voice choking off, "Well, I *am* a rebel."

He looked at her in surprise. "No, you're not. You're a model of good behavior." He said nothing about her work, which was not yet the caliber he knew Radcliffe was looking for.

Charlotte found her voice. "Is that how you see me?"

Brian thought a minute. He'd dealt with defiant rebels at the boys' school and she certainly didn't fit the mold. "Well, yes."

"That's so boring." She was distressed.

He could see her reconsider—not her approach to the essay, but her approach to him. "Don't forget this is their first impression of you. You don't want it to be their last." Charlotte now looked so discouraged he said, "Why don't you read some E. E. Cummings? I wouldn't imitate him, but he may give you some idea of an offbeat approach that might work. I understand your desire to do something different. That's okay. But this is false. Don't be cute. It won't fool Radcliffe."

He saw that his words hit harder than he meant and she was about to cry, but he was going to have to level with her.

But he surprised himself when he said, "Look, Charlotte. You don't need to bring me your college essays. You already have my attention. You all do. I know I've been asking you to take risks in your writing, to surprise me, to dig your feet out of the clay. But you've chosen the wrong place. Work with Mrs. Reed. She's the expert. All right?"

Her shoulders drooped and she rested her forehead in her hand, heaving a long, deep sigh. He was expecting her eyes to come back in some last flirtation he knew she meant to achieve, but he had no idea of the effect he'd had. He handed her the essay, still waiting for her to answer, but she got up and started to leave the room, swinging her arms in frustration. He looked away but his arm shot out and he caught hold of her arm just above the elbow as she passed him. "Charlotte . . ."

Charlotte stopped when she felt his hand but he wasn't even looking at her. He just held her arm as if it were part of an annoying shrub that needed pruning. "All right," she said. He let her go.

She ran down the stone steps to get her coat. This little foray into his room to win his approval had backfired. Maybe he had a cold streak. But she took her lumps. Mr. Parton always saw right through her.

When Brian heard the heavy oak door swing shut, he went out onto the porch outside his room and watched Charlotte walk along the flagstone up to the road. He had only meant to redirect her rebellion, not squelch it. She needed to break out but his words had come out all wrong. He was puzzled. Why had he needed to put her in her place? When he went back to his desk, he slammed his books around a bit.

In early November a rare, second Indian summer came, and Brian swam two miles every day when he got home. One day when he came back up from the beach he found a bunch of yellow rosebuds tied to his front doorknob. He put them in his bathroom glass and left them on the porcelain tank of his toilet next to the sink and forgot about them. One morning he was shaving and he eyed them. The buds had turned brown without opening. It was only when he threw them in the garbage that he noticed all the thorns had been snapped off.

Mr. Macready as a Variable

MR. MACREADY SEEMED an odd man to Charlotte. She'd never seen a man so talkative or so opinionated. She liked it because at least she knew what he was thinking. Or so she thought. He could not have been more different from her father except for his mood swings. One afternoon he appeared in her room, jocular and upbeat, and said, "Charlotte, it's time to learn how to clean a skillet. Come on." She dutifully followed him up to the kitchen.

He always had a story in which he was the star, and this was no exception. He told her about how he was an officer on a carrier task-force ship that had a sister ship in the South Pacific during the war. He used to enjoy giving directions to the ship's cook. Both ships used the same menu in their kitchens. But the other ship had dozens of men with stomach disorders and diarrhea and all manner of problems all the time, and there were no such problems on his ship. Well, almost none. "I finally went to their kitchen," he said triumphantly, "and realized they weren't washing their skillets."

Charlotte said, "My father said never get a skillet wet. Just wipe it with oil."

Mr. Macready shrieked, and Charlotte laughed. "What! You too?" he said. "It's a myth. Don't you realize the oil goes rancid and breeds bacteria? You have to scrub a skillet within an inch of your life and dry it. Never mind the oil. The other ship's kitchen began to scrub the skillets and the men's stomach problems all but disappeared. So scrub, girl, scrub." And with that he got out the steel wool, scrubbed all the pans happily, and handed them to Charlotte to dry. She kind of liked standing next to him, drying. It felt like family. His last words as he finished humming to himself were "I want these pots and pans kept just like this, Charlotte. It's sanitary."

"All right."

"Attagirl."

She went back to her room marveling at how a man could be interested in such a thing.

That night when she was reading to Peter after his bath, he complained that the seams on the insides of his pajamas were itching him so Charlotte told him to put them on inside out, and she noticed four odd bruises on the inside of his arm. She took his arm to look closely, and he pulled it away.

"Peter, what are those?"

"I don't know."

And even as Charlotte asked, she remembered the Sunday before, when they were playing softball with Peter and a friend. Charlotte was pitching and Mr. Macready was catching. She remembered how he grabbed Peter by the arm to show him where to stand. She'd thought at the time he was much too rough. She saw another bruise on the outside of Peter's arm from Mr. Macready's thumb. Should she say anything to Mr. Macready? She'd made friends with him at last and she was loathe to criticize him now.

The Macreadys had a bird feeder in the front yard and Charlotte took to filling it because Mrs. Macready kept forgetting. There'd been a killing frost and Charlotte knew that the ground was now frozen. That was when you had to feed them. She lay in bed one icy Saturday morning and heard the quiet four notes of the white-throated sparrow. She smiled. Was he asking for his breakfast? Four pure, sweet notes over and over: "Where is my seed?" As she listened, the words seemed to change and she decided his sweet song was a call for his mate: "Where is my love?" She put her coat on over her pajamas and went to get the birdseed. To her surprise Mr. Macready was up.

"What are you doing up so early?" he said cheerfully.

"Filling the bird feeder. Can you get more seed when you go grocery shopping?" She knew never to ask for anything unless he was in a good mood.

He looked at her pajamas and turned away. "Forget it. I don't want them crapping on my shrubs." Charlotte was startled.

"But they're dependent on us."

"Where'd you get that?"

"The Audubon center told me if you start feeding them they get dependent on the food and you have to do it all winter or they die."

"Well, you never should have started. I'm not spending good money on birdseed and I don't mind picking up the dead birds." She could see the pleasure he took in saying that last. She went back in, trying to account for his sudden mood switch. He was as unpredictable as her father. Did he have a hangover? That afternoon, with a dollar from Mrs. Macready, she walked to town and lugged back a ten-pound bag of birdseed. Mr. Macready was in the yard when she got back and to her surprise he was all smiles again. When he saw the birdseed under her arm, he said, "I like a resourceful girl."

Charlotte made a mental note. Stay on his good side, wherever that was.

The Broken Piano

THERE WAS AN unusual rustle as Miss Haddam and her cane walked down the aisle between the girls one morning in November. This was a rare event now, and they remembered how she used to start assembly every day with some thought, some philosophical rumination. The seniors had grown up with Miss Haddam's vision. The well-read and well-tutored might have found her thoughts sentimental, but Miss Haddam did something that busy parents were failing to do: she was laying down a system of values. It was the kind of thing educators said that young people needed if they weren't going to end up dying on Harley Davidsons, or playing bongo drums and scratching themselves in torn undershirts like Marlon Brando. Not that the girls saw anything wrong with bongo drums, undershirts, motorcycles, or Marlon, but parents believed these were the signs that things were getting worse. Although Miss Haddam used to reassure parents, "Remember, things always appear to grow worse between generations, but no one seems to notice that it's always the same worse. Believe me, the young are not so easy to corrupt, although that doesn't mean we shouldn't be vigilant."

Today, in a rare event, Miss Haddam led assembly. She began, "We live in an era that suspects silence. Even music is piped in so we don't have to endure a silent elevator. I hope Haddam girls will have the good sense to study in silence. Silence is the sound of thinking, the sound of reading, the sound of writing."

Miss Haddam wore thick glasses and they were always smudged, so though Brian noticed the seventh and eighth graders were quiet and attentive, the upperclassmen, who knew Miss Haddam couldn't see the back row, were not. Dana was rolling her eyes and putting her finger in her throat as if she were gagging. Charlotte laid her head on Maude's shoulder, who ignored it, and Theo actually slid inch by inch off her chair until she was on the floor as if out cold, crumbled in a heap at Cora's feet. Brian wondered why no teacher ambled over to restrain them. They always overdid everything. He loved it. Miss Haddam was still talking.

"We look through microscopes in silence. We study the forest floor in silence. Observation, examination, and scrutiny are done in silence. And most important, we're silent when we listen. Now, a school is not a silent place. Your voices fill the air, but what else? What do you hear when you listen?"

There was quiet. Not one girl raised her hand.

"My dear girls, your silence is commendable," she said, "but sorely misplaced. The point of my discussion is the clamor of modern technologies and modern music.

"Rock and roll, the radio, the television are cheap distractions. Study in absolute quiet. Turn off the radio so you can hear the whisper of your thoughts. You don't need Bill Haley or Jack Armstrong. Respect the power of silence. You can't see to the bottom of the lake until the water is perfectly still and the mud has cleared. Then you can see. It's the same with the human mind. Raucous disturbance will throw broken reflections back at you instead of yielding the secrets inside. Remember— silence is not a lonely thing. It is the sound of thought thinking itself. Perhaps it even has a voice.

"And one other thing. Keep your shirttails tucked in. Sloppy dress leads to sloppy living and sloppy thinking."

"God," muttered Dana to Charlotte. "She's getting senile."

"I don't think so," said Charlotte. "I like the way she talks."

But the issue of silence was about to humiliate Charlotte. That afternoon, Mrs. Chase called Charlotte into her office and said, "Miss Haddam has a favor to ask you."

When she got there, Miss Haddam's office was filled with papers. It was nothing if not sloppy, and Miss Haddam was at her desk.

"Mrs. Chase tells me you play the piano."

"Yes."

"Can you play the morning march at assembly for the next few weeks? The music teacher will be away."

"I don't take lessons anymore."

"I hear you play very well. It'll be good practice," said Miss Haddam.

Charlotte wanted to say, *Practice for what?* "Very well. I'll do my best."

As it happened, Charlotte wasn't a bad pianist, and Debussy, Grieg, Schumann, and Chopin had been friends in solitude many a day when she was growing up. She did know a march called "Harvard Is Marching Up the Street." But the first morning she played and students filed in, when she heard the demanding tempo of their marching feet she was so nervous that her left hand mislocated whole chords. It sounded like she was playing with mittens on. It was unheard of for Charlotte. She knew this piece. The students lined up in rows, as normal as you can imagine, but Charlotte knew what wasn't normal: the startled look on Dr. Dierig's face, the girls' snickers, eyes sliding and heads turning, looking in the direction of the piano. Charlotte was shaking, trying to act as if nothing was wrong, but the nerves in her fingers were like Mexican jumping beans. She figured she'd learn in a day or two, but no, every morning was just as bad. Her march was famous overnight. Her friends teased her, singing "Harvard Is Tripping Up the Street." Then, even worse, they fell silent.

The assembly march took on the aura of slapstick. A daily display of public failure. At first she practiced in the afternoon in the assembly hall. But knowing the sound could be heard downstairs in the library and the French and English rooms, all she did was make more mistakes. She might as well have been playing the music upside down.

The teachers couldn't stand her practicing either, and it got back to Charlotte that they were complaining. She went to Mrs. Chase. "Can't we find some other place for me to practice? I'm disturbing study hall in the afternoon."

"We can't move the piano."

"Mrs. Chase, I can't do this."

"There's no such thing as 'I can't.' "

"It's making my life a misery. I'm a laughingstock. I'm bothering everyone. Especially Mr. Parton."

"I know," said Mrs. Chase pointedly. "He told me."

"He did?" That was all she had to hear.

"He was the first one," said Mrs. Chase. "Why don't you come on Saturday? Practice when no one is here."

So Charlotte did, but she did something else, too. She brought Mrs. Macready's sewing shears with her. She was going to disable the piano. Cut some strings. Something. Anything. But when she was there, after she played all the pieces she loved without a mistake, she couldn't bring herself to touch the venerable old Steinway. Charlotte loved the piano and loved to play. She was proud of her ability. She noticed that the lyre, the part that hung down underneath and connected the three pedals to the damper, was loose. She pushed at it with her foot. Then she started to kick it. The lyre loosened a little more. She kicked harder and heard one of the brackets crack. One more kick and the lyre crashed to the floor. Charlotte crawled under the piano and stared at it. The brackets were detached, the wood split. The pedal rods were bent. No one could play the piano now. Repairs would take weeks. By that time the music teacher would be back. Lying on her back, she struggled to get the lyre up so no one would notice it was broken. But it was heavy. It fell over again. When she finally had it aligned she lay under the piano on the floor, and heard loud scraping and dragging sounds downstairs.

"Oh my God," she muttered. Someone was there. She tiptoed down the stairs and was walking toward the sound near the library when Mr. Parton rounded a corner and walked head-on into her. He jumped back and so did she.

"What are you doing here?" he said.

"I'm practicing—trying to learn that stupid march."

"Oh. I thought the roof was falling in."

"Oh . . . I upset the piano stool."

"Five times?"

"I was adjusting the swivel seat and it kept falling off."

"Oh." He looked her up and down. "C'mon. I'll take a look at it. It won't do for you to fall over, on top of all your other problems."

She could have kicked him. She hoped he didn't know anything about pianos. He took the stairs two at a time, went to the piano, and swiveled the top of the stool. It was fine. Didn't fall off.

Charlotte distracted him as fast as possible. "What are you doing here?"

"Moving the bookcases in my classroom."

"You too?"

"Moving them, not breaking them."

She caught her breath. "Why are you so mean?"

"Can't you take a joke?" He was smiling like he had a secret.

She looked at him, her mouth open. "It's not a joke to me, Mr. Parton."

He turned to go back down. She followed. "Why are you moving the furniture?" She sensed he didn't think it was her business, but oddly, he answered.

"Well, the glass doors are a distraction—to see into the library during class. It's more private now." If Charlotte hadn't been so terrified she would have noticed that he was embarrassed at being found moving the furniture.

The piano sabotage worked. Monday morning the girls marched in, and as soon as Charlotte put pressure on the pedal the lyre fell to the floor. Everyone looked. She stopped playing, feigned surprise, and after an awkward moment, Mrs. Chase said she could return to her usual place. She glanced over at Mr. Parton, and he looked at her as if puzzle pieces were falling into place in his brain. He knew. Charlotte felt as if black wolf spiders had crawled out from under her heart. She kept thinking about it. She had tried to murder a thing of beauty to save herself. How, how could she have done such a thing? What had come over her? What else was she capable of? For three days the piano sat silent, and to Charlotte it seemed a defenseless, wounded creature.

Everyone at school was affected. What she hadn't thought of was that new student tours included a music class. Now music classes were a bit awkward. And when she saw the moving men load the piano onto a big truck she wanted to run after it, yelling, "I'm sorry, I'm sorry, I didn't mean to. I'll fix it." But she had meant to. Now she was not only a chicken, she was a rat, and it lodged in her heart. And the worst thing was that everyone believed it was an accident. An old piano, with repairs long overdue. No one suspected her, not even Mrs. Chase. Her mother would have said, "I told you when you were ten years old you were selfish. You haven't changed." Charlotte thought she had, but this wasn't a good sign. Brian knew. Why didn't he nail her? Why did he just leave her to twist in her misery? She would have preferred to be caught. To face the music. But no, the girls marched to the assembly in silence. They didn't seem to care, but if a thunderbolt had struck Charlotte down, she would have said *Thank you. I deserved it.*

Hans and Brian Talk

BY NOVEMBER MORE than one girl had a crush on Brian Parton. He pretended to be oblivious but he needed some advice. He felt like he was living in a fishbowl. It was one of the flaws at Haddam that no teacher had a private office except for Hazel. Even his car was invaded in the morning by an alien being. He shared a sandwich with Hans Dierig in the Latin room. Hans had taught at Haddam for six years and asked Brian, "How are things going?"

"The girls are quick," said Brian, "but they certainly are emotional."

"What do you mean?"

"We even had tears in class once."

Hans was suddenly interested. "Really? Over what?"

"I don't know. Maybe I'm too severe. And they argue among themselves. There's some competition going on."

"Maybe it's for your benefit." Hans was watching Brian and added, "And there must be those who have a crush on you."

Brian was relieved he'd brought it up. "Only one, I think."

"Brian, you're too modest. Even I know of more than one," and he sat back with the same merry look he gave the girls.

"Well," said Brian, "only one I've noticed. What do you do about it?"

"Not a thing."

"Has it happened to you?"

"Yes. I like women and they always notice. Even now that I'm turning gray."

"This year?"

Hans nodded. "I'm picking it up."

"It's disconcerting, isn't it?"

"I find it appealing."

Brian eyed Hans. "Do you ever have inappropriate thoughts?"

Hans smiled. "I don't censor my inner life. I censor enough as it is."

Brian smiled back, crumpled his wax paper, and threw it into the wastebasket. Hans looked over. "Nice throw."

"In some areas my aim is true. You know," said Brian, "I looked up the word *infatuation* the other day. I'd forgotten it's also a verb. To infatuate means to inspire a foolish or extravagant love. I didn't do anything I can think of, but the feelings coming at me are extravagant. But foolish? I don't know. They seem authentic."

"Oh, they're not foolish."

"But are they accurate? They have this outline of you. They color in the outline with whatever fantasy they need. So it isn't really you."

"It's more complex."

"How so?"

Hans thought in silence. "When a student feels this way, one of the hard things to understand is how it begins, with the material, the daily congress, the chemistry . . . Anyway, they give you some power you didn't ask for and don't want."

"You're not talking about grades."

"No, that's a myth. This has different roots—"

Brian interrupted, "But of course you don't accept that power."

"You do nothing and that just makes matters worse."

"How could it?"

"Because this kind of love turns its face away. The teacher ignores it and his detachment beckons the student to come further."

"Oh, great. By doing nothing I encourage it?"

"The labor of teaching is to beckon them further."

They were quiet for a minute and Brian said, "You know, detachment can be appealing in a woman. It sounds like an absence, but it has a presence. Detachment has teeth like a buried snare, and it can take hold." They were quiet again. "But I don't know, Hans, I feel no power. I feel more like a victim." Hans smiled. "Thank God it's ephemeral."

Hans started to swing his foot back and forth. "It isn't always. In a school this small, Brian, everything is more intense. We're like a family. I have students I still hear from after six years, and the letters are a bit more than casual." He stared out the window as if Brian weren't there. "Why is it treated as some sort of dirty little secret? There's something erotic in teaching and learning. Have you ever been witness to that moment when one of your students starts to engage with the work? They start to like it and sometimes what I see on their faces looks a little like they're falling in love. With learning, I think. Or being taught. I've never quite known but there's an intimacy. Pliny said, 'Love is the best teacher.' But you won't find the letters of Abelard and Héloïse in anyone's curriculum. Now, there was an inappropriate love."

"Why?"

"The age difference."

"Doesn't that add to the eroticism?" said Brian.

"Perhaps. And if the Eros in teaching becomes too palpable, the taboo is threatened with possibility."

Brian said, "You should have been in class yesterday, Hans. The sophomores are reading *Romeo and Juliet*. It's too hot—twelve-year-old lovers. I won't include it next year."

"Don't drop it. How else will they know what they think? I envy you. Studying Latin doesn't touch the heart as a rule."

Hans had offered no challenge, but Brian felt the competitive tug and heard himself say, "Are you sure there's nothing? The Romans had hearts."

"Elegiac poetry is too difficult."

"What about Ovid? Augustus may have expelled him from Rome for *The Art of Love*, but it's wonderful."

Hans threw his head back and laughed. "God, maybe I am getting old."

Brian smiled. His memory never let him down.

"You know *The Art of Love*?" asked Hans.

"I doubt if there's any erotic literature I've missed or forgotten."

"How could I forget the *Ars Amatoria*? Miss Haddam would choke on her tea biscuits." Hans closed his eyes and said:

"The height of bliss is reached when, unable any longer to withstand the wave of pleasure, lover and mistress at one and the same moment are overcome. Such should be thy rule when time is yours and fear does not compel you to hasten your stolen pleasures."

"Nothing difficult there."

"You know it by heart?" said Brian with a grin.

Hans twirled his mustache. "The good parts, of which there are far too few. I've forgotten most of it."

"Reread it, my friend."

"Very well. And when I add *The Art of Love* to Latin Four, you can add *Lady Chatterley's Lover* to senior English."

Brian smiled broadly. "Out of the question, but I might try a short story. 'The Woman Who Rode Away' or 'The Horse Dealer's Daughter.'"

"C'mon. These girls could handle it."

"I'm not worried about the girls. It's me."

And Hans said, "Oh, well, you *do* have to be able to handle it."

The Linen Closet

IF CHARLOTTE HAD the normal distractions of an active social life she might not have been so drawn to Brian Parton, though she would have said it was *because* she was so drawn to him that she made little effort to develop a social life. Haddam girls came from widely scattered towns. The fact of her isolation on Flanders Point and her lack of transportation would have been a problem either way. But as it was, more and more weekends Charlotte's thoughts turned to him, where he was, what he was doing, and wishing she could see him. Brian, however, gave no thought to Charlotte's whereabouts.

One Sunday, when the Macreadys took the children to church, Charlotte explored the house in a way she knew they wouldn't like. With the dog sniffing her every step, she went into the Macreadys' bedroom and examined Mrs. Macready's jewel box. Every piece was neatly laid out on black velvet, every earring with its mate. On the night tables were family pictures in polished silver frames, and pictures of ancestors filled the top of the bureau—a considerable display. In the dressing table drawers, cosmetics were arranged like little treasures. No bills or newspaper clippings or dirty combs were thrown in the drawers in haste. Bureau drawers were lined with floral paper and sachets and there wasn't just underwear. This was lingerie. Lace garter belts, silk and satin things folded, nothing mashed in a jumble. Some still had tissue paper around them, waiting to be worn. Why would a woman who was pregnant have her drawers so full of things she couldn't wear? A promise, maybe. The stockings looked like they'd been ironed and there were delicate lace nightgowns, nothing like her mother's faded flannel ones. The closet was a revelation. Shoes arranged by type in neat rows, his and hers, and there were no wire hangers, only wood. Mr. Macready's suits were lined up evenly like slices of gray bread. The linen closet was a work of art, full of real linen and embroidered white-on-white coverlets, not a bunch of raggy towels and wrinkled sheets. Charlotte had never seen such a meticulous house, where things were treated as if they had some intrinsic worth. Charlotte had noticed Mrs. Macready's perpetual motion, how she always had something in her hand and her endless trips to put things in their place. Once when Charlotte's mother and father were fighting over their messy house, her mother had said angrily, "I'm not a housewife, I'm not married to this house." Caroline Macready *was* a housewife, though Charlotte wasn't at all sure it was worth it. She understood now why Mrs. Macready was so precise with her. Charlotte too had her place and her set jobs: fix supper for the children, feed them, bathe them, get them ready for bed, read them a story, and of course put everything in its place. Every night sitting in their pajamas, robes, and slippers, they ate the same thing—two soft-boiled eggs with cubes of toast mixed in, a glass of milk, and a Lorna Doon. Boom! That was it. When Charlotte asked why they had the same supper every night, Mrs. Macready said vaguely, "Oh, there's security in the predictable." This kind of security was stifling, Charlotte thought, though maybe it was preferable to the chaos that she'd grown up with. She didn't even own a bathrobe and slippers.

From the back of the linen closet she picked up a stack of pillow covers, and a thick envelope fell to the floor with a thud. She picked it up. To Charlotte's surprise there were nude pictures of Mrs. Macready in pin-up poses, and she was not the least bit pregnant. Charlotte would probably have just smiled to herself, thinking, I know something I shouldn't know, but she'd found similar pictures of her mother once, in the same place—the linen closet. This was interesting. Was there something about linen closets? She spread the pictures out on the floor, aware that the dog's tail was not wagging. She gave him a big smile and turned back the pictures. Did everyone do this? I knew sex was hidden, she thought, but I didn't expect it to be hidden everywhere. She couldn't wait. She put the envelope back and slid it under the linens. The dog continued to watch her every move. Dalmatians were supposed to be good watchdogs. He was watching, all right. Wandering up to the living room to look for a marriage manual, she said to the dog, "Sit. Stay." And to her surprise, he obeyed. Something else well taken care of.

When she went back to her room, she sat in the window seat and thought about the pictures. She felt an odd quickening and a small shift inside, as if her organs were making room for something new. The house was so quiet that when the furnace next to her room clicked on she was startled and reminded of empty houses when they had no more stories to tell, and of the last time she'd gone to her house in Eastport to clean it for the listing broker (and to have their dog, Plum, put to sleep).

She'd been the last one there. Her mother and sisters had moved to Washington, DC, her father long gone. The selling broker had said Charlotte only needed to leave it broom clean, but she scrubbed it down, not wanting anyone to see the dirt. She never enjoyed cleaning so much. Washing woodwork, scrubbing tiles, rinsing and drying windows. There was nothing she could do about the bullet holes her father had shot into the kitchen wall one night, but other than that, no trace of her family was left. Charlotte doubted most people would know the holes were from bullets.

She heard the Macreadys' furnace shut off again, and the house was as still as a tide at the turning. What secrets did this proud house hide? She felt as if something was about to happen and, beset with deep melancholy, she went for a walk on Nathan Hale Road, nervously pulling up sour grass and chewing it. She'd always spit it out before, but today, without thinking, she swallowed it down.

That night she was so sick that she threw up all the grass. Violent dry heaves followed, coming every ten minutes. When Mrs. Macready realized Charlotte was sick, she asked her husband to call the doctor, but he said, "She doesn't need a doctor. I can help," and went to her room. "There's something I learned in the navy, Charlotte. It may help." He followed her into the bathroom and stood behind her and pressed his hands against her gut so the muscle would have something to heave against.

He said, "I taught this to the men when they were seasick. It shortens the dry heave so you don't strain a muscle." Charlotte was mortified standing in front of the toilet in her plaid pajamas with him behind her, but she was in no position to refuse, and it did help. As soon as she got her breath she protested that she'd be fine, but he was so overbearing he said, "Don't give it a thought. I'm used to it." She had the fleeting thought that he wanted an excuse to touch her, but then she felt like an ingrate. He was only doing what he'd do for his own children. But the sixth time she dry-heaved over the toilet she was aware that he was getting a little too free with his hands. When he let go of her she gulped, "I think I'm better now, thank you," and rushed to her room.

She wasn't better, she was dizzy and trembling inside. She looked for a place to throw up, but the wastebasket in her room was wicker, so that was out. Finally she opened the window, and when the last two dry heaves came she thought her stomach would tear loose. She leaned out the window, pressing her hands hard into her abdomen the way he had. Ashen and weak, she fell into a quick, dreamless sleep. When she woke up she looked down the hall and saw the Macreadys' bedroom door close. Charlotte closed hers too, even though she didn't want to be cut off when she was sick.

She lay in bed and remembered another closed door at home when she was twelve. Her room at home was like a cavern under the eaves, and it had only one window, so it was darker than the others. Her mother had come in and gotten in bed with her. The light in the hall was on and there was a dark figure in the door. Although back lighting obscured his face, the man in the silhouette was her father. He came in silently and took her mother's arm and pulled her up. Not violent, just insistent. And Charlotte lay frozen, pretending to be asleep. What if he took Charlotte's arm and pulled her up? She was always afraid of that. Sleep would be long in coming because she was trying not to listen for sounds behind her mother's bedroom door. Thank God there never was a sound, because she was so afraid of what she might hear.

Dana's Boys

THEY WERE FREEZING on the boathouse porch, listening to Dana talk about her weekend at Princeton. Maude noticed that there was a certain sameness to her recitations. "Dana, how do you get so many boys?"

"I try to look available and inaccessible at the same time," she said.

"Be more specific," said Charlotte.

Theo gave Charlotte a look like, *Don't encourage her, she brags enough.* But Charlotte wanted to know.

"Okay," said Dana. "Let's say I'm at a party, or, to make it more difficult, I'm waiting for someone at the Princeton Club."

"Now you're talking about a pickup," muttered Theo.

Charlotte said, "Theo, it's not a pickup at the Princeton Club."

"A pickup is a pickup."

"God," said Dana, "I'm talking about being friendly. You have to talk to people. I have a drink. And then it's easy. I circulate around the room, not staying too long with anyone because I don't know anyone, and I make a lot of eye contact and try to put on an expression that conveys my intent."

"Which is . . ." Charlotte had grabbed her notebook and was writing.

"I'm hot, and I like it, and I want it." Maude and Theo looked at each other.

Now even Charlotte knew she'd been set up. She smiled.

"What happened to the inaccessible part?" she asked.

"You didn't let me finish. The other part is . . . but you're not going to get it. You've got to keep them off balance. Men are hunters. They always have been. They want to achieve you, not just fall into bed."

Charlotte rolled over and laughed into the bedspread. "Forget this. I could never do it."

"You can. Just be yourself. Someone will find you."

"I don't think so. Myself is generic wimp. Besides, it seems so sneaky, so calculated."

"It isn't. You have to trust in deceit. You can confess later, if you feel guilty, but why would you? It's just the initial call."

"Call?"

"You know. What Thomas Hardy says. 'The voiceless call of woman to man.' "

Charlotte stared and nodded slowly. Thomas Hardy knew about this? "Where'd you read that?"

"In *Jude the Obscure*."

"That's nice."

Dana smiled broadly. "It's more than nice, Charlotte. It's *it*."

A long, slow smile came to Charlotte's face. Dana didn't have an easy time in life. For some reason people always blamed things on her, but she was a treasure.

The Odyssey

At night Brian could be found in his apartment sitting at a large desk under the eaves, typing. It was an old partner's desk, and he sat at one side to do his own work; the other side held his students' work. The poems he had sent to a poetry journal had been rejected, but they'd asked to see more, so he was encouraged. Writing was his true calling, and he stared into space trying to find new words that could describe the feelings that came home with him from school—something stirring, vague, some new inclination, a quiet disturbance. He'd been pushing words around for two hours. He'd opened to random pages in the dictionary, the thesaurus, books of poetry, looking for something to use to get him started. He used to think he was cheating by looking at other's work for his ideas, but Henry Miller had written that he borrowed everything, cut things out, and copied them down, thinking he would use them, but "borrowings" were never used in the finished work. It was more like scaffolding—getting you in position. A safety net. He tapped his pencil on the pad and waited for his metaphor to appear. He believed the first responsibility of a writer was to show up. Show up at the typewriter. So here he was, and nothing. Nothing but Bridget. The one woman he'd known the best. He could say he knew her inside and out. He thought of Charlotte and the white sweater she'd worn that day. Now she wasn't even wearing undershirts. If this was her rebellion, it was wonderful. He threw down his pencil. Who am I kidding? he thought. Impervious, I'm not. I know what's stirring and it isn't my noetic self or my poetic drive. He got up and stared out over the black water.

He dug out the seniors' book reports and looked for Charlotte's. She'd just finished *The Odyssey.* It began, "Odysseus was an honorable, honest man." He laughed out loud. She was so naive. He scrawled across her paper in big red letters, "You missed the point completely! Haven't you ever heard the expression 'wily Odysseus'? The Greeks revered cunning. His very name means 'the hated one,' and he was a pathological liar. Think larger than life. I want to hear about character as destiny." He read the brief report again and wrote on the last page, "Dig deeper, Charlotte. You're mining for gold."

He sat back and a huge moth flew at the lampshade. He leaped up, grabbed a towel, and started snapping at the moth. "Take that, you little bastard," he muttered. Two misses and one hit and the moth lay twitching. Brian picked it up by the wing and flushed it down the toilet. He took good care of his clothes and pulled open his bottom bureau drawer, sprinkling mothballs into the corners. He shook out his blue sweaters, of which he had three, and refolded them, inserting a mothball into each one. He found it relaxing to fuss with his clothes. He went back to the red scrawl on Charlotte's paper and saw his writing looked angry. Take it easy, Brian, he thought. It's *The Odyssey.* She's eighteen. And he put the last page of her paper in the typewriter and wrote on the back:

Charlotte,

This is not a finished paper. It's time to stop thinking in terms of book reports. Perhaps I haven't made myself clear. As a senior, I expect you to begin literary criticism. You will have to do this continually next year. Literary criticism is an arduous, exacting process of analyzing, questioning, arguing, defending, writing. It is difficult but rewarding. You all say you forget what you have learned. What you have written on you will not forget. You have not begun.

The Odyssey *is well within your grasp, and there is a motherlode. You have not found it, nor have you been lucky enough to stumble onto it. Please redo this. Reread, rethink, revise, and rewrite. A complete overhaul. If you can back up your statement that Odysseus was an honorable man with proof in the text, my disagreement will have no effect on your final grade. If this is un-*

clear, see me after class. I don't expect you to get it right the first time.

When Charlotte took back her paper in class, he noticed that she read his comments as if they could be ingested. He started to discuss Emily Dickinson, and when he turned to Charlotte, expecting to see her upset, she looked as if he'd just given her a big hug. Women, he thought, and he turned back to the woman poet.

The Lamb Roast

Charlotte had come to think of her father as a simple no-show in her life, but lately he'd begun to reappear. In November there was a dinner invitation. Her sister Kathryn was fourteen, and she was taking the train from Washington. They were going to their father's apartment for dinner. It was a big deal, this dinner, the first mending of the rift between Jack and his "beautiful" daughters. Kathryn was spending the night and going back to Washington in the morning. Charlotte met her at Grand Central, and they took a cab to 17 Gramercy Park. She looked over at Kathryn as the cab pulled up and said, "Here goes nothing." Kathryn had none of Charlotte's ambivalence about their father, and she was feeling very grown-up to be in New York on her own, so to speak.

The first thing Charlotte noticed about her father's apartment was the strange furniture arrangement. The living room had the old Duncan Phyfe sofa under a painting Charlotte didn't recognize, and a large green table that her father introduced as the billiard table. There was a small bookcase full of books that looked familiar. Placed next to it was Bette, his fiancée. Charlotte preferred the Duncan Phyfe when it was olive green with hundreds of little nail heads around the edge, but Bette had recovered it with a red and yellow satin stripe. That was all there was in the living room.

The middle room was his office, with the usual clutter of typed papers, and Charlotte could see the small editing marks on the pages piled on the desk. The last room was a bedroom and kitchen combined, where they lived like a couple of eccentric pioneers with a four-poster bed and a Queen Anne bureau, the icebox, the stove, and the sink. The kitchen table was a large glass outdoor terrace table that Charlotte remembered from the old house, and they could see their feet through the glass. Charlotte noticed the fingerprints around the light switches. The wood-work was grimy too. Her father would marry another terrible house-keeper, but at least there were no clothes on the floor.

When they met Bette she smiled and kissed and hugged them warmly, as if she'd been a member of the family for years. Charlotte was surprised at the soft touch of Bette's ample arms, and she couldn't remember how her mother felt. They had two Siamese cats, which they treated like children. Charlotte had never thought of her father as a cat person, but he seemed to like them. They were amusing, and when the conversation lagged, everyone, even her father, turned to the cats.

Charlotte saw that her father still loved to cook and to sit down to eat what he had labored over. He asked them twice how school was going. He asked about the dog. Charlotte told him the dog was dead, and he told them with pride how Bette went all over New York for the exact right spices, olive oils, and French cooking tools. He sharpened a large Sabatier knife as he talked about their shopping. They hung every-thing on a dusty Peg-Board.

They were cooking a new lamb roast recipe from *Tante Marie*. It was made with mint sauce, not mint jelly, Bette said importantly. Charlotte knew without being told that they made everything from scratch. The roast smelled wonderful, but her father seemed irritated. Charlotte looked for the source but saw nothing overt, though she noticed her fa-ther turned the cookbook repeatedly, as if he couldn't find what he was looking for. Bette scuffled around putting crackers on a chipped plate and slicing a piece of Jarlsberg. Fortunately Bette was a talker, so there weren't many awkward silences, and there were always the cats. Char-lotte had to grab Kathryn's feet three times to stop her from kicking the table legs. Her father and Bette sipped on drinks with melting ice cubes. Her father had found a devoted drinking partner. Bette was ample armed, bosomy, and jiggly, and Charlotte noticed how sweet and solic-itous Bette was to their father. Bette's eyes seemed to wobble about as if her pupils were loose, except for when she looked at Jack. Then her eyes settled on him, at him, for him, as if her very purpose in life was him. How her father must love it. The attention he so needed. The opposite of their mother. Bette was better than Bess, thought Charlotte, thinking how odd that both of her father's wives had names short for Elizabeth. She was happy for her father. Though Bette had another little wobble—a startled, halting, unsteady way of moving that Charlotte recognized as a variation on a theme. Her father was unsteady too, after his accident, when it seemed his body had fused his joints together to keep him from falling down. He'd never really walked right again, but sort of stiff and a little off-kilter. And now the two hobbled and jerked around the stove, waving their French knives. Every now and then they would stop, pick up their watery drinks, take a sip, and stare at the oven door expectantly.

When her father bent over *Tante Marie*, his thick glasses slid down his nose. "I'll be damned, Bette. These French. Listen to this: 'Cook until done.' Jumping Jesus. If I knew when it was *done* I wouldn't need a cookbook. How are you supposed to know?"

Charlotte glanced at Kathryn. Her father and Bette discussed it. They opened and closed the oven door and peered at the roast.

"It's browning up, all right," said Bette.

Her father was intent. "The potatoes look like they could use a basting. We want a crust."

"A light-brown crust," said Bette sweetly.

Charlotte had forgotten what a production her father made of cooking a meal, every little detail attended to, every sensual nuance, every authentic turn of wrist and flip of fork an act of French choreography. Three hours of cooking, twenty minutes of eating. They opened the oven door, slowly, carefully, and in slow motion slid out the pan to do the basting. But when Charlotte saw little potatoes around the roast turning dark, it was worth it. Heaven. They were both hungry and kept munching on the warm cheese and damp crackers.

Her father put the roast on the top of the stove and pierced it with a French boning knife. He made a slice in the middle and said, "I think it's done."

But no, when he started to slice, only the back half was done. "This damn oven is giving uneven heat," her father announced, and Charlotte noticed the Jarlsberg was beginning to sweat.

"Let's give it another half an hour, Jack. That should even it out," said Bette. Charlotte glanced at Kathryn. Trouble brewing. Her father paced three steps to the left, a long stare out the dusty window, a swallow of whiskey, and four steps the other way, back to *Tante Marie*. A look at the oven, a look at Bette, an odd look up at the ceiling, and Charlotte heard a whisper in her head: "Whence cometh my help?" Only her father could see a lamb roast on a Sunday afternoon in biblical proportions, the covenant of the French cookbook about to be broken. She felt the back of the Windsor chair dig into the middle of her spine. She shifted. The chair hit her just wrong. She and Kathryn talked on, when Bette and her father had their heads in the oven, about *Rebel Without a Cause*. Kathryn had a thing for James Dean, who was dead. Charlotte tried to think of a way to talk about her English teacher, but there was no way.

The sun was setting. Yellow-gray light seeped into the windows and fell on the four-poster bed. It seemed like a different sun than set on Flanders Point. They played with the cats. Charlotte didn't like the ill-mannered Siamese. They had a slimy, rodent look, but they were better than nothing. She found herself looking at the four-poster bed. She thought when a man took a new wife, he should buy a new bed. The old one had too many secrets.

Her father sulked. He looked at the cookbook several times. Charlotte had a stomachache and Kathryn said, "Are there more crackers?" Their father wasn't smiling, but at last he took out the lamb roast. The juices in the pan were sizzling, and their father deglazed the pan with red wine. Bette, Charlotte, and Kathryn watched him carve, Bette bent from the waist, hovering. Charlotte remembered that carving was a ritual art with her father. But the worst thing happened. The meat was cooked but now it was tough.

Her father looked daggers at Bette. "Where did you get this meat?"

"From the butcher." Her eyebrows wrinkled up, worried but not afraid.

"Well, it's a bad cut of meat and a worse recipe. It's overdone—and tough."

Charlotte and Kathryn stared. They recognized the breathing pattern their father used when he was sober enough to try and control his fury, and Bette sputtered, "Well, it will be—" But she didn't have a chance to finish. Charlotte's father speared the whole roast with his long

Sabatier carving knife and dumped it in the garbage next to the stove.

"Jack, Jack," cried Bette. "The girls will love it."

"Daddy, I'm sure it will be great. I like it well done," protested Charlotte, and Kathryn said not a word. At least there were still the potatoes. But her father picked up the roasting pan and dumped the wonderful little brown potatoes and carrots and onions, the whole dinner going in after the lamb roast.

"No . . . no . . . " he muttered, seething. "This recipe's no good. It's not fit to eat."

That was it. They ate ginger ale and saltines instead. Her father hadn't planned any dessert. They could smell the lamb roast cooling in the garbage. They would have been happy to pick it back up, but they didn't dare question him. Charlotte was furious but she knew they were lucky their father hadn't thrown it at them. She wondered how much Bette knew.

Charlotte sipped her fifth glass of ginger ale. She wondered, does he get angry if their lovemaking doesn't go exactly to his expectations? What if Bette didn't measure up one night? Would he throw Bette in the garbage? This seemed like a good time to offer her father a distraction.

"Dad, I know you're hungry and mad about the lamb, but I have something urgent."

"What?"

"You raise money on Wall Street, don't you?"

"Well, yes, for investors when I'm not writing a prospectus—I do both."

"Haddam's in a financial crisis. They may close for good in January. Could you raise money for a school with investors?"

He looked at her seriously. "My investors come for profit."

"Oh. Well, I just thought I'd ask. You know a lot of people with money. I'm not even supposed to know about it—it's all hush-hush."

"How *do* you know?"

"I overheard the English teacher talking about it," she lied.

"I'm sorry to hear it, Charlotte." He paused and his look was a bit glassy. "Even sorrier about the roast. Next time we'll have a goose stuffed with prunes—can't go wrong with goose."

"Okay. I wonder if a college could reject you if after you sent in your application and took your SATs and everything—then suddenly, your school vanished."

"I don't know, Cookie, I don't know. But it's worth asking."

Charlotte noticed a couple minutes later he went to his desk, turned a page in his datebook, and wrote something down.

Could it be about Haddam? She didn't think he really cared—but he did have this Radcliffe fixation and maybe he did have wealthy clients.

Her father and Bette and Kathryn all walked to the corner with Charlotte when it was time for her to leave. Standing on Third Avenue, her father put two fingers in his mouth and whistled, a piercing shriek. He stumbled slightly on the uneven cobblestones. An old checkered cab cut across Third Avenue and rattled to a stop. She was surprised when her father reached to give her a hug, just as natural as anything.

"Have a safe trip back, Cookie," he said. It was perfunctory. The first hug she remembered, though. Charlotte threw a sympathetic eye in Kathryn's direction as the cab pulled away.

Going home on the train, she thought about her father's hug. It wasn't so difficult. Just open your arms and move. Charlotte had always made such an issue of it. It never occurred to her that it wasn't just that her parents didn't hug her—she didn't hug them. Charlotte could only hug children. She'd try it on Max. Boy, would Max be surprised. By the time she met her father again, she'd hug him hello. That was the way people did things. It was time for her to take matters into her own hands. It was part of growing up—part of being a warm person. She fell asleep thinking about the hug and the way her father seemed different. Maybe now that he'd touched her so plainly, she could stop worrying about how he touched her. A detached hug had freed her, given her new space to feel compassion instead of shame for her father. But he'd always be a little dangerous when he drank.

When she got back to the Macreadys' she remembered something wonderful about being pick-up small. The hugs were missing but she'd had something better. She used to be her father's frequent bundle. She was in his arms, on his shoulders, around his waist, or piggyback. He used to walk his property, taking long strides up the great sloping hill in front of his house and all around the fields of Flanders Point, with Charlotte attached to him. She'd forgotten the physical feel of his arms, of his shoulders, of his strength when she hung on, clutching the fabric of his shirt, or reaching to get closer and safer, with her arms around his neck. How could she have forgotten? But the hug brought it back.

She pulled on her coat and said to Mrs. Macready, "I'm going to walk over to the orchard. If it gets dark, don't worry about me. I know the way in the dark."

And she was off. She hurried. Something urgent was there. When she got to the orchard, she sat up on the fence near where she waited for Brian in the mornings, though now her back was to the road. The view from this upward perch was familiar. Air, water, wind, grass. The clouds were peach and gray with a hesitant, leftover blue darkening. She whispered at the sky, "You are my giant. I am your small girl. Max is your son. I am his keeper. He is my beautiful troll. I'll love him for you."

Charlotte's spot on the fence was as high as her father's arm. The memory of how he was in those days came back. She was on her father's shoulders, his hands holding her feet. She balanced herself, matching the rhythm of his stride, and to sit on his shoulders was like bouncing on small waves. She put her hands around his chin or circled them around his forehead, as if she were his hat or his scarf. Sometimes she rested her chin on his head. And always he moved her all around himself. These were not hugs. These were loose encounters. Resting, holding, balancing, perching, and clinging, limb on limb, better than hugs, more natural, more plain, more pure. He let her crawl and climb all over him. And he liked to scoop her up, and he'd straddle her on his right hip, or he'd pick her up and fling her around in circles, grabbing one wrist and one ankle; up and down through the air he spun her around, and she flew in arcs and screamed and laughed. She knew even then that he liked the way she wasn't afraid. She said, "Do Max, do Max!" and Max said, "No, I don't want to." And her father just looked at him. He didn't coax Max.

"Aren't you afraid, Charlotte?" her father said in front of Max, and she said, "No."

"That's my lion heart . . . such a brave girl."

Charlotte pondered as she sat picking at a deep empty knothole in the fence, and a great remorse fell over her shoulders. Did Max know that she'd stolen his share of their father's love when she was four? That she'd replaced Max? That her four-year-old heart had sung a little song inside, "I have something you don't have," over and over, like a jump-rope rhyme.

I'm guilty, Max. I wanted it all. You were cheated. And you were worthy. It's funny, Max. I love you for your quiet ways, so good in a man, so welcome. You accept my love with no bitterness. I should think you'd hate me. You seem to know he's not what you need. Not anymore. I may have gotten, but you knew. Because, Max, he made a myth of me. My heart is no lion, and I'm going to let him down. I get scared—lots of times. It'll hurt him, and it'll hurt me to disappoint him, but it can't hurt you, Max. You're the wiser, the better.

Air, water, wind, and field. Here I was—and Max was—and my father and my mother too sometimes, but now there's only me again, remembering my father's arms and the view from where he put me. Up too high. Charlotte climbed off the fence and walked slowly back to the Macreadys'. There was a voice in the wind. *Max, Max, come back. I stole him from you. Now it's your turn. It's your turn to have a turn. I love you. He won't hurt you. He only pretends. You're worthy and he's worthy. Father, come back.*

But Max, living with a borrowed family just like Charlotte, had a cold vision that was clear. He knew something Charlotte didn't. She hadn't stolen anything. His father had never given his love to Max, so Charlotte couldn't have stolen it—at least not from Max. Max knew it and his mother knew it. Charlotte had no idea. But maybe it's true that even if you steal something that isn't there, if you think it *is* there, you're a thief. Charlotte thought it was there.

John Donne's Flea

THE GIRLS WALKED down to Little House for their creative writing class with Hazel Pierce. Sometimes class was fun and sometimes it was like a confession session when they had to read their work out loud and pretend it wasn't true. Mrs. Pierce had this thing called free writing. When they first got to class each girl had to read a paragraph or two from something they'd read outside of class that had words that stirred them. Mrs. Pierce said it was to get them into the milieu of words. Then she had them free-write for ten minutes. Sometimes they couldn't think of anything, and today was one of those days. So she stood up and pondered a minute. "Write about the thing that your mother or father does that irks you the most, that you see as a character flaw, even if it's something they know about in a conscious way. Tell everything. A writer can't afford to be kind. You have to tell the terrible truth. We won't read in class, though." So they wrote. Charlotte wrote the following:

My Father's Eyes

Bathing suits are two piece now, and bathing suits are like shorts. When a woman lies down in the sun, after sitting and watching her children play at the water's edge, her bathing suit is wrinkled and damp from being crushed in the folds of skin where the top of her thigh and her hip meet. The cotton leg of her shorts sculpts itself up, curved a bit open even though now she lies down to get some sun. My father walks along the sand below her, pretending to concentrate on his cigarette and the windrows of seaweed washed up with the tide, but his head moves sideways as he tries to see under the raised leg of the woman's shorts. Behind thick glasses, his eyes slide sideways in a tense and focused momentary stare. These women are strangers. What does he think he's going to see? A little more? The patch of white nylon that covers her undershorts? He is furtive. No one notices but me. I watch and mark it well.

In the movies men watch women too, but it's different in the movies. In *East of Eden*, James Dean looks at Abra's hair when she isn't looking, and he wants to take her hair in his fingers. Stewart Granger looks at Deborah Kerr in *King Solomon's Mines*, and he wonders how it would be to kiss her. Gary Cooper looks down at Ingrid Bergman in *For Whom the Bell Tolls*, and you see in his eyes that he is already thinking how it would look to see her head on the pillow. I watch men's eyes in the dark and feel hot all over, and I learn what they love. I don't need to learn what they want. I have my father to teach me that.

Hazel Pierce stopped Charlotte in the hall that week and said, "Come see me this afternoon, after study hall."

"I'll miss my bus."

"I'll take you home." Charlotte nodded. Her essay was late for the third time. She'd get a lecture. When she went up to the assembly hall, where there were a table and chairs, the afternoon sun was stepping across the floor in seven horizontal rectangles from the seven small windows. In the morning the hall was dark, but once the sun crossed over and started its downward slide, the hall was glorious. She sat down.

"I'm sorry my essay is late."

"That's not why I wanted to see you. It's . . . you seem so overwrought, so distracted. It's not your habit to be late with work." She waited but Charlotte said nothing. "I know how isolated you are at the Macreadys'. It must be hard working for a strange family."

"They're not strange anymore."

"I know, but even so you can never relax."

"I guess," said Charlotte.

Hazel realized that sympathy would just let Charlotte agree with everything she said. Hazel would have to get her angry. "But Charlotte, don't you see how privileged you are? To go to a school like Haddam, to be studying with the caliber of teacher we have here, to live on such a beautiful patch of earth as Flanders Point?"

"Privilege? Mrs. Pierce, Theo and Dana come from privilege. I don't. You have no idea what my family was like. One of the reasons I love this school so much is because I can leave my stupid family behind. They shame me but I'm free here. Free to be me."

"What shame? I met your mother the week after you came for an interview. Her work representing the poor is groundbreaking. You come from an educated family, a good family. What shame is there?"

"My father used to fly this big army plane and he crashed it when I was nine. We were living on Flanders Point. He came home with his head all bandaged and he started drinking. We moved and we lived like slobs for seven years in a well-kept town. *We* were not well kept. My mother never did a lick of housework in her life that I could see. No, that's not fair. She used to sweep and leave the pile she swept in the corner of the room under the standing broom. But everything was backwards after my father's fall. My mother was never home, and she should have been. My father was home all day and shouldn't have been. Our house was filthy. Our yard smelled like garbage because my father burned our garbage in an old rusty drum instead of using the garbage collectors. The stink never went away because this black gooey ash stuff oozed out around the bottom of the drum. Rats started coming in the yard to eat the garbage." Hazel felt Charlotte's anger rushing out.

"We had rats in our basement. What am I saying? There were rats in my room. Can you imagine? I was leaving *cheese* for them near a hole in my floor by the radiator because, stupid me, I thought they were mice. We had fleas in the carpets. One summer we went to Cape Ann for two weeks and when we came back to the house I opened the door, took two steps into the kitchen, and felt an odd tickle on my ankles. When I looked down there were all these little black things jumping up my legs. They were fleas. Fleas! I had to run out, and the house had to be fumigated before we could even set foot in it."

"Where'd they come from?"

"Well, before we went away there were seven people and a dog for the fleas to feed on. I guess they lived on the dog or in the carpet. While we were gone they all multiplied, and they were starving, so they were waiting at the back door for us to come back." Hazel had to smother a laugh. "It's disgusting."

"Aren't you exaggerating, Charlotte?"

"Do you think I could make that up?" She was almost shaking.

"I'm sorry," said Hazel. This was not what she expected to draw out of Charlotte. She was hoping to get to the issue of Brian Parton, but maybe this was more important. Carefully, deliberately, Hazel said, "It sounds as if your mother neglected you. It's too bad. She could have held the family together if she tried. A mother always can."

Suddenly Charlotte stood up. She walked back and forth in front of Hazel. "But she did, really! She worked fourteen hours a day. She had a daytime job at a law firm, then another, nighttime job as someone's personal secretary, and a weekend job, too. God, all she did was work. She didn't have time to clean. My father was always so mad at the mess, but he didn't clean it. I was the only one, and only now and then. She supported the family for six years when my father was too sick to work. All he did was burn the garbage. Our house was a disgrace in the neighborhood, and we couldn't even hide the garbage because we lived on a corner. Everyone could see. But do you know what?"

"What?"

"It wasn't anyone's fault." Charlotte stopped and took a long slow breath. "I don't think so, anyway. I'm still not sure. Maybe it was just my father's destiny—to destroy himself, and his family went down with him."

"You're not down, Charlotte."

"If I'm not it's because of Haddam. Here I feel as if I'm home. As if we're all cared for. Sometimes I even wish this was a boarding school. I'd like to live here." Charlotte noticed Hazel Pierce was watching her, as if she'd done something right. Though Charlotte had no idea what.

"Miss Haddam would be pleased to hear you say that."

"But still, how do you get out of the black places in your life?"

"For example . . ."

"I don't know. There are black things I can't see that have power over me. It's not a presence or an aftersense. They have no beginning, no end, no boundary, no name. But without any appearance of force, they make me bleak and hopeless. All I can do is give in."

"Are you talking about depression?"

"That's what my father had but I don't really know what it is."

"I'm not sure I do either. I'm sorry I can't be more help on this."

But when Hazel drove her home, Charlotte felt better than she had in a while. Hopeful. As long as there's hope, there's hope, thought Charlotte. In the car Hazel said, "Charlotte, if you can step back a little you could write a funny piece about the fleas waiting for you in the kitchen of your house. To get yourself started, there's a wonderful poem by John Donne called "The Flea." I'll bring it for you to read."

And they read the poem in Hazel Pierce's next class. As they finished discussing it, Charlotte said, "You realize, of course, that these two people in the poem, talking to each other, are naked."

"Where do you get that?" said Maude, pretending to be shocked.

"They're naked," she repeated.

"How do you know?" asked Theo. Charlotte glanced at Hazel Pierce and got a small nod of approval.

"Well, picture it. The woman finds a flea on her. But you can't see a tiny black flea in all the clothes they wore in those days—yards of velvet and silk and wool. You can only see a flea on bare skin."

The girls stared at the text, then stared at one another, and they all laughed.

A Bunch of Sea Lavender

A T THANKSGIVING, BRIAN was looking forward to four days of uninterrupted writing. He set his alarm for six every morning, but Saturday he shut it off and woke up late. He'd been working on a poem to submit, but it wasn't going well. Henry Miller had written, "When you can't create, you can always work." But the assumption was work would produce something. He was discouraged. When ideas wore thin and words wouldn't come he wondered if he was really a writer or just a man with grandiose dreams and occasional bursts of words that would never constitute a body of work. He was sleeping too much. He should have been rested, but writing was physical for Brian. A tense pulse beat in his shoulders when he wrote on his yellow pads, and if something good came through, the tension built. There was a little heat. He thought of it as a pilot light, a small blue flame, his own gift burning. But it flickered so faintly sometimes, or too deep, where he had to peer hard to see or feel it, so uncertain seeming. What he was certain of was he had consistent trouble calling it up. All he could seem to do at the moment was read poetry and feed on the leavings of others. He opened Ezra Pound's collected letters to T. S. Eliot and threw it back on the bed, uninterested.

He stood in his room naked, staring at the rubble of books all over his bed. Stacking them up next to his pillow, he drew the covers down and got back in bed. Cold sheets reminded him there ought to be something warmer than books in his bed. He hadn't said a word to a soul for three days and the silence was getting to him. He needed to talk to someone—anyone. Lying flat he stared at his feet, and with the edge of his palms sculpted the covers around himself until he looked like a mummy. Outside a solitary crow barked. He threw off the blankets, got dressed, reheated yesterday's coffee, and went for a drive around the point. The tires thudded on the sandy washboard surfaces and almost skidded off the road on one turn, but he didn't slow down. Flanders Point roads were off-limits to the local police. No stop signs, no speed limits, nothing. He loved it. When he turned onto Nathan Hale Road there was a figure walking along in green boots. His mother had had a pair of boots like that for gardening. He slowed down as he drove past and recognized Charlotte. He backed up and stopped. She was wearing a long gray fisherman's sweater that looked big enough to fit him, and she was covered with dry mud. There was a pencil stuck through the braids on top of her head.

"Hi, Charlotte. Where are you going?"

"Back to the house."

"What's all that?" He nodded toward the huge bundle of some bluish-gray plant in her arms.

"Sea lavender."

"Where'd you find it?"

"On the island in the cove. It was low tide."

"You look like you've been wrestling with the mud king."

"I know. The mud was like quicksand sucking the boots off my feet. I kept falling." She knew she was a sight, but he looked amused and she didn't mind.

He eyed the lavender. "Did you leave any out there?"

"I sort of overdid it, didn't I?" she said with a big smile, and dropped the whole bundle onto the road.

He stifled a laugh. "Well, don't you want it?"

She bent over, rested her hands on her knees, and peered at it intently. "I don't know, should I keep it? I kind of like it."

"Won't it be full of bugs?"

"I don't think so . . . not this late in the season."

"What's on your sweater?"

Charlotte looked down at the sweater and let out a screech. There were little black bugs crawling all over the front. She started jumping around and grabbed at the sweater to pull it away from herself, jerking and tugging at it frantically. This time Brian laughed out loud. She looked like a hysterical, gangly scarecrow.

"Ick," she said, freeing herself of the last of the little flies, feeling like a total fool. She wanted to make him laugh but not this way.

He asked, "Why isn't sea lavender lavender?"

"It's lavender in August. It's dead now," she said.

"Nice, though."

She nodded and nudged the bundle with her boot. "You're in a good mood," she said, looking at him.

"Aren't I usually?" He saw a small shrug and she looked away. "Are those your clothes?"

"No."

Brian thought about getting out of the car and taking a walk with her. "I'd offer you a ride, but I don't know about all that mud."

"That's okay."

"Well, see you Monday, then. . . ." but he didn't move and Charlotte loved the long pause. What was he thinking, anyway? He lifted his hand in salute and drove off. She watched the car slip a little around the turn, and the tires squeaked. He was so controlled, so polite, so guarded in his tense way—no wasted motion until he got behind the wheel of that car. She liked the way he kept asking her questions. He never did that before. She picked up the sea lavender and shook out the bundles for any last bugs. And she walked back to the empty house singing *Sleeper's Wake,* her favorite Bach chorale from music class. She held the sea lavender at arm's length.

When Brian drove home new images suddenly appeared, images he could use. Botanical death was different, not ugly. Lavender to gray, moist to dry, soft to brittle. A quiet surge emanated from between his shoulder blades. The Muse tapping him? He went and rewrote the stanza he'd been working on that morning. The new words were muscular and seemed to stand up and announce their importance as if to taunt him. He wanted to scrape the lines up off the page, wrestle them to the ground, flatten them out, look for cracks to seal or bumps to plane off. He had scraps of paper everywhere, ideas, phrases from yesterday, an arsenal of words waiting for his use. He worked until after three and finished what he thought was his best poem. Sitting back at last, he threw his pencil over to the bed. His father would be horrified at the thought of spending five hours on twenty-six lines. But Brian was excited. He had to go out more. Ideas came from unexpected places and ordinary things. A bunch of sea lavender falling to the road. The briefest moment. He always forgot. *Get out. Get out.* Observations from the exterior would animate and illuminate the interior. That was the landscape he had to see. The one he thought was so barren. Wordsworth knew it:

> *There are in our existence spots of time,*
> *That with distinct pre-eminence retain*
> *A renovating virtue, whence, depressed*
> *By false opinion and contentious thought,*
> *Or aught of heavier or more deadly weight,*
> *In trivial occupations, and the round*
> *Of ordinary intercourse, our minds*
> *Are nourished and invisibly repaired.*

He would read Wordsworth's *The Prelude* again.

But instead he drove down to the beach, parked his car, and walked along to the marsh thinking about his poem, unaware that he was whistling. To his surprise, Charlotte was sitting on the retaining wall. Twice in one day. She had changed her clothes and her hair was down. He walked over slowly, and she looked up.

"You're back . . . "

"Cabin fever." He sat down and they looked at Haddam lying on the hill across the cove. They didn't talk. After a long, uncomfortable minute Charlotte said, "What are you doing here?"

"It's nice here."

"Are you just out walking?" she asked.

"I'm out looking."

"At what?"

"I don't know," he said, "whatever I see . . . the cove, the marsh."
She forgot her discomfort. "Do you need a guide?"

"Well, for a minute or two, maybe. Where would we go?"
Charlotte looked surprised. "You're already here."

"Kind of a mess, isn't it? I thought you might have a better spot."

"Oh boy," she said. "Do you have a lot to learn."

"So . . . we're even."

She looked at him, suddenly fearless. "No, Mr. Parton," she said quietly, "we're *not* even."

Her intensity startled him. "All right, all right, we're not even." But she looked at him as if she was, and he wondered what she'd do if he met her challenge, so he looked back. She looked away, and he was relieved. So much for her boldness.

She said, "I don't think you need a guide. Just stay and look and listen. The salt marsh always has something to offer." She got up to leave.

He held up his hand. "Shhh. What's that funny noise?"

She listened to the little grunting sounds in the reeds. "Those are clapper rails. They nest in the salt grass. They don't migrate until late in the season. They're all around but you can't see them."

"Are you a bird watcher?" he said, motioning her to sit back down.

"Oh no," she assured him, "but Flanders Point is like an Audubon sanctuary." She didn't know what to say next so she sat back down and turned to what she knew, pointing to the sky. "Look . . . a red-tail hawk."

He shaded his eyes. "Where?"

"There . . . "

"I see it. How do you know? It's so high."

"By the shape of the wingspread," she said.

"I wish I had binoculars."

"Here." She handed him hers and lay back on the wall, watching another small black speck in the sky. It was far higher than the red-tail. She sat up slowly, still watching. It wasn't a gull or a hawk. The speck was moving fast, descending, plummeting. Brian saw it too. "What's that?" He pointed and handed her the binoculars.

"A raptor of some sort," she said. "It can't be a hawk. It's folded and it's dropping too fast." She suddenly caught her breath and, keeping her eyes fastened on the plummeting bird, she reached over and gripped the sleeve of his jacket. "Are you watching?" she said.

"Yes."

"Don't take your eyes off it."

The bird changed direction and ripped down the sky in a wild, wingless streak, and then the wings were out and it swerved toward a mallard that was flying across the cove. The dark bird swooped in and punched the mallard hard with its feet, knocking the duck out of its flight. The duck fell and the bird changed direction again, flipped over, and flew upside down under the duck and caught it in its claws. Then it soared off with the limp duck in its talons. Brian turned to Charlotte and watched her following its flight.

"Wow, did you see that?" said Charlotte with an amazed smile. But he didn't hear her question because he was thinking that her smile could knock a star from the sky. "That was no hawk," she said. "Do you know what I think it was?"

"What?" He watched her face.

"That, I think, was a peregrine falcon. It had to be. I called the Audubon Conservancy about a heron I saw the other day, and the naturalist told me there was a falcon in the area. We were talking, and he said nothing escapes a falcon. The only bird that flies that fast and takes his prey on the wing is a falcon."

"How fast?"

"A hundred and seventy-five miles an hour."

"What?"

"Yup."

"Poor, hapless duck."

"Who cares about him?" said Charlotte. "There's always another duck. It's the falcon I love, so powerful, so confident, taking what he needs."

"You don't think it's cruel?"

She looked at him in surprise. "Of course not. No one ever said nature had a heart. Life is cheap in nature. It's just the way of things."

"Could you elaborate?" Now Brian was smiling.

But she misunderstood and said, "Falcons are rare these days. The naturalist wants to go with me to look for a nest. He said they're in decline because DDT is running off the land and getting into the water and the animals the falcons eat have DDT in them. Then it ruins their eggs. The Audubon is trying to get a law passed to ban it." She paused. "It's a once-in-a-lifetime sight, what we just saw. I'm so glad you were here."

"Me too." She was quiet then, but he could feel an intense energy spilling around her and it made him want to draw closer. "I have to go, Charlotte."

"Where's your car?"

"At the beach."

"Can I walk partway with you?"

"Sure." They started walking.

"Listen, I know a shortcut through the woods," she said.

"That's okay."

"C'mon, there's a neat cottage with a straw roof."

"Another time."

"It only takes a minute." She walked into the woods, looking back and gesturing for him to hurry up. "You've got to see this."

"Okay, okay."

He followed her on a faint path, pushing branches out of his face as she disappeared behind a boulder and called, "Over here. Look."

The path opened into a clearing where random spots of light slipped through the last leaves and quivered on the roof of a small, white-washed cottage. "Have you ever seen a straw roof like this, Mr. Parton?"

He walked over slowly. "It's not straw, Charlotte, it's thatch, real thatch. This came on a boat from Ireland or England."

"What's thatch?"

"It grows in the peat bogs of Ireland."

"People live in houses like this?"

"Yes. My mother grew up in one just like it." Lost in thought, he pulled off a piece from the overhanging eave. "Who owns this?" he asked, his voice thick.

"This is Larsen's woods. I guess the Larsens do." She was trying to understand the emotion stealing forth from this man who never showed emotion.

Brian looked at his watch. "We'd better go."

Charlotte led the way and they walked back toward the beach without a word. When they got to his car, he stood with his hands in his pockets but didn't open the door and said nothing. He looked at her and then looked away and then looked at her again.

Charlotte felt as if seconds were walking by and he was staring as if it was up to her to say something. Finally, she said, "What?"

And he looked away. "Nothing." He opened the car door and got in and she stepped back so he'd know she didn't expect him to drive her back.

When he passed the spot where they'd come out of the woods, he noted the location. He'd go back there one day alone. So far, he'd had no chance to pursue his dream of returning to Ireland, or even England, to teach school and live in a house with a thatch roof. He probably never would, although he was interested to know that Haddam sometimes exchanged students with a small girls' school in Devonshire—a sister school, he'd heard. Maybe in a year or two he could teach there and rent a thatch cottage.

When Charlotte got in the car on Monday morning Brian said, "Maybe one day you'll be a naturalist and work for the Audubon."

"No, but I love knowing about another world that I'm not part of, because when you know about it, even though you may not be part of it, it's part of you. Don't you think?"

"That's well put. But you do have good luck seeing such interesting things."

"It isn't luck."

"What is it?" said Brian.

"It's just being there—waiting. To understand the mystery of nature you have to endure the monotony."

"What's the mystery?" he said.

"How disordered nature is. Have you ever realized how often nature breaks her own rules? The other day I saw a squirrel eating a dead possum on Red Coat Lane. Since when do squirrels eat meat?" She still got nervous when he asked her a question.

"You do see more than the rest of us."

"I'm out a lot. In my tomboy days I was more comfortable outside than in the house."

"Were you a tomboy?"

"Yes. In the third grade I used to beat up the boy who picked on my brother."

Brian smiled. "You protected your little brother?"

"My big brother. He's two years older than me." Brian looked at her. "He was sort of shy in those days. My father treated me more like a boy in the family." She squinted ahead of her and said quietly, "I never realized that before." Charlotte had never talked about her family with Brian. She felt a different kind of openness in the car that morning. Maybe they would be friends. But she misread. Brian was oddly nervous and was only interested in distracting her away from himself. He was building roadblocks, not opening doors.

Meanwhile, Margaret Chase continued to find families looking for a certain kind of school. There were many parents interviewing at Haddam. And the seniors' diversions with old Miss Haddam continued. Margaret Chase would come to Brian's class and say, "Who wants to go over at eleven-thirty to Little House—prospectives arriving." One of them always volunteered. And as the school tours went on, Mrs. Chase sent a confidential memo:

> *To all Faculty:*
> *I'm happy to announce that in January we'll*
> *have seven new students. It's hard for students*
> *to change midyear. It took subtle arm-twisting.*
> *I expect you to bend over backwards to make*
> *them feel at home here.*
> *Can you wait until December for your*
> *November salary? The cupboards are bare.*

The girls noticed a new tension—no one knew why. Some new worry slipped around the halls with the teachers' footsteps.

Henry V and a Condom

ONE MORNING JUST before English class, Dana and Theo grabbed Charlotte as she came in the front door behind Mr. Parton, knowing she'd join in their latest scheme. They said in low, conspiratorial tones, "Follow us."

"What's up?"

"You'll see." They went into the English room, which was empty, and Dana motioned for Charlotte to come over to Mr. Parton's desk. She pulled open the center drawer. "Look."

"What is it?" said Charlotte.

"What *were* you, Charlotte, born yesterday?" said Dana.

"Yes, she was," said Theo. "It's a condom, Dodo."

"Born yesterday," said Charlotte ruefully. "I don't think I've been born at all. Let me see . . . " She examined it. The word *Sheik* was written on it. "Where'd you get it?"

"In my brother's bureau drawer," said Dana.

"You're not going to leave it here . . . "

"Why not? Since I don't have a boyfriend right now and I can't put it where it belongs, I thought I'd put it where everyone else does, in a drawer."

Charlotte said, "I'm not so sure about this." She also thought it was mean. But she didn't want to stand up against Dana.

"Let's see what he can handle," said Dana.

"Why does it always have to be something dirty?"

" 'Cause that's what'll shake him up."

. . .

They were reading *Henry V* in class and writing sonnets as part of a poetry project.

"Mr. Parton, I finished the poem I had to revise. May I borrow one of your paper clips?" said Dana.

Brian walked over to his desk holding his copy of *Henry V* open. All the girls saw was a split second's hesitation and then he reached in, took one out, closed the drawer, and put the paper clip on Dana's desk without looking at her. But they noticed he began to turn pages rapidly in his copy of *Henry V.*

Brian found a passage he knew well. "Turn to the prologue, beginning of act four." He was blushing, damn it to hell, and he could feel his undershirt dampen as well. Brian read deliberately:

> *"Now entertain conjecture of time,*
> *when creeping murmur and the poring dark*
> *fills the wide vessel of the universe."*

"Charlotte, continue."

"Me?"

"You."

Charlotte read twelve lines and looked up.

"Go on." Her voice wavered as words of great beauty slipped by, but all she could do was try to breathe normally:

> *"The armourers, accomplishing the knights,*
> *with busy hammers closing rivets up,*
> *give dreadful note of preparation."*

She stopped again. Brian swiveled around. "Why did you stop?"

"You usually take turns."

"It's your turn."

She flipped her hair and went on.

Suddenly he said, "That will do. Now, what's all this about?"

Charlotte froze. Did he mean Shakespeare or the condom? Did he think *she* put the condom in his desk drawer?

"I'm waiting, Charlotte." She bit her lip and didn't open her mouth. "Theo?"

"It's the night before the battle of Agincourt, and the French and English armies are getting ready."

"Right . . . go on."

Charlotte didn't hear the rest. She was trying not to cry, and she was getting hives. She heard him say, "I think you got more out of that than there is in it, Theo. Dana, read to the end."

Charlotte watched him move around the room, pivoting on his little platinum bead, unperturbed.

Brian thought about who did it while he taught. "Shakespeare uses the prologue like a Greek chorus in this play to create the fields of France in his tiny Globe theater. What strikes you about this passage? Anyone?"

The class was quiet. He saw Dana folding a piece of paper into a small square. A note was about to be passed. What made her think he'd miss it? "Does anyone wonder why the prologue is so extravagant?"

Charlotte thought, Try to act normal, and she said, "I'm struck by the way a scene that's boring can draw you in." *Yeah sure,* she knew Dana and Theo were thinking.

"But what was the figure that engaged you?"

"The figure?"

"The literary device."

"Oh. Metaphor?" she asked.

"Yes." He turned and saw Theo's pencil drop, and then she reached to pick it up, along with the little folded note on the floor by Dana's desk.

He ignored it. "The prologue is full of metaphors, isn't it?"

Charlotte pushed on, leading the class away from his embarrassment, as well as her own. She hadn't seen the note yet.

"The metaphor that caught my ear was the description of how slowly the night was passing . . . when Shakespeare compares the night to a witch." She looked for the lines. "He says:

> *'The soldiers*
> *chide the cripple tardy-gaited night who,*
> *like a foul and ugly witch,*
> *doth limp so tediously away.'*

"I love that."

Brian said, "Maybe it's too strong. Should language call attention to itself this way?" But the question went unheard because now Theo leaned in to Charlotte and pointed to her open text.

Brian's eyes flicked by as he saw the folded note sitting in the center groove of the book. He turned and went on though he knew no one was listening. "For tonight, I want an essay on why he takes such pains with the prologues."

Charlotte now held the note. Brian walked over to Charlotte's desk and stood over her. As her left hand held the note and draped over the left side of her desk she started to slide her arm back so she could read it. But Brian, with more calm than he felt, leaned over slightly and smoothly put his hand over hers, held it firmly, and with his thumb and index finger removed the note from her hand. He kept talking the whole time and slipped the note into his jacket pocket, his eyes on the text, never looking down.

Damn. Charlotte sank back in her chair and put her hand over her eyes.

After class the girls went downstairs to the science lab. The room was empty and they could talk.

Charlotte sighed. "That was awful and it was mean."

"It was worthy of us, though," said Dana.

Charlotte couldn't hide her disgust, muttering, "Never again."

Theo said, "It wasn't so original, your idea, you know, Dana. It's been done before."

"I think maybe it was. I took the condom out of the wrapper, unrolled it, and left it wet on his address book."

"What!" said Charlotte. "We didn't discuss *that!*"

"What's so terrible, Charlotte? *You* don't need to worry," said Dana.

"What do you mean? He thinks it was me. How could you even try to pass me a note when you know his peripheral vision is twenty-twenty?"

Dana looked at Charlotte with a small smile. "It wasn't a note."

"What was it?" said Theo.

"It was blank. I just folded up a blank piece of paper." Theo and Charlotte stared at Dana.

"Well, that *was* original," said Theo, and Charlotte left the room.

Brian drove home in a cold fury. He knew most men would have laughed it off, but to Brian's deep sense of propriety this was a violation, powerful and disturbing. And the blank note, though funny, was maddening. He had to concede it was a clever move, and only Dana would pull something like that, knowing he'd be too embarrassed to speak and discipline them; and then humiliating him with the note.

Charlotte was furious, too. She hated making a fool out of anyone. Once the kids in high school had played a joke on her, hiding her coat on a snowy day. They had sent her out to the bleachers on the football field, then to the gym. She finally found it on the floor in front of her locker. She never forgot what a fool she had felt and how it had hurt.

When she got home from school she threw her books on the bed and walked down to the salt marsh. What a great, silent place it was sometimes, and for a minute she forgot everything. The rushes that grew so tall in the autumn were eight feet now. They stood dry and brittle, rustling in the light airs of the cove. It was the sound of silk in her mother's dress, it was the sound of taffeta on her crinolines. When the tide moved in and the water curled and crept through the mud flats, lapping against the bottom of the reeds, it was like wet silk floating. Did other people hear it—the marsh and the tide like lovers whispering to each other in the corners?

She sat on the wall and watched the sun carve brooding, late autumn shadows. Brian had handled it so well. He kept his cool. He got the note. Yet still he'd been made a fool. She jumped off the wall, snapped off a cattail, and cracked open the pod. Maybe he shouldn't have engaged. That was the mistake. He should have been above it. They passed a note. Big deal. Why should he have even bothered with it? But any way she looked at it, he was not at fault. She snapped off another pod, and this time she blew the little pieces of milkweed into the wind, each one carrying a seed.

There was something else. Brian's hand over hers. When he'd taken the note from between her fingers a shock went through her as if she had no will of her own when he touched her and when he took what he wanted.

Before she went to bed, she wrote to her mother . . . not about the condom; her mother would be disgusted. About Brian Parton.

The Aftermath

THE NEXT MORNING it rained. Charlotte was not on the fence. Brian drove up the road toward the Macreadys'. She was walking on the road with her head down. If there was one thing he had grown to like about her, it was her honesty. He pulled over and she climbed in. They drove in silence, a loose windshield wiper making an odd racket.

Finally he said, "What do you know about it, Charlotte?"

"What do I know about what?" she said, and they both stared straight ahead as if the rain would whisper the answer. He wanted to say "Talk to me, damn it!" but he said nothing. Just before they got out of the car she said, "It wasn't me."

The episode was whispered through school. Girls kept staring at her and Dana. That night she was cold gray clay from the weight of it. She knew it was unimportant, such stupidness. But she couldn't sleep. The next morning in the car, unable to go on with the silence, she said to Brian, "I'm sorry about what happened."

"Forget it."

"I can't. I could have talked them out of it."

Brian put his foot on the brake and pulled the car off the road. He turned and faced her. "But you didn't, Charlotte. The whole female staff heard about it."

"We didn't mean to humiliate you."

"Bull. But I'm surprised at you."

Charlotte started to cry and said, "I'm not surprised at all. I was thinking about myself. When I have really strong opinions I can get people to listen. I didn't even try."

He hadn't meant to sound so sharp.

She got herself under control and said quietly, "It would be different if you were a pompous know-it-all, but you're not. You're fair."

Brian kept still. He was interested to hear this. It didn't sound like Charlotte pumping him up. He wasn't sure he was a good teacher. He hoped he was. This was feedback, even if delivered hysterically, and he listened.

Charlotte sat there sniffing, her head down. She looked miserable. Yesterday he'd felt like slapping her. Not today.

"I'm not angry," he said.

She gave him a look, "Yes, you are."

"All right, yes, I am." He liked the way she wouldn't let him get away with anything. He felt a lightness of heart.

"What are you going to do about it?" she said.

"I don't know. Probably nothing." He started the car but didn't move it. "What do you want, Charlotte?"

"Me?"

"All of you."

"Your full attention."

"You have it and you, above all, know it."

"I guess it's not enough," she said.

"What more is there?"

She paused and said, "Just more."

He looked at her quickly and turned away and Charlotte heard him mutter, "Damn!"

"What?"

"Nothing," he said, but she looked where he was looking and recognized the car that had just passed them. It belonged to the headmistress.

Margaret stopped him in the hall and said, "Come to my office before lunch."

When Brian sat down opposite her he suddenly felt like a prospective parent about to be solicited. Margaret was oozing warmth until she said, "I saw your car on the side of the road this morning. Was there a problem?" She was shuffling papers.

"No," he said.

"With the car? With Charlotte?"

"No . . . " Mrs. Chase opened her mouth to say something and Brian said, "Charlotte was trying to apologize."

"She does have special access, of course, doesn't she?"

Margaret was oiling her way up to something. Brian said, "She has no access at all, Margaret, though she may not see that."

Margaret stopped sorting her papers and looked him up and down. "Remember, it's your job to be sure that she *does* see that."

He ignored the slide of insinuation. "Your concern is admirable but needless."

"If you say so," said Margaret.

That day, the senior class was informed that they would be meeting with Margaret Chase and Miss Haddam on Saturday morning in Miss Haddam's house. Maude and Cora, who hadn't been in on it, didn't protest. Charlotte said to Maude, "Listen, why don't you say something? You don't have to be there."

Maude was a little cool. "Yes, I do. You're the one who should say I had no part in it. You know that. So I'll see you Saturday morning."

That night while Mr. Macready was still upstairs, Charlotte knocked on Mrs. Macready's bedroom door. And when Mrs. Macready opened it, she said warmly, "What a surprise. I thought you were Peter. Come in, Charlotte." Mrs. Macready liked Charlotte and had noticed from the first week that Charlotte took very good care of the children, an expert for a girl her age, though she was oddly careless about herself. There was usually something amiss, a bandage on one of her fingers, or a hem falling down, or shoes badly scuffed. Charlotte was pretty but she didn't act like it. It occurred to Mrs. Macready that Charlotte needed her more than she needed Charlotte. And one afternoon, she'd said quietly, "Why don't you give me your shoes, Charlotte. I'll polish them for you." Another day she said, "You know, Charlotte, if you can find some green thread in my sewing basket, I'll fix that hem." To her surprise, she found that Charlotte was very good at fixing hems. It was noticing that they were falling down that she wasn't good at. Mrs. Macready asked her husband to put a full-length mirror on the back of Charlotte's bedroom door, and she explained in her cheeriest voice, "Every morning, Charlotte, before you leave your room, look in the mirror, front and back, and check your clothes and your appearance. If you want people to treat you nicely, you have to look nice," and Charlotte had smiled, happy with the feeling that Mrs. Macready was such a natural mother, she was even mothering her.

Charlotte sat on the bed and related the events at school, ending by telling Mrs. Macready that she'd apologized to her teacher and he'd seemed to accept her apology, but it still wasn't over.

Mrs. Macready said "Why did Dana bring a *condom* to school?"

"She was just fooling around. The three of us did it, but it was Dana's idea."

Mrs. Macready was calm with all the children asleep and she didn't falter once. She said, "It would seem to me that you're equally to blame. An idea is only an idea. The three of you approved it when you acted on it. Only one pair of hands was needed to put the condom in the drawer but more than one pair of hands are to blame."

"You mean, even though I didn't say I approved—"

"Your silence was approval."

"But is it okay for me to be the one to own up to it, if that means the other two will probably get nailed too?"

"I'd admit it, clear the two who weren't in on it, and take the consequences, which may be the anger of Dana and Theo. I don't see any way out of this without pain."

"That's all right. I just want to make amends."

"To whom?"

"To my English teacher."

"Well, that's a different issue. I thought this was about your friends."

"My teacher, too. He's furious."

"You said you apologized. Just leave it be. He'll get over it."

Charlotte looked at Mrs. Macready gratefully and nodded slowly. The kinks were straightening in her brain.

"You make it so clear. Thank you."

"You're welcome, but don't make yourself crazy over this. Before you know it, it'll be forgotten."

But about this, Charlotte knew she was wrong. When she was thirty, she would still remember that she'd been willing to stick her finger in the eye of someone she cared about for the approval of someone she didn't.

"You won't mention this to Mr. Macready?"

"No."

But Charlotte had the feeling from his looks that weekend that he knew. She didn't hold it against Mrs. Macready. It reaffirmed her hopeful notion that in bed men and women could talk about anything and secrets would be shared. On Saturday she walked over to Mrs. Chase's.

When she got there, Dana seemed intent on stirring things up. Brian Parton wasn't there and Dana said, "Mrs. Chase, I think you should call him. He should be here."

The only response Dana got, however, was a raised eyebrow and a cold stare. Margaret Chase's dogs came over, sniffing and poking wet noses at Dana's knees. Dana hated dogs. "Get away," she said and then whispered, "That dog smells to high heaven." Charlotte thought, Good dog. You know who to bother. Sit on her feet, sniff her crotch, pee on her, jump up and slurp her mouth.

When Miss Haddam arrived, they stood until she sat resting her bony left hand on a walking stick.

Charlotte didn't know that Miss Haddam's way of reprimanding students was to start the meeting in silence until someone was too nervous or too bold to be still. Charlotte finally said, "Maude had nothing to do with this, and neither did Cora."

"Who did?"

"Well, I did . . . " said Charlotte weakly.

"Anyone else?" Miss Haddam and Mrs. Chase looked at Dana and Theo.

Finally, Charlotte added, "It's not for me to say."

Theo looked miserable but said not a word, and Dana was looking ice picks at Charlotte, who had no way of knowing that Dana was already on academic probation for borderline grades.

Miss Haddam spoke, "Charlotte, perhaps you don't know the Haddam way yet. At times like this, my dear, the truth is your only friend." Charlotte was mute.

"Dana?"

"I don't know how it started."

"Theo?"

"It just sort of happened."

Miss Haddam truly believed in the "Love mercy" part of the Haddam code and she was rarely severe unless the issue was cheating. "I'm inclined to let this pass," she said with an odd edge.

Mrs. Chase said, "Forgive me, but uhh, I think, well, I'm not inclined to ignore this, I mean." If the torch was going to be passed, it was going to be passed. "You will all stay after school for a week and, uhh, clean up the science lab, and you will write essays to Mr. Parton on . . . collective conscience and . . . individual responsibility in the Greek polis."

"Polis?" said Charlotte. "What's that?" She saw how nervous Mrs. Chase was with Miss Haddam.

"A city-state in ancient Greece," said Theo.

"Oh."

"I want citations. Hand them in tomorrow." The girls stood up to leave.

"I think Friday suffices," said Miss Haddam. Mrs. Chase stiffened. "The point, Margaret, is for the girls to think. They can't think in one night."

"Of course they can," said Mrs. Chase with a tight smile.

"Friday would be better. And I would like to add something." Charlotte thought she heard an impatient sigh from Dana and Theo. Only Charlotte sat back down, noticing the aged quaver in Miss Haddam's voice and the feeble tremble of her chin. "Dana, Theo, I've known you since you were seven. You're part of this family. Charlotte, I don't know you as well, but you are, too. This episode was silly. But it goes to the heart of what you have yet to learn. With independence comes consideration. I usually talk about responsibility, but this is different. It shows a callous disregard for a man in authority who's come to teach in a woman's place. It may be awkward for him. But he has an outstanding reputation. He's not here for your entertainment. *He* did not complain about this. When asked, he shrugged it off. I do not. Nor does your headmistress." She paused. "You can go." And they left.

Mrs. Chase said, "I wasn't aware of Brian bringing any reputation at all." She was wondering what Miss Haddam could possibly know that she didn't. Margaret had done the background check. One year's experience? "He hasn't even been certified!"

"They don't know that."

They sat in silence and Mrs. Chase realized that Miss Haddam wasn't going to fade quietly. Miss Haddam said slowly, "This class will graduate from college in 1960, won't they? I'll probably be dead. But they're going to change the country."

"Every generation thinks they're changing things, but actually what they're doing is preserving the status quo."

"It may be different this time," said Miss Haddam, thinking Margaret's an odd view. "Margaret, when one sails a ship and has a hand on the tiller, one is automatically responsive to the needs of the ship without thinking. One day when you need other people to help you say, 'Tighten the mainsail halyard,' and they look at you oddly and say, 'What's a halyard?' By the time you explain, you have already fixed it. Doing things through other people is difficult. I need you to consult with me often. If not, the experience I've gained will vanish when I do."

Margaret Chase was devoted to Miss Haddam and tried to emulate her, but clearly she had a lot to learn. She had never had one of Miss Haddam's lectures directed at her. "You're right. I'm a good sailor, I know what a halyard is, but it's also true I've never sailed a ship this size."

Walking back to Dana's car, Charlotte said, "The tension in there was so thick, you could taste it. What was that all about?"

"The transfer of power. We were being used."

"I'll say. You certainly couldn't accuse them of subtlety, could you?" said Charlotte.

"By the way," said Dana, lighting a cigarette, "thanks. You almost got us expelled."

"I don't think so at all. That was tame."

"Think again."

"What's Periclean mean?" said Charlotte.

The girls looked at her.

"You know . . . Athens, Socrates, Pericles . . . Have you forgotten?"

"I'm new here, remember?"

"I'll help you, Charlotte, it's great stuff," said Theo.

So the essays were written but when Charlotte handed Brian hers in the car, he said, "Give it to Margaret Chase. I don't need to read it."

She sat forward. "Stop the car. Stop the car!"

He pulled over and said, "Charlotte, I don't care for this melodrama one bit."

"Wait. Let me talk. You did it to me the other day. Give me the same time."

"Go ahead."

"You're wrong to dismiss us. *Read* our essays. We've written them because we respect you. You have to respect us too. To slam the door is . . . immature. We want another chance."

He looked away. She dared to put herself on equal footing, where she knew she didn't belong. It was interesting and that made him angry and he looked back at her and said, "Just who do you think you're talking to?" thinking she'd crumble. She held his look. No more was said. Later, when he pulled into the drive he said, "Very well, I'll read them." And it was done. It was a payment dropped into a void and the whole episode left a crack in the girls' solidarity. Charlotte could feel it and she thought she'd lost something. She had, but what she'd gained was worth more than what she'd lost. She just didn't see it.

And no one, not even Charlotte with her special access, knew what else good had come from it. Brian was on more solid ground. In a new way, he could, as Hans had said, "Handle it."

Blue Heron

AFTER THEIR FIASCO, the girls were on good behavior and Charlotte expected things to go back to normal. But Brian was different. It was as if he'd hung a sign on his suit that said DO NOT DISTURB—GO AWAY. The free-flowing talks in his car stopped and she knew she'd have to win his trust again. She had no idea how, so instead she tried to put him out of her mind. She found small success. Thoughts and images about him slipped in from the margins and pushed up from below, surprised and tricked her. She tried to change her perspective. This was nothing. She was nothing. He wasn't much more.

From the Macreadys' she had been watching a great blue heron in the evenings. Silent, he stood in the cordgrass every day when the sun went down. He appeared the day after the condom episode, and he'd been feeding there for two weeks. The mystery of his stillness drew her out the door. She went to the wall at the water's edge and climbed down. She stood as still as she could and stared at him. If the heron saw her, he gave no sign. But she wanted to get closer, and she picked her way through the rocks till she was far into muddy grass that reached past her knees. With the sun almost gone, she stood in his place and the heron looked like a thin, gray, fading shadow leading in the night. She moved a step and stopped again. She was learning to be still and not go too close, and even as she learned he allowed her to come closer. At that moment he lowered his head, and with his reedy leg bent strangely backward—kiddershins, it was called—he took a cautious step away from her.

Just this once she wanted to stir him further, to be acknowledged, and moving like a heron herself, she stepped forward. With his familiar absence, the great heron opened his wings and with a dry clatter he lumbered up. And there was quiet again as his great wings stroked the dusky night and he flew. Charlotte turned to follow his dark and dignified silhouette throbbing to the west. She watched till he was gone and went back to the house. The next day she saw from the kitchen window that he was back in the same spot, standing mute and still. What a good, steady bird, she thought, and she turned to the little ones, who clanked their spoons on the table in a game while they waited for their eggs. She loved the sight of the four of them fresh from their bath, wearing pajamas and robes and slippers, waiting to eat like good little children. It was predictable and it was secure, as Mrs. Macready had said, and it didn't feel stifling to Charlotte. It was reassuring for the moment. But Charlotte preferred the restless, ever-shifting boundaries between the sea and the marsh. More than predictable, the tidal wetlands were so vast and eternal they could accommodate, even welcome, the unpredictable, like a great heron that didn't follow his kind in the flight south. This was more than reassuring—it was reliable.

The Gold Pencil

CHARLOTTE WAS DEVELOPING a hypersensitivity to the world around her that was troubling. Little things affected her that no one else seemed to notice. If she didn't like the way a glass felt on her lips, she would get another glass. If the seams in her stocking slipped off her heel, she would feel it and had to fix it. Her underpants had to come to the exact right spot across her lower back. She couldn't wear earrings because they made her ears hot. The droning sound of the Macreadys' icebox drove her to unplug it when she was fixing supper for the children. If someone chewed with their mouth open, she wanted to get up and leave the table, though of course she couldn't be so rude. Faucets that didn't feel right in her hands were irritants. The handles of teacups strangled her fingers, too. At suppertime, the children laughed when she got static shocks on the icebox door so loud they could hear the tiny snap that made her jump out of her skin. Charlotte laughed, too, but it wasn't funny. She knew her mother would say again, "Get a grip on yourself." She had a grip on herself, and it was too damn tight.

She was getting a thing about tight clothes, too. She pushed her sleeves up because she didn't like anything around her wrists. She never buttoned her coat. Jackets and cardigans flapped open and loose behind her as she walked. She unbuttoned her blouse two buttons so nothing would pull at her neck. She could feel the labels on the back of her sweaters and ripped them off. And it was true that wearing a bra made her back itch, but her refusal to wear one was more a manifestation of this growing need to be unbound. She kept these things to herself, of course. But sometimes she thought she should have been born in the wilderness so she didn't have to wear clothes, just spiderwebs tied around her with strands of myrtle.

And her hypersensitivity was not only to irritants. Of major importance were pens and pencils. She felt a keen and sensual pleasure in her fingers from using her Esterbrook pen. She would copy things over just to feel the soft, wide nib slipping along. And pencils had to have the right soft lead with a grainy scratch. She liked the slight resistance and the tiny musical *slish* of the lead scratching along the vellum. Pens and pencils belonged in her hands, and stationery stores drew her inside the way clothing stores drew in other girls.

She came to class on Mondays with a fistful of yellow pencils, and over the course of the week they'd end up on the floor, in her mouth, or dropping out from between the pages of her books. Sometimes she'd grab her hair, give it a quick twist on top of her head, and anchor it with a pencil stuck through it like a chopstick. It was interesting what Charlotte could do with a pencil. Brian had noticed that when other seniors asked to go to the bathroom, Charlotte asked to go to the pencil sharpener. If he was ever in need of a pencil, which he almost never was (he had his own thing about pencils), he would look in the desk where Charlotte sat. Her discards would be there. He reminded her to come to the midterm with a good supply, and he was amused after class one day when she picked up his gold lead pencil to make a note and her eyes lit up with pleasure. "I love the way this feels in my hand and the way this writes." She had said it as if it was of the greatest importance, or as if she would eat it.

But Charlotte was exhausted. She took no comfort in the small sensual pleasures of life now. Not even the soft sound of the tide working through the cordgrass soothed her. There was a constant pull toward Brian that she must not give in to, and she bound herself in. But rarely did half an hour pass that he did not intrude on her thoughts. She was tired of being resistant and at odds with herself; her self-control was what was out of control. What she longed to be was compliant. Her long walks in the salt marsh turned into silent monologues as she talked herself out of the urge to walk in Brian's front door. Only the sight of a marsh hawk quartering along the water would pull her free. She wanted Brian's hands on her, all over her, to quiet her; her thoughts turned increasingly sexual.

She approached the English midterm with exhilaration and dread. The only way she could talk to Brian was through her work. She wished he didn't grade it. She had yet to get an *A*. If nothing else, she told herself, she was learning more than she ever had. Did it make a difference that her motives weren't pure? Was love pure?

Friday morning he handed them the thin blue exam books. All essay questions. She began quickly, pressed too hard, and snapped the lead on her pencil. She picked up her spare. After ten minutes that too broke under pressure. She reached over to Theo's desk, indicating that she needed a pencil. Theo nodded absently.

It was a number 3 pencil. Charlotte hated those. It was like writing with a needle. They weren't allowed to leave their seats during the exam. She put down the number 3 and looked up. Brian was watching her. Caught in this foolish agony over nothing, she sighed and resolutely picked up the nasty pencil, remembering how her father used to say, "If you don't bend, you'll break." She looked at Brian as if to say, "I know, I know, I'm crazy."

But Brian took two long steps toward her, pulled the gold pencil out of his breast pocket, and handed it to her with a look of quiet forbearance. Turning back to her test, she felt her knees turn warm as if she were kneeling in a white-hot sun. She thought the rest of her legs would dissolve too and she would slide off her chair. If she went limp at nothing, what would happen if he kissed her? When the test was over and she handed him back his pencil, he was distant and didn't respond to her thank you.

In keeping with Miss Haddam's honor code, nothing was locked at Haddam, and the seniors discovered where the students' confidential reports were kept. Maude saw Miss Haddam go to an old cardboard carton and pull out a girl's report. The box was labeled USED CURRICULUM NOTES, and Maude realized that Miss Haddam was so hard of hearing that she hadn't realized she wasn't alone in the office. These weren't just grades, they were highly specific evaluations. When she mentioned it to the other girls the pressure built up. They were all curious about what Brian thought of them, and it was too much to resist. One afternoon, they assembled after school and sneaked in and each read his comments. Charlotte read eagerly.

Charlotte sometimes gives evidence of having a very clever mind. I doubt that she knows it is there. She consistently thinks shallowly and much of her written work is weak, with indifferent grammar and sloppy execution. When quality is present, it is concealed. I am not sure that she can distinguish between her good work and her bad. She does well on exams where she does not know she is thinking. If she ever develops any power of self-evaluation and applies herself seriously, she will do excellent work.

She put the report back in the folder, stunned and chagrined. He'd lifted her up. Now he slammed her down. She was sloppy and shallow? What could be worse? She'd known all along that Brian didn't think she amounted to much, but she was puzzled by how angry he sounded. Angry at her for not being good enough. At least he didn't say she was dumb, just that she wasn't using what she had. She would have to work harder. The other girls were reading avidly, and with a leaden pressure squeezing in her chest, Charlotte picked up Hazel Pierce's report, although she didn't really care to read anymore. Mrs. Pierce knew Charlotte better because of the short stories she'd written the year before.

Charlotte seems to be in a highly emotional and nervous state this year, and her work has been erratic as a consequence. It is impossible to find out through her stories what her beliefs, ambitions, and standards are, for they are done hastily, although with occasional brilliance. Her writing is an attempt to present herself in a favorable light.

Indeed, her entire concern is with herself to a degree that would seem disturbing if one did not take her youth and the current transient quality of her emotions into account. I think efforts should be made to take her out of herself, into a wider world of ideas, ideals, and different points of view. If we cannot do this we are failing her. She seems to be seeking her own reality, which is admirable, but she is confused in her search and disturbed by her own capacity for pain.

Beliefs, ambitions, standards. Charlotte never even thought of such things. She sighed. It was time to get serious. The girls were thumbing through other reports but she couldn't read anymore. She'd been stung by Brian's comments, but Hazel Pierce's left her raw and bleeding. There was a deep ache beginning that she didn't understand, and in her blindness she thought it was because she had disappointed her English teacher. And she turned in the wrong direction—toward him. I'll get serious, she thought. I'll work harder. I'll write neater. It was to Hazel Pierce that Charlotte should have turned, for here was a woman who understood her. Who could have shown her the way. Charlotte missed the path completely that day. But whether she thought so or not, Charlotte was no fool, and understanding was not that far away. And it would come in an unusual form. The form of unexpected trouble and unexpected help.

Fog on Flanders Point

CHARLOTTE HAD BEEN waiting so long for her mother to answer her letter about Brian Parton, she figured her mother must be pleading a case in court. But that night when Charlotte went up to the kitchen to get some saltines, there, propped against the lamp in the hall, was a letter from her mother. She forgot the saltines and hurried to her room.

> *This is your mother speaking. Don't ever write a letter like that again. Yellow lined paper, worn-down pencils and crossed out words are not acceptable. If I ever receive another letter presented in this fashion, I will throw it away without even attempting to read it.*
>
> *I did, however, struggle through it. You are the only one of your siblings who has the privilege of private school and I suggest you forego the melodrama, stop complaining, forget about your English teacher, and get a grip on yourself.*
>
> *Your mother*

She threw the letter on the bed table and watched the paper refold as if it were alive. She stared out the window but there were no lights on the water. Fog was moving in. She pulled on her duffel and walked out the door into the wet night. She'd go to the low marsh to let the tide take her. She would wander over a cliff and be washed against the rocks. Her mother used to say, "I never worry about Charlotte. She can take care of herself." *Maybe you should worry a little, Mother.*

She ran along Willow Lane to the dunes, and willow branches

dragged across her shoulders and caught in her hair like wet fingers. Gray, dripping ground fog thickened over the Point. She stopped to listen for the foghorn and heard the sound of water slapping on paper as it dripped on dead leaves. Under a branch she turned her face up and let the water drip onto her face. "Please, God, help me . . . I can't figure everything out alone, and some day I *will* be worth worrying about." She picked up a small sharp stone, like the kind she used to draw hopscotch on the sidewalk, and scratched angry letters that she could barely see onto the road—MOTHER; LOVE. And she walked away.

When Mrs. Macready went down to say good night to Charlotte the room was empty. She sat on the bed and looked at the spartan furniture. She should make it more feminine for Charlotte. She'd hang organdy curtains after the baby. Mrs. Macready went up to the library, where her husband was reading. "Have you seen Charlotte?"

"No. Why?"

"She's not here."

He shrugged. "Maybe she went for a walk. She does that."

"On a wet night like this? It doesn't make sense. She takes college boards tomorrow and she said she was going to bed early. It's eleven o'clock."

Mr. Macready knew his wife wouldn't rest until everything was in place. "Why don't you call the headmistress? She might be over there. If she isn't, I'll go look for her."

Mrs. Macready called Margaret Chase. Charlotte wasn't there. Mr. Macready got his car keys.

When she got the call, Mrs. Chase was concerned. On occasion she'd seen Charlotte walking at dusk like some restless shorebird looking for a nest. She was responsible for Charlotte. Why would she have gone out again after dark? A problem with the family? Where would she go? Could she have gone to Brian Parton's? Mrs. Chase wondered if Charlotte had it in her to do something like that.

"Hello, Brian, this is Margaret." There was an odd pause.

"Yes . . . "

"Was everything all right with Charlotte in class today?"

"I think so. Why?"

"She's disappeared from the Macreadys'. They're worried. I have company. Would you call and let Mrs. Macready know we're aware and show some concern?"

His impulse was to say no, but he said, "Of course," wondering what he had to do with it, but he called.

"Mrs. Macready, this is Brian Parton. I'm Charlotte's English teacher. I live on the Point and—"

"Have you seen her?"

"No, but I know some of the places she goes. You could try—"

"Would you take a drive and see if you can find her? It's pretty raw out there."

"All right." Damn, he thought. He took his time getting dressed.

Charlotte knew every twist and turn on Flanders Point. She walked careless and tumbling, unaware of any danger, numb. What did it feel like to hug a parent full on, head to toe, pressing close, as if the love was so strong nothing could come between, as if she had the right to think about her mother, *This mother is mine . . . I nursed here, my cells built up one upon another inside her. My mother, my love . . . with her distant heart, her preoccupied mind, her presence not present.* Charlotte hadn't missed her mother since she left. She missed her sisters and her brother. It was fruitless to be with her mother. Nothing was given. Well, not nothing. There were cello lessons and piano lessons and riding lessons and art lessons, but nothing Charlotte needed.

In the fog the field by the salt marsh was an alien landscape pierced by ghostlike trees, and when she climbed up on the retaining wall her foot slipped and she hit the side of her head hard on the stone. "God-damn," she muttered. A lump rose above her ear and she clenched her fingers. The nails gouged into her palms. There was an eerie purple light from somewhere, maybe reflected light from the town, and the color-drained reeds were hushed. There was stability here and her feelings against her mother dissolved. Lawyers were busy and overworked. She must not be so hard on her mother. Her clients needed her. Her father seemed to spend his life trying to save himself but her mother—she was saving others. Charlotte softened. She lay down on her side on the bumps and seams of the wall, folded up her knees, and clasped her arms around them, and on the purple wall that ran like a gash along the side of the marsh, she fell into a cold sleep. A small trickle of blood ran into her ear and the fog meandered in, slipped under her collar, crept under her skirt, fingered its way up her sleeves. Dampness clung and she breathed the icy mist into her bloodstream and through the chambers of her heart and the cold crept to the marrow. She was a dim shape in a fog of exhaustion and spent storms, a fog that dripped around the edges and spread over the night, a heedless winter fog that worked its way in slowly.

Brian couldn't see more than twenty feet off the road, the melancholy foghorn of the Eastport lighthouse and a random bell echoed over the water. He drove to the marsh. Charlotte gave him regular reports on the birds: terns, sandpipers, and cormorants. Pintail ducks and mergansers came through, rested for a few days, and left. She'd seen a nighthawk in a tree near her house, and marsh hawks, egrets, and gray herons. She'd started a list and said the way to find them was to keep your ears open and your feet moving and never make eye contact. Once he'd seen her standing in the cordgrass looking through binoculars. He pulled the Buick to the edge of the field, went down to the wall, and walked along it. Feeling foolish, he called her name when he saw a dim lump lying on the wall.

"What the devil," he muttered. She didn't move. He put his hands on her face and hair. "Jesus, you're soaking wet." When he couldn't rouse her, he jumped off the wall, slid an arm under her knees, and picked her up. She was limp and he moved fast, crossing the field with long strides. When he set her down, her legs buckled and he caught her up and put her on the front seat, got in, and drew her against him. Her face was frost white, and dark strands of wavy hair were pressed flat on her cheeks as if the night had carved them itself, marked her with no mercy.

At the Macreadys' he opened the car door and she didn't move so he picked her up again and said, "You're okay, Charlotte. I'm taking you home."

"I am home," she said but she didn't open her eyes and he carried her through the garage. Mrs. Macready came down the steps.

"Where's her room?" said Brian. Mrs. Macready pointed.

"Where was she?"

"Lying on the marsh wall. What happened?"

"I have no idea."

Brian put Charlotte on the bed and she fell sideways and started to shake all over.

Mrs. Macready moved quickly. "Help me get her clothes off." She tugged off Charlotte's skirt.

Brian took off her wet shoes and socks. Her feet were like blocks of ice. Mrs. Macready sat her up, struggled to get her coat off, and threw it on the floor. In one swift gesture, she pulled Charlotte's damp sweatshirt up over her head. Charlotte swayed on the bed in a nylon half slip.

"Good Lord, Charlotte, no underthings?" said Mrs. Macready. The mass of wet hair on Charlotte's shoulder released a sudden rivulet of water that ran over her collarbone between her breasts to her waist.

"Look, I'll wait outside," said Brian quickly and he turned away.

"Don't you dare leave. I'm eight months pregnant. I need help. Pull down the covers. Hurry."

Brian stripped them back to where Charlotte sat supported by Mrs. Macready, who laid her back and said, "Get her covered. I'll get some towels."

Brian tugged the covers the rest of the way down from under Charlotte and then drew them up. He didn't like the violent shaking. He knelt and reached under the covers to rub her feet and she cried out. He stopped rubbing and held his hands around her toes. If it hurt, that was a good sign, he thought.

Mrs. Macready came in with a towel.

"Do you have any alcohol?" said Brian.

"Rubbing?"

"Drinking."

"In the living room, upstairs."

Brian went up. He poured brandy and, feeling like a Saint Bernard, he brought it down. "Hold this. I'll prop her up," he said and Mrs. Macready held the covers around her while he lifted her shoulders, sat behind her, and leaned her against him.

"Charlotte. Drink this." she took a sip and pushed it away. "Charlotte, it's Mr. Parton. Drink this." she opened her mouth and drank.

Brian lay her back down and pulled up the covers.

"There's blood on the pillow," said Mrs. Macready, and she saw a bruised scrape in front of Charlotte's ear. "She must have bumped her head."

Brian sighed. He wanted to leave and said, "Maybe a doctor should—"

"Perhaps, but I think she's all right."

"I'll be going, then." He couldn't wait to disappear.

"Wait a minute," said Mrs. Macready. "I want to look up hypothermia in *Merck*'s just to be sure. I'll be right back."

Brian looked around. The room had little to recommend it but there was a huge window that faced out toward the salt marsh. Books were piled up. He recognized the sea lavender hanging from the nails in the cinder block. In the corner was a graceful tree branch resting upright that reached the ceiling. He couldn't imagine how she got it in the room. Hanging on one of the branches was a bird's nest, a hanging pouch shaped like a teardrop. Brian walked over to look at it. He'd never seen a nest like it. In the bottom of the nest was half a small blue egg. He touched it with his finger and it was like a tiny piece of open sky in the shadow.

Looking out the window, he was reminded of D. H. Lawrence's story "The Horse Dealer's Daughter," a romantic, irresistible tale. He felt like the young doctor who had rescued the girl from her attempt to drown herself in the lake, had brought her home, taken off her wet clothes, dried her, and covered her to warm her frozen body. And though he had done only what any doctor would have, when she awakened from her close call, she'd fallen in love with him, he felt tied to her, and they had married. Brian shook his head and looked over at Charlotte. What a fool he was, borrowing his fantasies from D. H. Lawrence.

He walked back and sat on the bed, noticing the letter on the bed table. He read it and winced. Refolding the letter, he hid it partway under the lamp and looked down at Charlotte. He had no desire to leave at that moment. Mrs. Macready came back in and said, "We've done all we can. I don't think she should take the exams tomorrow."

"I'd let Charlotte decide," said Brian.

"She'll catch pneumonia."

"If she can stand, she'll take the SAT's. Mrs. Chase is picking her up at eight o'clock. I'd wake her at seven."

"If you think so," said Mrs. Macready.

"I do. I'll be going now." He started to leave, then turned around.

"It might be less embarrassing for Charlotte if you didn't tell her I brought her home. I don't think she even needs to know I was here."

There was a pause and he was surprised to see that she was looking for something to trust in his request. And she said, "All right."

The Good Wives River

H E DROVE AWAY troubled by the mention of him in the letter. But Brian's misgivings were overshadowed by a certain curious pleasure at helping, at being the one to find her, of his importance in someone's life for a change. She wasn't really irritating. He thought of her swaying on the bed. He had certainly never expected God to grant his secret wish to observe her breasts in a way that would not alarm her. He remembered the day after the hockey game when he threw the hasty prayer upward, then quickly forgot it. Maybe there really was a prayer list as his mother had told him. And perhaps his internal mutterings had floated up one day after a field hockey game, had been inscribed on the prayer list, had suddenly come to the top, and since it was his turn to have an answered prayer, this whole thing was his fault. He smiled to himself, picturing a heavenly conference room and the daily meeting of the Answered Prayer Committee, a busybody assembly of less-than-immaculate archangels with muddy feet and uncombed wings. His request was up for discussion. (Most never made it this far.) An angel would say: "Well, he can just undress her if that's what he wants. When she's in his car or something."

God would say, "Teachers don't undress students."

The angel would say, "Well, just make it look innocent. Maybe she falls into the cove and he rescues her and . . . you know."

God will answer, "Too melodramatic!"

An angel will retort, "Besides, you fall into *rivers,* not beach coves."

So another angel yells out, "There's no river. How 'bout fog? That gets you wet."

God, anxious to end the meeting and impatient with such adolescent prayers, would say, "Good, she's out in the fog. You fill in the details. Put it in work."

And there it was. An answered prayer. What a cad he was. Here was this girl in pain with no one close by, and he was making a mockery. He drove around and around the point in the purling fog with the buoy chiming and the lighthouse sounding its horn, and it was as if he drove back through the years to when his mother was alive. Never would she have written such a letter. He could still remember sitting on her lap. When he leaned against her he would lie under her neck, his nose under her chin. He would breathe deeply and silently and touch the two bones that crossed like a hard ledge under her throat. Beneath these bones she was soft everywhere, rippled like fragrant summer earth tilled before planting. The August after she drowned he'd gone one afternoon and lain in her garden on the same earth where she had knelt, humming to herself and batting the bees away as she pinched back dahlias and staked the hollyhocks.

He remembered how his life had closed around his father after she drowned. His father. So silent, so dark, wanting nothing from Brian. Not before, not after. His father, whose only pleasure was a glass of port after a spartan supper. His father, who sat erect, barely opening his mouth when he ate, careful, tidy, dabbing at his lips under the mustache, never letting too much food in at a time. His plate was given quick scrutiny. Nothing unhealthy must enter the sacred vessel. Nothing must touch. Brian wanted to lick butter off knives, slather it soft into warm biscuits, stuff them in both cheeks, and then stuff more in the middle to chew on. His father hated excess. But Brian wanted a full stomach, full of warm butter and biscuits. Pleasure from food was not tolerated, and if Brian made a sound when he ate he was silenced. By the time he went to college, he had almost forgotten the pleasure good food could bring.

There was so little left of his mother after all these years. His father always dominated his memories, stern, disapproving when his mother took a nap on Sunday afternoon and let Brian curl up next to her on the bed. He remembered how he tiptoed into their bedroom the afternoon she died and took her shawl to bed with him. He slept with it, drawing in every last molecule of her scent. The next night he slept on his stomach with the shawl under his hips. Then he slept with it between his knees. He wrapped himself in her shawl every way he could think of, hiding it in his closet during the day so it wouldn't be washed. Her smell grew fainter and mingled with his. And a week later, when the woman his father had hired to help with the house found the shawl and washed it, Brian finally cried. He told God he should have taken his father and not his mother. He told God he would never forgive him, and he swallowed his betrayal hard, down where it lodged in his heart and against his father and life and God.

His father didn't sleep in his mother's bedroom for a long time, and Brian knew he was grieving. But his father didn't speak. Brian had gone to the living room sofa one night and stood fearfully by his father, trying to say something to him, to share his pain, his fury with God. He had actually picked up his father's hand and held it and his father hadn't thrown him aside. But he couldn't open and he'd held Brian's hand limply, and he stared at his son as if he was a small intruder. Brian's past was a fiction, he told himself, and he knew better fiction. That was where he would live. He didn't want reminders of how irrelevant his life was. How irrelevant it had always been. Even Bridget, who claimed to love him, had gone off without consulting him to have her vile abortion. He had no part in his father's life; he had never seemed to give him pleasure.

And he hadn't been there for his mother when the waves dragged her under. He was such a strong swimmer. He could hold his breath for a whole minute and ride the waves. Small but strong, his grip was vise-like. But he hadn't seen the waves take her, hadn't heard his brother call. He remembered the ugly rope burn across her back that had ripped the straps off her bathing suit when she was swept under the safety line that ran down the beach wall. His brother left him there and had run to get his father, while Brian had crouched down listening for her breath. The beach was deserted. He thought maybe the breath had been knocked out of her, and he waited for the next breath. He watched her lying unconscious, facedown on the sand. He remembered the terror he felt when he realized that there was no breath, and he grew frantic. How could life vanish so fast? The only thing he could think of to do, an action to take, was to turn her over. He'd taken her by the shoulders and pulled with both hands, reaching for her waist to move her sideways, and he felt as if he were administering some vile abuse on the soft limbs he loved. He hadn't finished turning her when she sputtered for a second, breathed, then stopped again. At that moment his father and brother ran up behind him. He turned around, his mother now on her side, and his brother screamed, "I told you not to touch her, not to do anything, you idiot!" Brian started to cry out, "But she just breathed, she just breathed," but his father silenced him with the quick flick of his hand that Brian always hated. He was quiet because he was terrified that his moving her had actually stopped her breathing, and there was a sudden white moment of uncertainty as to whether she had breathed after he'd turned her or before. His father stared in disbelief and crouched down and felt for a pulse. "It's too late, it's too late," he said, and Brian couldn't believe it, and couldn't act, couldn't say, "Try, do anything, do something, press her chest"—which is what the words rolling in his mind were telling him to do, yet nothing was tried. He always saw that red mark on his mother's back where her skin had been torn and tiny drops of blood slowly appeared. And he remembered the small band of white skin on her finger. The day before, she'd lost her carnelian ring.

She used to cook fish on Friday and Saturday mornings. She buried the fish heads around the edges of her peonies for fertilizer. That summer she died, she'd lost her ring with the cabochon carnelian. She looked everywhere. Her father had given it to her. She was afraid she'd lost it at the beach, that her finger had contracted in the cold water and it had slid off into the sea. Brian looked everywhere too, even clawing through the soil in the garden where he'd seen her pulling up the chickweed around the peonies the week before. But it was never found. After she died, Brian took care of her garden in the summer. Not like she had, of course, but he remembered some of the things she did. Her astilbes stopped blooming because he didn't know to separate them in the fall, and he forgot to dig up the dahlia roots and store them for the winter. They died in a killing frost. But her azaleas bloomed and the poppies kept coming and the peonies slowly spread, pushing up their straight shoots like stiff red fingers every May. Even without the fish heads they did well.

And the thing that could still bring Brian to his knees happened eight years after she died. He was seventeen, graduating from high school, and he hadn't done much in the garden the year before. He was busy with girls. But one day he stood in the middle of his mother's garden, thinking about her, wondering, remembering. He studied the dozens of peony shoots, thinking how he'd miss this most beautiful of all her flowers. The stems were almost a foot tall, turning bronze and pushing up to the sun like dry Japanese brushes. There, wrapped in the tallest stem in the tiny rust-colored leaves, was her carnelian ring. When he saw it he knelt in the dirt in a sort of trance and stared and stared. He wanted to scream at someone, "Come look, come look!" but he was loath to disturb it—as if for a minute she was there, and as if his memories of her would shatter if he dared to interfere. After a long time, after dark, afraid it would be gone in the morning, he took it between his fingers and since that day he'd never been without it.

Whether it was the dense fog in the cove or a painful inner fog, Brian got lost on the way home from the Macreadys'. He didn't mind. He was patient and he drove slowly around the Point, relishing the rolling, drifting white blindness that closed and opened, closed and opened in his headlights. Perhaps this was heaven.

But when he finally walked into his apartment, the phone was ringing. It was Margaret Chase. "Do you have any news about Charlotte?"

"She's okay," said Brian. "They found her. Or rather I did."

"You did?"

"Mrs. Macready asked me to go out and look for her."

"I hadn't thought you to do that much—"

"I knew where to look, so I brought her back."

There was a moment of silence. "Did she say why she disappeared like that?"

"Not exactly."

"What's that mean?"

Brian heard a certain edginess. "She was unconscious."

"What!" There was a short pause. "How'd you get her back?"

"I carried her." There was a longer pause and Brian enjoyed it.

Finally she said, a little too carefully, he thought, "Thank you very much. It's nice to know we can count on you. If this girl starts running away, we'll have to move her in with me." Brian said nothing, doubting that Charlotte had "run away." She said, "I wouldn't say anything about this at school."

"Of course not. Good night, Margaret."

When Mr. Macready returned, he poured himself a long bourbon. He wondered what had sent Charlotte out that way. She was an odd girl, stubborn and uncompliant at inappropriate times, although she had good manners and he liked her spunk. He could do worse than have his daughters grow up with minds of their own like hers, and he went down to Charlotte's room. "Where was she?" he asked.

Mrs. Macready was reading a thermometer.

"In the marsh somewhere." Charlotte was on her side. The covers were pulled down and Mr. Macready looked at her bare back. Mrs. Macready covered her quickly and said, "I've got to lie down. Will you sit with her? If she starts to shiver, come get me."

"All right."

Mr. Macready sat at Charlotte's desk and finished reading his *Wall Street Journal*. She turned and lay on her back, throwing her arm up over her head. He sipped his bourbon. After a while he got up and went to the hall. It was quiet. He went back in. Charlotte didn't move. He fussed with her covers, and when she didn't stir he slowly pulled the covers back to her waist and stared. Seconds passed before he pulled the covers back up and left the room. Charlotte woke up and turned to face the door. Who had stood there? She'd sensed someone pulling the covers down. She got up, unsteady, and leaned into the hall. The door to the Macreadys' bedroom was closing. She knew who it was, and she felt her dislike harden and deepen, but she liked the covers being pulled down.

Brian picked Charlotte up at the fence on Monday and she had a bad cold. She was distracted, her mouth turned down.

"What's the matter?" he asked.

"Nothing."

"How were the SAT's?"

"I left in the middle."

"What happened?"

Charlotte stared straight ahead. If there was one thing she didn't want, it was Brian feeling sorry for her. "I don't know," she said. "They made me stop."

"I don't understand."

"It was nothing. But I suppose you'll hear about it. I was in the middle of the English, and for some reason I started to cry. I just couldn't stop. The monitor came over and pulled me out in the hall because I was disturbing the others. He wouldn't let me back in."

"Did you take the math?"

"No. Dr. Dierig was there. He was so nice. He drove me home."

"What will happen?"

"They said I could take them again if Mrs. Chase writes the College Board." She sounded despondent.

"I'm sure she will," said Brian. She blew her nose in a wad of Kleenex. He slowed the car, looking over at her. "You have no idea why you were upset?"

Charlotte looked down and shook her head slowly.

"I'm a good listener," he said. But Charlotte didn't answer.

That day Brian walked over to Miss Haddam's with Hans Dierig and asked him, "What's the story with Charlotte? Why does she live with the Macreadys?"

"Hasn't she told you?"

"I never asked."

"Her parents went through a nasty divorce two years ago. I heard about court appearances and other things I only half believe. She has some sisters and a brother and the family moved this summer. According to Mrs. Chase, Charlotte refused to go and her mother said she could stay on at school if she lived with a proper family. Mrs. Chase knew the Macreadys."

"And her father?"

"The few times she's mentioned him I've gotten the feeling she adores him. It was odd, though. Last year I asked the girls to write something from their own life in Latin. Two sentences—then we read them in class. I'll never forget what she wrote. She wrote—" He stopped and they stood in the path that wound along the cove, and the wind lifted his thinning gray hair, and he called the words to mind. "She wrote: 'My father would have killed my mother given half the chance, but he never got half the chance. I threw his guns in the Good Wives River." Everyone stared at her, and she joked and said her life was too boring to write about so she made something up. The girls believed her."

"What's the Latin word for *gun?*"

Dr. Dierig chuckled. "She made one up. She was new last year. The first semester she didn't talk much, she didn't smile. She was hunched when she walked, she got somber straight *A*'s, and she just watched. The second semester she started to change. She made friends. This glorious smile appeared. She even stood taller and straighter. She must have grown five inches. It was as if she'd finally taken a deep breath and she found she had more length. Her grades slipped a little, but I was pleased. It was like watching someone recover from a long illness."

"Is there a Good Wives River?" Brian asked.

"Not that I know of."

In the spring of 1952 the Good Wives River flooded its banks. It was a beautiful bright night. The full moon carved out sharp and muddy rips on the rushing, swollen river. Charlotte and her mother had hurried from the house after midnight and driven the back roads to the stone bridge. They took her father's weapons after the doctor had come to take her father. Charlotte understood that this was a symbolic act and nothing more, that he could get more guns, and with the cold, flinty twist of a sharp instrument Charlotte felt her mother's adamant fear penetrate her. But this shadowy perception entered through her mouth and nose, her eyes and ears, organs that can on occasion take in and bypass all the entries to the mind. She saw her mother's restless eyes and nervous hands as she twisted the watch that hung loose on her thin wrist or clutched her sweater till it pulled out of shape. She heard her mother blowing air from her bottom lip like a frightened whale that had been under the water too long. She felt the weight of the black steel Luger as it lay in her lap and the press of the open shotgun across her thighs while her mother drove to the river. And seeing and hearing and feeling, she learned well and she smelled the steel and the spring night when she threw in the guns.

The Good Wives River rushed along in such a rage there wasn't even a splash. She couldn't see what happened to the shotgun or the Luger after the water took them, but in her mind's eye, she saw the shotgun twist and turn up and over, knock and hit things, while the heavier

Luger sank and sloshed along the river bottom, moving inch by inch. That was the night she understood, though no one said it to her, that her father's real weapon against her mother wasn't his guns. Sex was what her mother feared. His weapon that could never be thrown into the river. And this was her mother's legacy. In the dark of Charlotte's heart grew the knowledge that sex could be a weapon and intimacy might be a fatal encounter. The closeness Charlotte wanted was no cause for rejoicing. Maybe there was even danger.

There was more that Charlotte knew. That her mother was never there, when her father needed her to be, by his side, in his bed. That her father was made impotent by her mother's absent heart. That he could not reach her any more than Charlotte could, that he too could not touch her. He could force her in his sad fury, and maybe did when he came into Charlotte's room and pulled her mother back into the bedroom with him, leaving only silence behind the closed door. He had loved her once, but now he used himself as the weapon.

That night when the river crested, her mother stood on the bridge and tugged her sweater closed, and the empty sleeves dangled. Charlotte bent over the wall and listened to the reckless flow of water, the rush, a snap, a hiss, a crack as the water gouged out new and wider banks, ripped out overhanging shrubs, tore them loose. The moon still gave light. Branches and logs ruptured the surface. All that was in the water's path felt its powerful assault and all things either held or were swept away. Mother and daughter were above and held. The guns were swept away.

Charlotte sniffed and sucked on cough drops for a week, fighting off a cold. She didn't want to miss a day of school.

That first morning, she had asked Mrs. Macready, "What happened last night? I woke up in bed with hardly any clothes."

"What do you remember?"

"Nothing that makes sense. You and Mr. Macready and, I think, my English teacher talking in my room."

"You were soaked when you got home. I put you to bed. What happened? Were you lost?"

"I don't think so."

"Let me know next time you go out so late, won't you?"

Charlotte said, "Was Mr. Parton here too?" Mrs. Macready looked distracted. "I'd be mortified if he was here. He wasn't, was he?"

Mrs. Macready turned to leave the kitchen. "Of course not."

At school, however, Charlotte noticed something odd with Brian that she liked and that made her nervous. But it was a good nervous.

In class she would be watching the text while Theo or Maude read from an impossible Henry James story called "The Beast in the Jungle," and she would look up to see what Brian was doing—he'd be looking at her. Before, if his eyes met hers for even a second, he'd pivot away, but sometimes now he didn't. He stood there, everyone else's head buried, trying to get through the swamp of James's ornate prose or getting ready for some improbable question, and Brian was watching her as if he were looking for something. What made her nervous was blue eyes. Blue eyes were different. She couldn't read them. She couldn't figure out how to get in. Brown eyes were so clearly an entrance, with just a thin, wet membrane protecting a dark window. You could go in deep and feel your way to someone's heart, or slip into the folds of their brain where dreams were born. You could start something. But blue eyes threw you back like a thin curtain of ice. She couldn't get used to the one-sided eyes.

The most exciting thing, though, was the way he turned his head, still looking at her. And that last second before his eyes followed his head was like a message for her that he didn't want to turn away. An eye smile, like a little good-bye, a link. She knew she was making too much of it, but still, in all the movies she'd gone to, watching men's eyes, she'd never seen a man do it. This was his alone. But what was he doing? Did he know how she felt? Why was he responding all of a sudden? It was one thing to have a crush on him, but these small tugs were pulling her heart loose. Actually, a lot more than her heart. She said nothing to anyone. She couldn't believe he meant anything, and then suddenly he stopped. And that was when her heart, which had been trying to keep its place, pulled loose its mooring and wandered off in his direction. This didn't feel like a crush anymore. It was bigger. All she could do was follow. What she felt now she would never write to her mother. Sometimes she felt physical vibrations in her body. Her bones were singing. But since he now ignored her, she knew that whatever it was he'd been looking for, he hadn't found.

$\mathcal{M}argaret\ and\ \mathcal{B}rian$

Not long after the episode with the condom, Margaret Chase invited Brian for dinner. When he got there he was surprised he was the only guest—if you didn't count the rank weimaraners. They both shuffled over, made a perfunctory sniff at his crotch, and left him alone. Though he rubbed their heads with a show of affection he would have preferred to kick them in the face. Mrs. Chase's greeting was not perfunctory but warm and breathy, and Brian had the odd feeling that she was sniffing around at something, too—though hopefully not his crotch. When she went into the kitchen he smelled his hands to make sure the dog odor hadn't rubbed off. She called from the kitchen, asking him to make a fire in the fireplace, and he was glad to be given something to do. Not quite sure why he was there, he discussed school issues with Mrs. Chase, most of which were financial. Through dinner there was discussion about the traditional spring theater production, involving the entire upper school, but always called just the "school play." She wanted *A Midsummer Night's Dream* this year, and for the next year she wanted two productions. She thought this could lead to new fund-raising, but Brian quietly disagreed, telling her it would interfere too much with serious study. So dinner was largely full of the small talk he disdained. After a while he realized there was something hanging in the air. This evening was not without some purpose, and then he was glad to let the small talk spin out rather than get into whatever it was.

After two pieces of homemade rhubarb pie, which, she explained, her housekeeper had made, he helped Margaret clear the table and do the dishes. They were few. She had reheated a pot roast cooked the day before, she said apologetically, but no apology was needed. Brian thought food was better after it had been sitting around for a day or two, taking on its character, and he ate heartily. At one point, he spotted Mrs. Chase putting a piece of bread on her fork to mop up the gravy, and he gratefully followed suit. Standing next to her he dried the silver and studied the enormous old-fashioned kitchen with pots hanging everywhere, black iron skillets on white walls, soup ladles, worn knives, chipped bowls, colanders, and enough copper to mint pennies for a week. She must have had an elaborate lifestyle before her husband died, he thought. She must be used to getting her way.

After dinner they went back into the living room and she said, "Why not put another log on the fire. . . . " He did, hoping to make his lack of enthusiasm clear. Mrs. Chase poured Courvoisier into a snifter and handed it to him without asking if he wanted it. She may look sloppy, he thought, with her scuffed-up, worn-down oxfords and her dusty, dry hair that looked like it could catch gnats, but she does have a sense of the good things in life. Things he wished he could afford. If she were younger he was sure this would be a prelude to seduction. Wine, brandy, doing the dishes together, a fire, a moist December night. He wondered when was the last time she'd had sex, and he waited for her to raise what was on her mind. Apprehensions were washed down with the brandy.

"There's something we should discuss, Brian." He put his glass down. "There's a rumor going around about you and a female at Haddam."

His eyebrows flew up. "What?" But before she could answer he said, "There is no substance, and I *know* you know it, to this nonsense about Charlotte."

There was an uncomfortable pause. "It isn't Charlotte," she said. "It's Hazel Pierce."

"What?" This time he practically shrieked and then he stifled a laugh. It wasn't funny, though. Brian knew the damage careless words could do. "Where's it coming from?" he asked.

"The girls."

"One girl in particular, by any chance?"

"Not Dana, if that's what you mean."

Brian stood up and stared into the fire, fingering the loose change in his pocket. He didn't really give a damn but knew he should and had to act as though he did. "Mrs. Chase—"

"What happened to *Margaret?*"

"Margaret, perhaps there is no place for me at Haddam."

"Don't be ridiculous."

"Hazel is married. Happily. She lives *on campus*. Her four children are all over the school. We have a professional relationship that a colleague might envy, but that's only to the good for Haddam. Hazel and I have a natural affinity because we teach from the same bias. I'm really shocked." He stopped. He shouldn't overdo it.

She waited. His denials had so far not included reference to any female relationship of his own. Surely if there was one, he would bring it up now. She sipped her brandy, enjoying listening to this man of few words use so many words. And her next step was going to lead him back to discussion of Charlotte. She liked cornering him.

He said, "A single man in a woman's place . . . the whole community has only two men. Could it be just that—pure and simple?"

She considered. "Calumny is not pure and never simple, but to answer your question, I don't know. It didn't help that you brought Charlotte home when she ran away," she said and then muttered, "like the spoiled brat she is."

There it was, thought Brian. "Oh? Did she run away? I wasn't aware of that." Maybe this was what Margaret really wanted to pick at, thought Brian, and he felt an inconvenient tenderness toward Charlotte. There were brats at Haddam, but Charlotte wasn't one of them.

"Whatever. But *you* knew where to find her in the middle of the night," she said.

"At your behest, I recall."

"*No* . . . no, I never asked any such thing."

Brian could see he wasn't going to convince her. "I helped because I knew where she might go. She tells me about her favorite bird-watching spots when I drive her to school. Something *you* arranged, Margaret."

"Perhaps I should disarrange it."

"Perhaps you should."

"The girl will do anything for your attention."

Brian gave her a cold stare. He'd never felt anger like this toward a woman. "That night had nothing to do with me and she doesn't know I was there."

Suddenly Margaret said warmly, as if teasing, "You're a natural lightning rod, Brian; adjust your behavior accordingly."

"There's no 'behavior' to adjust."

Mrs. Chase was silent, wishing he'd sit back in the chair. He was wound tight as a spring. She crossed her legs and he heard the silky slide of her stockings. She reminded him of a black widow spider stepping back before a strike. "Just be careful," she added.

Infuriating. "That's what you say to someone who's engaged in something. Do I have to say it again? I, Margaret, am not."

"I didn't mean it the way it sounded."

Not much, he thought. What Brian hadn't picked up was something that even Mrs. Chase had not faced. The person on the staff most interested in Brian was Mrs. Chase herself, and she was using this episode to engage further. She hadn't thought about the significance of the way she so often sought him out about the smallest matters, nor had he. He thought her frequent questions to him were a kind of studied amateurism and a penchant for improvisation. Nor had she realized that when the girls' teacher reports had come in, she read all of his before giving any notice to what the other teachers wrote. And there was the way she felt most content in staff meetings when he was there, sitting quietly with his hands in his pockets and his legs crossed, not saying a word. Brian would have been surprised. But there it was. Now they were sitting in front of her fire, sipping brandy, and she was taking pleasure in his agitation.

For Brian was unsettled indeed. He was beyond reproach and here was reproach. He rose to leave. "I'll be going, Margaret."

"Please stay and have another drink." He didn't understand that to Margaret, anything was better than indifference, and she was having the time of her life.

"Thank you, no. I don't know what to do about this, so I'll do nothing."

They said good night. He drove home past the house where Charlotte lived, something he'd never done before. The light was on in her room.

Mrs. Macready had told Margaret every detail of that night right after it happened and it had been festering in Margaret's mind. By appearing to tip him off, to protect him, she'd keep him ever more distant from Charlotte. Though what she really wanted to do was to dirty Charlotte in his eyes. To belittle, expose, and degrade her, so Brian would simply turn his back in the future. This was at least a start. It was for Charlotte's own good, of course, she reasoned.

Hazel and Brian

THE NEXT DAY, Brian walked over to Little House and knocked on Hazel's door. He envied her private office. No one else had one. She had a way of getting what she wanted. She also had a way of talking that always made him think they were becoming friends, and then he wouldn't see or hear a word from her for weeks. But one thing he had learned was that she could be trusted with a confidence. He sat down opposite her and said, "Hazel, I remember one day you said students just pass through. What they embrace with passion one week is replaced by a new great passion a week later."

"So it goes, but that's not to belittle it."

"I know. And when one of them seems to adhere to one passion?"

Hazel shifted. "Just remember it isn't real."

"Why isn't it? Is a young person a fraud?"

"No . . . just unreliable. You're young, you tell me."

"Don't insult me."

"What's real, it seems to me, is the wonder of their newfound capacity to love and to give. That's what they're enamored with—that they're capable of love." Damn, thought Brian. She's focusing right in. "It's not the same as love," she added, now hinting at condescension.

"You seem so sure."

Hazel studied him, and her chilly manner vanished. "I'm not sure about anything ever, but in Charlotte's case, her love isn't love. It's transference. She's looking for her father."

Brian rubbed his hand through his hair and looked down. "Maybe it's her mother she's looking for."

"That's possible."

"Maybe all love is transference of one kind or another."

"Well, don't get caught in countertransference. Turn your back. It's all you can do."

"Oh, I already have. This is just a quick look back to see if I'm being followed."

"Think of it this way, Brian. It can be a teacher and pupil, a boss and employee, a doctor and patient. There's an Eros in the *hierarchy* on top of everything else, but it's universally generalized."

"I don't follow you."

"Imagine a psychiatrist is treating a patient. One day he opens his mail and there is a letter signed by one of his female patients. It says, I love you, I love you, I love you, and I will always love you. The psychiatrist pauses and thinks, Really? Am I so wonderful and so charming? Can she mean it—what have I done to deserve such love? And as he's reflecting on the letter, he turns the envelope over and sees that the address is clearly his, but it's addressed to *Occupant*."

Brian smiled. "I see what you mean, but so what? People fall in love all the time without any hierarchy at all. If this hierarchy is so powerful and seductive, you wouldn't find just one student in fifty falling in love with the teacher, you'd find half of them succumbing to passion."

She just looked at him and then said, "I don't have all the answers, but I do believe Eros is deeply embedded in the act of learning. Men and women who discover knowledge and truth together are in danger of discovering each other."

He said, "How about having dinner with me, Hazel? We can compare notes."

"No, you can have dinner with me." And they drove up to the cottage beyond the hockey field where she lived. Brian learned over dinner that she'd divorced two husbands and didn't think four children was enough. She was also the first person he'd talked to who knew Miss Haddam well and had real respect for her and the school. Hazel also told Brian she had been blacklisted during the McCarthy hearings, as had her second husband, who lived in New York. Her fiction hadn't been published in five years.

"So are you a Communist?" asked Brian.

"No. I have Marxist sympathies, but no, Stalin stole our revolution."

"You don't look like an idealist," said Brian with a slight smile.

Hazel glanced over and changed the subject. "Tell me what you think of the girls."

They spent the rest of the meal talking about the upperclassmen, and when Brian got up to go home he realized that although she acted engaged, warm, interested, it was only an effective pose. She was really quite distant, almost cold. However, he had a more balanced view of the school and his role with his students. He hadn't realized how much he needed to talk to someone. She made detachment seem not only desirable, but easy. But no sooner was he back in the classroom than he re-engaged. Maybe he really didn't belong at Haddam. A college appointment would afford more distance from his students.

$\mathcal{P}lum$

CHARLOTTE RETURNED TO writing her mother neat, short, "nothing" letters. And her mother wrote her old-fashioned notes with sentences that started with words like *tis* and *twas*—one of her mother's eccentricities. In Hazel's class, she wanted to write something mean about her mother but she was afraid. On the boathouse porch she asked Theo, "When you hand in your work for Mrs. Pierce, do you ever write about your suspicions about your father and his love affairs?"

"Yes, and I embellish them wildly to make them sound like fiction. Hazel knows, though."

"Aren't you afraid?"

"No. Hazel says you can't afford to be kind. You have to tell the terrible truth. Just change names."

"What if your mother saw your work? What if she peeked and read them? Or your father? They know you like to write."

"Hazel says no one ever recognizes themselves in fiction. You know how people are. They try to be honest, but people always tend to give themselves the best of it."

"Theo, sometimes I don't know what I'd do without you," said Charlotte.

Theo smiled. She loved the way Charlotte looked up to her. And she knew Charlotte was even a little jealous, but always in a good way. "Sometimes I don't know what you'd do without me either."

So Charlotte wrote about her mother. She didn't bother to change names. Her mother deserved it. And she didn't embellish but she wrote with a deep ache in her heart. This was one of the black places. A shapeless place she could never go.

Her mother left in September for the last time. It was a different leaving because this time everything went with her. Old boxes got tied up again. Papers filled the trash. Balls of dust were found under all the furniture. Her mother was always leaving, even if only for an hour in the old station wagon. This time Charlotte refused to go, even though this time her mother took the family with her. Charlotte was tired of the leaving feeling. She thought—by letting her go without me, my mother will never leave me again. Her mother exacted her price, though. Not because her mother was vindictive. She wasn't. She was just careless, with a familiar absence of noticing, an absence of attending. It was just her way. But still, the price Charlotte paid was dear. Her mother left the dog, Plum, behind. She asked Charlotte to take care of putting the dog down.

Her mother was a woman who got on trains and disappeared for the day, or who got into her crumbling Ford wagon to leave for a few hours. She'd even been known to get on a bike, though pedaling was not her style. The train took her to Columbia where she was getting another law degree. The Ford took her to her job. And the bike, Charlotte didn't know where the bike took her mother except away from her father's fury. Still, this kind of leaving Charlotte understood. The leaving Charlotte hated was the other kind. The kind she couldn't watch with her eyes, but she could feel in her stomach, that if attended to, if given any notice, stung her like a wolf spider, a tiny scrambling dark hurt that crawled into her heart and dug out the tiny stitches she had sewn there.

When she wanted her mother's attention, she had to say her name more than once. And there was the distance in her mother's eyes—always.

But it's the dog Plum you should know about. How Charlotte killed her dog. It was not some terrible stabbing or shooting thing she did, or some drowning with a rope and a great stone. It was simple enough, and all she really did was watch Plum die.

Charlotte wasn't the minister of death. Though perhaps she couldn't pretend it was not she who led Plum along to her appointment. With a graying piece of clothesline tied around her neck, they went for a walk, a long walk. If Charlotte had the strength to do this thing her mother had left her to do, certainly she could do it with her own two feet and walk Plum slowly out to the end.

Her dog was old, a drooping dull black Labrador with wrinkled calluses behind her elbows and a jagged scar on her side where a stranger's car had ripped her. Only her forehead still shone, polished to a fine black sheen from the years of loving strokes from her sisters, her brother, herself. Plum was a fine member of the family. With the good breeding her mother and father insisted on. She wasn't a mutt. Plum was a thoroughbred. She had been the runt of the litter grown strong with all the children playing with her. And Plum had children of her own. Forty-eight to be exact. They earned their keep. Her father sold them. In Charlotte's town Labradors were the dog of choice. One of Plum's sons, the pick of the litter, they heard had gone on to be a champion.

It was too much to bring Plum to Washington, DC, said her mother, and there was no room in the car. Her mother was to start a new job after the divorce. She told Charlotte she had meant to take Plum to the vet to have her put to sleep, but she just didn't have time. Since Charlotte would be in the old house for two more days before she moved in with a family near school, would she take care of it? When her mother drove away in September, she left Charlotte some money to take the bus to the vet and to pay for the service he would perform. It was typical. Her mother thought they let dogs on the bus. But then she didn't know about practical things. So of course Charlotte didn't take the bus.

Charlotte and Plum walked the two miles to the vet, and Charlotte talked to Plum. She told her how she loved her noble head, still proud, always gentle. She sat on a wall along the way and thanked Plum for the many times she had defended Charlotte. When she was little she had long braids because her father wouldn't let her cut her hair. Some mornings when her mother would do her braids she would comb so fast the tangles would make Charlotte scream. And Plum would walk over to her mother, her head swinging quietly back and forth, and there would be a growl, a low soft moaning growl telling her mother to let Charlotte be. And Plum would sit by Charlotte watching her mother until she was finished, not threatening, just gently reminding her mother not to hurt. And when her brother Max grabbed Charlotte's arm and pounded on it until she cried, Plum would come over more quickly. With her mouth slightly bare, just enough to let her brother feel the hardness of her wet teeth, Plum would push her muzzle against her brother's leg, warning him to stop. Charlotte held it in her heart, how this aging female dog, mother of so many, would not see her hurt without making her disapproval known.

"Thank you, old girl, for looking out for me," she said, and rubbed the black bump of knowledge. Plum could not cheer her when she was alone. Some things Plum didn't see any more than Charlotte did. Though there were many times when Plum shuffled into Charlotte's room and slept on the floor by her bed all night. But what Plum did see was something Charlotte would carry forever.

They walked on toward the vet. It was a long walk but, Charlotte thought, not long enough. Her loafers scuffed and Plum's back swayed as she walked. Charlotte looked at the houses, the porches. The older Victorian houses had full wraparound porches, welcoming. Newer houses had smaller porches as if they were an afterthought, and when she went down the long hill toward the last mile, the new little colonial houses had no porches at all. Just cold cement steps and the door. Why did the good things disappear? She had no way of knowing that these new little houses were featuring air-conditioning, and the contractors knew that once people got a taste of air-conditioning they wouldn't want to sit on porches in the summer.

Charlotte crouched down and put her face in Plum's neck. She always smelled so good. Sort of a soft, dusty dog smell, a neutral kind of odor, almost sweet. They arrived at the low red clapboard building of the vet who had given distemper shots to all

Plum's sons and daughters. They went into his examining room, and Plum hung her head low in disappointment. The room was clean and white and polished. There was the antiseptic smell and the sound of Plum's nails on the linoleum floor, but Plum was quiet. Charlotte could not do this. It would have been better if her mother had decided that Charlotte was too much trouble, and if she had put Charlotte down in her careless haste rather than ask her to finish this up.

The vet bent low and picked old Plum up and put her on the table. "Hello, old girl, old Plum, how are you today?" He took her muzzle and rubbed it kindly. "Yes, you're a good person, aren't you?" He always called the dogs good persons. He moved her shoulder and laid her down on her side. Charlotte took the old clothesline off from around her neck and stood opposite the vet, behind Plum's head. She looked up at Charlotte while the vet stroked her gently. Charlotte petted her and smoothed the top of her head. Plum didn't like the steel table, but she never had. She didn't struggle. She had no knowledge of what would come.

Plum laid down her head. She was tired from the long walk. Charlotte stood by her head and mumbled, "Good Plum, good Plum, good girl." The vet took a large syringe. He lifted the loose skin near Plum's heart, inserted the needle, and started to push the plunger down. At the digging of the needle Plum looked up at Charlotte but did not whimper. Charlotte stroked her head over and over as she lay it down again, blinking slowly. She looked up at Charlotte one more time, and Charlotte cradled Plum's head in her arms. The vet drew out the syringe and Plum's head grew heavy, heavy, and Charlotte said, "Good Plum, good Plum." She wanted tears to wash Plum's face as she died. But there were no tears. Charlotte could find none. She looked at the vet. His hands were in the pockets of his white coat and the room was still. Plum was dead. The best "person" she'd ever known. Charlotte put Plum's head on the table. The vet looked at her.

"I'm sorry," he said.

"Thank you," said Charlotte

She went to pay at the reception desk, and she had the feeling the receptionist knew what Charlotte had done and was watching her. Perhaps the woman only wanted to express sympathy. She might understand, but Charlotte didn't think so. Charlotte didn't look up and left quietly.

Hazel Pierce gave Charlotte her first *A*. Afterward Charlotte was so surprised she asked Mrs. Pierce, "How come when I wrote about something so awful it's worth an *A*?"

"Charlotte, people like to read about bad behavior. That's what's interesting."

Charlotte just said, "Oh." And Hazel did something she'd never done before. She showed her pupil's work to another teacher. She showed it to Brian. She asked him after he'd read it, "Fact or fiction?"

Brian said, "Fact. For sure."

Mr. Macready Makes a Pass

THE DAY AFTER Charlotte's first *A* the weather went wild. Snow, ice, and wind came hard and fast out of the north, and a storm surge at high tide sent the water to the top of the marsh wall. The cordgrass was submerged and even the phragmites showed only feathery tops trembling in the churning whitecaps. Charlotte worried about the marsh hens. Surely they'd all drown. Everyone was caught off guard. School closed early, and for the first time, Brian took Charlotte home. He drove at a crawl, forgetting which house it was, and she pointed ahead, momentarily stunned that he'd forgotten where she lived. She kept forgetting that just because she was thinking about him, he wasn't thinking about her. Why was that so hard to remember? As she got out of the car he said, "If the snow is deep tomorrow, I'll pick you up here. I have chains."

"How deep is deep?"

He looked annoyed. "Tell you what. I'll pick you up at the fence, regular time."

Later in the afternoon the bitter gray wind died down, and the swirling snow lessened to a kindly float. After spending half an hour getting the little ones into snowsuits, boots, mittens, scarves, and hats, Charlotte helped them build a snowman. Mrs. Macready had come into the mudroom to help, and Charlotte noticed that she was getting so pregnant she could hardly bend over. It was still snowing lightly and Mr. Macready got home early. Mrs. Macready suggested he take Peter sledding, and Peter looked quickly at Charlotte and said, "Can Charlotte come, too?"

"Sure," Mr. Macready said.

They walked to the steepest hill in the orchard, dragging two Flexible Flyers. There were several boys there and the slope was already packed hard. At first Peter went down with his father and Charlotte went down alone. It was a great, quirky, uneven hill, and what made it exciting was the stone brook at the bottom. You could think of nothing else and had to swerve hard at the end to save yourself from a crash in the rocks and ice. Then Charlotte went down with Peter and Mr. Macready watched.

Suddenly Peter said, "Can I go by myself?"

Mr. Macready said, "Okay. C'mon, Charlotte, you come with me. We'll race Peter." Peter was already pushing off. Charlotte hung back a second, then got on the sled. She sat in front and Mr. Macready got behind her, put his knees up, and extended his legs around her so he could steer the front bar with his feet. Charlotte felt this was awkward, but it was so much fun she forgot about it and they went down again and again.

The other boys were sledding on their stomachs. Peter said, "Daddy, I'm going to go on my stomach," and he ran behind his sled to get a running start, flopping himself onto the sled head first. Mr. Macready got on his stomach at the top of the hill and said, "C'mon, Charlotte, push us off and get on top. Hurry up!"

She laughed. "No, I'll fall off . . . you go."

"Nonsense," he said. "Your extra weight will add speed. C'mon, girl!" She thought this a little familiar, but not sure if she had the right to say no she climbed on top of him and down they went after Peter. Charlotte laughed because it was hard to balance on Mr. Macready on a moving sled. She had to hang on to his shoulders to stay in place. She forgot everything in the reckless rush of the sled careening and thrill being flipped over when they came too close to the brook. She lay there breathing hard and covered with snow, and then she realized Mr. Macready was staring. Feeling silly, she got up.

"C'mon," she said, heading back up to the top with the sled. To her relief, Mr. Macready said it was time to go in. She and Peter went down one more time while Mr. Macready waited at the top of the hill.

It was dark when they walked back to the house, each of them quiet. Charlotte thought what a wonderful family thing to do, this was, and even though she tried not to compare Mr. Macready with her own father, she was reminded how withdrawn her father was after his accident. The father she had loved so much, who let her stand on his shoulders at the beach and jump in the water, never came back. Neither her father nor her mother would ever have considered sledding or building a snowman. When they got back, she hurried to the kitchen to get supper ready for the children. Mrs. Macready came into the kitchen once, looking sweetly at her watch, but Charlotte knew nothing would be said. Everyone was in good spirits and she felt golden.

After the girls were in bed, she curled up with Peter on his bed and read from *The Adventures of Augustus*. Peter liked to touch, to hug, to tickle, and more than once Charlotte had seen him work his way in between his noisy sisters for a measure of his mother's affection. And Charlotte noticed how his dark, watchful eyes rarely blinked. She expected Peter to be his father's favorite, but Mr. Macready was not affectionate and had a rough way. He grabbed Peter's arm too tightly or ruffled his hair so hard his head got shoved around.

On the last page of the story, she insisted Peter get under the covers, but he knew how to prolong the bedtime ritual shamelessly, and he started to tickle her. She twisted away and grabbed his hand.

"Peter, enough. Not now. It's late."

"Yes!" he cried, jerking his hand free. He leaped on her stomach and tickled her neck furiously with both hands. Charlotte's laugh rose in quick, high-breaking gasps. It was teacups shattering, loons calling, crystals breaking on slate as she laughed and squirmed without holding back. "I love it when you laugh like that," said Peter.

"Peter," she gasped, "quit it!" and she sat up and tried to grab his hands, but he was too quick and sat on her stomach again, going for her neck. Suddenly, she saw Mr. Macready standing in the doorway. She jerked down her skirt.

"Peter," he said sharply, his eyes on Charlotte. "That's enough. Get off her and get in bed." She sat up, embarrassed, and straightened her blouse.

"Charlotte, what have I said about this kind of thing at bedtime?"

Charlotte thought of sending a huge gob of spit at his chin. She knew how to do it too, but she mumbled, "Sorry, I forgot." She left the room. He was so nice in the orchard, but now he was so rude, and she could feel his eyes watching her walk down the hall. How long had he been standing there? There was something about him that gave her the creeps. When she closed her door, locked it, and turned out the lights, the clouds broke and moonlight rose, a strong, thick blue. She went to the window and the motionless night was so cold and hard and deep, it seemed the cold might crack the frigid sky. Nothing moved. Even the moon seemed worried and frozen in place, as if to keep from snapping off in the cold and falling into the naked, shivering trees, with their jagged shadows crisscrossing the snow. The beauty of the cold took her out of her room toward the sky. She let her thoughts rotate into the black. Mr. Macready's sharp words at the door had reminded her of something. A shadow standing at the door. A long time ago. She dropped her clothes in a heap on the floor and got into bed with nothing on. She couldn't get to the memory that hovered.

I scrape at my memory. I dig at the past. But the surface is swept clean. There is nothing amiss, but the blanket wool creeps through the tiny openings in the weave of the sheets. I feel everything on my skin and something rubs wrong. Irritates. Little tortures share my bed. Tiny wool filaments of pain. The moon joins me unconcerned. The light is a blue I could slice and store in a shoe box. A blue I could save and bring to Brian one day and say, "Here are your eyes." Why isn't the moonlight amber like the sun it reflects? Just this angular blue that moves on my blanket like an arm approaching me. It's sexy to lie between my sheets with nothing on. Dana was right. When I pull back the blankets, does the moon see my smooth skin that burns from the tiny strands pricking at my sleep? Is my secret wantonness revealed? It is too much. How can anyone sleep without pajamas?

Charlotte had lost track of time when she got up in the dark to put on her pajamas. Maybe she'd been asleep. She got back into bed and heard a quiet step shuffle outside her door. She turned her head and stared at the door. Oh no, she thought, he's come to lecture me again. But then she heard the same quick steps move down the hall. Why had he stood listening? How odd. Sometimes he came into her room if the door was open, or if it was closed he always knocked and told her something special she had to do the next day. It was normal. Mr. Macready usually treated her fairly; there was nothing to worry about. Everyone made mistakes sometimes, and he didn't stay angry. If she wasn't performing well, surely he'd let her know. But this was different. He just stood there and didn't knock.

She lay still, unable to sleep, and just then she heard a little knock on her door. It could have been a dormouse tapping. She got up. It was Peter.

"Charlotte, could you come lie down with me until I fall asleep? I'm scared."

"Okay." Charlotte climbed onto his bed, he under the covers and she on top, and bundled herself around him in a way she hoped he'd like. His clinging was sweet, and it stirred something inside that she'd forgotten about—or maybe never known. He lay his arm on her neck, and she felt it grow heavy and still and slide back to her shoulder. She didn't remember the warm feeling of another body touching hers. It was wonderful, indescribable, and lodged in her heart.

She got up early the next morning and walked to the marsh to look for the marsh hens. She found three nests, empty and ice encrusted, but that was normal. Rails were reluctant fliers, but surely they'd headed inland for safety. Then she found three carcasses washing against the wall. She'd never seen them up close, and she studied their delicate webby red feet, frozen stiff. Nature could be so wasteful.

Brian had come to Haddam hoping to find more time, no distractions, and peace so he could write, but how little he knew. It was tension, confusion, and a vague yearning that drove his writing forward now, and he realized contentment just put him to sleep. Maybe peace was for dead people. He began to think that the inner agitation that moved just beneath his rib cage, and just beyond his perception, was something he should nurture. He thought to esteem his discontent, because when he mixed it with the restless energy that made him pace in class, and then sat down to write, his fingers seemed to swim across the page. They moved in subtle rhythms, forming letters with small pushes and rolls, like a microcosmic tide, coming and going, word waves pushing against white vellum. Some inner tension pressed for recognition, and maybe this was the source of his poetic drive. He remembered reading Wordsworth's description of a poet as a man "pleased with his own passions and volition." And then reading *The Prelude,* and over and over, Wordsworth referred to his "terrors, pains, early miseries, regrets, vexations and lassitudes." Was this what Wordsworth was pleased with?

This was not the conventional view, but Brian thought perhaps there was more to be said on Wordsworth.

Brian was careful to stay away from identifying his own discontent, however. The mystery was part of it. Not knowing what hunger was there. He would work at his desk, hours would vanish, and he would look up and find pages of an unfinished poem. And there was something else good that came. At least he hoped it was good. He found that he didn't need the constrained security of the traditional forms of poetry he so loved, and the iambic pentameter that had been ticking in his brain like a metronome for years, loosened. He wrote free verse, imposing no form on his words. They found their own form, a new, organic simplicity. His ear was attuned to this new sound, though he didn't entirely trust it because he didn't see himself as a simple man, but complex and cerebral. He was writing against type. And he wished he had a colleague to read his work. Hazel Pierce was published, but he was afraid to share his work with her. What if his was no better than the girls'? He didn't think anyone could say if his work was good or not, though the poetry journal editors thought they could. He wondered what they used as a measure. He sent off poems regularly, and the rejection letters rolled back with equal regularity. Did he need connections? Tenure at a college? One little break? Ten little breaks? He didn't know, but each turndown was like a small bloodletting.

And while Brian wrote, there was an emergency at the Macreadys'. The fifth child was due January 15, but in early December Mrs. Macready was rushed to the hospital, and the baby was delivered six weeks premature. Charlotte was at school when it happened, and she came home to an overwrought neighbor staying with the children and general chaos. A housekeeper was brought in the next day, and she stayed every day until six, when Charlotte took over. She was used to the routine by now, though she was uneasy without Mrs. Macready. It was too much responsibility. However, she did what she was told.

Mrs. Macready was in the hospital three weeks, and one night, the day the children had hung cranberries and popcorn on the Christmas tree, an incident occurred. The children were in bed, and as was Charlotte's habit, she was studying at the kitchen table. The Macreadys never returned to the kitchen after the dishes were done. Charlotte could spread out in bright light. She went downstairs for her *Webster's* and was startled to find Mr. Macready in her room. She hadn't heard him come in through the garage door. His topcoat was on her window seat. "Oh, Charlotte," he said, "I was checking to see if the heat is coming up." Before she could answer he said, "How's everything at school?"

"Fine." There was an uncomfortable pause. This was Mr. Macready's usual time for the bourbon he called a nightcap. She wondered if he'd had it. He walked to the window and looked out. When he picked up her hairbrush from the desk and moved it to her bureau, the hair on her forearms stood on end. She didn't move. He sat on the edge of her bed and examined a little book of Elizabethan sonnets Mrs. Macready had lent her, which was on the bed table. He ran his fingers around the edge of the binding and slid his fingers between the pages, flipped a few, noticed his wife's name on the inside cover, and closed the book with deliberation.

"That reminds me, Charlotte. Sit down," he said and patted the bed. Charlotte took a step back. "There's something I've been wanting to talk to you about. Mrs. Macready and I don't think you should be running around without a bra. Mrs. Macready's been meaning to talk to you about it. It's not proper for a girl your age."

Charlotte turned, furious, and went out her bedroom door and left the house. Half running and half walking, she hurried down the same cold country road they'd taken with the sleds. *How dare he. That creep, that creep. I always knew he was a creep.* But she felt guilty too. The wrong person had noticed her—the absolute wrong person.

In front of her was Brian's apartment, and the windows glowed yellow. When she got to his door, she stood in the dark listening to the night wind running across the pines. She didn't know what she was listening for. A restraining voice? Advice from an owl? Did she dare knock? Would he be angry? She knocked.

Brian opened the door. "Charlotte, what is it?"

"Can I come in? It's important."

Brian glanced at the dark windows of the main house and said, "Well, just for a minute." He looked at his watch and an icy blast blew in. "Don't you have a coat?"

Charlotte stepped in. She was out of breath and it was hard to talk.

"Mrs. Macready's away. I just had to get out of the house. Mr. Macready . . . " She started to cry.

"Charlotte, sit down." He took her hand and led her to his reading chair. He sat on the edge of the sofa and said a prayer to himself. "Did something happen?"

She stopped crying and smoothed the skin under her eyes. "Not exactly, but I think something would have if I hadn't left. I don't know. I was afraid." She saw the relief in his eyes. "I know I shouldn't have come, but can I stay here for a while?" She looked around. She felt as if she had stepped into her dream. She stared at a photograph of a dark-haired woman under the desk lamp.

He was saying something. " . . . can't . . . here, you know better than that. If anyone knew you'd come here, you'd be expelled and I'd lose my job."

Charlotte said, "I'm sorry, I'm sorry." But she also felt a deep relief.

"Do you think you're projecting?" said Brian.

"What's that?"

"When someone experiences some fear and projects it onto something else or attributes it."

"I'm not afraid of Mr. Macready. He's proper. He can be rude and he likes his way and he's thrown a couple of temper tantrums with his wife, but he's just temperamental." She paused a minute, thinking about other things she'd noticed. "He's a little rough with his son, though."

"What do you mean?"

"Well, he gets too physical. He sort of jerks him around. Peter's scared of him."

Brian didn't know what to say. "Are you comfortable living there?"

Charlotte thought of how she liked Mrs. Macready, how sensible she was underneath her nervousness. She thought of the marsh she loved that stretched below her window. The birds that lived there. The new clothes dryer. And she even liked Mr. Macready sometimes. Up until now. "Yes . . . yes. I really am."

"Do you want me to call the headmistress? That's where you should go."

Charlotte shook her head. "No, I knew I'd be safe with you. Would you drive me back?"

"Back? Is that wise?"

"There's no other place."

Brian looked away. "Okay. Let's go. Here, put this on." He picked a navy sweater up off the sofa and thrust it at her.

"That's okay."

He rolled his eyes. "Put it on, for God's sake."

"Okay, thank you."

He got his shoes and a windbreaker and drove slowly back, hoping she'd tell him the details, but she sat silent and hunched down. Trouble seemed to follow her around, but at least she wasn't slumped against him, drenched with fog. Before he reached the Macreadys' she said, "You can let me out here, Brian. I don't want him to know where I went."

She didn't seem to notice she'd called him by his first name. He stopped the car and let her out. "Are you sure you'll be all right?"

"Yes. There's a lock on my door. Thanks."

Brian said, "Oh, that's reassuring," but she didn't notice this either and he drove away. He had a sense of Charlotte as being a strong, resourceful girl. So why was he again "rescuing" her? Her coming to his apartment was dangerous. The headmistress would think he had invited this in some way. And a barrier had just been breached. He'd refined an aloof attitude with her after his talk with Hazel, but he'd have to be even more aloof or she might come again. He wondered if he should scold her, but he decided the less he made of it the better. More disturbing, he found her trust appealing. Charlotte was not the only one living a solitary life, and she was so insistent. "I knew I'd be safe with you," she'd said. Back in his room, he turned to his writing but his typewriter remained quiet. He called his friend Eben, who taught Radcliffe girls at Harvard, but he wasn't there.

On Monday when he picked her up he asked, "Everything all right?"

"I'm okay," she said. "Mrs. Macready comes home from the hospital tonight."

"Maybe you should think about finding another place."

But Charlotte was in no rush. Nothing must disrupt her rides to school with Brian.

Jack Delafield Makes an Offer

I N THE MIDDLE of the morning one icy day in December, Mrs. Chase and Dr. Dierig were standing in the office, watching the handyman sprinkling sand over the ice patches on the walk, and a man appeared. Neither had seen a car pull up, so they watched him with some puzzlement. He came down the walk dressed in a black bowler and a black topcoat with a white scarf tucked neatly into the collar. The man looked distinguished in an old-fashioned way, but he also looked a little unsteady, as if he was afraid of the ice.

"Who do you suppose that is?" said Hans.

"I don't know," said Margaret Chase. She was surprised that the gentleman pulled open the heavy oak door and walked right past her into the receptionist's office, as if he knew exactly where he was going. Mrs. Chase didn't think the unsteadiness was from trying to protect his patent leather shoes from ice and snow. She suspected he'd stopped at a bar on the way.

"I'd like to see Charlotte Delafield," he said abruptly as she followed him. Mrs. Chase ignored his rudeness, extended her hand, and said, "I'm Margaret Chase, the headmistress. May I ask what this is about? Charlotte's in class."

"It's a personal matter. I'm her father."

Mrs. Chase took a dislike to him, and saw Hans Dierig's surprise when she said, "I'm sorry, we have very strong feelings that the girls are not to be interrupted in class." On the contrary, Haddam was known for flexibility in such matters. "It's easy enough to make an appointment. I'm afraid you'll have to wait until class is over."

"Make an appointment?"

Mrs. Chase looked at her watch and wondered what could be so urgent he didn't even take off his hat. She tried to recall what Charlotte's mother had said about him and only remembered the general impression that he was difficult. "English class will be over shortly," she said with exaggerated politeness. "Perhaps you would be comfortable waiting in the foyer. There's a little time between classes, and if it's important she can be excused from her next class."

He said to Margaret, "May we speak alone?"

"If you wish." When they were in her office, he didn't sit at first, but walked to the window and stared out over the sound. Normally Margaret fussed over parents and tried to make them feel important, but Mr. Delafield made her uneasy. Finally, she said, "May I take your coat?" and she leaned close and breathed in. It was faint—the alcohol odor. Without a word, he gave her the coat and sat down opposite the desk. Abruptly, his demeanor changed to one of confident ease.

He said, "I hear you have a serious cash flow problem. I may be able to help."

Mrs. Chase was startled and wary. "Where did you hear that?" He lit a cigarette without answering and then looked impatiently for a place to put the match. She got up and gave him a small saucer and sat down again.

"Do you remember a student named Amanda Colter?" he asked.

"No."

"She graduated from Haddam ten years ago. Six years ago, just before she was to graduate from Sarah Lawrence, she was killed in a head-on collision with a truck on that damn new highway."

"Where . . . what highway?"

"I-95. Her father is a client of mine. I'm an investment analyst on Wall Street, and a financier. I do a lot of business at the Harvard Club. We were discussing Haddam the other night."

Mrs. Chase was suddenly attentive.

"I told him you were looking for an immediate infusion of capital. Fifty thousand dollars is a great deal of money, but he has a great deal. So far, there is no memorial for his daughter. I think I can convince him to lead a fund-raising campaign with a challenge gift to create an endowment."

"This would help over the long term, but—" began Mrs. Chase, but he cut her off.

"I understand you need hard cash to meet the banknotes. He's also offered to grant an interest-free loan."

"What if we can't pay it back? Too much debt is killing us as it is."

"He's used to risk. Personally, I don't think he would care if it was paid back."

Mrs. Chase wasn't quite buying all this, so she performed as a reckless innocent, saying, "If he could make the gift outright, we'd name the school after him."

Mr. Delafield looked superior. "That's a little much."

"What do you mean? Harvard is named after John Harvard. Yale, after Elihu Yale, Duke was *renamed* for James Buchanan Duke. What's the difference if we become Haddam-Colter?"

"He's a very private, unpretentious man."

"He must want something."

"Why not just the grace that comes from an unselfish act and a prize awarded yearly, named for Amanda, and presented at the awards ceremony?"

"We don't have an awards ceremony. Miss Haddam doesn't believe in them."

"Maybe she should start."

She certainly couldn't call him tactful. She recalled Charlotte describing her father as a sad and broken man once. He seemed very composed to her. Not sad in the least . . . and quite attractive. "This is all rather sudden, Mr. Delafield. You didn't say how you heard about this."

"Nor will I," he said, and she saw him look pointedly at her legs.

"We're concerned about rumors." They sat in silence and Margaret realized her heart was racing. "Is this a real possibility?" she asked.

Mr. Delafield smiled oddly and said, "Yes. Can you arrange for Mr. Colter and me to meet with the board of trustees and the bank?"

"I can."

"How is Charlotte doing?"

She was caught off guard. "All right."

"As bad as that?"

"Academically she's doing well . . . quite well."

"And her chances for Radcliffe?"

"Good, considering she came here so late."

He mashed out the cigarette. "Is there anything you can do to help things along?"

She flushed in embarrassment. This man was arrogant, but he was effective and focused. Maybe he hadn't stopped at a bar. "No one pushes Radcliffe around," she said, "but I know people."

"I'm counting on it."

As if he hadn't raised the topic, Mr. Delafield stood up. "I also need you to excuse her from school for a few days in January so she can testify at a court hearing for me."

"What kind of court hearing?"

"Her mother has sued me."

This was impossible. "That is between you and Charlotte. Class is about to break if you care to see her."

"I do."

Mrs. Chase went to the English room and told Charlotte her father was waiting for her in the vestibule. Brian overheard and saw anguish on Charlotte's face. As she hurried off, he said to Margaret, "Everything all right?" He got a curt, "Oh yes."

Jack Delafield said, "Hello, Charlotte. Where can we talk?"

"What is it? Is Mom all right?"

"Yes . . . after a manner of speaking," and Charlotte didn't miss the sarcasm. Last time she'd seen him he was so affectionate. What now? She said, "I'll get my coat. We can go down by the boathouse." They walked down and she noticed her father's expensive-looking shoes. How unlike him not to have those rubbers men wore. She didn't think he drank this early on a weekday, though she could tell her father was making an effort to distract her from something with brittle small talk. She hadn't felt this emanation from him since she was fifteen and he'd left the house. She waited and he said, "You know, your mother is taking me to court in two weeks."

Suddenly she felt sorry for him. "She mentioned it."

"Do you know why?"

Charlotte did, but she said, "No."

"She wants more child support."

Lie, thought Charlotte. "Well, Washington, DC, costs more than Eastport, I guess."

"Your mother wouldn't know what anything costs. If she tried to balance her checkbook, even with her limited brain, she might, but apparently that's too much to ask." Charlotte turned away. It was back, the old, scarring venom toward her mother. "And I'll be goddamned," he went on, "if I finance her endless God-will-provide schemes."

"What schemes?"

"The car for Max, for one thing."

Charlotte turned back to him. "But Max bought it himself. She just paid for the insurance." To this he said nothing. Never could handle it when the truth didn't cooperate. "Well, what is it you want me to do?" Charlotte said, quietly hoping to calm him down. When he was this angry she knew he needed to discharge a gun or throw a lamb roast. What could she do to redirect him? she wondered.

Brian walked onto the porch outside his room while his class wrote an essay, and he watched Charlotte and her father talking.

But then Charlotte's father caught her off-guard. "I want you to testify on my behalf, that I can be relied on without the child support being increased."

"I can't say anything against Mom."

"I'll take care of that. But I want your assurance you'll say nothing against *me.*"

She couldn't be tactful. "How can you even ask me that? She told me that you haven't sent anything in a year, and that your letters are awful."

"Is that what she said?"

Brian could tell they were arguing, and Charlotte gestured suddenly and walked away. He saw her father reach for her arm and pull her back, and Charlotte jerk her arm away. Maybe she could handle him.

Her father grabbed her wrist.

"Look, Daddy, I don't want to be involved."

"You already are, my dear. Your name is in the papers."

"Will you let go of me—"

"Your mother is *not* going to ruin me."

"Ruin you! What are you talking about? That's paranoia. She won't ruin you. She doesn't have a mean bone in her body." And she managed to jerk her wrist free, daring to say, "I think you're out of touch with reality."

"Haddam hasn't improved your manners, I see."

"Don't talk to me about manners."

Her father looked surprised at the change in Charlotte. "If you don't do it voluntarily, you can be subpoenaed, you know."

"And I have no doubt you'd do it . . . "

Brian left his class and went out to see if Hans was teaching. He was. Mrs. Chase wasn't in the office either. Damn, how could she let Charlotte alone with her father when she knew the situation? Brian started down the steps toward Charlotte and her father, not sure what he'd do when he got there. The minute Charlotte's father heard the sound of his shoes on the stone steps he stepped back, motioning Charlotte to follow him. Brian noted with a certain chill that this father conveyed no sense of embarrassment—just that he didn't want to be overheard. They came up the steps and Charlotte looked at Brian with hopeless resignation, but with no fear that Brian could see.

But when Brian walked back into Dovecote, Charlotte and her father were nowhere to be seen. He heard their raised voices in the music room. It wasn't a shouting match yet, but Brian went to get Hans out of his Latin class. Outside the room he said quietly, "Hans, Charlotte's father's here."

"I know. I met him, sort of."

"He and Charlotte were arguing down in the boathouse. Now they're arguing in there. I don't know what's going on but I think someone should go in and ask him to leave."

"I thought Mrs. Chase was with them. I'll do it. Tell my class I'll be back in a few minutes."

Charlotte and her father turned when Dr. Dierig entered. No one said anything for a minute and Hans said, "Mr. Delafield, perhaps you could continue this another time. The school is small. Voices carry."

"Excuse me, I don't think we've been introduced," her father said coldly.

"I'm Dr. Dierig. I'm assistant headmaster and I teach Charlotte Latin." With that he smiled broadly at Charlotte as if nothing was out of the ordinary. The tension in the room, however, was anything but ordinary.

Charlotte's father turned to her and said, "Give me the address of the family you live with. I'll see you this weekend."

"Remember, I didn't say I'd do it." She should have closed it off right there, but for some reason she didn't.

"You'll do it. May I have that address?" And Charlotte realized her blunder, but it was too late. She glanced at Dr. Dierig and could tell from the look on his face that she should say no more. She gave her father the Macreadys' address, confused by his belligerence in front of her teacher. She shouldn't have been. It was the old pattern; he treated Charlotte the way he used to treat her mother.

"Mr. Delafield," said Hans politely, "did you have a briefcase?"

Charlotte watched her father look Hans up and down. This was the father she knew, the one who was wondering if he'd found someone to fight. She could feel it in her bones, the way he took the measure of the moment, but he turned and said, "I can show myself out, thank you."

After he left, Hans saw Charlotte's hands trembling and he put his arm around her. "When did all this start?"

"My mother wrote me that papers had been served. I'm *going* to appear in court—for her. But how could I tell him? He's got a terrible temper, and he already thinks everyone's against him. I don't have the heart to hurt him. I just can't. I can't, I just can't." She was about to cry, and Hans hugged her and then let her go.

"Litigation brings out the worst in people. I'm sure it's not you he's angry at."

"I know. He's just taking it out on me because I'm here. But it still kills."

"It must be terrible."

And suddenly Charlotte straightened. "Well, I can handle it." Hans, however, wasn't so sure. He hadn't forgotten the stories about the guns.

That afternoon Mrs. Chase met with Hazel Pierce, Brian, and Dr. Dierig about the situation. The meeting was short and to the point. Normally Brian would not have been included, but as he had been involved in the morning events, he was now.

Mrs. Chase said, "The school is about to be caught in the middle of a nasty, disruptive court case. After speaking to Charlotte's mother today, I'd like your advice. She says legally we have no responsibility, but the father may try to serve us with papers for blocking access to her, or for some other, God-knows-what reason. Any trumped-up reason can be claimed, and once a charge is made you have to defend yourself. But our interest is Charlotte's welfare. I think the best way to keep her out of harm's way is to make her less available to him, extricate her from her living situation at the Macreadys', and have her live with me for the rest of the year. I don't want her out of my sight. Our other choice is to do nothing and hope it all blows over. But Charlotte's mother says it would be in her father's interest to create some diversion with his daughter to distract the court from the real issue, which is him."

Hazel said, "I think Charlotte is vulnerable no matter where she lives. I'd leave her at the Macreadys'."

"She likes it there?"

"Yes and no. She likes the children and Mrs. Macready," said Hazel.

"Hans?"

"Move her."

"Brian?"

Of course Brian could say nothing about Charlotte's coming to his apartment. "Well, there's something else. Charlotte talks about the Macreadys' when I drive her to school and she thinks he may have a drinking problem."

"Who? Her father or Mr. Macready?"

"Mr. Macready."

Mrs. Chase had chosen the Macreadys and she was defensive. "So does her father, I gather, so of course she's hypersensitive."

"Not necessarily," said Brian.

"Oh yes . . . What we might think of as normal drinking she'd see as a problem. She's no judge."

"But her perception is what counts," said Hazel.

And Margaret Chase said, "I'm going to suggest the move as soon as possible." Hazel was shaking her head but Margaret didn't see.

Brian said, "Shouldn't someone ask Charlotte first?"

Mrs. Chase said, "No. Her mother gave us the go-ahead. Charlotte has no choice in the matter. We'll rally around her."

Brian cringed, doubting it was Charlotte Mrs. Chase wanted to protect. This would not end well. When the meeting was over Hans muttered to Brian, "Looks like Charlotte is still dodging bullets." Hazel Pierce overheard and said, "You have no idea, Hans. Once she and her brother called the police to the house and when they got there they found her father lying on his bed with a shotgun on his stomach and his toe somehow lodged in the trigger." And she told them about a new short story Charlotte had just handed in about his suicide attempts, his threats. A woeful story.

"I think you underestimate her," said Brian. "She's bulletproof."

That night Charlotte slept a deep, hard sleep. She'd forgotten how her parents' conflicts drained her. Neither seemed to have an inkling of what they were asking her to do. She wondered if Max was involved. Please let Max be in it too so I'm not alone, she thought. But Max wasn't named in his mother's papers. The way it turned out, though, Charlotte needn't have worried. The day of the hearing her father didn't show up in court. Since he lived in New York, Connecticut had no jurisdiction and couldn't force his appearance. Her mother was awarded a judgment against him, which meant that the next time he came to Connecticut, if anyone knew about it, he could be arrested. Charlotte figured he'd never come, and even if he did her mother couldn't do much from Washington.

Christmas in Boston with Eben

BRIAN DROVE TO Boston for Christmas vacation with his friend Eben Armstrong. Eben was only three years older than Brian, but Eben's career was well ahead. He'd finished his Ph.D. and was an associate professor on the tenure track at Harvard. Brian didn't see his own slower pace as any cause for envy. Lying about his age, he'd served in World War II and Eben hadn't. Brian had also taken time off to work for the post office in Boston and read his way through the western canon on his own before going back for his master's. Brian missed their long talks, their nights at the bars in Boston, the book clubs, and Eben's many female friends. Eben had written he was getting engaged. That did trouble Brian a little, and he brooded on the drive up, wondering if his teaching in this tiny school had derailed him for good.

When Brian got to the apartment, Eben embraced him warmly and then looked him up and down and said, "For Christ's sake, have you been growing again?"

"Cut it out," said Brian, embracing his friend. "Why do you always forget that I tower over you?"

It was an old issue between them. Not that Brian was that tall, six feet, but Eben was five foot five. He tossed his duffel in the corner and Eben poured him a bourbon. Brian said, "The place looks different."

"I decided it was time for more than bat wing chairs and Danish modern."

"Looks very substantial and very vacuumed. But I want to hear about the girl," said Brian.

Eben handed him a picture of her. "Where should I start?"

"Where'd you meet her?"

"She was in my first lecture course two years ago."

Brian stared at Eben. "She was your student?"

Eben nodded.

"Your first class?"

"Well, I'd been junior faculty for two years, but this was my first big course."

"Well, what's the story?"

"Not much of a story, really."

"I'd still like to hear it," said Brian. "Isn't this the scenario we both swore would never happen to us?" He sat back and Eben shook his head with a little smile as if he'd just lost a friendly bet.

"Well," said Eben. "It's just one of those things. In September the head of the English department had a stroke. He was doing a 200-level survey course. Some Radcliffe girls took it, mostly sophomores. I was sort of his heir apparent, so they asked me to step in. A hundred students gave a comfortable anonymity. I didn't even grade the papers. Anyway, the first lecture, while going over the syllabus, I checked out the women—you know me, I like women but . . . just looking. I got used to the coughing, the incessant sniffling, the throat clearing. They're always sick, it seems. And there's this sea of eyes on you, or no eyes, just the tops of their heads as they take notes. I noticed one pair of eyes that never looked down. No notes. I kind of liked the way she looked at me. So engaged. Anyway, I remember one day, she *didn't* look at me, not once. Next day, same thing. So I ignored her too. She's used to my looking? I don't look at her once."

"Big mistake," said Brian.

"I know, I know, but wait. Immediately her eyes are back on me. So you begin to feel this sort of dance. The next lecture I ignore her again."

"Oh, Eben."

"Then came the note."

Brian put his drink down and sat forward, resting his elbows on his knees. "Predictable."

"Could I meet her outside of class? I have office hours. Few take advantage. We met in my tiny office. I couldn't tell if this was sincere, and not knowing made me wonder. We met several times at a café where students hang out. But other teachers were there with students. It was a campus hangout for everyone. All work, but I was feeling some interest. At least once each meeting, she'd give me this look, and before I knew it I was beginning to wonder what she'd be like in bed."

Brian was shaking his head and smiling.

"But I was still seeing Janice, and I thought that was serious."

"Well, then—"

Eben held up his hand. "The semester ended. She disappeared without so much as a thank you. It pissed me off. Then she showed up in the spring. She was auditing. No more work meetings. When she wasn't at the lecture I was disappointed. She used to wear her hair different ways, but always with a plaid ribbon. She liked black. She wore black a lot. By now, we both knew we were interested. Oh, her name is Pamela. Anyway, she graduated and I was relieved. At least I hadn't encouraged her. Then I got a letter. She was coming to Boston to look for a job, and would I have lunch with her? There was a phone number. I called and suggested dinner instead of lunch, figuring she'd know the difference. She's younger but only a few years. It seems okay to me."

"Any repercussions?"

"No. How would anyone even know? Anyway, there it is. A tale of increments."

Brian sat back. "I think it's a wonderful story. I know eyes like that."

Eben gave him a look of feigned surprise. "In high school?"

"Any one of the girls would tell you it's no different, but it's very different." He leaned in, teasing his friend, "Not that I don't love women too," and he slumped back in his chair again, "but I'd never do a thing. You know me. My biggest weakness is a strength in a case like this. If I'm ever going to find a woman to share my bed, I'm going to have to be more aggressive."

"That's what you said last year."

"One thing," said Brian. "You said at the beginning that you weren't aware this was happening."

"Oh." Eben sat pondering again. "The heart is such a double-crosser. I was affected by this girl, but my heart kept telling me I wasn't. I saw myself as blameless. It was bullshit. There's some sort of self-deceit mechanism, a truth blocker. Pam said she never would have been so bold if I hadn't encouraged her. But I don't see it."

"If two people are attracted, what's the difference?"

Eben got up and pulled off his heavy sweater and started folding it and refolding it as he talked. "You know, Brian, I feel for the first time—ever, I guess—that I'm not alone. All my life I had all these sisters, and my mother, and they were so close and they seemed to share everything. Every now and then I was invited into their world, but I held back. I shared nothing. Not with my father, not with my worthy sisters, not with anyone. I always felt as if my soul was . . . " He stopped. "I don't know what I felt. Maybe that's it. I didn't feel. I was in this hollow, empty cave, never leaving, not *daring* to leave, to show myself. So far back out of the light that I was almost lost to myself." After a pause, almost hypnotized by the ritual of folding, he said, "Have you ever wanted to grab hold of a woman and say, listen to me, listen to what I feel, tell me who I am, tell me what you see, but you knew you just couldn't. Men don't do it. You kept your fears, your worries, your misery, your needs, even your joy, to yourself. And there was this silence inside at the same time as there was this calling out, but neither was ever heard."

Brian was uncomfortable but he said, "Not exactly. I feel isolated from women but I think that's just the way life is. Are you suggesting it's a fiction?"

Eben pondered. "The fiction is the silence. The stalwart, closed-mouth demeanor. Maybe you're not as emotional as I am, but when I listen to something like . . . oh, Mozart's Requiem—say the *Lacrimosa*, it overwhelms me. With Pam, I'm not afraid to show it. She's changed me. I feel free, if you know what I mean, more like I belong."

"Well, you belong to a woman."

"It feels more like I belong to life."

"So does Pam have a friend?"

"Of course. It's already arranged."

After breakfast the next day they went for a walk along the Charles River, and Brian didn't notice the biting wind or the way Eben huddled in his layers of scarves. He asked, "Do you think the Eros in teaching is inherent?"

Eben paused. "Plato said it was."

"You can never say 'Plato says.' Remember all his words are put into someone else's mouth." Eben rolled his eyes. This was like the old days. "So do you think the Eros is inherent?"

"If the spirit is willing."

"I'm not talking about willing spirits, Eben. Your spirit wasn't willing."

"Oh, are we talking about me?"

"Yes, we are."

"All right, all right," he said. "I think Pam and I were equal—we *are* equal. Your thing is different."

Brian turned to him. "My thing? There's no *thing.*"

"If you say so." He stopped and stared over Brian's head. "All right. I'll be serious. If you think in terms of teaching as a shared journey of discovery, instead of just a job, look what's involved: sharing of knowledge, hunger for understanding, desire for approval, opening of another spirit, penetration of one mind into another, the mystery of the unknown, the pleasure of success, mental intimacy in shared moments of revelation, maybe even climactic moments."

"That's a lot of sexy words."

Brian noticed a slight smile as Eben went on, "Internal changes, growth, expansion, opening, tapping into unconscious longings—well, most of those words describe an erotic relationship. If you hung them all out on a clothesline and picked only three, you'd have enough to produce a spark, a thin column of smoke, maybe even a small flame."

"You make it sound like there should be a fire extinguisher in every classroom."

"Nah. Other words like self-discipline, tedium, restraint, disinterest, objectivity, distance, annoyance, exhaustion, prior commitments, morals, maturity, honor, and ethics have to be hung on the line, too. I don't know about this Eros thing, I mean, it's an interesting idea, but whatever one says, involvement *is* inherent because doors are being opened, not closed. And there's no telling what will come through those doors."

Now even Brian felt the icy Boston wind and he said, "Let's go in." They walked back quickly without speaking. Once back Brian said, "One more thing. Unfortunately, undermining the safe distance between my students and me is my extended engagement. It's not like a big lecture class, Eben. I see them every day. It's almost one to one. I know them better than you ever knew Pam. There's no chance of anonymity."

"Well, bear in mind, the gross inequality will preserve the distance."

"How do you know the *in*-equality might not just be the appeal?"

"I don't. I suppose there are teachers . . . and *teachers*. But I know you, Brian. The moat around you is wide and deep. I'm not worried."

"I know. I'm just talking."

"Just remember—detachment is the key."

"I know, but there always has been a problem with it."

"What's that?" said Eben.

"Detachment calls forth the very thing it refuses to have anything to do with."

Eben stopped, considered, then shrugged. "Still not worried—not about you."

And Charlotte's Christmas

THE SAME TIME Brian drove to Boston, Max and Charlotte drove to the new house in Washington, DC. Neither one had seen it. It was a split town house with no property to speak of, and the ambassador to Thailand lived in the other half. Charlotte was relieved to see her mother in a decent house for a change, although it was as messy as always. But Charlotte would remember that Christmas as the last time she saw her grandmother and the first time she understood her mother.

Her grandmother had been visiting, and in the old days she had been Charlotte's partner in playing cards. Every game Charlotte knew, her grandmother had taught her. It had been three years since she'd come for a visit, bringing her contralto voice and her Boston elegance. But the voice that used to be as rich as molasses was weak and quavery now, and her jaw trembled when she sang. Charlotte stood behind her grandmother when they did the dishes. Time and poverty had stolen her elegance. Now her white hair was a loose, falling-down bun, and her faded housecoat quivered at the hem as she washed a pan with vigor. Charlotte knew she'd have to wash the pan again. But the odd thing was her grandmother's feet. Her ankles seemed to have sunken into the soles of her feet as if her ankles were standing directly on the floor and her feet were vestigial organs that just rolled sadly up and around the ankles like old socks.

When they finished the dishes they played cards on the Duncan Phyfe sofa. Charlotte saw that her grandmother held the cards gingerly and didn't slap the pack. Her hands were so raw her fingertips were split and bleeding. She took hold of one of her grandmother's hands and gently turned it over. The skin was cracked open. Charlotte said, "Grandma, you mustn't do dishes anymore. Why didn't you tell me? You have to put Vaseline on your hands," and she went to get it. Her grandmother told her it never seemed to help, but Charlotte dabbed it around the splits just the same. They put away the cards. "Have you tried sleeping with cotton gloves and Vaseline?"

"Yes, dear, but I can't sleep with gloves on."

"Try. It will help." Before she went to bed, Charlotte rewashed the frying pan. Then days after Christmas, something woke her up early and she went down to get a glass of orange juice. Standing by the icebox door she heard someone crying in the living room. She went to see. Her mother was on her knees, bent over, feeling with her fingers for broken and scattered pieces of the vase that had held a place of honor in every house they'd ever lived in. A collection grew in front of her knees. Her nose was running and dripped on the rug.

"Mom, what is it? What happened?"

"Someone was straightening up and put the catnip into the vase on the mantle. The cat must have knocked it over."

Charlotte knew it must have been her grandmother. The vase was blue and white with an Oriental scene—tall, solid, wider at the tip than at the bottom, a graceful, elliptical shape, big enough to hold headstrong lilacs, a clutch of top-heavy peonies, rigid magnolias, and quince blossoms or prickly juniper berries in January.

"Can't we glue it back together?" said Charlotte.

"I don't see how. It was a wedding present from the man I was seeing when I married your father."

Charlotte's neck straightened slowly and her eyes narrowed on her mother's face.

"I know, but I was in love with this man. We were having an affair."

The way her mother said the words "your father" made Charlotte feel as if he'd been her father before he was a husband, as if Charlotte had loved him first, as if she'd chosen him. The pieces on the floor curled like blue shells. Charlotte had to know more and like a suicidal moth she asked, "You didn't love Daddy when you married him?"

"No, I had once, but not then."

"But then why—"

"He wouldn't take no for an answer and so I finally said yes. He said he couldn't live without me. I wrote a letter explaining that I could not marry him, but I never sent it because the other man never asked. He sent four wedding presents instead. I cried all the way through the ceremony."

"I thought you eloped."

"Yes. The presents came later."

Charlotte felt the black heart of the earth heave open. How could she have done it? Years flickered through her brain, years of the way her father looked at her mother. The need. The bleak hope. The drinking. The silences. The dark furies, the hot nights, the cold suppers. "What were the other presents?"

"The crystal bowl from Steuben and the porcelain figure skater. Edward said it reminded him of me. And my pearls."

His name was Edward. A pearl necklace. All the treasures she had. What kind of man would love a woman and let her go? What kind of a woman would settle and marry a man just because he was insistent? No wonder Charlotte's mother didn't love her. Charlotte wouldn't settle, and in that she was like her father.

What a terrible mistake. Because of a stupid cat and a broken vase Charlotte knew her family was a lie. Maybe even the happy years on Flanders Point hadn't been happy. She went down to the cellar to talk to Max, but he'd just finished building a new stereo speaker and he was listening to a song called "Nina Never Knew," his favorite Sauter-Finegan piece. She yelled in his ear, "Do you want to drive back a day or two early?"

"No," he said, pointing to the speaker.

She went upstairs, got into bed, and pulled the covers over her face. Her warm breath would put her back to sleep. The sound of Sauter-Finegan's horns drifted up. Her mother was downstairs typing. On and on her fingers hit the keys like feet that hit the road running. She was fast, faster than anyone Charlotte knew. Her father used to say, "It's not that your mother's so smart, it's just that she works so damn hard."

Charlotte remembered the day she had climbed into the attic to help her mother pack. They were throwing things away, and Charlotte opened a box of old, yellowing letters bundled with rubber bands. When she picked up a bunch, the rubber band had snapped off. They were all addressed to her mother at Radcliffe, all the same. When she asked her mother what they were, her mother got quiet and put aside her packing. "They're from my father."

"But there's hundreds."

"He wrote every day. Almost a thousand. Out they go." She sighed. When her mother had gone down the rickety stairs Charlotte read some of them. They were so full of emotion they made Charlotte uneasy, and she stopped reading. Now she wished she'd read more and she wondered.

Later that night a story came and Charlotte wrote it down. She would hand it in to Hazel Pierce. But whose voice was this? It was not a voice Charlotte knew.

I used to walk to the Queetchie Reservoir in the winter. It was a wild place and no one went there. Twice I saw a man's footsteps in the snow, but I never saw another soul. The stillness was ancient and complete, and the sound of my own voice was startling. Even the birds were hushed. I had a place underneath the sycamore tree, a mottled white spire in the winter that spread along the north bank. It broke away from a wall of gray hemlocks that stood like an old Indian council. It carved out a space of its own. It stood aside. I had to do the same if I was going to live.

One cold November day when I was fifteen and the last of the leaves had blown hard and thick around the storm drains, I went to the sycamore and came up with a plan. My father expected me to go to college at home in Chicago. I think he was afraid I would leave him. I was afraid I would not. And here is the thing I did right under his nose. He was a freemason. Without telling him, I applied to Radcliffe and then went to the freemason meeting house and filled out the forms for the scholarship they awarded to a senior each year. There was some luck involved. The day I went, the secretary was out and the person who gave me the form had no idea who I was. Where it asked for parental consent, I signed my father's name. The regular secretary would have told my father for sure.

Then I waited. In March I got into Radcliffe. In April I won the scholarship. Now I had to tell my father, this man I loved and feared. My sister told me he walked past my mother when he got home and came looking for me. My brother had seen him watch at the window when I was at choir practice. At dinner he addressed his comments to me. But I didn't want to hear. I wanted to go dancing. I wanted roses on my wrist.

I walked to the reservoir. The water was higher than I'd ever seen it. The branches of the sycamore were nervous in the wind, and angry black waves chopped against the granite dam that held the water back. The sodden body of a dead loon bumped against the dam wall. It looked as if the smallest disturbance would crack the dam, and if I jumped in the water the whole thing might go. But I knew I had to leap—up and out. I told him that night.

But even Radcliffe wasn't far enough away. He wrote me every day for three years. The letters came in identical envelopes, like thin sharp white shells rolling in as predictably as the tide, sliding up to the windrows on the beach, cutting and slicing as they swept in, delivered by his dark power to turn back life. Three years of letters. His long fingers reached across the miles and my throat was scorched, my hands scalded when I opened the letterbox in the dorm and it was never free of my father. Boils erupted all over my back. Oozing painful ruptures leaked clear liquid when I slept. The doctor said they were very odd. He told me they appeared to form the pattern of a cross on my back. They were there for months.

Finally, I threw the letters in my bureau drawer unopened, but I still heard his voice.

"Don't forget me. I have the answers."

"You are more beautiful, more loving, more gracious than any who follow you."

"I am the one who loves you best."

"I know what you need."

"Don't ever leave me."

"You have gifts no woman has."

"Your beauty takes my breath away."

Sometimes I spread them out over the floor and swooped

down on them like a harrier, scanning, peering, looking for some bit of fresh life, some change, but like a valley of dry bones, the white letters held no movement, no recognition.

I was hurrying across the quadrangle in a bitter nibbling wind when they told me there was a call from home. My father had gone through the ice at the reservoir. It was only luck that an engineer was walking the edge of the dam and saw my father walk slowly out to the middle, his black topcoat and black derby and black walking stick sharp and thin, tapping against the white, or he might not have been found. This was not part of the plan. I went home for the funeral. When I got back to school and opened my letterbox, his last five letters were there. The ice had swallowed my father but hadn't silenced him.

That spring I met the man I left my father for, the man who took me dancing and kissed my lips in the dark, whose secret whispers stilled my father's voice. He left letters in my letterbox, too. He too thought he knew what I needed. And this is where our story begins.

And Charlotte remembered there was a second carton of letters tied up in bundles with ribbons. These were from Jack Delafield to her mother. Charlotte never read those, and those her mother saved.

Charlotte wasn't sleepy and she got up and packed her suitcase. She went down to her mother's study and picked her way through the piles of legal documents. It seemed they were always an inch thick: complaints, returns, affidavits, notices of counter complaints, writs of habeus corpus, writs of mandamus.

"Mom, I'm taking the train back to Haddam this afternoon."

Her mother stopped typing. "Why?"

"I can do my research better in the library at school."

"Can't you wait for Max? It's cheaper to drive."

Charlotte didn't answer. Her mother said, "All right, dear."

There was a minute of silence, and her mother sat with her good posture, her shoulders square, her thin hands resting on her knees. Charlotte noticed that the sleeves of her robe were frayed and a little dirty. Her hair was pulled back and fastened with a pink rose, always the rose, and flyaway wisps rambled around her face. Her mother was such a strong woman but her appearance was always so fragile. It wasn't just her father who was to blame. She knew now. It was her mother, too. And knowing it softened Charlotte to her mother, though she wasn't sure why. She wasn't quite ready to leave.

"Mom, if you loved someone once who didn't love you—or not enough—and you knew how much it hurt, why did you get so mad when I wrote about my teacher? I should think you would have understood."

"I did understand. That's why I was so angry."

"What?"

"I didn't want you to make the same mistakes I did."

"Maybe it wouldn't be a mistake."

Her mother considered, looking at Charlotte in a way that made Charlotte feel important. "Maybe it wouldn't. It's possible, but not very likely." Her mother always left the door open a crack for alternatives. Not just because it made her seem reasonable, but because she really believed them. It was one of the things Charlotte most loved about her mother. And in spite of the way people behaved sometimes in her court cases, her mother never got cynical. She believed in people and she was naive to a fault. Just because she was experienced didn't mean she was worldly. And her mother lived by her own rules.

"Could I have some money for the trip back?"

"Get my purse."

Her mother offered to drive her to the station, and when Charlotte got out of the car, she thought about hugging her mother, but she wasn't quite ready.

The Macreadys were away, and it was after dark when she got back. She went out and walked down Nathan Hale Road. Brian's windows were all dark. She'd thought she'd feel that this was home. But she felt like a visitor on the Point. She wasn't sure of home.

$\mathscr{H}owl$

THEO BOUNDED INTO English the day after Christmas vacation clutching a small book in her hand. She said, "Mr. Parton, before we start class, I have a poem I want to read out loud . . . or, well, just the first few lines anyway. Okay?" He suspected she was up to something, but unconcerned, he gestured for her to begin. Waiting until the others were seated she read:

> "*I saw the best minds of my generation destroyed*
> *by madness, starving hysterical naked, dragging*
> *themselves through the negro streets at dawn*
> *looking for an angry fix, angelheaded hipsters . . . *"

Brian walked over with sudden interest and Theo handed him the book with a look of triumph.

"What are you reading?" said Maude.

"She's reading *Howl*, Maude. How'd you get this?" he said, examining the book.

"My father's a lawyer. He was in San Francisco and everyone in his firm was talking about it and reading it. It was banned. He read it on the plane and said as long as I promise never to write like this, I could have it. He says it's a big nothing."

Howl is *not* a big nothing," said Brian. He was standing still, reading, and the girls didn't say anything. Suddenly he said, "This is the first copy I've seen. I hear that Ginsberg has put himself on the literary map with this poem."

"Can we read it in class?" said Cora.

Brian handed it to her. "I don't see why not, but there's only one copy. If you want to take turns reading it at home, then we can discuss it after class. But it's not available in stores."

"Why?"

"Remember the problems Whitman had with obscenity? Same kind of problems. Theo, I'd like to borrow this overnight."

"Sure," said Theo. "I read it last night."

"What did you think?" he asked, genuinely interested.

She sighed and said, "I thought, What a sheltered world Haddam is. The poem is raw and dark and shocking. But I believed every word and it's brilliant."

Charlotte was turning pages. "Listen to this introduction by William Carlos Williams. It says, 'Hold back the edges of your gowns, Ladies, we are going through hell.' "

"I didn't read the introduction," said Theo, "but it's hell, all right."

Brian teased her. "Theo, how many times have I told you. *Read* introductions. Position yourself."

"But when I'm reading for pleasure I don't want a position. I want the words to wash over me and take their own position." Charlotte handed the book to Brian and looked at Theo with wonder. How she wished she could think like Theo, who was saying, "It's funny you mentioned Whitman, Mr. Parton, because there's a poem in there about Whitman too. He calls him 'graybeard.' "

"Ginsberg knows this is revolutionary. It's probably poetic justice, no pun intended, that the poem was seized, and Ginsberg's been charged with obscenity. Remember how Whitman said, 'I draw back the veil.' And what we found behind Whitman's veils? More veils. Maybe Ginsberg draws back the last veil. Anyway, it's a bold thing to do in today's climate—" he paused, considering his words, and then he muttered almost to himself "—with the crazies still on the loose, blacklists still everywhere, and book-burning crypto-fascists coming out of the woodwork." He looked up. "Don't forget what Charlotte told us in her Whitman report. He was actually tarred and feathered in one town." Suddenly he turned back to Theo. "Is your father on the case?"

"What case?" said Charlotte.

"The trial in San Francisco," said Brian.

"Oh, no," said Theo, "but his firm represents the publisher. That's how he got a copy."

"Lucky for us," said Brian, and he sat on the edge of his desk and started reading to himself again. He seemed far away, as if he just slipped through a magic door. They'd never seen him lose himself in class like this and all eyes were on him. No one noticed the long silence as all the tension left his motionless frame. They were seeing a different man at that moment. He looked up, unembarrassed, unblushing, and said, "You know, girls, it's a reminder of the power of words. The power of art. Sometimes you get so bored reading what I assign. I know it. But poetry is still important enough to get you arrested. Words are important enough to be carved into stone, rolled onto papyrus, stored in hidden caves for millennia. Don't ever get bored with poetry, with literature. Spend your life reading. Every one of you. Read and you'll stay in touch with the souls driven to write, souls that couldn't leave silence behind. Nietzche tells us 'human beings are amazed about themselves. . . . They cling to the past,' and I tell you literature is our stories, our cultural memory. Never, never yield to the massive amnesia that's part of the culture we call modernity. To be fully human, as Auden tells us, continue to 'break bread with the dead,' go back to Homer, read the canon, even if it takes a lifetime . . . and it will." Then suddenly he *was* embarrassed and he fell silent.

None of them had heard him talk like this, forgetting to toss around his clever quips, and suddenly sincere and impassioned. Even Dana was moved.

So they all read *Howl*, taking turns, and were amazed at the world out there waiting for them. They talked about it for days, shivering on the boathouse porch at lunch. Theo said, "This is *Leaves of Grass*, all right, a different *kind* of grass," and Dana and Maude and Cora laughed and Charlotte had no idea why they were laughing. No one, however, wanted to have a class discussion with Brian.

But they did want to read the new confidential reports and, ever watchful, they found a time when the office was unguarded and read the midterm evaluations. Charlotte didn't go with them. She couldn't bear to read again what a disappointment she was to Brian. She should have gone. He wrote:

> Charlotte seems to have developed some powers of self-evaluation and has certainly applied herself seriously. She has done so well that I am moved to wonder if my previous report was either fair or accurate. Charlotte's "shallow thinking" is really a healthy naivete, a yea-saying, an unanalyzed acceptance of things through excessive goodwill. We could use more like Charlotte. And she has a strong intuitive sense that she is as yet unaware of, that mediates her naivete.

Charlotte's wasn't the only report that admitted a certain lack of understanding in his earlier assessments. Generosity was making an appearance in Brian. The women around him, staff and students, were drawing it out.

$\mathcal{O}wl$

THE FIRST WEEK of classes after the break, Mrs. Chase called Charlotte into her office and suggested that she move into her house in two weeks. Charlotte protested, but Mrs. Chase wouldn't listen and she added, "Both your parents have agreed."

"My father, too? What does *he* know?"

"Is there anything for him to know?"

"When did you talk to him?"

"Last month. He's interested in your welfare—like any father."

Charlotte wished she'd kept her mouth shut about Mr. Macready and his bourbon. She should have known it would alarm her mother. Thank God she hadn't said anything about him coming into her bedroom. Now she'd be driving to school with Mrs. Chase. And living with her.

In the car that morning she told Brian. He acted surprised and didn't tell her that he thought Mrs. Chase was doing this for reasons of her own.

"So," said Charlotte, "we have ten more mornings to discuss American poets." They both did a lot of talking those mornings. Brian was giving her outside reading, and everything he suggested she had read by the next morning. He didn't see it as giving her special treatment. She asked. They talked a lot about *Howl* and she told him how she used to memorize things to say to him on three-by-five cards.

He smiled and said, "Am I so terrifying?"

"Not now."

"Maybe I should be."

On the last morning he found her sitting on the fence clutching white narcissus. She looked like Humpty Dumpty ready to fall.

"Where'd you get those?"

"Mrs. Macready. She forces them."

"What's that?"

"Oh, I don't know. She grows them in the basement or something."

"You okay?" he said.

"Yup," she said, and was silent.

"I saw something you would have liked yesterday."

"What?"

"A great blue heron flew across the cove with a branch in his beak that must have been bigger than he was. It was something," he said.

"Last fall I saw one every day for two weeks. Maybe it's the same one."

"Are you sure? They migrate, you know."

"Not this one. My Audubon guy said he must have lost his mate. He wouldn't leave without her. He's probably disoriented. I never thought he'd survive the winter." She stared at her narcissus, feeling desperate and overwhelmed, afraid she would cry. She wanted to hug him in the worst way.

Later in the day he found a beaker from the lab on his desk full of white narcissus. He rubbed his forehead back and forth with his fingers. God knows I don't need this, he told himself, and I don't want it. But he left them there in the beaker until the petals curled brown and the stems were gooey and rank. The custodian threw them away.

The night Charlotte moved to Margaret Chase's house there was a howling, blowing storm. Charlotte put her clothes away, listening to the sleet on the windowpane. Good-bye, Brian. The fierce wind moaned under the eaves. She was confused and didn't know what was expected. It was one thing to earn her keep at the Macreadys' because it evened things out. But now she was a guest. What a terrible thing to be. She would have to be perfect, polite, friendly, neat. What if she was hungry at midnight? Could she get something to eat? What about laundry? Should she buy her own soap? What if she needed shampoo? Mrs. Macready knew how to handle things. She'd ask Charlotte on weekends, "What can I get you today? Any food cravings? Personal stuff?" She was cute about it. Now Charlotte was owing. Should she offer to fix supper every night? What? She needed advice. Theo would know what to do. She always knew what was correct. When you knew the rules, you could pick which ones you wanted to break. While she ruminated about the difficulties ahead she heard a tapping on the window, a branch bending in the wind.

Charlotte put on her pajamas, found the bathroom down the hall, stopped by Mrs. Chase's bedroom, and said, "Good night, Mrs. Chase." When there was no response, Charlotte was at a loss. Mrs. Chase had said, "I'll show you around the house later," but she'd forgotten. Sheepishly, Charlotte tiptoed back into her room and got under the covers. Hard pillows. Damn.

She heard the tapping sound again, sat up, and looked toward the sound. It came again. Such an urgent, deliberate tap didn't sound like a branch. She got up and opened the window. No branches were anywhere near the window. The icy, damp wind blasted her pajamas, and suddenly, something flew in with the wind. Charlotte jumped. Oh God, she thought, not a bat. She whirled around and ducked, following it with her eyes. But it was a brown bird with a large head, circling the ceiling. She crouched by the window and the bird flew round and round, calm as could be, and then lit on top of the open closet door. Charlotte heard two tiny clicks. Now she could see it, and she thought her heart was going to leap right through her ribs. It was an owl. A tiny, wet brown owl with little globs of ice stuck to brown and white feathers. The strange clicks came from the little talons gripping the wood. A water rivulet ran down the closet door.

The owl was no more than six inches tall, small enough to stand on the palm of her hand. She sat on the floor and watched for long cold minutes. His black talons grew out of wonderful knobby, wrinkled feet that clutched at the door's edge. It must be hard for it to balance on a flat, square surface instead of a small round branch. If only she had the big tree branch she'd put in her room at the Macreadys'. It would have been perfect. But the owl looked content. As if it were nothing to come into a strange place and just make do with whatever was there. Charlotte understood. Athena had sent this owl. It was her owl, saying be wise, be patient. The bird blinked once slowly and looked at her as if she was a tree. The owl didn't move again, but its tiny little chest rose and fell rapidly. Ice crystals melting off its wings spread a puddle on the floor. She knew already what this owl was. It was a saw-whet, nature's smallest owl. Maybe it couldn't fly in the wind, or maybe it was lost. She left the window open, tiptoed over to her coat, spread it over her blankets, and crawled into bed. She would stay up all night and keep vigil with the little owl who'd knocked on her window to come in out of the cold. Charlotte stared in magical wonder. This was a sign, a good sign.

In the morning the owl was gone. She got up, stiff from the cold. She looked everywhere, but it was gone. Was it a dream? But no, she got on her knees and felt the floor under the closet door. It was still damp from where the ice had melted off the owl's wings. How had it gotten out? It was not uncommon for a bird to fly in an open window. But to fly out was something else. But then, this was different. This was no accidental visit. This was her secret. A welcome from a small stranger. No one would believe her anyway. Not even the Audubon guy. This was between her and God.

Charlotte didn't sleep well in Mrs. Chase's house. She kept waking up and imagining Brian's head on the pillow next to hers, then she'd lie awake for hours. She cried at the slightest thing. She fell asleep in math class. She kept losing things. She tried to study and instead found herself inventing dialogues in her head, as if she were in his car. Brian still suggested extra poetry readings for her, but it wasn't the same. They never had time to talk and there was no way she could arrange it. *He* had to, and of course he didn't.

She finally got her period in the middle of the night, made a mess of the sheets, washed them herself in cold water, scrubbing by hand, so Mrs. Chase wouldn't know, and muttered, "A little late, God, like about five years, and thanks for nothing."

At least she had a figure now. One day she found two unappealing, brand-new bras laid out on her bed. How dare Mrs. Chase take such a liberty. She hid them and vowed not to wear them. And her mood blackened.

She felt like a charity case and offered to do the dishes and clean the kitchen every night after supper. Mrs. Chase said, "That would be most appreciated." Fortunately they didn't eat together that much because Mrs. Chase was out a lot. Charlotte felt a new isolation and wasn't sure where to turn. Her letters to her mother grew longer and she made sure they were neat. Her mother wrote words of encouragement and Charlotte read them more than once. She also saved them. Dana wanted to know details about Mrs. Chase's living habits. But Charlotte wouldn't talk. She said, "She isn't living and she has no habits."

"The old battle-ax," muttered Dana. "I bet her family has been here for three hundred years. They were probably paupers from debtor's prison."

Maude, who almost never criticized a teacher, said, "Have you noticed how she always makes Mr. Parton sit next to her in student court?"

"She has a crush on him," said Theo, eyeing Charlotte. "And what about the way she watches with those beady little eye flicks, and those chin thrusts?"

"Her chin reminds me of Ol' Witch Hazel in 'Little Lulu,' " said Cora.

Charlotte added, "A chin that juts out like that could do real damage if you bumped into it in the dark," and to Charlotte's surprise everyone started to laugh.

Enjoying Charlotte's new malevolence Dana said, "Maybe that's why they call her battle-ax. What I've noticed is how when she turns to Brian, that fake smile of hers changes to a hungry smile."

Charlotte was thinking—it had never occurred to her that Mrs. Chase liked Brian that way.

Mr. Macready's Return

CHARLOTTE HADN'T BEEN back to the thatch cottage since the day she'd shown it to Brian. Today she returned, and just at the boulder by the path she found a large clump of pure white snowdrops pushing up through the dense leaf matter. She'd never seen them so early before. They were singular flowers that didn't usually grow in clumps. She loved the way anything could happen in nature. The cottage looked the same, and the thatch roof held a damp winter color. She went to the door and pulled on the padlock. To her surprise, it popped open. The door must have been unlocked all this time. And then Charlotte made a mistake. She opened the door and went in.

There were three small rooms. The walls were whitewashed stucco with brown water stains. Dark beams crossed the ceiling. She pictured Brian's mother living here under the thatched roof. There was a huge spiderweb across two of the beams with a spider sleeping in the center. Did spiders live in the thatch? She wondered if they dropped down in the middle of quiet conversations.

The windows were coated with years of hard, dusty grit but the afternoon sun pushed on through. There was a cot in one room and an old wooden icebox that once held huge blocks of ice. The little living room had a window seat like the one she used to have at the Macreadys', but it was high as a table, perhaps not meant for sitting. There was a small fireplace, and a bed of ashes had turned black and gummy from the bits of rain that got past the flue. The house had the smell of neglect, but it was not a bad smell, she thought. Rather like dry fields. And the house was oddly warm, as if it had been used recently. Maybe it was the thatch. Charlotte climbed up on the window seat and lay back humming to herself. The sun was high and sharp and warm, dribbling through the bare branches, leaving shadows like faint web work on the floor. She took off her sweater, balled it under her head, and lay in her undershirt. She thought about her father. She always felt his presence—sometimes good, but sometimes like a raptor looking for her. She slipped into her favorite inner space, daydreaming about Brian, and she didn't hear the door when it quietly swung open.

The sound of shuffling feet startled her up. Mr. Macready was standing near her. The first thing she saw was the old gray work gloves on his hands, so wrinkled and leathery they looked like talons hanging limply. She clutched the sweater to her chest.

"Well, Charlotte, is this the secret place you come when no one can find you?"

"No, I've never been here before." His eyes were not friendly, and something turned in the back of her mind. She hadn't seen him since she'd left. She'd thought she'd left on good terms. She was uneasy. He pulled off his work gloves, and his hands looked suddenly pink and naked.

"What are you doing here?" he said sharply. "This is private property."

"I might ask you the same," she snapped and stood up. And with a good deal more bravery than she felt, she started to put on her sweater.

He grabbed it out of her hands. "The property belongs to me, for your information. And you, my dear, are trespassing."

"I was just exploring and the door wasn't locked," she said, suddenly polite and frightened. She was remembering other things about him now.

Mr. Macready stepped closer to her and said with an odd, taunting voice, "Well, I'm just exploring too, and look what I found."

With a suddenness she hoped would startle him she said, "You haven't found anything. I'm leaving. Get out of my way," and she tried to push past him. But he grabbed her by the shoulder and shoved her back.

"Who the hell do you think you're talking to?" he said, and he grabbed a handful of her hair. Charlotte felt the shocking strength of his arms forcing her back to the window ledge.

"What are you doing?" she cried, trying to free her hair.

He held her sweater up to her face. "You've been asking for it all year, running around the Point dressed the way you do. There's a word for a girl like you."

He pushed her back on the window seat, and with the length of his body he leaned against her hard. "Get away from me," she said. "You smell . . . " But suddenly she knew what he was about to do. She wanted to spit in his face, but instead she started to cry. "Don't you dare, you can't! I've got my period," she said in shame, sure then he wouldn't touch her.

But he said, "Is that so?" and she could hear excitement in his breathing, as if he wanted her to fight. But he held her arms above her and Charlotte couldn't free herself. He was too powerful and pinned her motionless with ease. Instead she went suddenly limp and said, "Is this the way *elite* Catholics teach their daughters the facts of life?"

"What?" He threw her sweater aside, brought back his free hand, and slapped her hard across her face. She gasped and then his hand was up her skirt and her arm pulled free and she grabbed his hand and they went back and forth—him pinning her arms and grabbing at her pants, and it was so horrible and animal and frantic and rough that Charlotte felt her mind start to fall into some odd, struggling grayness, as if she were leaving her body. She couldn't tell whether her pants were on or off, and she thought she saw a smile. But it was impossible. She couldn't close her legs because he stood between them. Both her hands were held together in his grip, and before she could fight anymore, with a clumsy rough move he pressed himself into her.

She drew in a sudden breath. And then something so strange and horrible. She felt almost nothing, no pain, just intense pressure and his weight on her and his chin above her and his throat straining and his alcohol smell. Suddenly oxygen starved, she thought she would choke and she gritted her teeth and closed her eyes. He didn't move. He just held himself hard against her. Why didn't that hurt? Only her arms hurt, pressed so far back in the socket she thought they would rip out. She heard him mutter, "I knew you were no virgin." Wondering how he could even think, let alone speak, she heard a sickening animal sound as he pushed himself off her and she felt a slight leaving but . . . her mind worked at split seconds. Was it over? She felt nothing. He stepped back and her lungs grabbed deep for air.

She turned on her side, drew her knees up to her chest, and pulled her skirt over her shaking legs. But what she saw when she looked at him, she'd never forget. He *had* been in her and her blood was on him, and he was wiping it off with her sweater like a hunter cleaning his knife after he dressed his kill. It was her blood, and now it seemed her brain bled. A tight, metallic, acid blood thing dripped in her throat that must have run down from her brain, and her throat burned. He was staring at her and she knew his eyes must be threatening. And then the door banged and there was a rough striding sound of crunching twigs and leaves under his boots. Then silence.

Oh my God, how could this happen, what have I done . . . what have I done? She had to get home. She stood up and blood ran down her leg. She took off her undershirt and stuffed it between her legs and pulled her underpants tight to hold it in place. She pulled on her sweater backward so the blood smear was out of sight and ran through the woods the back way, praying Mrs. Chase wouldn't see her come in.

There was a red slap mark rising on her face when she looked in the bathroom mirror, and her back and shoulders ached. She soaked in the tub, thanking God it was not a stranger who found her. She counted off fifteen seconds and realized he hadn't been in her that long. It was more like eight or nine. The tub water was pink, and while her mind turned, looking for some reason, some logic, she kept going back to the day she'd left the Macreadys'. Two more bruises had appeared on Peter, one on either side of his collarbone. Charlotte had seen Mr. Macready shake Peter hard. Maybe he'd left his thumbprints. Confused, wondering if she should tell, wishing she could get advice from Mrs. Macready again, who always seemed to know the right thing, she'd finally shown her the bruises, even putting her hands on Peter's shoulders, saying, "They almost look like thumbprints." Mrs. Macready was vague, Peter said not a word, and Charlotte left the next day, to a noticeable coolness on Mrs. Macready's part. Maybe she'd confronted her husband and he knew that Charlotte told. She closed her eyes, trying to think of something she loved, trying in her mind to follow the marsh hawk's flight, trying to forget what she had seen. It couldn't be over at age eighteen.

What did he mean she was asking for it and she was no virgin? She was. Or was she? Was that why it hadn't hurt? She remembered how hard she hit the front of the saddle on the down stride sometimes when her horse carried her over a stone wall. She'd bruised herself more than once. She counted off nine seconds to herself and opened her eyes, alarmed that the water in the tub was turning darker.

She let the water out and rinsed herself again. Going to bed on layers of towels, she tried to sleep. Was she torn or was this her period? She counted off nine seconds over and over. Only nine. She slept, a drugged, shocked sleep of escape, of forgetting and remembering, of not believing, and the blood kept coming. She got up ten times to change. At six in the morning she went into Mrs. Chase's bedroom, surprised to see her reading in bed.

"Mrs. Chase, excuse me for bothering you so early. This is embarrassing, but I got my period for the first time last month. And I have it again and I think something's wrong. I'm bleeding too much."

Mrs. Chase sat up in her red flannel nightgown. "How much is too much?"

"I've gone through two boxes of pads during the night."

"That's too much, all right."

"It's the clots that scare me. I keep finding these big clots."

"Do you have any pain?"

"No."

"I'll call the doctor."

"Is it a man?"

"Yes."

"I don't want a man." For the first time she saw a look of sympathy on Mrs. Chase's face.

"Charlotte, I understand, but that's all there is."

The doctor's arrival was Charlotte's second humiliation. Before he left he sat on Charlotte's bed and said, "I think this will stop of its own accord. But your color tells me you're anemic and can't afford to lose much more blood. No more aspirin for your cramps. Aspirin thins the blood."

"I take aspirin every day for my headaches. I have for years."

"I see." He studied her a minute. "Your family is where?"

"Divorced."

"I meant where are they located?"

"In Washington, DC." She liked his quiet way. "Have you seen this before?" asked Charlotte.

"Yes. It happens sometimes when a woman gets her period late in life."

"I just got mine last month."

"That's very late. It's almost as if the ovaries go haywire when they finally start to function. There's also a new theory that a hemorrhage can be caused by emotional stress, but I don't hold with that. If the bleeding doesn't slow by tomorrow night, I may bring you in for a transfusion. I don't want you out of bed or standing up. Mrs. Chase has a bedpan. Use it. Each time you stand, the bleeding may start again. Is this clear?"

"Yes."

"Here's my phone number if you have any questions later." Then he said, "Something puzzles me, though. Charlotte, I've seen hemorrhages like this before. I apologize for asking you such a personal question, but are you a virgin?"

Charlotte's mouth tightened. She looked down and she could feel something wanting to get out. She clamped it down. What could she say? He knew she wasn't.

"Well, yes, I mean technically, but I rode horseback for years and I was a jumper and I don't think I'm a virgin because . . . " She had to give him some reason. Girls didn't go around with a mirror checking. "Well, you know."

"I see." He waited. "What aren't you telling me?"

"What do you mean?"

"I think you know what I mean," he said kindly and let a long silence pass. He counted on her youth to break the silence. But she was mute. "I'd like to see you in my office in two weeks. Do you have a way to get there?"

And her voice broke when she said, "I can . . . work it out."

Charlotte bled for ten days. They brought her in for a blood transfusion. Dr. Swann wasn't there. Only a technician. A needle-small rape this time on the back of her hand as they dug for a vein, and Charlotte screamed. They said it wouldn't hurt.

The teachers came to tutor her. Maybe it was only because she lived with the headmistress, but she felt looked after as she never had before. Mrs. Chase ate dinner in the bedroom with Charlotte often. Maybe Mrs. Chase got lonely, too. No one but Dana and Theo knew about the hemorrhage. Dr. Dierig came for Latin and German. All the teachers came and laid out her studies. Except Mr. Parton. Mrs. Chase brought his assignments home. Charlotte thought it was odd and hurtful that the teacher who lived so close was the one who never came.

What Charlotte didn't know was Mrs. Chase was keeping him away. When Brian heard from Dr. Dierig that the other teachers were tutoring Charlotte, he knew what was on Mrs. Chase's mind. And it angered him. The breath of Mrs. Chase's suspicion was fanning a harmless spark to life, and it was starting to give off heat. He thought about it for a couple of days, that she was missing much too much, and decided to go see Charlotte that evening after supper. He told himself it was not so much to see Charlotte, but to challenge Margaret. She could be so damned arbitrary.

When he arrived at Mrs. Chase's door, she was perfection. "Brian, how nice to see you."

He was crisp. "Thank you. I came to tutor Charlotte."

"Oh, of course," said Mrs. Chase. "She's in my daughter's room. I'll show you."

"Charlotte," she said, "Mr. Parton is here." She was dressed, lying across the bed, and she sat up. He noticed she was wearing his sweater. He'd forgotten all about it.

"Hi, Charlotte." Brian turned to Mrs. Chase and gave her a calm look of dismissal as she left. He sat forward in the chair next to the bed. "How are you?"

"I'm much better. I'll be back at school soon. You must be busy," she said.

He looked at her, his anger toward Mrs. Chase remaining. "I wasn't informed of the tutoring."

They looked at each other for a moment and she said, "You weren't?"

"No, and I don't expect you to tackle T. S. Eliot alone. We'll start with 'The Hollow Men.' Here." He leaned over. "Read it this far to yourself, then we'll read it together." He handed her the text. The silence would drive Mrs. Chase to distraction. He skimmed it and then watched Charlotte. Her face was gaunt with grief. What from? he wondered. Charlotte looked up. "I'm sorry. I can't read when you're watching me."

He smiled. "We'll read aloud."

When he left, she lay back and felt the love stealing forth. It wasn't dead. It was moving along the inside walls of her chest, back toward her exhausted heart again. She had to trust.

Brian remembered how radiant she was before Christmas, standing in front of her class giving her report on Whitman, never looking at her note cards. Now she looked sick . . . diminished. Something had happened to Charlotte. He asked Hans Dierig why Charlotte was home.

Dr. Dierig said, "Some sort of female problem."

"Will you tell me next time you go? I want you to give her something." Brian was tired. This small, "unpressured" girls' school was so intense. He was worried about Charlotte. And about all his students. He seemed to know both too much and not enough. The girls took more out of him than the boys. At this rate he wouldn't last three years. He forced himself back to his own work.

He was reading Ford Madox Ford, and wondered why he never seemed to get his fill of reading, of entering the minds of others. He couldn't deny the hunger of his intellect was sometimes greater than either his emotional or physical hunger and it made no sense, because he loved women and was lonely in a way that he hadn't felt before, and yet he did nothing to change his life and instead indulged his addiction to reading. Or was it misreading? Ford Madox Ford said, "A man marries a woman to finish his conversations with her." A woman to examine consciousness with, to talk to, and then to lose consciousness with. A woman to embrace head to toe, to be joined at the lips and joined at the hips, molecular and spiritual, body and soul. He wondered if a woman could imagine what it was like for a man to sink into the warm folds of her body. How could anything be better than the male experience? Not that he'd had any lately.

The next night Dr. Dierig brought Charlotte a volume of poems by E. E. Cummings from Brian. "To read for enjoyment," he'd written on a note tucked into the pages. She slept with the book under the covers.

She expected the bad dreams. She didn't expect the nausea and the curious electric fingers. Something odd had happened with Mr. Macready, this numb, stillborn rape that was over so fast, but still he was *in* her, that was all that counted. It remained an act unmarked and Charlotte had a growing need to tell. She wanted to call her mother but she was afraid her mother would prosecute the man. Her mother always wanted to set things right. This could not be set right.

She felt stinging electric discharges from the ends of her fingers and an odd quiver just above her knees as if her legs were about to buckle, as if her knees were dizzy. One afternoon, she picked up a clean notebook, opened to the first blank page, and words started to come as if some magnetic field sparked her fingers. She wrote:

> journey from rape,
>
> I'm bleeding and I scream. This is the voice inside with a message for the voice outside. I address you God. God of Anger. Why do you hold on so tight with your green nails. You howl through my heart and you sneak into every fold and fingertip until I burn. My nail beds turn blue with you and I cover them over with pale polish. You slither around the blue tips of my fingers, snarl, and aim your deadly course for my center.
>
> Do you wish to kill me? I won't have death. I'm good at hiding. You won't kill my heart because you will never find it. I seal my sternum around my heart. I stitch my ribs together. This I say to you while the shocks come through my fingers into all that I will ever give you. Words, just words.

The charges in her fingers were spent for the moment. She picked up the E. E. Cummings and opened the book at random. The first line she read was, "Come a little farther. Why be afraid."

She sat up. A poet had just tapped her on the shoulder. There was comfort here. *That's* what poetry was. She read the poem, closed and opened it again, and read,

> *the moon looked into my window*
> *it touched me with its small hands*

She read and read. So many short poems. Then she picked up her notebook, turned to the last page, and wrote "Journey to Love." She would write her entries backward and forward until they met in the middle. She'd heal herself with E. E. Cummings. Breathe in, breathe out. Read in, read out.

But it was not so simple. The dark days shimmered with dappled light on the floor of the room from which she never stirred. Outside she watched the delicate icicles, like crystal fringe dripping from the old viburnum under her window. She read, worked, thought, slept.

When she went back to school, she couldn't retain what she heard in class; it was as if she'd have to learn how to think all over again, to shut out the inner world she used to love, but where now she was staggering and craving sleep. Her performance slipped and she had the feeling again that Brian knew something. She couldn't even look at him.

Theo noticed and stayed close to her at school. "Are you okay? You're not yourself."

Charlotte just kept saying, "Oh, my parents are fighting." But she was getting scared. The wound was hardening and scarring and she was afraid that if it had time to set, it would never be undone. She touched wood when her fingers were electric, the desk, a chair back, the banister, and she tried to identify what hurt. Sometimes it was like an awl that dug her throat and she almost choked. And the weird sensation that her knees were dizzy and about to give way kept happening in the halls between classes. There was not one day that Mr. Macready didn't muscle his way into her thoughts. Had he made himself a companion for life in nine seconds?

One moonless night, unable to do one sentence of Latin, she took the E. E. Cummings and started at the beginning.

> The poems to come are for you and for me and are not for mostpeople. . . . You and I wear the dangerous looseness of doom and find it becoming.

She wished she could put words together like that. Her mother would have huffed, "Always melodrama with you," but Charlotte couldn't do this alone, and because it was Brian's book, it seemed like his voice behind Cummings and she listened. Late that night, when Flanders Point was thick with cold and black as pitch, Charlotte opened to the back part of her journal, for the first time, and began her journey to the center.

·   ·   ·

Me and the mockingbird are awake tonight. He sings his
soft song. Not his robust daytime aria, but a throaty verse,
self-conscious, hesitant, hushed as if to say, "A night owl is
hunting. I am at risk if I sing at this hour but there is something I must say."

What is it, dear friend? I listen, but I cannot hear. Do you
sing of love? You must. What else would drive you to this
melancholy trill that sounds so like my own . . . risking death
to sing your heart. Me. I lie in silence thinking on the day.

She waited for the next song but the mockingbird was quiet.

She kept her appointment with Dr. Swann. "We'll just talk," he
said. Grateful, she sat down. He was a friend of Mrs. Chase, and his hair
was gray. She liked his white lab coat with the bulging pockets.

He studied her. She had color. She looked like a different girl. He
drummed two fingers on the desk blotter. Finally he said, tenderly he
hoped, "Do you want to tell me about it?"

She stiffened. "What?"

"Who raped you?" He watched her closely and saw her teeth clench
behind her lips. He sat forward. "Charlotte, this is not something to hide
or cover up. You'll find no scar where you were raped, but that's not
what I'm worried about."

"What are you worried about?"

"The scar it will leave up here." He pointed to his forehead. "And
in here." He pointed to his heart.

"You don't need to worry about the scars on my heart. Scar tissue
is stronger than unbroken skin. Everyone knows that."

He gave her a rueful look. "Yes, but they can form troublesome ad-
hesions. Do you have a boyfriend?"

"No."

"But it's true, isn't it?"

She nodded and felt as if a clamp that had held her shoulder blades
together too tightly pulled out, and her bones slid back to a normal position. She sat straighter and her eyes brimmed.

He heaved a long sigh and looked up at the ceiling. It could have been
his daughter sitting there. "What a world. Charlotte, I think I under-

stand your decision to hide this. I even respect it. But I don't agree with it. Is there a reason?"

"If anyone finds out, so will the person I love, and then he'll never want me."

"So it wasn't whoever the person is . . . that you love?"

She shook her head emphatically. "Besides, my mother's a lawyer. She'd make a huge fuss . . . I mean a legal fuss."

He thought of his daughter again and realized he would want it hidden, too. "Can I be of help?"

"Well, there's something I've wondered about."

"What?"

"Could it happen in nine seconds?"

"It's possible."

"What would that mean?"

"The boy could have become impotent at penetration . . . Boy?"

"Man."

Damn, he thought. That made it worse. "Yes, it could be nine seconds."

"But it's still rape, isn't it?"

He chose his words carefully. "As long as there's penetration, there's rape." He saw her draw back.

"I hate that word." He thought she meant *rape*. She meant *penetration*. And she remembered that all the knives and all the scissors at home had the ends snapped off. Her mother was afraid of sharp points, of implements that penetrated. It was her mother who left her with her fear, not her father or Mr. Macready. Without even knowing it, innocently, her mother had passed something to Charlotte. And without even knowing it, Charlotte had picked it up.

She asked, "What if it didn't hurt?" and watched him as he thought that over and hated that he was picturing the whole dirty business.

He said, "That is also possible."

"How?"

"The presence of moisture would eliminate painful friction."

Charlotte thought this over. "You mean the blood?"

"Yes."

"God, this is disgusting. What *was* the bleeding, anyway?"

"Coincidence. Rape rarely brings on a hemorrhage like yours. It had already started beforehand, didn't you tell me?"

She put her hand over her eyes and shook her head. "Yes."

"Charlotte, are you certain this man won't do it again?"

"Yes."

"You're safe?"

She nodded and sat back. "Dr. Swann . . . I feel a little better telling you."

"This kind of thing loses its power if it's shared."

"It's hard to share with a man."

He nodded slowly. "Yes, I imagine it is."

She stood up. "Thank you for everything, Dr. Swann."

"You're welcome. You can call me anytime. Here's my home number. My daughter went to Haddam, you know." He walked her out to the waiting room, careful not to put his hand on her shoulder as he sometimes did with his young patients. That evening he called Mrs. Chase. At some point in time he was going to tell Mrs. Chase, though not yet. He invited her to dinner the following week, and then asked what Mrs. Chase thought was an odd question. "Margaret, how's the faculty now at Haddam? How many male teachers?"

When Charlotte got home she went to call her mother, but she couldn't bring herself to do it. Only Max could she trust. She called him but no one answered the phone. That night, Mrs. Chase said, "Some of your teachers have told me you're depressed and overwrought lately."

"What teachers?"

"That's not important. Did something happen when you lived at the Macreadys'?"

"Of course not."

For the next few days Charlotte tried to pretend, to act cheerful, but trying was not enough. She was a misery to everyone, and even Dana, who had plenty of her own dark moods, said, "God, Char, snap out of it? You said your rides with him were terrible, anyway."

"What? What do you mean?" said Charlotte.

"Quite a lot, Char, and you know it," said Theo.

"I can tell you miss him," said Dana. Charlotte ignored her. In her state of despair she began to see Margaret Chase in a newly negative way. Her dense perfume gave Charlotte a scratchy throat and Mrs. Chase had the chilly, almost frozen DAR look of a laced-up puritan who would personally pin the scarlet letter on Hester Prynne's chest. There was a pasted smile-for-all, real smile-for-the-few look. It had always been there, but now Charlotte saw it every day. She'd noticed that her friends didn't love Mrs. Chase even a little. She was no Miss Haddam.

It was about this time the girls noticed a plaque had been mounted in the reception area of the main building, Dovecote. The only thing they thought odd was that there was no fanfare, no celebratory event. Maude had to ask her mother, who taught in the middle school, what it was, and even so, her mother was oddly vague. The plaque read:

TO COMMEMORATE THE ESTABLISHMENT OF THE

AMANDA FAITH COLTER

MEMORIAL ENDOWED SCHOLARSHIP AND TEACHING FELLOWSHIP

A GIFT OF HER FAMILY TO THE FAMILY OF HADDAM ACADEMY

AMANDA COLTER, 1930–1950

The students discussed it excitedly at first, but since the faculty was noncommittal and none of them knew Amanda Colter, the plaque soon became part of the everyday scenery.

Radcliffe Says No

W<small>HEN</small> M<small>RS</small>. C<small>HASE</small> heard from the director of admissions at Radcliffe that they were accepting Theo and Maude, but *not* Charlotte, she was more than troubled. She was scared. She'd practically assured Mr. Delafield that Charlotte would be accepted. He'd brought in Amanda Colter's father with an unheard-of interest-free loan and he'd made it clear what he expected in return. Now this. She could have fixed it so Charlotte was not competing with Maude and Theo, neither of whom were enamored of Radcliffe. She had written a very good recommendation for Charlotte, but there had been three little words—*at times inconsistent*—that she could have, should have, left out. Three damning words could have cast a seed of doubt.

She'd also convinced Charlotte to forego the trip to Boston for an on-campus interview. Brian had told Margaret in the fall that he'd give Charlotte a ride back from Boston if she planned her interview near the holidays, and Margaret had never even told Charlotte about his offer. Instead she told Brian, "Oh, she's being interviewed here by the Radcliffe Club," trusting Brian wouldn't pursue it with Charlotte. And he hadn't. Charlotte's interview was with an alumna named Helen Pigott who recruited for Radcliffe and who lived on Flanders Point. Margaret knew her to be a martinet, overbearing and condescending, and sulky when Margaret beat her at tennis all summer long. Charlotte had told her the interview with Mrs. Pigott had not gone well and Margaret said, "Don't worry, seniors always feel that way." Why hadn't she complained to the director of admissions about Helen Pigott's high-handed attitude? If it had been her own daughter, Faith, she would have been on the phone immediately.

After the interview Charlotte had come into her office downcast and said, "Mrs. Pigott started by saying Radcliffe takes two kinds of students. Geniuses and well-rounded girls. She asked me which I was."

Appalled at the woman's arrogance, Mrs. Chase said cheerfully, "What did you say?"

"I had to say I was well-rounded even though I know I'm not. Maybe being the editor of the yearbook will help, but I don't think so because then she said, 'Well, we have our quota of well-rounded girls for next year.'"

"That's absurd. Recruiters aren't privy to that information. She just wanted to see how you'd act under pressure."

Charlotte said, "Rude pressure, I thought. Then she asked me what I was reading for enjoyment at the moment and I told her the truth. Irwin Shaw's *Young Lions*. She said, 'Balzac is more appropriate for a Radcliffe girl.' I didn't know what to say then, so I said, 'We'll be reading *Pere Goriot* in French this semester.' And she said, *'Ça fait combien des ans que vous faîtes les études en français?'* and I said, *'Quatre ans.'* But I should have answered in a complete sentence. She didn't even answer."

"When a Radcliffe graduate does the interview it doesn't carry as much weight as the admissions office. Don't worry. Your recommendations and your essay will get you in. They haven't turned down a Haddam girl yet."

Charlotte looked despondent. "But I can tell she didn't think I amounted to much."

"Did she say anything when you left?"

"She asked me if I ever went walking on Flanders Point. I told her I did. That I was doing a bird count on the Point for the Audubon."

"Oh? Are you?"

"Yes," and Charlotte added shyly, "that's a Radcliffe thing, isn't it? A lady with field glasses and big muddy shoes and her hair in a bun sounds sort of Radcliffe." Charlotte was thinking of her mother and had meant it as a joke, and Mrs. Chase cringed as she remembered her unkind response: "But, Charlotte, your hair is never in a bun."

Mrs. Chase knew she was responsible and she took a hard look at her first reaction of relief. Brian lived in Boston when he wasn't at Haddam. Radcliffe was right across the Charles River. A girl as resourceful as Charlotte would find him with ease. Not, however, if she wasn't there. And Mrs. Chase couldn't deny the adversarial nature of her feelings toward Charlotte. She'd felt it long before she moved Charlotte away from the Macreadys'. Her only regret was telling Charlotte that a Haddam girl had never been rejected. She didn't want to hurt Charlotte, just get her out of the way. But the thought that she had it in her to destroy a student's chances because of a competing interest in a man flew by so fast that it vanished before Margaret caught hold of it. Such self-realization was beyond Margaret Chase. It was not to be beyond Jack Delafield, however.

When Charlotte got the letter, she was stunned and humiliated. But some new reflex in Charlotte that would not have been there earlier in the year rejected this rejection. She thought of the poisonous little woman, who must have been all of four foot eleven, who had treated her like dirt. If that was what Radcliffe produced she'd go elsewhere. Though she knew Miss Pigott was not typical Radcliffe. Charlotte's mother was an outgoing and gracious woman. Charlotte remembered that when women clients came to the house in the evening, her mother was businesslike, but she was gentle and calming and helped them not to be afraid. She took matrimonial cases only because the women needed help, and she was wonderful with these women, who were usually uneducated, working-class, abused by their husbands and confused by the legal system. Charlotte liked the Radcliffe graduates she knew, but she didn't have to go there to be like them.

She called her mother collect when Mrs. Chase wasn't home, and to her surprise she was so nervous when she told her mother she hadn't gotten in, her voice broke, but her mother didn't seem upset.

"Radcliffe is only one of many. You got into two top schools. I'm a little annoyed that Radcliffe didn't see your potential and take a chance on the daughter of one of their graduates, but it's their loss. It doesn't matter that much in the long run."

"You think it's not important?"

"I think it's not important." Charlotte thought she should have been relieved, but instead she wanted to cry. Why didn't her mother want her to follow in her footsteps—to be like her?

"You're not disappointed?"

"Well, of course," said her mother, "but only because you had your heart set on it. I didn't."

"I'm glad," said Charlotte. But she wasn't. She wanted to say, "But I so want to be like you," but she kept still. She was desolate beyond words. Charlotte was her first daughter and it didn't matter.

Charlotte was surprised again when she told her friends and they didn't think it was anything to be upset about. After all, she was accepted at Bryn Mawr and Vassar, and apparently her peers didn't have the inflated thoughts about "Harvard men" that Charlotte did. They urged her to go to Bryn Mawr with Maude. But the thought of being so far from Cambridge and the Charles River, where her mother and father had fallen in love; Beacon Street, where her mother had been born; Boston, where Brian lived, made her heartsick. This changed her life forever. Max would say it was destiny. Accept it. And she did. She had no fight left and not a tear was shed. And Mrs. Chase knew she had not done well by Charlotte Delafield. What she didn't seem to notice was with what ease she forgave herself, and she turned her attention to how she would appease Charlotte's father. She spoke to the director of admissions at Radcliffe and was surprised to learn that Helen Pigott's daughter had been turned down a few years back. That was useful information. A scapegoat, perhaps.

A Midsummer Night's Dream

FATE HAD PULLED Charlotte into Brian's life the night Mrs. Chase called him when Charlotte was lost in the fog, and he learned more than he wanted to know. In a few short days he found that what Hans Dierig had predicted was true. The better he got to know a student, the more he cared. And she watched him with growing intensity. Though he felt a certain tension, he pushed it aside. When she had appeared on his doorstep in December, there it was again. The tug, an interest, a need. Whose? he wondered. His or hers? And when she moved to Margaret's he even missed their morning rides. That was when he began to keep an eye on her. It was peripheral. Nothing he couldn't handle. But it wasn't fate that cast Charlotte as Titania in *A Midsummer Night's Dream*. Nor could it be called fate when Brian appointed her as his assistant director—to make up for the fact that she hadn't gotten the prized role of Puck. He also thought Charlotte was troubled because of Radcliffe, and maybe a vote of confidence from him would help. He'd find some way to talk to her about it, help her put it in perspective. He asked her to give the play a close reading over the weekend.

"Well," said Charlotte, "I read it again last night. It's not so innocent."

"Did I say it was?"

"No . . ."

"So, what do you mean?"

"Did you see the moon last night?"

"No, why?"

"It was so bright I read it by moonlight, and it's not just a comedy. It's about love and jealousy and what people do in the dark and stuff. Does Titania sleep with Bottom?"

"Do you mean in the carnal sense?"

"Yes."

"Some critics think so. Most don't," he said.

"I get the feeling she does."

"Well, we won't play it that way," said Brian. "Maybe it's better to read the play in daylight."

"And the lovers, they're all sleeping together too . . . in the woods. They even say so."

Brian wasn't sure what passage she was referring to and said, "Where?"

"Oh, never mind."

Monday after class he said, "Charlotte, can you wait a minute?" She stood by his desk and he said, "I went over the play and cut a lot. I need you to stay this afternoon. I'll give you the cuts and we'll give them to the cast on Wednesday."

"Okay," said Charlotte, thinking how nice it was to be needed. Later they worked upstairs at a table in the assembly hall, red-lining the script while the wind rattled a loose shutter and squirrels ran over the roof. The sun was low in the west and moved across the floor and disappeared. She'd expected to be his "gofer," but nothing like this. And even though it was the time of day when Charlotte would have given anything for a pack of peanut butter crackers, she didn't say anything. It was a small thing, perhaps, to endure discomfort for something more important, but this was the day Charlotte discovered seriousness. And to put herself last, not first. They worked on. Mrs. Chase wandered in frequently, switching on the hall lights when they hadn't realized how dark it was. Charlotte thought her behavior odd. At six-thirty, Brian excused himself and came back with two cups of lukewarm coffee. Charlotte was shaking with hunger and she didn't like coffee, but with milk and sugar it was like food and she drank it gratefully.

Finally Mrs. Chase said, "When will you be done, Mr. Parton?"

"Another hour."

"Be sure to shut off all the lights when you leave." Brian picked up a slight impatience. "Don't worry," he said. The work had taken longer than he thought because Charlotte questioned and argued. It made him think harder and he liked it. He wasn't that keen on the whole project. Charlotte was. Perhaps he shouldn't belittle a school production.

Over the course of the next few weeks, two things gave him pleasure. One was Theo. Her mischievous view of life and her droll assessment of the foibles of her peers made her the perfect Puck, and by the second day of rehearsal she *was* Puck. She never just stood there like the others. She moved. She bounded over the stage, asking him every day, "When are we moving this thing outdoors?" She needed more space. She was utterly charming and the glue that held the play together.

The other surprise was Charlotte. She'd had a dismal winter—sick, working hard but distracted, hypersensitive and depressed in a way he couldn't put his finger on. Suddenly a new Charlotte emerged. Almost buoyant. It happened so fast at first he wanted to drive her to school again and ask, "Will the real Charlotte Delafield please stand up?" She seemed confident, a steady, strong, and exacting stage manager, jumping up on stage, pushing, pulling the girls into position, encouraging them, performing for them, demonstrating, cajoling, rolling her eyes when they forgot their lines for the umpteenth time, fussing over everything, trying to be tactful as she insisted on her own way. He found himself encouraging her, backing her up. If there was a look of pique from the student being directed, he always said it was his wishes Charlotte was carrying out. Her eye for blocking was better than his and he consulted her often. She came up with an idea for the tedious wall scene between Pyramus and Thisbe, suggesting they build the wall out of big stuffed pillows instead of cardboard so the two actors could peer through the famous chink, lean on the wall too hard, and it would fall over; try to sit on it and it would give way—slapstick silliness right out of the Marx Brothers. Theo and Charlotte argued over it, Theo saying it wasn't Shakespearean, Charlotte saying, "It's laughs we want." And when the pillow wall was constructed and first tried out, the sight of Thisbe, played by a six-foot Swedish girl named Katrina, leaning her elbow on the top of it as she slowly sank till she pitched headlong over her fellow actor, Brian thought, was worth it—Shakespearean or not. Even Theo laughed and said, "You win."

Then with the speed of a chameleon, Charlotte stepped out of that role and into Titania. She moved with ethereal grace like the fairy queen she played—a far cry from the knock-kneed, gangly girl who crashed into desks and emptied the pencil sharpener. An imagination appeared. On her first report he'd criticized her earthbound plodding, her lack of daring, and her incessant caution. Now he knew he hadn't been fair. She scrambled up on stage, giving the girls things to do with their hands. "Bits of business," she called it. When he said, "Where'd you get that?" she said proudly, "In acting class last summer." And the girls welcomed her ideas because they felt so awkward standing like sticks. At times he had the odd feeling she was getting over something, escaping. He didn't know from what but her energy was as contagious as Theo's and the two of them turned the afternoon rehearsals from tedium into small, daily adventures. Of course Theo took no direction, and Charlotte had the good sense not to offer any. The competition between them was evident.

Four weeks passed. Brian looked forward to rehearsals more than class. All year he'd felt the girls studying him. Now he studied them, their ways, their interactions, their boredoms, their intrigues, their enthusiasms, what made them laugh, what jealousies, what resentments. It gave him new insights into what Eben meant when he said he "adored" women: Eben didn't mean he adored them just for the sex. He liked them as people, as friends. And Brian couldn't help but notice that during these afternoons of immersion in the play, he was most content when Charlotte sat at the table in front of the stage next to him. Charlotte might never rise to Maude's level of scholarship, but she had a creative gift, an aesthetic sense, a vision. No one knew it, but *she* was directing the play. And he let her because she made him look good.

But someone was watching. Mrs. Chase stood in the back, where the cavernous shadows of the assembly hall obscured her presence. Silhouetted against the lights on the stage, Brian and Charlotte leaned in to each other, he like a young tree and she like a supple reed bending toward him in the wind. When Brian sat at the director's table and Charlotte stood prompting, sometimes her long hair brushed his shoulder as she leaned over his director's book. Charlotte brought Brian coffee. Once he brought her tea. One afternoon Mrs. Chase saw Charlotte turn to him suddenly and Brian said, "Hold it," and she whispered and pointed and gestured as if *she* was directing *him*. It was oddly intense. Mrs. Chase saw the girls watch with interest, maybe envy, though she didn't care. The thing that Margaret cared about was that she rarely saw Brian anymore.

Margaret Chase was so highly tuned to the unseen, dancing molecules that passion sparked that more than once she went over and stood quietly behind them. Their interest in each other was palpable, and the erotic air they stirred swirled over her arms and wrists and face. All year she'd noticed how Brian's cloistered background and a shy, cerebral demeanor of repressed arrogance held both students and faculty at a distance. But now it was Margaret who was held at a distance. She thought Brian was doing it on purpose. Taunting her. She noticed how pretty Charlotte was looking, and she stopped her outside on the terrace one day, took Charlotte's chin, and turned it to the sun. "Charlotte, you're not wearing makeup, are you?" Charlotte bristled. "Of course not, Mrs. Chase." That afternoon Mrs. Chase went into Charlotte's bathroom and looked in her medicine cabinet.

When the days started to get warm, rehearsals moved outside and Brian and Hans had to work hard to keep everyone's mind on Shakespeare. Hans was the faculty consultant, which they'd never had before, but Miss Haddam was hesitant about giving the entire responsibility to a new teacher. Early April was spectacular that year. The trees hadn't leafed out yet, but the sun was warm and the great shagbark hickory trees were heavy with starlings that swooped en masse in great black clouds, and the rapid flutter of a thousand wings sounded like walls of waves crashing on rocks—mysterious, powerful, heart-stopping. When the starlings flew, rehearsal stopped and all eyes turned upward. Even Brian watched. "They're wonderful," he said to Charlotte.

And to his surprise she frowned. "I suppose, but they don't belong here. They're English and the guy at the Audubon Society says they're wreaking havoc on American songbirds. They're predators of a sort, you know."

"I thought you liked the predators."

"The raptors, the night hunters, not the stupid starlings."

"Oh."

One day, Mrs. Chase stopped by to dismiss rehearsal early because a violent wind was whipping up, and thrilling, dark cumulus thunderheads were churning in behind it. Brian was in shirtsleeves and Charlotte was wearing his tweed jacket with the collar turned up and the sleeves coming down over her fingers. Margaret was disgusted. She looked much too appealing. What was Brian thinking of? This simply would not do. She listened for comments in the halls, hints of envy, whispers, jokes from the faculty. She heard nothing but that didn't mean it wasn't going on. Thank God the play was only a week away.

And Charlotte shed her androgynous cocoon forever with the cherry episode. Everyone was excited because that morning the costumes had arrived, lush, authentic, and professional. No one knew that Dana's parents had paid to rent them from a place in New York. During a break, the girls were devouring the contents of a large bowl of cherries that Hazel Pierce had brought over from Miss Haddam's kitchen. The girls spit seeds at one another. They made a mess but no one seemed to mind that day. They were working on the scene where Titania falls in love with Bottom because Puck has put love dust in her eyes. Unfortunately, the king and queen of the fairies have had a spat and at this point, Bottom's head has been turned into a donkey's to humiliate Titania. Maude, playing Bottom, put on the great paper-mâché donkey's head for the first time while Brian and Hans and Hazel were chatting, spitting cherry pits into their hands, and enjoying the girls' antics. Brian had asked Hazel to come to rehearsal for weeks, but this high-spirited afternoon was not the time he would have chosen. They heard Charlotte say, "Maude, come over and lie down. I want to try some new business." Brian and Hans stopped talking and watched. The big head had been made in the art department and had an open muzzle so Maude could breathe and be heard. While Maude grumbled that it hurt because it sat wrong on her collarbone and she couldn't see, Charlotte got Maude down on the floor to do the scene where Titania is fawning over Bottom in the forest. She said to Bottom, "Or say, sweet love, what thou desirest to eat."

Then she put a cherry in between her teeth, knelt forward, put her arms about the clumsy ass's head, leaned in, and with her front teeth holding the perfect red cherry, she delicately deposited the cherry onto the narrow opening of the donkey's mouth, where it lodged. Everyone got quiet. Brian looked around to see if Mrs. Chase was there. No sign of her. Though poor Maude was oblivious, Charlotte's intent was unmistakable. Titania said, "I have a venturesome fairy that shall seek the squirrel's hoard, and fetch thee new nuts."

And Charlotte swept her arms around the donkey head, again leaned over, removed the offending cherry with her tongue, and ate it herself. Dana caught Brian glancing at Hans, who had a big smile on his face. Brian stood up, glanced at Hazel Pierce, who was trying to keep a straight face, and said, "Okay. Back to work." And he said to Charlotte aside, "Leave out the bit with the cherry." The girls heard and groaned, "Killjoy . . . " But they knew nothing like that could stay in. Not with Miss Haddam in the audience.

But then, when they began the scene again, Charlotte played Titania *more* amorous, not less. She took Bottom's hands and pulled them around her waist; Maude jerked her hands back, and they went back and forth playfully. Finally Titania, as if to settle the matter with Bottom, pushed Bottom down, climbed on top of him, and sat astride, calling out her lines of ardor. Bottom's huge donkey head was bobbing up and down and everyone laughed as they wrestled on the floor. Brian spotted Margaret Chase watching from the office window. Horrified, he moved fast. "Charlotte . . . cut!" he yelled. She sat back instantly because he sounded mad. "This isn't *A Streetcar Named Desire* you know. What kind of cheap nonsense is this? You're supposed to be charming, not vulgar. Shakespeare would retch!"

Charlotte froze. He wasn't kidding. Mr. Parton was angry and he never got angry. "Get up," he said. "Start over and get your mind out of the gutter for a change." Hans reached over and touched Brian's arm in surprise. The girls were silent now. Charlotte felt as if her skin was burning off her bones and she stood up and said, "Excuse me. I'm not taking that," and to everyone's surprise, she turned and ran off into the woods. There was a moment of quiet confusion as the girls looked after her and then at Mr. Parton. He turned to Hans, who just shook his head. Brian dropped his script on the table, trying to cover his embarrassment and decide what to do, when out of nowhere Margaret suddenly walked past him and muttered, "Do *not* follow that girl into the woods."

But Brian was already thinking he would do just that. "Okay," he called out to the cast, "that's enough for one day. Tomorrow we'll work on individual scenes. I'll put a list up in the morning. Learn your cues, girls. Time is running out." He waited a minute, letting the girls disperse, and then he walked into the woods. If he'd looked back he would have been unhappy to see all eyes had turned to watch him go after Charlotte, except for those of M.   aret Chase, who walked quickly back to her office.

Brian found Charlotte far up the path sitting on a rock, her sweater draped over her head, as motionless as a stage prop. The minute he'd entered the woods, his calm returned and he was braced for tears. He asked her quietly, "What were you thinking of?"

She pulled the sweater off her head. "I was *completely* in character."

"You certainly were. You know, Charlotte, you have more experience than the other girls, so I give you license, but you have to show more restraint. You can't have it both ways."

She didn't move, didn't even seem to be breathing. "How could you call me vulgar?" she said hotly. "How could you? I don't have a vulgar bone in my body."

"I know."

"Well . . . then . . ."

He sighed. "What can I say? Your parents still see you as children, *their* children. The play wasn't written for children but we have to present it that way. Do you understand what I mean?"

More silence. Delicious silence, he thought to himself.

"I certainly do. No cherry pits—no touches, no kisses, no fun." It was like a petulant slamming of doors. He laughed in surprise and saw that she was about to laugh too, and like an utter imp she looked up at him and protested, "It wasn't vulgar, it was innocent."

He believed her, but he said, "Like hell it was."

"It was unconscious, Mr. Parton."

"It was conscious, Charlotte."

"It was intuitive."

"It was aware."

"It was right," she said and started to smile.

"It was wrong," he said and finally stared her down. When she dropped her eyes he felt a bit of relief and a lot of disappointment. A flock of starlings roared in and set the branches above them trembling. Brian, who was thinking all the wrong things, sighed and looked up. He should fly with the starlings. "I have to get back. Rehearsal's over. We'll work inside tomorrow. Are you still on board?"

She flipped her hair. "Of course."

"I'll say one thing about your moods, you're not in danger of boring anyone. Do you have a ride home?" She nodded. He was surprised, thinking she would have leapt at the chance. "Play it with restraint, Charlotte. It'll be much more interesting." And he left realizing neither one of them had said they were sorry. He'd thought to find her weepy and wounded but Charlotte was changing before his eyes.

As he expected, Margaret was waiting for him in the deserted English room. "What's going on, Brian?"

"How do I know?"

"You're a bright young man with a good future . . . and I think you know damn well." Brian refused to say a word. She pushed again. "You didn't handle that very well."

"No, I didn't, I should have let it pass. I was much too harsh."

Margaret looked at him in disgust. "That's *not* what I mean. Disengage, Brian." And she left. She had a hunch that the reason he'd overreacted was because Charlotte had aroused him and that scared him. Intolerable. Obscene, infuriating. But still, she could use his fear to squash Charlotte, who at the moment seemed to have his full attention. Not for long, thought Margaret. It was her responsibility to break this up. She let two days pass, continuing to watch rehearsals from a discreet distance, and was pleased to see she'd driven some sort of wedge between them. Brian was more distant, Charlotte a little subdued and much too compliant. But Margaret saw confidence under the compliance and she wasn't taking any chances. A little more cold water on Brian was called for. The play was that weekend, so she'd do it today. Snuff out any remaining interest, grind it under her heel. She asked him to walk her over to Miss Haddam's after lunch. They took the path through the woods from Dovecote to Little House. The breeze from the cove was freshening, and terns scolded in some raucous new excitement.

"Brian, there's something I'd like you to be sensitive to. There's talk and innuendo about you and Charlotte."

"Really?" Brian tried to sound amused but he felt his color rise.

"Yes. The play has thrown you together, and I think it's general knowledge that Charlotte has a crush on you."

"I see no sign of it," said Brian. "But I do see a deep commitment in her work on this play."

Mrs. Chase raised her eyebrows. If there was one thing Brian was not, it was naive. "I doubt if her commitment is to the play," she said archly. "The comment was made to me that there might be a question of who has a crush on whom." She heard him draw in a deep breath, and suddenly she softened, and not just because of her feelings. He was the best teacher she'd ever worked with. Coming to Haddam at the last minute with no résumé, he'd already established himself in a position of leadership with the faculty, though she doubted he realized it. His imposing way belied a modesty that continued to surprise her. His comments on his students' confidential reports read like harsh but funny poetry. And one by one, the girls were responding to his demands and reaching to keep up with him. She had no wish to accuse. "It's just a word to the wise, Brian. You know how vulnerable your age makes you to this kind of rumor."

"Thank you for the cautionary words, and forgive me, but I'm appalled to hear them." Which of course he wasn't in the least.

However, it wasn't Margaret who got in the last word. It was Hazel Pierce, and Brian was shaken by her reaction. There was a note on his desk full of encouragement and glowing words of praise for his direction of the play, followed by a separate enclosure that said,

Brian,

I came across a poet named Haniel Long in a 1930 anthology Lyric America *last night, who wrote this poem. I don't know who he is but thought you'd enjoy it, pursuant to our conversation awhile back.*

> *Sometimes I have nervous moments—*
> *there is a girl who looks at me strangely*
> *so much as to say,*
> *You are a young man,*
> *and I am a young woman,*
> *and what are you going to do about it?*
> *And I look at her as much as to say,*
> *I am going to keep the teacher's desk between us, my dear,*
> *   as long as I can.*

> > *A charming little poem, don't you agree?*
> > *H. Pierce*

Brian was annoyed that she didn't come to him in person. He realized he'd overreacted to Charlotte, but the last thing he would have expected of Hazel was that she'd leave a snide note. Hazel's circular approach would normally have engaged Brian. He would have taken it as a perverse form of goodwill, but instead he was left feeling exposed. She was baiting him and, though tempted to go over and protest—disguising it as some sort of teacher's amusement—he thought better of it. He never said a word and avoided her. Which was too bad, as Hazel had meant it as a caution, not a reproach. Of all people, she should have known her written words might be misconstrued but she didn't give it a thought. Nor did she make any effort to seek him out.

Venus Touches the Moon

THE LONG-AWAITED dress rehearsal ran late on Friday and Brian said to Charlotte, "Wait for me. I'll take you home." The hell with Mrs. Chase.

They drove in silence at first. The sky was a pristine, cloudless gray with a soft pink smog horizon.

Brian pointed. "Look, the evening star," he said.

Charlotte looked over. "It's mine, you know. The moon gave it to me yesterday."

Brian looked over. "Who are we today? E. E. Cummings?"

"You said you are who you read."

"And do you accept everything I say?"

"Almost."

"And you read E. E. Cummings?"

"Of course. It was your idea," she muttered, embarrassed now.

He smiled but she didn't see it. "What am I going to do with you, Charlotte?"

"Just drop me off at the dungeon, I guess."

Brian laughed out loud and Charlotte sat forward. She felt an internal rush with his laugh, and suddenly she remembered how she used to make her father laugh. When her father laughed it was like a kiss. Here it was again.

"The dungeon," he said. "That bad, eh?"

"Mrs. Chase is a pain. Drunken Mr. Macready was better than her."

The Buick cruised by Mrs. Chase's house.

"Where are you going?" she asked.

"Your star seems to have disappeared. I want to see where it went."

"I think it's behind us." She twisted around but the moon and the star were nowhere to be seen.

"Are you driving to the beach club?" she asked.

"Yes. Have you been down there?"

"I grew up on Flanders Point. I learned to swim at that beach."

"You grew up here? You never told me that."

"It was in the happy days of my family, before my father's accident. My parents even knew the Armbrusters." She remembered the beach days, how they didn't allow inner tubes in the water at the beach club, and she and her brother used to race down to the beach holding pillowcases wide open until they were full of air, and then they'd twist them shut with a big rubber band and go floating in the water together. Those were the summers when her father put her up on his shoulders and dumped her backward into the water. Was it already determined when she was building sand castles at the beach that ten years later she'd be driving here at sundown with someone she loved? The thought of it left her weak.

He stopped the car in front of the stone wall and looked at the small crescent-shaped beach, where great, sheared-off rocks formed cliffs on either side. The evening star was next to a white silver moon. The day had faded down until the points of land were like great black arms around the crescent but the sea, flat as a mirror, still reflected mysterious light. It was the slack, still moment when the tide turned. A post lamp by the tennis court threw a dim circle of light onto the sand, and it was so quiet that when Brian suddenly opened the car door Charlotte jumped.

She got out and followed him onto the wall. The beach was a melancholy place now, with a desolate winter beauty that held the colors of cold minerals and damp stones.

Brian looked up. "There's your star."

Charlotte was chagrined. "It isn't really a star. It's a planet."

He looked over at her in surprise. "Oh, *planet*'s a clumsy word. I prefer *star.*"

With a curious melancholy Charlotte's memory tugged her back to something Max had told her last year, some phenomenon in the sky to look for this winter. She remembered.

Brian stepped onto the sand.

"But the name of the planet isn't clumsy," she said. "It's Venus."

"Really? That I like."

"Tonight is a rare event and tomorrow night, too." She watched him, ready to share but oddly nervous.

"What do you mean?" he said.

Charlotte wanted to tell but she was afraid he'd scoff again. Brian turned and said, "What?"

"Nothing."

"Charlotte, cut it out."

She looked at her feet, at his face, at the sky, and said, "Well, once every twenty-four years Venus touches the moon. I mean . . . it appears to. You see how the star is right there touching the bottom tip of the crescent almost as if it's sitting on the point?"

"Yes."

"This is the night Venus touches the moon."

There was a long silence. Finally Brian said, "If you're making that up it's a very nice image."

She didn't answer.

"Is it true?" His voice was strangely husky.

"Yes, it's true. My brother knows the stars. He told me to watch for it this winter. I'd never make it up."

"No, no, you wouldn't," he said so low she could hardly hear. She felt she was going to lose her balance on the wall.

"Every twenty-four years," he said. "That's wonderful."

There was silence again and she didn't disturb it. "Next time it happens I'll be fifty-two," he said.

"And I'll be forty-two," she said.

Brian turned and stared at her and walked slowly down to the water's edge. She watched him make shallow moon shapes in the sand with his shoe. She was touched that he had let down his guard, wasn't acting like a teacher. It seemed such a generous gesture, as if maybe he was thanking her for something. She wished she was bold enough to go over and take his hand. But he wanted restraint. She mustn't take advantage. So she just stood quietly, while he stared out over the water. The light from the tennis court seemed brighter as the night grew darker. Finally she said, "What are you thinking about?"

He turned to her and then seemed embarrassed and looked away again. "How pretty you are." From the corner of his eye he saw her head tilt sideways like that of a nervous robin on the grass listening to the earth. In the next breath he said, "I better get you home." They went back to the car. He drove slowly and she didn't know what to say.

"How do you think the play turned out?" he asked in a bland voice. She was relieved.

"Much better than I thought. Everyone is working hard for you."

"You got over your disappointment about Puck?"

"Yes. It's not me."

"Dr. Dierig thought you should be Puck, but he was voted down. I thought you were upset, though."

"I was, but Theo's a natural." Charlotte slid the blue gingham bow off her hair and held it in her hand.

"You were indispensable, Charlotte. Thank you for never complaining. No one but me knows how hard you worked."

"That's okay. It was fun."

He paused. "Yes, it was. You seem to have the theater in your blood."

"Do you think so?" He nodded. "I learned something, though," she said. "I like directing more than performing."

"How so?"

"Promise not to tell?"

"Not a word."

"I like telling people what to do."

He smiled to himself. They were almost at Mrs. Chase's, and the hairbow was still in her hand. Hoping the dark would impair his famous peripheral vision, she leaned forward casually as if she was fiddling with her shoes and placed the still-tied bow on the floor of his car. He kept a neat car. He would find it in the morning.

Brian's Buick stopped at the entrance to the Chase driveway and Charlotte opened the door but before she got out, she knelt up on her seat, leaned over impulsively, and with her face right next to his, said, "Thank you for letting me do so much, Mr. Parton. You don't know what it meant to me," and she kissed him on the cheek. Then she turned quickly and climbed out of the car. Though his voice was barely audible, she heard him mutter, "See you tomorrow."

As Charlotte walked up the driveway she noticed her hand was rubbing her forearm oddly, as if her hand remembered something that she didn't. She stopped, looking at her arm, and suddenly she knew what it was. When she'd leaned in to kiss him on the cheek, he had gripped her arm above the wrist as if to say, "Stay a little . . . don't go yet." She turned and stared down the dark, empty road, thrilled but in despair. She'd been so nervous, she'd totally missed his signal; that is, if it was a signal. She went to bed early but she lay for hours going over that moment in the car—that spot of time that came and went like quicksilver, that both of them had let slip away. Normally she would have thought she was imagining, but her arm could still feel his grip.

When Brian got home he knew he'd made a mistake but he was just as certain that he would never do it again. There was a letter from Eben.

February

Dear Brian,

Remember our talk at Christmas? I went back to Plato's Phaedrus *to see what I thought was so important about pedagogical Eros, and found a very small passage that made a rather large impression on me. I'd recalled it as being more significant than it seems now, but then I came across an essay by a scholar named Jonathan Poole. (He's our age, but clearly is ahead of us both.) He too was struck by the* Phaedrus *passage. I think it was his thoughts that I confused with Plato's. Anyway, I enclose the* Phaedrus *passage, and the paragraph Poole wrote with my own insertions in parenthesis. I send it along because you seemed curious about the feelings of the girl for you. According to Plato (or rather, Poole's interpretation), the teacher is not exempt from the desire for greater intimacy. BE CAREFUL MY FRIEND and*

Good luck (whatever that means . . .)
Your friend, Eben

And on the next page Brian read:

The dialectician selects a soul of the right type, and in it he plants and sows his words founded on knowledge, words which can defend both themselves and him who planted them, words which instead of remaining barren contain a seed whence new words grow up in new characters, *whereby the seed is vouchsafed immortality,* and its possessor the fullest measure of blessedness that man can attain unto (italics supplied).

Brian, interpret "dialectician" to be teacher . . . possessor of knowledge. Then we go to Poole. It seems to me he holds back from actually making the claim that there exists a tempting causal nexus between student and teacher that can stumble into love. Poole says:

Here we glimpse the extreme ambition of the philosopher (teacher). It is to find a living element for the immortal stamp, or seed, of the mind. It is a desire for perpetuation by spiritual means, in a living respondent. The desire is simple enough, yet no desire is quite as demanding. It informs the homoerotic *paideia* of the Platonic dialogues; it may touch on longings for extreme intimacy or incorporation. . . .

Isn't he suggesting that Eros lies in teaching, and the extreme ambition of the philosopher (teacher) is the desire to stamp or seed his mind—"sowing, dissemination" (insemination), "extreme intimacy, incorporation" (penetration)—in a living respondent (in, not on, is an important distinction)?

A stamp, of course, implies an indelible marking rather than entrance into, but even so these markings have the effect of awakening, arousing, exciting the disciple until the mind (maybe the true homeland of desire) softens, expands and opens (see?), offering a receptive matrix upon which the teacher presses. (Ah yes, the receptive matrix . . .)

Anyway, that's how I read it. If I misread Poole he'll never know and I ask your forbearance. I suppose if I hadn't fallen for one of my own students, I wouldn't be so concerned with this, but I did and so I am.

Brian sighed. "Thank you, Eben. Your timing falls into the realm of the uncanny." Brian grabbed a piece of white bond paper and dashed off the words,

> *Eben, got your note. Many thanks, though there is lessening interest on my part. I don't know where you got such an idea. I'm a committed believer in the incest taboo, but I appreciate your concern just the same. And I still envy you the love that you found. Someone in your position certainly has the right to love someone in hers or what's a heaven for? It's different here, though.*
>
> *In haste,*
Brian

If ever Brian believed in his innate ability to say no, it was now. Eben's note had cleared his mind—or so he thought. He was no dreamer and knew his place and couldn't remember the last time he'd had such a sense of well-being. Nevertheless, he did not sleep well. Saturday, at last, was the performance of *A Midsummer Night's Dream* and at noon that day he found a short letter from Eben in his mailbox, written in all capital letters.

> *DEAR BRIAN,*
> *EVER SINCE I'VE KNOWN YOU, IT'S BEEN YOU THE REALIST, AND ME THE ROMANTIC, YOU THE PRAGMATIST, ME THE DREAMER. I NEVER THOUGHT I'D SAY THIS BUT SOMETHING HAS CHANGED. PERHAPS YOU AND THE TRUTH NEED TO GET ACQUAINTED . . . SORRY, I MEAN REACQUAINTED.*
>
> *YOUR FRIEND ALWAYS,*
EBEN

Margaret Chase Says Yes

JACK DELAFIELD WAS not one to accept Radcliffe's refusal at face value nor would he leave the matter to Margaret Chase. He believed in the basic incompetence of people. After a phone call with Margaret he called the admissions office at Radcliffe. He called at lunchtime and played it as a curious inquiry about his daughter's application, identifying Charlotte as a legacy student so they'd be polite. The woman that answered sounded young, and she said she was an undergraduate intern helping out in the office. The staff was at lunch. This was just what Jack had hoped would happen: getting hold of someone inexperienced whom he could manipulate. Incompetence could be a plus. He chatted with the girl about her major, her plans, if she liked her classes at Harvard before he got to his query about Charlotte's record.

After mentioning that his daughter had been turned down, he said, "I'm calling because I had asked my daughter to share her application essay with me last fall and she forgot and she doesn't have a copy. I wonder if it's possible for you to pull her file and send me a copy of the essay. I imagine its an odd request but she told me with pride how she'd written it about me and it would mean a lot. Could you do that for me?" And like tumblers falling into place under the touch of a master safe cracker he heard the words, "I don't see any harm. Give me your address. I'm sure I can locate it and, if you like, I'll just send you the essay. We don't need it at this point."

"That would be very kind," he said, constantly amazed at what a little honey could do dealing with women. But a second bureaucratic misstep occurred a few days later. The large envelope from Radcliffe that arrived was not just Charlotte's essay. It was the whole file: records, recommendations, everything. When Jack read the teachers' letters he quickly picked up the damaging words "at times inconsistent" in Margaret's recommendation. "Well, I'll be damned," he muttered to himself. "That bitch." Margaret Chase had destroyed his daughter's chances. For what possible reason? He looked at the date. It was after he'd met with her the first time but before he'd arranged for the Colter loan. *She won't get away with this.* Fate had dealt him a winning hand and he would play it out. Quick to engage with another's cunning he considered his options. He had the power to meddle with the Colter loan but it was Margaret Chase he was after, not the school. He called her.

"Margaret, there's something I'd like to discuss with you privately." He was pleasant. "I'll be in the country tomorrow evening. Could I stop by around six or so?"

Margaret did some quick thinking. She'd had a short conversation with him on the phone about the rejection, but she knew that wasn't the end of it. Tomorrow was Saturday, the performance of the play. There was a cast party she wasn't planning to attend, then Charlotte would be out overnight at Theo's. She asked him, "Are you coming to see the play tomorrow?"

"What play?"

"Our play—*A Midsummer Night's Dream.*"

"I didn't know about it. Is Charlotte in it?"

"Of course. I can't believe she didn't tell you." She let it sink in. "Come as my guest. It starts at six on the front lawn of Dovecote. Then you can come back and we'll talk afterwards. Charlotte will be at the cast party. If it's not too late, we'll have dinner." He deserved the full treatment. Besides, no one got up from the dinner table angry, although she didn't know what Jack Delafield was capable of. In her mind, if he accepted her invitation, then it wasn't anything serious.

Normally Jack would have preferred to talk before she tried to soften him up, but he might learn something about Charlotte and Margaret's relationship, so he agreed.

The play was a hit with the parents, if for no other reason than that the breathtaking costumes added status to the school and the reassurance of its ability to put on such a production. There was a languid westerly breeze from the cove, blowing in behind the performers, so their lines came floating forward loud and clear all the way to the back row. But more memorable were the idiosyncrasies of the young cast as they struggled to live up to their professional costumes. One was the incongruous sight of Puck, who was supposed to be a tiny sprite, but Theo was five feet ten inches. She towered over most of the cast even without the peaked and petal-shaped headgear she insisted on wearing, which made her over six feet. Then there was the image of Cora, who played Helena and was completely undone by the long, opulent skirt she wore. She kept stepping on the hem, tripping over it, and had to be caught and steadied more than once when she started to fall. Nerves, thought Charlotte, and saw the parents trying not to laugh, and when Cora left the scene almost in tears, thinking she'd ruined the whole play, Charlotte hurried over and said, "Cora, don't let it throw you; it's funny. Play it for all it's worth. This is a comedy."

"How?" said poor Cora.

"Just let yourself trip, look annoyed with yourself, which you are anyway, and the audience will laugh."

"I'll try," she said, dubious.

"It'll work. I don't know why we never thought of it. I'll tell the others so they relax." And Charlotte was right. She told Theo and Dana, "If Cora trips, react. Roll your eyes, use it." Charlotte didn't know if it would help the play but she knew it would help Cora and that would help the play. And it *was* funny. Sure enough, the tension onstage and off dissipated.

The other costume problem produced no visible reaction, but did not go unnoticed by the parents. When made up, Charlotte was transformed from a girl with a nice face to a stunning Titania, with flowered braids circling her head like a crown. But the costume, a white gauzy fabric tied with ivy garlands like the White Rock Girl's (ideal, of course, thought Charlotte), which had appeared safely opaque during dress rehearsal, was elusively transparent when backlit by the late-day sun. Charlotte and the cast members had no idea. Jack Delafield leaned over to Margaret and said, "Did you approve this costume?"

"I never saw it," said Margaret, horrified. Charlotte was surely wearing something underneath, but you'd never know.

"Do something about it," said Jack Delafield.

"I certainly will," she said, excused herself, and walked to the back, where, to her annoyance, Brian and Hans were watching. They'd become inseparable over the last few weeks and this too irritated her. She had an almost obsessive resentment of sharing Brian's attentions with anyone, and why the hell wasn't Brian backstage? She walked over. The last thing she wanted to do was point this out to Brian, but when she looked at Charlotte from his viewpoint she figured he already knew. Infuriating. She said, "Brian, for God's sake get someone to tell Charlotte she needs a slip. Her father is throwing a fit."

"It's nothing, don't make a fuss."

"You heard me. Who's dressing them back there?"

"The music teacher."

"Well, hurry it up, I don't want her onstage like that again and I won't have that girl embarrassing the school. She probably did it on purpose." Hans pretended to be oblivious but he relished seeing Brian challenge her. "She doesn't know a thing," Brian whispered. "Don't embarrass her now."

"That's *not* the point," she said, and then muttered under her breath, "Stop enjoying it and do what I say, damn you." She wanted to smack him when she saw him smirk.

Hans was in a state of shock. This was a Margaret he'd never seen. Brian walked back and said to the music teacher, "Order from Chase. Sun's coming through Titania's costume. Transparent. Get a slip on her. Use your own if you have to," and he swiveled and went back to stand in the rear.

During the act break Jack studied the program and saw that Charlotte was the assistant director to the English teacher and he was suspicious right away. All was quiet on the lawn while the parents waited for the third act to begin, and Jack saw Charlotte and Mr. Parton standing apart, looking at each other though not speaking or moving. He watched. Suddenly, two great blue herons swooped onto the lawn like thunderous, windy gray shadows and landed just in front of Dovecote. People stopped what they were doing and looked in awe at the two enormous herons, who with their vast wings still spread took three bounding duet-like steps, surveyed the crowd quickly as if they were reedy young dancers on the wrong stage, and then lifted in graceful unison and soared up and away, majestic, over the cove. The eyes of everyone followed the mystery of two of the biggest birds anyone had ever seen. Jack looked at Charlotte to catch her eye, but she'd dashed over to Mr. Parton and they were talking, excited, as they hurried to the side porch and watched the herons until they were out of sight. Charlotte and Brian walked back to the cast and Jack noticed how intensely Charlotte looked at her teacher before he turned away, as if they shared some secret. He sat back thinking. Charlotte must have a special relationship with this teacher. Charlotte was living with the headmistress. And Jack had also noticed the way Margaret Chase seemed to check on the English teacher's whereabouts in the audience frequently, too frequently. Was there a connection here? Was Charlotte in the middle of something?

As naive as Charlotte's mother had always been, a trait she'd seemed to have passed on to Charlotte, Jack was cynical. His own need for women made it impossible for him to believe that a man and woman of any age could have a friendship without sex. He left his seat and during the last act, no longer interested in the play, he stood in the back to watch the students and faculty and how they behaved. He saw nothing more to reinforce his suspicions, but then he didn't really need more. He could invent.

Margaret Chase left the campus later with Jack and he followed her home in his car. The folder from Radcliffe was in his briefcase. When they drove in the driveway he remembered her house. He even thought he remembered years ago seeing her on the tennis courts in the summer. Inside, the house was cavernous and poorly lit, but welcoming. They had dinner at a pine table in the kitchen, with old brass candlesticks at one end, and Jack had the feeling that Margaret had wealth, maybe tied up in a trust, but she had no interest in spending it, either on her house or herself. She did, however, have a full and comely figure that reminded him a little of Charlotte's mother's and a bosom that must have been her pride in younger days.

During a lull, he said, "Margaret, as a legacy student *and* applying from venerable Haddam, doesn't it strike you as odd that Charlotte didn't get into Radcliffe?"

"Well, three out of the five girls applied. That's never happened."

"Were the others legacy families?"

"No."

"And did they choose Radcliffe?"

"No, it wasn't their first choice."

"But, of course, it *was* Charlotte's, which you knew."

"Yes, it's disappointing. Her recommendations were outstanding."

"Oh?"

"Yes, from her English teacher and her Latin teacher . . . "

"Anyone else?"

"Well, I wrote one, of course."

"Oh, I'm not concerned about yours. Yours would be unimpeachable."

"Yes."

"I'd like to see them."

"Who? The teachers?"

"No, the recommendations."

Margaret shifted. "Unlike school reports, these are confidential." She began fussing with her hair.

"You know," he said, "sometimes admission decisions are made as much by what isn't said as what is, or even sometimes by an unfortunate choice of affirmative words. Could that be the case here?"

"Oh, no. We go over them together with a fine-tooth comb. The school's reputation was built on the girls' college admissions."

"Not on feel-good plays with overdone costumes, I'll warrant."

She wanted to close this off. He was looking for something, and she could feel a web being spun.

"Have you called the admissions office?" asked Jack.

"No, what point would it serve? If you wish, I still can."

"No. I've already spoken with them."

She looked startled and stood up suddenly. "I'd like to hear what they had to say, Jack, but let me clear the dishes first and we'll talk in the living room."

He poured the rest of the wine into his glass and left the kitchen.

"I'll be a few minutes," she said.

"No rush." Now he knew that she knew, so from here on in, he'd just let this play out her way.

Margaret was shaken. She left the dishes on the table and went up the back stairs. She had to keep this man busy, distract him—start pouring brandy or something. She didn't know any man who could stay clear with brandy on top of a bottle of Bordeaux. And only partly aware of her actions, she took off her suit, her bra, her girdle, and put on a green velvet dressing gown.

She went downstairs and saw no reaction to her change of clothes.

"So what did they say?" she asked.

"They were noncommittal."

She handed him a snifter of Armagnac, took hers, and sat down next to him.

"But her file was sent to me," he said.

"What file?"

"Her application file. The whole thing. Recommendations and all."

There was a long silence. What could she say now. "How did that happen?" she said. "Did you ask for it?" Maybe she underestimated him.

"No. I think it was a mistake."

"It certainly was," she said, indignant.

"But I do know this, Margaret." He bent toward her, leading with his chin. "There's only one reason she was turned down. And you know it too." She said nothing. "It was you. I read your recommendation."

"And it was excellent."

"Not quite."

"Well, three little words. That couldn't be the reason."

"It's a code, Margaret. I do prospective interviews for Harvard. The words *at times inconsistent* mean you can't rely on this girl—pass her by." Margaret got up and started to walk to the bar. He grabbed her wrist. "Sit down." He almost threw her back.

She said, "Jack, Charlotte's work has been inconsistent, radically so, this year, but her grades were fine when the application went in, her SAT's were high. Everything was in place. My comment didn't mean a thing. There was very stiff competition this year."

"I don't buy it, Margaret."

"Well, that's just too bad. I've done nothing but help your daughter. No one has ever been invited to live in my house. In December, she was going to go to Radcliffe for an interview, with almost no money, and I even arranged for her to get a ride back with one of the teachers who lives in Boston. Of course, then we changed plans, but—"

"What teacher?"

"What?"

"Who lives in Boston?"

She felt a jolt of alarm as she realized her blunder but it was too late. "Mr. Parton . . . " and Jack gave her a look that chilled her to the bone. Feeling panicky she said, "Look, this is a complete misunderstanding. . . ." But Jack knew he could do anything now. She got up again and he pulled her back down again, but not so rudely this time. She felt the change. He sat thinking.

"There is no misunderstanding, Margaret." She didn't answer. He didn't move but he was looking her over. "Take off your shoes," he said. She did.

"And your stockings."

"Not here," she got up again, "in the bedroom . . . "

"Here." His face revealed nothing but confidence. Margaret found it interesting. She took off her stockings and garter belt and dropped them on the floor. He studied her further and the tension was so erotic Margaret wasn't breathing normally anymore. She'd found him attractive from the start, so she wasn't going to protest.

"And your pants." She did so as modestly as possible and sat down. But then, he pulled up her dressing gown while she sat there, spread her legs, unzipped his fly, and, with intense concentration, slowly put himself into her without so much as a word, as if she were inanimate. But she was anything but, and thinking to get into the spirit of the moment she allowed herself to quickly undo the top of her dressing gown. He barely noticed as he started shoving back and forth like a rutting moose for a hyperactive minute or two; then he moaned a bit and released her. Not exactly pleasant. She threw down the skirt of her dressing gown as he zipped himself up.

"And just what was that supposed to be, Jack? A get-even fuck?"

Jack was appalled. He lit a cigarette and looked her over again. "We're not finished." His arrogance infuriated her.

"Oh, yes we are. Get out of my house."

"I'm not going anywhere just yet, Margaret."

"How dare you."

"I dare."

To her dismay, she found his attitude exciting. She forgot Charlotte, Brian, and Radcliffe. She sat quietly trying to discern what she was feeling and then carefully, remembering how her husband had adored her breasts, she pulled the top of her gown down to the waist and said quietly, "Well, I'm ready when you are, Mr. Delafield."

But she was not ready for what happened next. Though he refused to move from the living room, he removed her dressing gown, took off his clothes, laying them deliberately across the sofa, and started to examine her body. He touched her and pressed and fondled and tasted in a way that seemed to her like lovemaking of the highest order. He moved her every which way, got her on the floor to look at and probe and moisten her secret places with his mouth and his fingers. She'd been married twenty years but never handled like this. She was beside herself and had the sensation that this man was feeding on her body, but it was not so much a hunger she felt from him, nothing raw or urgent or animal; she was not a meal, she felt more botanical, and this was a slow sipping of nectar. It left her unashamed and unembarrassed, pure and free. It was pleasure he was after, not just his but hers. Every now and then he moved her head where he wanted something, but he always returned to her. She had a secret orgasm that she didn't reveal before he finally entered her, and then there was another.

They lay on the rug, not touching, sprawled next to each other, staring at the ceiling. She looked over and he was rubbing his chest. What a wonder a man was. "If that's the way you get even, Jack, let me sin again."

He didn't answer. "It felt more like love than anger," she said.

"It wasn't love for you, rest assured. There are those of us among my sex who love the female body and we know how to enjoy it. That's all it was."

"I see. Is there any way to tell who those of you are?"

He laughed, content to enjoy her admiration. He had not gotten even yet. But let her think so, he thought to himself. She'd still done a fine job of derailing his plans for Charlotte. And there was the teacher. And there was Charlotte.

Presently, he got up, got dressed, helped himself to a swallow of Armagnac, and left without so much as a good-bye. And Margaret's sixth sense was not operating. She had no idea what, if anything, would be next with Jack Delafield except that she was now in a worse position than before.

After the Play

WHEN THE PLAY was finished things returned to normal, and at first there seemed to be a new normal. Not since the days when the school was young and Miss Haddam had gathered her students to her in pursuit of her own moral vision had there been such a hum, such spirit. The school felt more important, even to the faculty, because the student body had found a deeper sense of community. If Mrs. Chase had been more seasoned, she would have known this moment was so seductive that now she could rebuild, bring in the parents, set up committees for a capital campaign. But on this score she was no more effective than Miss Haddam. With the immediate fiscal crisis past, and without a new vision and the kind of driving leadership that under Miss Haddam had been a life's obsession, the moment passed. And like a tide pulling back, everyone felt a loss, an invisible and inevitable depletion.

Brian was no exception. Each class folded back in on itself. The seniors read Nathaniel Hawthorne and Brian fell down into the dark heart of Hawthorne. He drove to school shrouded in Hawthorne's blackness, thinking to himself, Black and more black, ten times black. His daily visits to the pool at the Y became erratic, and he had difficulty keeping his mind on his classes. He wondered what was bothering him, but in his introspection, he was looking in the wrong places. He'd connected with Charlotte. If Brian had seen it happen to a colleague he would have cautioned, "You know, once you interact as equals, the moral taboo dissipates like so much smoke," but he didn't apply it to himself. He thought he missed the rehearsals, the momentum, the project. What he missed was Charlotte. Because there was a sudden reversal going on. While Brian wallowed in unfamiliar pain, Charlotte unexpectedly turned away. She accepted that she'd been lucky to have the special time with him. Being so close to him had taken away intrusive memories and she felt a new sense of control. Maybe she was getting over him. And more important, maybe she was getting over the other thing. She wrote in her notebook:

> i first saw the light in the middle of the night, in a spotlight just switched off. i trust the light at night. no false reflection of myself, only shadows that can take hard looking,
> ill be fine. i don't need Brian's favor. in some ways, i'm more grown up than he is. i'll figure out which ways later.
> And the other thing. Mr. Macready seems to be fading too, or numbing down . . . i think.

Charlotte was learning both to quiet the clamor of her inner life and block what she despised, though the hidden inner conflict left her lethargic and she fell asleep when she got home from school. But it couldn't last, because while her conscious mind was rebuilding, maturing, strengthening, her unconscious lay quietly, knowing what it needed, what fantasy it would insist upon, and waiting for the right moment to reach up and reclaim it. It was just a matter of time. Perhaps it's understandable that this overly introspective girl, who was beginning to look outward, and this newly introspective man, who was making attempts to see inward, would intersect at just the wrong turn and make it hard for either of them to choose the right road—if there is such a thing as a road labeled "right."

And almost immediately, her naps brought a dream, a terrible dream. She was running from a man with a knife in the woods. That was an old dream, but in this one, she made it to safety in a small house and slammed the front door and locked it. But the door turned into rubber and the shape of the man's figure pressed into the rubber and then his arms and shoulders pushed into the rubber and tried to grab her. What she remembered so clearly was the feel of this man's body merging through the rubber against her as she pressed back against the rubber door to keep him away and just then, as she looked down, she saw the outline of his hand with the knife moving in and pushing against the rubber door. And she woke up gasping. Theo had told her dreams were wish fulfillment. Impossible. She didn't want this to happen.

She asked Theo about her dream. "The wishes come in disguise, Char."

"I don't get it."

"You want a man to pursue you. You want a man so close you can feel him pressing against you and his arms around you."

"Not that way."

"I know. But the wish triggers a latent fear . . . of men, of sex, of intimacy. So your unconscious writes this man into your dream as a threat, a killer, instead of a lover. Part of you believes sex is dangerous, maybe even a fatal encounter."

"That's sick."

"It's more common that you think. You just have some things to work out. You should do what I do."

"What?"

"See a psychiatrist. You'll understand your dreams. Believe me, it helps."

"Do you have dreams like this?"

"Sort of. It's important. Wishes and fears have to be expressed. Your dreams are like an escape valve."

But Charlotte misconstrued. She thought maybe Theo had been raped, too, in Italy, the summer before. She had no idea these insistent dreams were ideas from her childhood, tangled and twisted beyond her conscious reach. And she gave up her afternoon naps.

So things built up. One day Theo and Dana were arguing about Hawthorne in Brian's class. Maude was watching, amused, and Charlotte was trying to get a word in. Brian said to Dana, "Hold it. Now you've slipped into sophistry."

"What's sophistry?" asked Charlotte.

Without looking at her he said, "Clever disputation, expert argument, semantic chimerism through the deployment of fallacious argument . . . that is to say, adroit rather than sound."

Charlotte threw her pencil to the desk. "Do you do this on purpose?"

He turned to her. "Do I do what?"

"Use these fancy, obscure words and then when we ask you what they mean, you race through more fancy, obscure words?"

The girls were frozen; nothing moved, not a chin, not a hand.

"There's always the dictionary, you know. It's a far better source than I."

"Don't talk about dictionaries. You go so fast we can't even hear the *word*, let alone take the time to spell it and then look it up after class."

She saw his blush deepen. Any minute she was going to cry, but she couldn't stop. "I want to know what it means when you use it *now,* not when I have time to look it up—when it's too late and I won't remember the rest of what you said because I didn't know what you meant in the first place. We don't take notes in here, you know."

"Perhaps you should," he said calmly, and he turned away to collect himself. She was spoiling for a fight. But in a way, she was right: he expected too much from all of them. He was showing off—she caught him and he took it hard.

Theo broke the silence. "Mr. Parton, I hope this doesn't add insult to injury, but you *are* hard to follow sometimes."

Brian turned back to Charlotte. "I apologize, Charlotte. I've gotten used to how quick you all are and sometimes I overdo it."

Charlotte stared at the floor, crying. She didn't want to sniff like a stupid ninny, but her nose was about to drip, so she sniffed and said, "I'm sorry. I didn't mean to be so rude. I'm sorry." God, she thought. What's wrong with me?

She looked so miserable it occurred to Brian to give her a hug, so he avoided looking at her. But when he drove home he puzzled at his curious impulse to protect her—from what? He knew Charlotte had been wrong—a brat. If a boy had challenged him so rudely he would have cut him to ribbons, humiliated him without mercy (he knew how). But with a girl his impulse was to make amends.

She came into his room the next day, limp and upset. He sat in painful silence. Finally she said, "Does the word *sophisticated* come from *sophistry?*"

"Yes," he said, relieved.

"I thought *sophisticated* meant 'worldly.' Something good, something to aspire to."

He studied Charlotte and saw she was a little shaky. "I suppose. But *sophisticated* means 'not natural.' I don't think sophistication is anything to aspire to."

She nodded quietly. "Cora told me I could be expelled for the way I behaved yesterday."

"Occasional bad behavior doesn't warrant expulsion," he said.

She didn't know what she'd done to deserve his patience, but she felt as if this man, who never seemed to understand anything about her, understood.

But the next day he was at it again, pivoting and pacing, throwing words around. She wanted to go up to him and say, "Words, words, words. You act as if you don't care what anyone thinks. But you do. The only reason you were nice yesterday was because you can't stand anyone being angry with you, even me. You're a fraud, Brian Parton. I wear your sovereign indifference as an ornament." But it didn't help to get angry with Brian because she wasn't angry at him—she was angry at herself. And after that they were barely on speaking terms.

A Spring Floodtide

APRIL DRIFTED BY. Charlotte couldn't stand his silence and her hard-won, carefully composed demeanor of cheerfulness cracked open like a seed pod. She had to find a way to him. Before she would have gone up to him and said, "Can we talk a minute?" But now she felt as if she'd dug herself a hole and she had to be devious. One morning after assembly, she went up to him and said, "Are you back to swimming in the cove yet?"

"No, the water's too cold in the spring."

"You can take it," she teased and she walked away. But her body was trembling inside as if preparing for flight. Dana said trust in deceit but it made her feel sick.

That day when Brian got home from class, he put on his trunks and ran down to the beach and dove in. He lasted about three minutes. This was serious, dangerous cold. But rubbing himself dry, he felt wonderful. Why did he find such bliss in this shock? Perhaps there was something perverse in it. Icily, lethally cold, the water healed him a little every day, as if cold could cauterize, but he had no wound. Not that he could see. He cleaned out his locker at the Y and started swimming in the cove again every afternoon and he said to Charlotte in the hall, "You were right. The water's bearable."

That day she couldn't concentrate. Friday afternoon she set out. The sun was sliding low and her figure cast a long shadow as she cut across the field that led down to the water behind Brian's apartment. Black cormorants flew low and fast in threes and fours. She stood on the beach. A spring flood tide had brought the water in higher than she'd ever seen it. On the sand was a blanket, a dark robe, and a notebook. He was swimming close to shore, one hundred feet away. She said, "Thank you, God," and waited for him to come out before she approached.

"Hi, Charlotte." He blushed deeply and grabbed his towel.

"Aren't you freezing?" she said, hoping to sound lighthearted.

"Yes." He rubbed himself, drying his chest, his back, his arms, his legs. She was wearing her white sweater.

When Brian put down his towel Charlotte forgot what she'd planned to say. She couldn't help it. "Oh, Mr. Parton," she said and reached her arms around him. "I miss you so much. It's terrible. Please come back."

He put his arms around her in dismay and suddenly realized she was crying, and without meaning to, he held her close. She was sobbing uncontrollably and instinctively he pressed her against himself from his shoulders to his knees. It felt like nothing he had ever experienced, as if her body was crying into him, her bones, her heart, her soul, her life spilling some terrible pain, and, as if he had some share in it, he held on, completely overcome. Finally he closed his eyes, lifted her arms, and with taut control moved her gently away. He put on his robe. Why did it feel so wrong to do the right thing?

Her face was hidden behind her hair and he regained himself. "My car is awfully quiet without you, I do agree."

"Oh, you don't understand." She fell to her knees on the blanket. "You must think I'm nothing but a worm, a mealy-mouthed worm."

He almost laughed. "No, Charlotte, that's not what I think, though when I first met you, you were a bit of a mouse." He braced himself and crouched next to her.

"Do you still think I'm a mouse?" she said, her head down.

"No."

"Then what?"

"I don't know," he said. "You tell me."

"I've tried so hard to be what you want, to think for myself, to challenge and be skeptical and you never notice. You never *see* me."

"I see you and I notice everything." How could she say that? He'd given her more than any of the other girls. He dug into his soul looking for words with no reverberation, no false promise.

"You notice my work," she said, "but that's not what I mean. It's me you ignore, especially since the play."

"Is that what you think?" She was shivering. "Here," he said, "take the blanket."

They stood up and he shook the blanket and put it around her shoulders. She gripped it closed and stood there like Hiawatha, staring up at him. Her need seemed real and her feelings so naked and honest it raked his soul, brushing aside years of cover.

"Listen, I should go in," he said.

"No, there's something I have to tell you. I'll die if I don't."

She would ruin everything. "No, listen to me," he said. "This doesn't need words."

"But there have to be words. What has no words doesn't exist, has no being at all."

He turned and stared at the horizon. "That's a very ancient argument, Charlotte."

"What do you mean?"

The wind picked up and he said, "It goes back to philosophers before Plato, but if that's what you think, I've misled you badly. Words are not reality. They're only half the story. They only re-present. Do you understand?"

"No."

"Well, neither do I, but listen—some people would say what's happening here is a cliché but I don't think so. It's authentic. People's lives cross and crisscross. Sometimes, whether we want it or not, contact is made." He was looking for closure, a way to leave her whole. This could not be. "What I'm trying to say is, I understand. I have thought of you. Is that enough?"

He'd gone too far. She would say, "No, it's not enough," and it would continue. The sky was ablaze with pink and peach and scarlet and the sea rippled as if scattered roses were moving over the surface.

She looked up at him. "It's enough," she lied, and he moved slightly with the hurt of her words.

"We should go," he said. "If you don't freeze to death, I will," and they walked back up in silence. Maybe this was a welcome silence.

That night Charlotte woke up every hour with her dreams. Bad dreams again, of dangerous men and sewage pipes cracking and spewing forth. What was the sewage? She asked Theo.

"Sewage? I'd say it's dirty things." Charlotte said no more.

Charlotte's Peepers

School was almost over and the girls were trying to think of some prank of pranks to play on Brian. It wasn't so important now to humiliate him, just have fun. And it was the bounty of Flanders Point that inspired them. Dana had said, "C'mon, girls, we need one more trick to remind Mr. Parton of . . . "

Charlotte said, "Of what?"

"Of how dangerous we are."

"There's nothing dangerous about me," sniffed Maude. She was past the prank stage now.

"Me either," said Charlotte.

"You are so, Char, because you never give up."

"Wrong. I've given up. He's beyond reaching. You know, Dana, neither Maude nor I has ever been kissed, but we're a whole lot more grown-up than you are." But the next words out of her mouth were "Why don't we do something to make him laugh instead of embarrass him?"

"Like what?" said Dana.

"We could put peepers in his desk drawer instead of a drippy condom."

"What's that?" asked Dana.

"You know, spring peepers. The ponds are full of them now."

"Never heard of them."

"What! How can you miss them? They've been whistling and singing all night the last two weeks."

"Oh, that racket. I thought it was crickets," muttered Dana.

"Not in April," said Cora. "Even I know that."

Dana said, "If you can find a way to put the peepers in his pants, I'm with you; otherwise, forget it. I'm not touching a damn frog."

Charlotte took great pleasure in ignoring her. "Theo, if you could come over one night, we'll go out and collect them."

"How about tonight?"

"Really?"

"Yup. I'll pick you up."

"Okay. Bring a flashlight," said Charlotte, "and a little fish net if you have one. It gets dark around seven-thirty."

So that night Charlotte and Theo drove toward the sweet, high-pitched whistles at Black Pond on Flanders Point. Tramping through long grass and scrub growth, Theo muttered, "How can you see them in all this stuff?"

"You search. Shhh." They stopped where the grass merged with small pools at the pond's edge. Two shadowy figures surrounded by a pure and throbbing soprano song. Charlotte said, "Here's what to do. Sit somewhere on a dry spot and listen for one, single voice. They start to separate out when you get close. Crawl toward one sound. Don't turn the flashlight on until you think a peeper is right in front of you. Keep your net ready."

"Don't they jump away?"

"No. Be still, wait, and shine the light low, across and through the grass, but not in his eyes. He'll stop singing when the light goes on, but he won't move. You can't see him because he's camouflaged."

"Then how—"

"Stare where you think he is. When he starts singing again, then you'll see the movement of his white throat that bubbles out when he sings. Then you'll realize you're looking right at his tiny head."

"Okay—"

"Then plop the net on him. We'll drop him in a pickle jar."

So they crouched on the moss at the pond's edge and crawled over muddy rocks and scratchy downed trees and moved aside twigs and dry grass—creeping, stopping, creeping again. It took Theo half an hour to "see" her first peeper singing, but she got him. Then with a "search image" in her mind, she found five more peepers in fifteen minutes and got them all. "This is fun," she said.

"I know. They're gorgeous."

That night, Charlotte hid them in Margaret's basement in a jar filled with grass and mud. Driving to school with Margaret, she hid the jar in her book bag. The girls met before class and shook the eleven little peepers into Brian's middle desk drawer. Dana just watched, but Charlotte could tell the green-and-brown-spotted peepers had won her over.

Of course, it was dark in the desk drawer but even Charlotte was surprised when in the middle of class the peepers started to sing. Maybe they thought it was night. Brian got a weird look on his face. His eyes moved slowly in an arc as if he were searching the inside of his head. He gave them a sly look, walked over, and opened his desk drawer. Immediately the sound stopped. For ten seconds, there was quiet. He bent over, his face almost into the drawer, and muttered, "Well, I'll be—" when all hell broke loose. The peepers started hopping and leaping, hitting him in the face and chest, and he yelled, "Whoa!" jumped back, and burst out laughing. They were suddenly everywhere, flying in every direction. They were heroic, leaping five feet in the air like so many panic-stricken grasshoppers—just much nicer.

The girls helped catch them, cupping them with their hands, then screeching and letting them go again. When they were all caught except two leaping at the glass of the French doors, Brian sat down. "Charlotte, will you get those, *quietly,* please?" and he looked around at them with a rare smile. "That was wonderful . . . just wonderful."

Charlotte stole a look at Theo and then at Dana, who was trying not to smile. She took the peepers down to the science room, and the biology teacher was fascinated. Everyone went to see them, and during study hall they began singing again. Charlotte heard a ninth grader at the next table whisper, "It's Charlotte's peepers." Everyone in the library could hear them, and kept looking over at her, smiling. Charlotte couldn't remember when she'd been so happy.

When she got home she walked to the pond, shook the jar, and they hopped away. A guardian angel attended me today, she thought. It was perfect, and she'd never seen Brian laugh like that.

Margaret Chase, however, never said a word. Dinner was more than awkward. Something mean hung in the air, something hard and sharp, punctuated by Margaret's chin thrusts. But this time Charlotte thought it was telling. Mrs. Chase *was* jealous. After all, it was hard to get a rise out of Brian, let alone a laugh. Charlotte had just done both. She'd have to be more guarded than ever. Dana was right. Margaret Chase *did* have a thing for Brian, and if so, she had it in for Charlotte. She couldn't be living in a worse place and she couldn't do a thing about it.

But the whole event served her in another way. The underclassmen brought her bird's nests and cracked eggs, odd mushrooms and wildflowers they didn't recognize. It was as if they knew her now and looked up to her. She'd acquired a reputation and, to her surprise, it had nothing to do with her directing the play. She felt stronger, safer, a new self.

The Bearing of Reality

CHARLOTTE GOT UP early on Sunday to read *The Waste Land*. Mr. Parton had said it was hard. It wasn't hard. It was hopeless. She had started the night before, but after a few lines, she was reading words and thinking about something else. Maybe in the morning with different light on the page, with a different hour in her bones, she'd understand it better. Please, Eliot, don't be so difficult that I fall asleep. She stretched out on the rug in her bedroom and read. But the poem rose from the page like a mountain, Annapurna, maybe, shrouded in a curtain of word sounds, a calm eminence waiting to be scaled. She dug herself in, hoisted herself along, clawed at the words. Damn, poetry was work, but then, it was good work, she thought remembering not to be impressed with herself just because she was reading poetry and not watching *Captain Video*. She pushed on. This was murder.

She started flipping pages. Skimming and then pressing the pages flat she started to read another Eliot poem, *Four Quartets*. There was more white space on the page. Maybe it was easier. The subtitle was *The Dry Salvages*. They were islands off Cape Ann. She knew Cape Ann. She read more closely and suddenly there were goose bumps on her brain. Here was a connection between her and the poem—words about the past and memory and the way forward, about grief merging into relief, about a past that's never finished, about fog cowering in the fir trees, wrinkles on the sea, and the ocean tossing up human losses. This was uncanny. The sea had tossed up her loss, *too*. The old dinghy. And she'd *seen* fog in the fir trees. It did cower in the marsh on windless nights.

Here was a point of entry. Brian might accuse her of skimming off the top, of ignoring Eliot's meaning, but she found her own meaning.

So stirred was Charlotte by the words that she didn't take up her pencil to write them down, as she always did. These words were too beautiful for her to appropriate, to put in her journal. She would feel like a thief. T. S. Eliot owned these words. She didn't even dare to borrow them. But she could argue with the next heart-chilling words. Humankind, Eliot wrote, could not bear much reality. *But you haven't explained what you mean by reality.* And that time was no healer, that she could never face "it" steadily. *Oh, Eliot, don't be so harsh. Time* must *be a healer. It always is. And I can face it.* But she had to prove it, act on her own behalf, mend inside, heal what was hidden. Finally, Eliot's poem prodded, to find her way forward, she had to go back. Not since Mr. Macready had assaulted her had she been back to the marsh. She lay still, frozen, and then she turned over and stared at a jagged crack in the ceiling. That was new. There was also something disturbing in the air, something going wrong somewhere outside. Her muscles fluttered under her skin in anticipation. But she shrugged it off. Charlotte had no use for claims of premonition. That was Theo's thing. What stirred her fear was the vile memory of Mr. Macready, that's all. A little more courage was needed, but the poem offered no more.

Determined, she opened a book Brian had given her, telling her they wouldn't get to Wordsworth in class but she should read Book I of *The Prelude*. There was a story about a boy who sneaks out at night and steals a small boat and takes it out alone on a lake of black water. She found the part Brian had marked in red.

> *One evening—surely I was led by her,*
> *I found a little boat—*

"Her?" Who was "her"? She went back a few lines and saw that "her" must be the evening, that is, nature. She knew now why Brian thought she'd like it. Wordsworth was a wanderer, a nature person. She kept reading. The boy in the stolen boat ends up seeing a great black shadow of a mountain crag in the dark night, a looming "grim shape" and imagines that it comes alive, and it "like a living thing strode after me." Overwhelmed, the boy races home. And the next lines reminded

Charlotte that she was not alone with her trouble, even if, unlike the boy in the poem, hers was not imagined. Both she and this boy had trespassed on someone else's property and both were marked by their trespass. She read the lines over and over.

> *my brain*
> *Worked with a dim and undetermined sense*
> *Of unknown modes of being; o'er my thoughts*
> *There hung a darkness, call it solitude*
> *Or blank desertion. No familiar shapes*
> *Remained, no pleasant images of trees,*
> *Of sea or sky, no colours of green fields,*
> *But huge and mighty forms, that do not live*
> *Like living men, moved slowly through the mind*
> *By day, and were a trouble to my dreams.*

Eliot, Wordsworth, Cummings, too. *We're all connected and I belong, we all belong.* Wordsworth and his imagination, Eliot with his depression, she with her wound, and now she found her courage. Time *is* a healer and it was *time* to act. She closed the books, put on her pea jacket, and hurried out toward the tidal marsh.

The dull, motionless morning had shifted into action, too, and now a disheveling easterly wind swept the point. Sudden gusts dipped and troubled the surface of the water spreading patches of wrinkles. Max said sailors called them "cat's paws." Max knew these things. She hurried along toward the Macreadys' but when she neared the house, she realized she had no idea what to do when she got there, so she turned south and went to look for the dinghy, her own version of Wordsworth's little boat. She was picking her way through tidal pools when she heard children's voices. Stepping through the rushes she looked out over the water. Two little figures sat in a tiny boat. The tide had just turned and was running out. With a jolt she recognized Peter and his friend Tommy huddled in her old dinghy. They were drifting toward the open sound.

"Peter!" she cried. A flock of ducks rose out of the salt grass, calling their alarm, and then a boy stumbled out of the rushes.

"What the devil are you doing?" she said.

"We're taking turns."

"Are you crazy? With no oars?" She was incredulous.

"We don't need them. It drifts back in."

"Not now it won't! Can't you tell the tide's turned and the wind is up?" She was about to ask his name when she heard Peter call, "Charlotte, Charlotte!" His voice was shrill with worry as he stood up, and the boat lurched.

She screamed, "Peter, sit down! Don't move. I'll get help. Don't move. Sit *absolutely still*!" The boat was almost four hundred feet from her, but she could see the fear on his face. There was no time to get help. She turned to the boy. "Run," she said. "Get Peter's mother. That boat is drifting out with the tide. Tell her to call the coast guard. Tell her to come with a rope! Hurry!" The boy ran off. Charlotte kicked off her shoes, pulled off her jacket, and stepped into the icy water.

Peter yelled, "Char, it's leaking! What should I do?" but he stood up too fast and the boat rocked. He grabbed for the gunnel, lost his balance, and pitched into the frigid water. Tommy started to reach out and Charlotte screamed, *"Tommy!* Don't move. *Don't move!* Sit still!" The boat had already drifted too far for Peter to paddle back, and in horror Charlotte saw that he was struggling. She leapt out over the shallow water until it was too deep for leaping, then frightened that she wouldn't get to him in time she yelled, "Tommy, don't take your eyes off Peter no matter what. If he goes under, don't look at me, watch the spot where he was; you have to guide me!" She started swimming to Peter as fast as she could. He paddled and splashed, trying to hold his chin high as he spit water and cried and choked, but his jacket was heavy and his shoes were pulling him down.

"Peter," Charlotte screamed. "You can swim, you can swim. I'm coming! Swim, Peter, *swim. You can do it!"* She was still fifty feet from him when she heard him choke and cry out as he slipped under, his small arm slapping the surface. Charlotte knew this tide. It didn't run fast, but it was strong and it would take him. She'd have to judge it. Her eyes stayed on the choppy water where Peter had vanished, but in her mind's eye she was under the water trying to guess how many feet an eight-year-old would be pulled. Was he struggling or was he limp? She had to get it right the first time.

Forgetting Tommy, she dove and the water, needle-sharp and cold, crushed her bones as she pushed herself down into its darkness, whirling slowly about, reaching, feeling with her arms, her feet, in every direction. *Please, God, help me.* She kicked to the surface, gulped more air, spun in the water, and saw odd bubbles ten feet from her. Peter. She was close and she dove again with all her strength. This time she touched bottom and moved along, opening her eyes. The murk was hellish black. He could be five feet from her and she'd never even see him. Where was he, how close, how far, and then, just before she kicked back up again, she felt something: a tiny slip of a touch, like little fingers, brushed her forearm. Blindly she grabbed and had his hand and then the slick wet fabric of his jacket. She dug her fingers in as hard as she could, fighting the need in her lungs, and kicked back up, breaking through the surface with an ungodly shriek: "I got him!" She could feel her legs stiffening in the icy water but she wasn't afraid. She didn't need prayers or luck now, just power. Because she knew what to do and thank God, Peter wasn't struggling. He was limp. She put him in a chest carry and side-stroked for the shore, beating, pushing, surging, fast, fast, not thinking, just swimming.

Charlotte stumbled out of the shallow water, hardly able to lift Peter, but she got him to the salt grass and laid him down. God, where were the Macreadys? She glanced out at the dinghy and yelled, "Tommy, are you okay?"

"Water's coming in!"

"I know, but don't rock it. Be still!" He was crying.

She looked at Peter. His face was gray and his lips were purple. No breath. Charlotte put her hands over her face and thought, Calm down—you know how to do this—focus, and then she took off his jacket quickly, frightened at the feel of his limp body, laid him on his stomach, turned his face carefully to the right, climbed over him, and bent in concentration. Her thoughts sped back through dark opening doors as she started to press and rise. It was two summers ago. She was a junior lifeguard at Pear Tree Point. The lifeguard was teaching her artificial respiration. He lay on his stomach and her knees straddled him, his back warm and smooth against her legs. The lifeguard was saying, "That's right, Charlotte, harder, you have good hands, harder, keep it smooth. Keep the rhythm going even after they start breathing." She remembered and pressed with both palms over Peter's rib cage. She rose, pressed, released, sat back. *Again: rise, press, release, sit back.* She kept on, touched by the smallness of Peter's back and the feel of his fragile ribs bending into his lungs like rubber. She kept on, steady and firm, and suddenly water ran out of his mouth. She hadn't even heard the footsteps crashing behind her, and without a word Mr. and Mrs. Macready dropped to their knees beside her. Peter coughed and gagged, and there was a terrible screech Charlotte would never forget as his lungs ejected the watery death. She rose, pressed, released, sat back. Tears ran down her face. He sputtered again, and this time a human sound came out with the water. More presses, and with sudden agitation, he grabbed his throat, gasping.

Suddenly Charlotte remembered Tommy. She looked at Mr. Macready and jerked her thumb back over her shoulder.

Mr. Macready looked and said, "Jesus, Tommy's out there!" Mr. Macready and the other boy started running along the shore toward the boat and Tommy started yelling. Mrs. Macready thrust a blanket at Charlotte, then knelt, wrapped Peter in another blanket, and sat with him in her arms in the deep grass. Charlotte heard calls and footsteps and splashes as Mr. Macready retrieved the dinghy and got Tommy in but she didn't look up. She stared at dried mud and rippling gray grass, her mind clear, white, centered. Peter was shivering violently, but he was alive. Mr. Macready stepped in front of Charlotte and leaned down. "Thank you. Thank you, Charlotte, for what you did. What can I say?" and he put his hand on her shoulder as if everything was just fine. Charlotte jumped and scrambled away in a rage.

"Don't touch me. Don't you dare put your hand on me. I didn't do a thing for you. I did it for Peter. Peter and his mother. I'd never do anything for you!"

Mrs. Macready was watching, and shocked, she said, "Charlotte, what's the matter? Peter might have drowned. Kevin just wants to thank you. What is it?"

"You can ask him what it is. See if he'll tell you." And Charlotte was almost ready to say it herself but a station wagon pulled up, slammed to a stop, and a man jumped out and hurried over to Peter.

"How's he doing?"

Mr. Macready said, "I think he's all right but we should take him to the emergency room just the same."

They all got into the wagon and Charlotte said, "Should I come and explain what happened?"

Mr. Macready said, "We know what happened. We'll call you later. I'd sure like to know where they got that damn boat." And they drove off to the hospital, taking Tommy and the other boy, too.

Charlotte stared at the dinghy lying on the rocks. There was one more thing she had to do. And she had to hurry before they got back. She ran to Mr. Macready's workshed, the room that no one was allowed to enter, and reached for the black iron latch. When she went in, she cringed. His tools were lined up like weapons on the walls. She counted sixteen rasps and fourteen blackened files. Sinister-looking push drills lined up on a workbench. Of sharp chisels she counted ten, and a dozen screwdrivers. Locks, padlocks, and chain locks. Plumber's wrenches and slip wrenches looked lethal enough to smash skulls. There were pliers and wire cutters. Hammers waited and vises were anchored to the table edges. There was a wall of saws: hacksaws, rip saws, crosscuts, and back saws. There wasn't anything in his shed that couldn't inflict pain. She froze. A car was coming. How could they get back so fast? She looked out the window. The car kept on going and she turned around quickly. The place gave her the creeps. This didn't look like a workroom, it looked like an obsession. There was a problem in this room. She picked up a sledgehammer, surprised at the weight, and hurried back to the marsh. When she got to the dinghy, she flipped it over, raised the sledgehammer over her head, and slammed it down so hard the iron head plowed through the wood as if it were paper and hit the rock with a shriek and a spark. The handle tore out of her hands. "Ow!" she muttered. Another blow and the dinghy lay in two halves. Charlotte's arm was stinging and she collapsed next to the wreckage and started to cry uncontrollably. She felt as if a familiar giant fist were pushing up through her throat, choking off her air, but maybe this time it would push on through. And in the dark of her mind, images churned. The one she'd been living with of Mr. Macready's arms pressing her back in the sunlight seemed to move aside for a new one: just as vivid, just as visceral, like waves it came and it was the light touch of Peter's fingers on her arm in the black water. Such a little touch. He wasn't even conscious, he didn't know she was there but it didn't matter. She *was* there. A fragile life had touched her and it was more important than those terrible hands that pinned her. She stopped crying and remembered swimming hard, pulling him through the bitter water, lifting him, and bending over his ribs to get him to breathe again. She was breathing again too, deeper, freer, and her mind expanded and rotated away from the man and his violation. And then not noticing that she spoke aloud the words she was thinking, she uttered to the wind, "I didn't save you, Peter; you saved me."

Leaving the Center

CHARLOTTE LAY ACROSS her bed staring at the dark pink buds on the crab apple tree outside. Surely T. S. Eliot hadn't meant face it— *him*—directly. When she heard a car door slam, she got up and looked out the window and something gritty emerged from under her tongue. Mrs. Macready was coming up the walk alone, and then Charlotte heard voices and footsteps coming up the stairs and a knock.

"Come in," said Charlotte.

Mrs. Chase was tense. "Mrs. Macready wants to talk to you." Charlotte wasn't sure what to do. Mrs. Chase could smell a problem the way Charlotte could smell garlic. "Well?"

"I'd like to speak to her alone. Could you ask her to come up here if she doesn't mind?"

Mrs. Chase looked pinched and left the room. When Mrs. Macready came in, she hugged Charlotte, a long hug, wonderful, and said, "I don't know what to say." She closed the door. "Tommy told us the whole story. He said Peter was gone . . . he was drowning."

"I know. Is he all right?"

"Oh, he's fine, but how are *you?*"

"A little shaky."

"I can imagine. How did you do it—how did you find him?"

"It was just luck. I was a junior lifeguard for three summers. I never rescued anyone but I trained a lot."

"I can never, never repay you." There was an awkward pause. "But there's something else."

"I know," said Charlotte.

"I asked Kevin why you screamed at him and he said you must be in shock and you weren't rational. Is he right?"

"No."

"I didn't think so. What happened between you?"

Charlotte winced when she saw the pain on her face. Had she guessed? "I don't know what words to use that won't cause you more pain."

"Try."

"All right." She gathered herself in and held herself back, sitting on the edge of the bed. "You know the thatch cottage on the old Larsen property?"

"I saw it once when Kevin bought the property."

"Well, one day last winter I was looking for an owl's nest and I found the cottage. The door wasn't locked and it was like something from a fairy tale so I went in."

"And . . . "

"I was there awhile and your husband found me. We had words—I mean, we argued because I didn't belong there. Anyway, he was furious and—" suddenly she remembered a word her mother used to use "—he assaulted me."

"He hit you?"

Charlotte was so intent on getting this out she forgot that he'd hit her, too. "No . . . well, actually, yes, but that's not all. The other." She could tell Mrs. Macready understood, but still she had to say the words. "It was a rape." A slow, sinking defeat spread over Mrs. Macready's face.

"Is it true? He actually did it?"

"It was completed."

"When was this?"

"After I left. February."

"I wouldn't have thought he had it in him. Oh God. God. I'm sorry, Charlotte, so sorry." She sat on the bed heavily, as if her weight were more than her legs could hold.

"Forgive me, Mrs. Macready, forgive me for telling. I'm so sorry."

"You have nothing to be sorry about."

"But neither do you," said Charlotte. "I never should have told you about the bruises on Peter's collarbone. Maybe your husband was getting back at me for that. It wasn't my business and I was *never* going to tell about this."

"But that wouldn't have been right." Charlotte didn't answer, just waited. Mrs. Macready sighed and covered her eyes with her hand. "I sensed something in Kevin, awhile after you left, some dark, edgy mood. But this . . . " She looked out the window. "Can you ever forgive him?"

Charlotte sat back with a start. "Of course not! Can you?"

"I guess not." She paused. "What is it with these warrior men of ours?"

Charlotte was shocked. What a stupid, romantic view, she thought, and then she wondered—did Mrs. Macready like his aggression? Was this her dark side?

"What do you want to do about it?" said Mrs. Macready, and a sudden coldness in her voice hit Charlotte in the chest.

"Nothing. I'll never tell anyone, not even my mother. But I guess you had to know. I remember you said silence was an act of condonement . . . remember with the condom thing?"

"It's hardly the same." The coldness vanished, even though she looked as empty, pale, and bleak as an early winter sky. "I can't believe it. How can you live with a man for ten years, love him, sleep with him, and still not know him? How is it possible?"

"Oh, you *can,*" said Charlotte and she knelt fervently in front of Mrs. Macready, forgetting herself, taking her hands. "You can. It happens all the time. People have hidden lives and dreadful, painful secrets. When I was home for Christmas, I found out that my mother was having a love affair with another man when she married my father. She didn't even love my father. Maybe that's why he was an alcoholic. I don't know, things go so wrong. Please forgive me for being part of what's going wrong for you. If I'd never come, if I'd never seen, if I'd never told, everything would have been all right."

"Charlotte, what are you saying? Everything wasn't all right. I remember you telling me just before you left how people's paths crossed. Maybe there's a reason."

"I feel like it's my fault."

"Well, I feel like it's my fault," said Mrs. Macready. "I need time to think." And she was quiet. Charlotte studied the way the afternoon light in the room carved the edge of her profile like white marble. What a pretty woman, thought Charlotte, a sweet woman who taught her how to polish her shoes, put on rouge, make a bouquet out of goldenrod and yellow roses in October. "Arrange the world a little," she used to say.

But Charlotte's sympathy was only soft accompaniment to a sharp certainty that she'd turned a corner. Charlotte had held the power to keep still, just as she had when she wrecked the piano, but this time a sudden event had usurped her power and tore out the truth. With a searing relief her anger danced away with a hiss like water on an overheated grill. It's not that she was innocent, she thought to herself. No one was innocent. Not one person. But she wasn't guilty either. And how wonderful to let go of the center, to pass on through and let responsibility lie where it belonged.

Mrs. Macready said, "Charlotte, I have to go. You know, it's odd. If you'd saved Peter at the town beach, swimming out in that icy water, you'd be a heroine, and there'd be newspaper coverage and interviews. But Flanders Point is another world, isn't it? It's so private, no one will ever know but us."

Charlotte looked at her. It was the least she could do. "No one will ever know."

Mrs. Macready hugged her again, and she was crying quietly. Charlotte started to cry, too. "I'm sorry, Mrs. Macready, I'm sorry for everything."

"Oh, please, Charlotte, don't say that. I'm sorry, too. It's just a mess. Good-bye. Take care of yourself."

"I will." And Mrs. Macready left.

When the sun started to slide, Charlotte went downstairs and Mrs. Chase said, "What was that all about?"

Suddenly emboldened, Charlotte turned to Mrs. Chase, looked her up and down, and, reaching deep inside, said serenely, "It concerns me and me alone." And Charlotte walked the Point for the first time in months. How odd that it was harder to say that to Margaret Chase than anything else she'd said. But Charlotte was afraid of Margaret Chase. The cove breeze puffed softly around her and the gusts sounded like someone saying quietly, *hush, hush, hush*. She was so tired. Maybe adrenaline was borrowed energy and you had to pay it back. She thought of Brian. She thought of Max. He always got out his telescope when he was upset. "I turn to the stars, they're always in order," he'd said once. But Charlotte couldn't see it that way. She couldn't rely on the order of nature. Its famous harmony. What a laugh. There was no order. Sure, there had to be some coherent structure, Max would insist, but as for the rest, the charts and graphs and formulas systematized, categorized and memorized—this was a man's need to secure his place, control his life, like another religion. *Nature does not, will not follow. It is heedless, breachable, unjust, and random. Elms splitting in two in an icestorm are ruptures. The squirrel eating meat an aberration. The heron staying for the winter a dislocation. The ice-coated owl flying in my window a mishap. My old dinghy, an omission. Mr. Macready's act, a transgression. What is the balance? Where is the logic? What order, what control? There is no safe harbor. I just have to rely on myself.* But I'm not doing so badly, she thought.

That night at the window she heard tiny screams. She sat forward and listened. Thick beating sounds and high, terrified shrieks ruptured the stillness and she knew it was the screams of a rabbit dying in the claws of an owl. And in the woods below, as a dark shape bent over its prey, thrilled, she pressed her ear to the night as if she were taking its pulse. Was it a great-horned? Still eavesdropping she heard something new, the delicate sound of a tiny body breaking and the crunch of the beak on a bone. She smiled. He was feeding on the spot. Another secret revealed. Unmarked, predictable sudden death. Harmless death. Not an acre of ground on Flanders Point was unstained with blood, not a yard, not a foot. Nightly, blood seeped into the soil. The soil gave it back. What could be more normal? Quiet returned, deep, full quiet, and she sat and listened to the wind soft-walking through the treetops. Poor rabbit. But she'd be all right with rabbits screaming in the night.

You Can't Hold Back Spring

SPRING ON FLANDERS Point was creeping into everyone's bloodstream. The mountain laurel was blooming down the hill to the sea wall and delicate yellow wintercress pushed up through the leaf cover in the woods. One day Brian had even spotted a pristine white flower he'd never seen before walking to Miss Haddam's with Margaret, and she'd said, "It's trillium but that's poison ivy all around it. Have a care." No one wanted to study inside. The French doors were thrown open wide and Brian was beginning to think the idea of a poetry reading at graduation was ludicrous. He, of course, was responsible for it. He'd already argued with Theo, Dana, and Charlotte over their choices, excluding the sensual. Now they were working on their own poems to read and he just couldn't get them to pay attention. On these clear breezy May days the sudden warm sun made the blood quiver in anticipation. He sighed. Four of them were sprawled on the grass in a most unladylike way. Only Maude sat properly. Old Miss Haddam, the arbiter of skirt lengths and rouged lips, would have had the stroke that killed her if she'd trembled by. He sat on the porch steps outside the English room pretending to read Dana's poem. But Brian wasn't interested in Dana's poem. He was interested in the horizontal bodies lying on the grass just a few feet away. The girls knew he was looking.

"Mr. Parton, how can you read homework? Don't you have spring fever?" asked Charlotte. "I do."

He acted as if he hadn't heard and Charlotte stretched her arms over her head. Dana said, "To heck with the spring part, I just have fever."

This was impossible. Brian stood up. He rapped the back of his book sharply on the porch railing and without a word jerked his head sideways as if to say, *get back inside.* He swiveled and walked back in through the wide open doors. They dragged themselves up, glancing at each other in delight, and straggled in. Once at their desks, they behaved impeccably. Brian was a wreck but he carried on.

After class, he went to the faculty bathroom and splashed cold water on his face. There was another place he could have splashed, but it was over now. He wondered if Dana put them up to these things. He'd seen Hans at the window upstairs. Had anyone else seen? Later Hans stopped him in the hall and said with a droll smile, "That was quite a performance out there."

"You've got to give them an *A+* for trying."

"I wish they'd pull that with me."

"They're incorrigible," said Brian.

"I think it's charming."

"They're brats."

Hans studied Brian a minute. "They do take advantage of you, I agree. And you can't do a thing, because then you'd have to admit they'd gotten you."

"And they haven't. But this is not in the teacher's manuals and I'm beginning to think these young women are hazardous to my health."

The next day they were at it again. They'd celebrated May Day, an archaic Haddam tradition where they donned white sheets knotted and tied and they danced around this pole holding streamers in one hand and wafting willow wands in the other. In class, Theo raised her hand and said, "Mr. Parton, is the Maypole we erect and dance around on May Day a phallic symbol?"

"Why don't you look it up after school today, Theo, and do a five-hundred-page report for tomorrow? You can tell *us.*"

Maude glanced wryly at Mr. Parton. "Five hundred pages?"

He blushed. "Five hundred words."

The last Friday of classes was a half day. In the afternoon the seniors covered the campus and put everything in place, as if taking an inventory of the school and their years there. They replaced library books, cleaned beakers in the lab, swept the art room, washed paintbrushes. It was an old tradition, leaving the school spotless for graduation, their first nurturing act as they became alumnae. Saturday afternoon there was a picnic lunch with the teachers and next year's seniors, and although Margaret Chase tried to keep Brian at her side, at one point he slipped away and went to talk to his senior class. He found them standing on the stone steps and he joined them.

"I thought you'd never get away from her," said Dana.

Brian glanced back. "I'm her security blanket." They stared at him. As they reminisced and talked about colleges Brian noticed that Charlotte was wearing a bewitching blue sundress with a bare back. It looked brand new and he wondered if she'd picked it out. Hans appeared and joined them, and if Margaret Chase hadn't called them all back up, they would have spent an hour off by themselves, these five seniors and the two men they adored. After dessert, Charlotte came up to Brian and said, "I'm going down to the boathouse to clean up. Wanna come?"

He had nothing to do for the rest of the day. "Thank you, Charlotte, but I have a meeting." He expected a protest.

She hesitated, surprised because he'd looked at her so many times when they were all talking, she'd thought it was a sign. She searched his face and he seemed closed off again. "Couldn't we at least say good-bye in private?"

"Won't it be easier to say good-bye here?" he said.

"No . . . but okay. We can say good-bye tomorrow."

He saw her disappointment and said, "We'll find time," and walked away. He heard her running down the steps to the boathouse and he turned to watch. Damn. He should have given her that. Even Eben would have said, "You can relax now."

The air was glowing and the gray and white buildings of old Miss Haddam's Academy shimmered on the hill as if to remind him, *remember me.* Graduation was the next day. Unwelcome. Where had the year gone?

One Thousand Fireflies

Two new teachers were at Mrs. Chase's house for an informal dinner that night and Mrs. Chase included Charlotte. After supper she cleared the dishes quickly and excused herself. She was still thinking about Brian refusing to go down to the boathouse. She knew he didn't have a meeting, and was convinced he wanted to talk. His words said no, but not his eyes. She'd simply picked the wrong place.

She wouldn't have another chance and she braided her hair in a French braid and, in a rush unrecognized, a hurry that had more knowledge of her desire than her heart perceived, the unrecognized hurry of a secret rendezvous, she hastily tied on a ribbon. Her mother once said that she looked older with her hair back and braided. She looped a cotton scarf over her favorite sweater, took her binoculars, and told Mrs. Chase she was going out to look for Orion's Belt . . . Orion the Hunter, she thought ruefully. That's not where she was going. She closed the front door and started toward Brian's. She'd dressed for him, choosing the V-necked sweater because it dropped a little low and that might interest him. She'd pulled on the scarf and tied it loosely with the image of him pulling it off. He thought she was naive. He thought wrong.

She walked and her loafers crunched on the sandy road. Though she was off-balance, the road was steady and the direction clear. What reason might she give for her appearance? She could hardly say, "I'm here to have the conversation you keep avoiding." Maybe she should try, "I'm here to find my dream." But this time she made no plan.

She passed the fence where she used to wait for his blue Buick. It ran around the field where she'd learned to ride a two-wheeled bike. Her father used to run behind her, holding on to the seat, convinced that the bumpy meadow grass would teach her balance faster than the black tarmac. He was right. He yelled, "Pedal, pedal, don't look down, look straight ahead," and he would let go without telling her. Her mother sat in the grass watching, calling, "Jack, Jack, not so fast." And here she was, ten years later, at the same meadow in a dark wind, walking past her past. When she rode her bike over the field in those days, was it already set that she would return ten years later? She stopped and watched and listened. High and faint, the night whistled like a blackbird spilling wind from its wings to change its course. She wondered if she should turn back or even if she could, when the marsh wind nudged her toward the welcoming dark. *Toward you, my captain, I too change my course.*

All his lights were on, the glowing yellow from his windows spilling onto the stone steps. She was shaking, her heart ready to flee, but her feet stood firm. She raised her hand, looked up at the stars, and knocked. When Brian opened the door he took a deep breath with his head sideways and eyes closed.

"Charlotte, what are you doing?"

"I've got to talk to you."

"This minute?"

She wished she'd stayed away. "Yes."

He opened the door and she stepped in. Sitting on the sofa, he gestured to his reading chair. She closed the door and sat, pulling her knees up and wrapping her arms around her ankles. He was wearing worn chinos and an old plaid shirt, partly unbuttoned, untucked. His hair was rumpled and he was in his socks. It made him look young. She thought he might have been asleep.

"I'm sorry. You have to let me say good-bye. There won't be time tomorrow." There was an awkward silence. "Now that I'm here, I've forgotten everything I wanted to say."

"Do you want some three-by-five cards?"

She looked down and shook her head.

"I'm not expecting anything, Charlotte, so you can sit quietly until you feel better."

"I never meant to bother you," she said.

He sat forward slowly, his elbows on his knees, his smile skeptical, but his eyes were serious. "Don't give me that. You certainly did and you know it."

Charlotte's mouth was so dry she could hardly talk. "Could I have a glass of water?" she managed to say.

He went into the kitchen. Charlotte looked at his desk but the picture of the dark-haired woman was gone. She heard cupboards opening and shutting. He came in and handed her a glass of ginger ale and said, "Even if what you said was true, *bother* is the wrong word. You are disturbing sometimes, but you're not a bother."

He sat back in the far corner of the sofa and watched her. Her hair was braided in some complicated way that he'd never seen before. The change from when he'd first met her couldn't have been more striking. Even in her obvious misery, there was a subtle glow.

"I'll say one thing for you, Charlotte. You have a lot of guts."

Charlotte was determined that she wouldn't cry like the idiot schoolgirl she knew she was.

"It isn't guts. It's love, and I don't know what to do with it." He drew back. "Sometimes I think I'm going to choke. My throat starts to close trying to keep it in."

"When you throttle feelings they do choke you. I learned that when I was ten years old," he said.

"What happened when you were ten?"

He paused, debating. "My mother drowned in a swimming accident."

Charlotte wasn't sure what to say. "How do you ever accept something like that?"

"Accept? You ponder it. You hate it. You have no choice but you never accept it."

She thought quietly and said, "Sometimes I wish I could just climb in your jacket pocket and stay with you."

He knew she thought this was a bold thing to say. She had probably planned it. But her innocence was not feigned and it disarmed him every time.

"Charlotte, I can think of a much better place for you than in my pocket, and that's the gulf between us that will never be crossed."

"What do you mean?"

He paused. "I don't know a lot about women. I think you all figured that out this year. But I do know about men. When a man loves a woman, he doesn't want her in his pocket. He wants her in his bed."

Charlotte opened her mouth and drew in a quick, hard breath. The sudden heat she felt between her legs reached up to her face until her cheeks grew hot. How could words do this? She'd never felt anything like it.

"Well," she muttered, "that's what I meant."

"No, that's not what you meant," he said kindly. "If I thought you had, I wouldn't be sitting over here. Even I can take just so much provocation." Charlotte was speechless. She couldn't believe what he was saying.

"May I do one thing that is probably improper before I go?" she asked.

"What?"

"May I hug you good-bye?"

There was a pause. "If that's what you want."

"Can I have what I want?"

He tried not to smile. "Just that." He couldn't imagine how she was going to do this, and he would do nothing to help her. But as if she had done it a dozen times, she climbed onto the sofa and kneeled next to him, facing him, not sitting alongside him as he expected, thinking he would put his arm around her shoulder. Charlotte had something quite different in mind. She faced the back of the sofa on her knees, sat on her feet, and shifted sideways against his leg. Then moving the only way she could, she lay herself against his chest with her head just under his chin. With a delicate movement, she put her arms around him.

He breathed deeply and put one arm around her lightly. He left the other stretched across the back of the sofa. Neither of them moved. After a while, with her head still under his chin, she said, "Are you comfortable?"

He started to laugh, and though he made no sound, she could feel his chest moving.

She looked up at him. "Are you laughing?"

He pushed her head back down. "No, but you're really something." They sat in silence.

"There's something I've been wanting to ask you for a long time," she said.

"Go ahead."

"It's embarrassing."

"Then don't ask."

"No, I want to."

He drew his head back a little to look at her, but changed his mind.

"When I was out in the fog that night before the SAT's, wasn't it really you who found me?"

"Yes."

"Did you carry me home?"

"Sort of."

"What does that mean?"

"Well, I had my car."

"How did I get in bed."

"I put you there."

She didn't say anything for a minute. She had never heard his voice so soft. "It wasn't Mr. Macready, then?"

"No. He wasn't there."

"Why didn't you tell me?"

"It would've looked bad. People talk. I'm young. I'm single, teaching in a girls' school. How was it that no one could find you but *I* did? That would have caused the wrong kind of talk."

She nestled closer and he held his breath until she was settled. The warmth of her body seeped and melted into the places where she touched. He thought he even felt her heart beating, but it was probably his own and of course she was still not wearing a bra. So nice.

He said, "You remember that day on the beach?"

"Of course."

"I knew you'd come."

"You did?" She started to raise her head again, and he held it in place. He believed in his strength but he couldn't take too much more. What good was strength when he had no wish to be strong? He mustn't let her face get close to his or he would surely lose his honor.

"Yes," he said. "I wanted to try and deflect your feelings, but instead I ended up doing just the opposite. I accepted them."

"How can you say that? You never gave me a chance to talk. You blocked me. Do you know how hard it was for me to be still? I'm not still. I don't hold back. My heart is there for the taking."

"That has not been my impression," he said.

"But I've never *ever* said to you how I feel."

"Not in so many words."

"It doesn't take many words." She wanted to sit up and look at him but his hand on her head seemed to ask her to be still. "I love you. And I've thought a lot about it. I think you're in my destiny." He didn't answer. She didn't move. "Why don't you say something?"

"I'm thinking," he said.

"Good."

He laughed. "Not good. I'm touched but I'm not at all convinced that you are in mine."

"That's all right. I'll wait."

"I don't think you have a choice," said Brian.

"Well, of course, that's the whole issue, isn't it?"

"I don't follow."

Now Charlotte didn't answer. Finally she said softly, "Never mind." Silence returned.

Brian felt her hand move on his spine, exploring the contours of his back, and this was no sweet cuddle. This was a hesitant sexual caress, a shy but unmistakable first step. He held still and his own desire took on separate life, deliberate, airborne, as if feelings had arms, arms that could lie her down and press her close. This long embrace could hardly be described as a hug. He picked up her braid and studied the woven strands. The ribbon was loose. The braid was coming undone and so would he if he didn't get up soon. Yet now she was still and he relaxed. There was something he wanted to know also. The other girls were coy, they were kittenish, but Charlotte, though flirtatious and provocative and closer to him in many ways, was still the least accessible. And recently he'd seen something in her eyes that made her look away, when before, her gaze was so direct it was he who looked away.

"Charlotte, what's the problem with your father?"

She pushed herself up slowly and sat back. "What do you mean?"

"Why is he so—difficult with you?"

"I can't talk about him sitting this way." She sighed and went back to the chair. Distracted she pulled off the scarf around her neck and dropped it on the floor. Brian saw a red flush on her chest as she sat back.

"I hate my father," she said, and a long minute passed before she went on. "And I love him so much I can hardly stand the power he has over me. I would do almost anything for his approval. I think he ruined his life. He reached too high and brought the wrath of the gods on us all."

Brian was struck by the flat, lifeless sound of her voice. Usually her voice was buoyant, rising, falling, changing direction like the quartering flight of a hawk. Now her words were like dead leaves.

"During the war my father wanted to be a fighter pilot. When the army wouldn't take him he joined the Ground Observer Corps. He spent nights watching for planes that never came. He wanted the planes to come. When the war was over, he bought a plane from the army. My brother said it was a beast of a plane, heavy, powerful, used to train fighter pilots, an AT-6. That's what my father had wanted to do. Shoot men out of the sky."

"Why didn't the air corps take him?"

"He's so nearsighted his glasses are like milk bottle caps. Anyway, that winter he flew to Chicago. The weather reports were bad. He had all the stuff, the flying jacket, a leather flying cap, goggles. I'll never forget how he looked when he took off. The ground shook from the roar of the engine and everybody on the field stopped to watch his ferocious plane taxi along the runway. But he flew into a snowstorm over Lake Michigan and the plane crashed. They said there was ice on the wings. He could have landed on a road and saved himself but someone on the road would have been killed. At least that's what the paper said. Maybe he wasn't a good pilot. Maybe he fell asleep. Even he doesn't know what happened." She stopped.

Brian waited. "Go on," he said.

"He tried to land in a cornfield but the plane caught a frozen rut and bounced over a barn. The glass canopy shattered on his head and split his skull open. The Chicago newspaper called my father a hero. I don't see why, though. He was sick for years. He was depressed. He drank. He was violent. He had guns. A different man. We used to call the police in the middle of the night if he hadn't ripped the phone out of the wall. No one could manage him. He was in and out of mental hospitals." She sighed. "Today he's better. He works on Wall Street. But he's still dangerous." She stopped.

"How old were you when it happened?"

"Eight."

"Was he ever violent with you?" She pulled the sleeve of her sweater down over her hands as if she were cold. She looked at Brian and the fear was right there.

"In a way," she said.

He hesitated. "I'm not sure what you mean."

She looked away. Brian closed his eyes. It was as he thought. He sat forward and rested his elbows on his knees, holding his head in his hands. It was she who'd spoken but he who felt exposed. Her short, cold sentences peeled away layer after layer of his immunity. He hadn't meant to come this far, and he rubbed his hair as if to clear his mind. "Never mind," he said.

"No, it's all right," she said suddenly. "I've never told anyone. Maybe he won't have the same power over me if I tell it." Brian sat back. He was solemn. "But it's not what you're thinking," she said.

"Charlotte, I didn't mean to ask. You don't need to say."

"My father never struck me. He never touched me. But there was something in his eyes when he looked at me. His eyes touched me. Not at first, but later. I was fourteen. I was fifteen. I was old enough." Brian could see her eyes filling with tears. Her words faltered. "My mother started sleeping in my room. She was terrified of him. I guess I was, too." Tears ran down her cheeks but she wasn't crying. They just spilled over and she didn't notice. "I was afraid one night he'd come into my room, grab me by the hand, and take me into his bed instead of my mother. I had the feeling he was thinking about it and he'd kill me if I said no." She stopped and closed her eyes hard. "But the worst thing is . . . please God, forgive me . . . I'm not sure I would have said no."

She put her hand over her mouth suddenly, as if to stop the words, and then said, "He put bullet holes in the house, in the kitchen, in the bedroom. But he couldn't help it. He was sick. He was alone. My mother was in her own world. He used to turn to me—in other ways, I mean. He needed *someone*." Her sobs rushed out and she put her head down on her knees, covering her face with her hands. "It makes me so ashamed. My family is a mess. I'm afraid I am too."

Brian sat motionless, shattered.

"Charlotte . . . " She didn't move. He got up, took her hand, and led her back to the sofa, then paused, feeling awkward, and said, "I don't know how you were sitting before, but can you sit that way again?"

She wiped her eyes on one sleeve and her nose on the other. He sat down and she curled her arms around him. But this time she clung to him. And he held her with both arms, waiting for her to stop crying.

"Charlotte. What you told me is terrible. I can't imagine what it was like. It could have been worse, I suppose, but there is nothing worse than what the mind imagines. Try to remember that your father never touched you. He kept his honor. You kept yours. He was sick but he didn't hurt you. Focus on that. If you spend your life suspicious of your father, hating him, suspicious of men, you'll never be free. There *are* men like Mr. Macready but that can't be your expectation. You know, I'm not sick or violent. I'm a quiet man, but a man nevertheless. I've had thoughts, too. I even tried to tell you on the beach. But I didn't act. I picked you up and put you in bed once, and then I left. Remember? A man can do it. You tested me more than once. You know, you once said . . . how did you put it . . . you were disgusted with Mr. Macready because he looked at you as if you were undressed. Men do that. I do it. You've just never seen it. It's not disgusting, it's normal."

He stopped and thought. He wasn't used to talking like this. Had he said too much? Because he was ashamed. How was he any better than the creep Macready?

"You know, Charlotte, men are not after 'just one thing,' as you said, they're after the whole thing. A woman, love, sex, tenderness, a friend, a partner. Don't grow cynical and harsh like Dana." He stopped again. He felt guilty because what he said wasn't true. How many times had he wanted just one thing? But she needed to hear about the good side right now. She was so quiet he was beginning to think she was asleep, when she said, "Do you know what bird sings in the middle of the night?"

"I don't think any do."

"Listen."

He listened hard and heard a faint trilling song. "What is it?"

She sat up and looked at him. "A mockingbird. Sometimes they take a chance and they sing at night, even though they put themselves in danger from the night hunters."

"How do you know?" He was surprised by the thought of kissing her.

"One was keeping me awake last fall. I called the Audubon Society. They told me." She felt his shirt where her face had been. "I think I got your shirt wet."

"I'll never wash it," he said with a shy smile.

She looked down and it felt to her as if all the blocks, the barriers, the achings, the hidden longings, the games, the eyes, the ignoring, the pretending, the let-downs, all had crumbled, and he was there a foot away from her, waiting. The pull was strong but she couldn't move, and the thought of taking his hand and bringing it under her sweater would never do.

"It's getting late," he said.

"Five more minutes." And she lay back on him as she'd been before and said, "Do you ever get a feeling inside like a burning in your lungs . . . a great warmth that comes with no warning when something good happens?"

"I'm not sure," he said.

"I'm sure. There's mysterious feelings that go on under our skin. There's a universe, another landscape, a real place. You expand and contract and your insides do sudden things." She sat curled in her spot and he said nothing. She talked into his shirt. "It's a weather system. Sometimes there's a wind that circles around your rib cage and it finds small empty hollows it whistles through. Or it's the opposite, not air, but a tide lifting your organs and swelling, filling every red space until you can't get a deep breath. Do you get that?"

"I'm not sure . . . "

"It's a physical world or cellular. When you're afraid, your body opens like a giant crack in the earth and something falls and your blood flows out of control and drums a warning. Or when you're mad it's like a stone being thrown down hard and you clench before it hits. Clouds happen, rain wets you, fog hides you, and there's a cool moon feeling that steals around when you do something good. It's huge in there—Cosmic."

"Maybe we should start the day with a weather forecast from this world so we can bring our rubbers."

"You can laugh, but . . . "

"I'm not, I'm not, I promise," he said, laughing.

"Well . . . even if I can't speak it, I can feel it, it's there." They sat in a comfortable silence. She looked up and all she could see was his jaw above her forehead. "Don't you have it, too?"

It seemed a long time to Charlotte before he said, "A smaller one. Do you know what time it is?" he said.

"What?"

"It's after ten."

"I've got to go." She got up. "Would you drive me home?" she asked.

"I'll walk you back," he said and went to get his shoes. Charlotte looked in the mirror by the door. Her hair was a mess. She pulled the rubber band off and undid the braid. Brian was in the hall door with his shoes in his hands and he watched. She combed with her fingers, and then with rapid curling motions rebraided her hair. Brian was surprised that something so complicated was finished in twenty seconds. He wanted to say, "Do it slowly, let me watch." But he sat and put on his shoes.

Outside, there was no moon but the stars were so bright it looked as if they'd just been dipped and polished.

"I can't believe you said that," said Charlotte.

"What?"

"That you've undressed me—although I like it."

"Did I say that? Sorry. Men do that. Haven't you?"

"What? Undressed a woman?"

He laughed out loud. "You know what I mean."

"No," she said. "But I think I'll try it."

They walked on. She glanced over and added, "In fact, maybe I'll start right now."

"Oh, no, you don't," he said and ran ahead of her. She laughed and kept walking. His decorum, his stiffness lay in a heap like a discarded monk's robe. She caught up to him and he said, "Let's just forget it."

"But I want to try it."

"Well, don't get yourself in trouble."

"I've already gotten myself in trouble."

"Oh, when was that?" he said archly.

"Never mind." Her voice was brittle.

They walked and the night wind hurried along the shore, working up through the black hemlocks that lined the beach, and the long branches creaked and sang, twisted and rubbed into one another like arms.

"The wind never stops here, does it?" said Brian, and their footsteps were like the slow ticking of antique clocks.

Charlotte could feel her shyness return, and before it bound her she said, "When did you know how I felt about you?"

He said, "Are any of those stars up there yours?"

She looked at him. "No, but I know some."

"I bet you do." The night was so clear he could see the dusty sweep of the Milky Way and he said, "It looks as if God has cast his field with seeds of light."

She looked at the horizon; her eyes were caught suddenly by sparkles in the grass below. It looked as if the stars had fallen into the field, where fireflies hovered—not dozens or hundreds, but thousands of fireflies. "Look." She touched his arm and he stopped. "He *has.*"

Brian looked. "My God . . . I've never seen anything like it."

"Neither have I."

"Is it a migration?"

"I don't know."

They stood and stared at the mystery for a long time, then walked in silence. They were almost at Mrs. Chase's when he said, "I'm going to leave you here." The lights from the house filtered through the trees and lit the old, cracked road.

"Thank you for not treating me like a fool," said Charlotte.

"When I saw you at the door I wasn't pleased, but maybe things need to be said sometimes."

There was a long silence. Neither moved.

"After tomorrow, can I call you Brian?"

"I don't think you have to ask. You have a friend."

"We couldn't be more different, though," said Charlotte. "You're so temperate, so patient, so logical—"

"I've got a few years on you."

"Not so many . . . You wait for the right moment, the perfect time. . . . "

"Which never seems to come," he said. "And you'd propose a flight to the moon while hurrying through a revolving door."

There was a long silence, but not awkward this time, and he said, "Good night, Charlotte."

"Good night." She watched until he was out of sight, and the sound of his steps was gone. She stood in the clean-swept night and thought to the sky, Thank you, God, for letting me have this. Maybe I'm a thief, but I think this was given to me. I hope I'm not a thief. If I am, please don't punish me.

She allowed herself a small measure of peace that night sitting on the front steps in the dark, her head resting in her arms, turned inward and lost to the night sounds she knew so well. She thought to herself, My life would never have been complete without this man. I've never loved anyone the way I love him, no matter what my mother thinks. All through my stupid problems and demands, my overstepping, he never belittled me. He was patient and he listened. He gave. And no matter where I go from here, I'll be his. He'll just never know it. It could have been you, Brian. She raised her head and looked down the road. *This love is still following you, still searching for you. Maybe love is still going to find you and it will be mine. But no.*

She looked up at the night sky again before she went in, and her inner landscape seemed doubled—as full as the sky above and as empty as the night below. *I am two consciousnesses now, my friend and my love—I am me and I am you.*

When Brian reached his apartment he walked right on past. He didn't hear the mockingbird still singing in the hedgerow. He didn't feel the marsh wind nudging his shoulders. He didn't see the stars swing low or the fireflies move slowly inland. His eyes turned inward, examining the turbulence. When she'd pulled off her scarf, he'd seen her shapely collarbone was asymmetrical and he wondered if that accounted for her endearing but gangly walk. But her fingers had been knowing and graceful braiding her hair like Titania. This night she had asked for nothing. He almost wished she had asked for more and he was so bombarded with images he missed the beauty of the night around him and must have been a mile past his door when he noticed he'd wandered halfway around the northern loop of Flanders Point and wasn't very far from the Macready house by the marsh. He turned and walked back. The sky was turning light when he fell asleep.

Graduation

GRADUATION WAS A modest affair and the people stood around after the ceremony. Everybody was buzzing because Miss Haddam had brought in an unusual speaker, her friend Margaret Hamilton. She had played the Wicked Witch of the West in *The Wizard of Oz*. And she'd started her talk with the words, "We might as well get it out of the way first. I know you all want to hear the laugh," and she let rip the wonderful diabolical witch laugh that no one could forget. After that the girls were stepping about on cloud nine. It was such an un-Haddam thing.

Hans muttered to Brian, "Miss Haddam seems to have acquired a sense of humor."

Brian, too, was acquiring a sense of humor, though muted, and he was feeling more comfortable with strangers, able to greet parents graciously. Last year at the boys' school he'd dreaded graduation because he had to talk to people he didn't know and had no interest in. Not this year. The girls, with their white cotton dresses and white bouquets, looked innocent and chaste, and Brian loved that they were nothing of the kind. Haddam had hatched an intriguing bunch of late bloomers, whom he hoped would question the world and stir it up, though he also knew most would never fulfill the potential they held today. People just didn't. He especially cherished Maude, who was class valedictorian by a wide margin, but had disdained the distinction. As she refused to accept, the award fell to Charlotte, who had surprised them all by ending the year on a strong note. Theo and Dana had faltered badly, and Brian didn't know why but suspected it had to do with boys. Charlotte didn't mind getting the distinction by default. She was proud just the same, and Brian thought she deserved it more. Straight *A*'s came naturally to Maude. Charlotte had to work for them. And even though she too had stumbled in the middle of the year, she'd pulled back out. It killed him that she hadn't gotten into the college of her choice, but then he never had, either.

He looked around and Charlotte was standing with Theo's parents. He went over.

"Congratulations, Charlotte. Where's your mother? I'd like to meet her." He put his arm around her affectionately and then felt awkward removing it. He had to get the rhythm of the social touch and detach.

"Oh, she couldn't come," she said cheerfully and they walked away from Theo.

"Really?"

"She's at the court of appeals in Hartford on some case."

"Couldn't she postpone the appeal?" Charlotte turned away but not before Brian saw her troubled look.

"I guess not." She shrugged.

Brian pushed on. "That's a damn shame." Charlotte didn't say anything and Brian waited. He could feel the tension of her holding— holding tight, too tight, chin up, mouth down.

"What's such a shame?" she said. "Judges don't wait. And someone was depending on her." Charlotte tried to smile.

Brian knew he'd found the door that Charlotte never opened, but now was not the time. There would never be a time.

"My father's here," she said suddenly.

"Your father?" Brian looked for some recognition of what they'd shared the night before, but there was none. "Where?"

"In the straw boater, talking to Mrs. Chase." Brian looked over and Charlotte's father was listening to something Mrs. Chase was saying, but he was watching Brian.

"Do you want to meet him?" said Charlotte.

"I feel like I already have. I'm going back to the English room. Why don't you meet me there in five minutes?" He walked into Dovecote.

Charlotte turned to her father. He glanced at Charlotte repeatedly but he seemed intent on his conversation and was not actually looking at her. Brian had said five minutes, but she didn't wait. He was standing by his desk and handed her a slim book with a soft cover called *The Grey Fox Review*.

"What is it?"

"One of my poems was published. It may not seem like much, but it's hard to get published."

Charlotte was startled. "I didn't know you wrote poetry."

"Now you know." She dropped her chin and hugged him, then stepped back. He smiled at her and said, "Don't give up poetry, Charlotte. It's a great gift what the poet gives us. Don't underestimate it."

"No chance," she said. "Don't forget me."

He said, "No chance."

She couldn't move. "I'll be back to see you next year. I'll be grown-up and we can have lunch like real people."

"You're already grown-up."

"Oh, God . . . " she said suddenly, her voice breaking.

He blushed. There were footsteps in the hall. "Good-bye, Charlotte."

They stood for a second, looking at each other. Someone was coming. Charlotte saw her father standing in the doorway. He looked at them with suspicion. She said, "Dad! This is Mr. Parton, my English teacher."

"Mr. Delafield . . . " Brian said and extended his hand, but to his chagrin her father ignored it. Seconds passed before Charlotte noticed, but under her quick look of disapproval her father reluctantly extended his hand. Brian forgot his momentary embarrassment in his surprise at the power Charlotte had over her father.

Mr. Delafield said, "How do you do?" with pointed sarcasm and looked around. "Is this the English room?"

"Yes," said Brian.

"It seems somewhat devoid of books."

"Reference books have been reshelved. Would you care to see the library? It's big and the view of the cove is spectacular."

"I think not," said Charlotte's father. "There's no need for mawkish good-byes, either," and with a dismissive turn he said, "We should be going, Charlotte." He took her elbow and she calmly removed his hand, stepping away.

Brian felt her fury at her father's rudeness, it was as if she would hurl spit or scratch his face, but she said, "I know. Good-bye again, Brian."

Brian said, "Excuse me, Mr. Delafield, Charlotte and I would like a minute." Her father didn't move.

"Dad . . ."

"I'll wait in the lobby."

She whispered, "That'll show him."

"We don't need to show him up. I think he adores you."

"I guess, but he gets all twisted out of shape."

"There's a lot we never got to talk about, Charlotte."

"There is?"

"Yes. I should have been more help. I'm afraid I let you down a bit."

"Oh, no . . . you made my life bearable. You've given me so much."

"No, meager input." He was going to hug her one more time, when Jack Delafield reappeared.

Brian said, "Thank you, Mr. Delafield. Good-bye, Charlotte," and he turned away, fiddling with stuff on his desk, and he glanced sideways at Charlotte so her father couldn't see. His look was fleeting but she thought he winked at her.

"Good-bye, Brian. See you at Thanksgiving," she said.

She walked out with her father, who said, "You're on a first-name basis?"

Charlotte lied. "It's an old Haddam tradition, after graduation."

"Odd," he said.

Outside with her father she felt such a pain in her stomach she almost doubled over, and somewhere in the corner of her mind she thought, My father knows more than one way to hit. Then suddenly he seemed to cheer up and said he had to leave and that "a friend on Wall Street may have a job for you this summer, but in any event, I want to see you before you go to Bryn Mawr." Fat chance, thought Charlotte. He walked to the car that was waiting.

The minute he was gone she opened the book Brian had given her and looked on the inside cover. He'd written something.

For Charlotte,

Surely these things lie on the knees of the Gods.
Homer, The Odyssey—*Book I*
Yours, Brian Parton

Underneath the inscription, written in neat black ink, were strange and beckoning letters unlike any she had ever seen. She pondered their mysterious beauty and realized Brian had written Homer's thought in ancient Greek as well. She touched each word lightly with her finger.

ἀλλ᾽ ἡ τοι μὲν ταῦτα θεῶν ἐν γούνασι κεῖται.

The Knees of the Gods

AFTER GRADUATION WITH no one around and two weeks before he went back to Boston, Brian was at loose ends. He was the last one to leave and he walked the rooms of Dovecote alone. He was so used to the tumbling clatter of his students' feet that he'd never noticed the almost sweet sound of his own footsteps and the small, musical creaks in the old floorboards. Suddenly he had time to listen and think. He'd spent nine months in a community of women. Women of different minds and ages, different hearts and demeanors, women with engaging problems and contagious joy as they left notes in his desk, ripped the Stevenson sticker off his car, lolled on the grass for his benefit, left lipstick kisses on the blackboard, and demanded so much attention that at times he felt like a body servant to the upper middle class. Every day drained his energy but it refilled quickly and the debt was repaid. If perhaps the scales tipped out of balance on the giving side, that was his job. He cared and he liked them.

The empty library seemed desolate now, as if the school had lost its life, and so had he. He knew he didn't matter much in their lives, but maybe he'd left a mark on some. He felt less irrelevant than before, and though his new family was gone, his old family remained: the books, the stories, the characters that beckoned him with no letup. He never got enough of books. It was the words, alive on the pages long after the writers had gone, words that countered the silence and called like distant relatives, unmet ancestors, and old friends, telling their lives, their loves, and their troubles. Myths, legends, and fairy tales. Stories about what happened. What could happen. What might happen. Did it matter? It mattered to Brian and now to some of his students. But Brian also knew that he'd missed something by immersing himself in books. It was time to start giving the books away and live a story of his own.

That night he went out and walked past the field where he and Charlotte had seen the fireflies. He knew he'd made a difference in her life. She had put a thank-you note in his mailbox before she left and he'd reread the line, "I know I'm not part of your life, but you are part of mine. With your poem just published, I take you with me." There was never any question of his going near her, not really, but it would be a relief to go back to Boston, where she had no presence, no ownership, no power. He always thought saying no was a virtue. Where had he gotten such an idea? It was too easy. Life wasn't supposed to be so predictable and safe. Wait, endure, save, deny, sacrifice, he was taught as a boy. By the nuns, by his father. Store up credits in Paradise, build up a Heavenly savings account. Save another soul in Purgatory with each new abstinence, each coveted denial, each turn from the sensual life. He'd never believed it, and thank God in Jesuit schools he was allowed to read anything he wanted, so he knew it wasn't true. One thing about the Jesuits, they believed they could take on anyone, so they were never afraid of the powerful, "wrong" ideas the students might pick up.

He still thought of Bridget sometimes. Poor Bridget. She'd swallowed it all. The nuns told her she mustn't wear patent leather shoes because boys might see her underpants in the reflection. She must never ride a motorcycle. This was foreplay. The vibrations would arouse her. Were bicycles safe? French kissing was tantamount to intercourse. A tongue must never enter her. He had argued like a good Jesuit. He had tried to show her that only a guilt-ridden mind, deprived of a natural sensual life and obsessed by it, would even think of such things. That maybe purity was not in denying these things but never thinking of them in the first place. She didn't get it. It was too late. She'd been taught young. What fun it had been trying to convince her and he had very dear memories of how sweetly she had tried to be open-minded, to no avail. And how she must have suffered. No to pleasure, no to desire, no to touch, no to sex, no to love, even, or maybe yes, but just for a minute or two. It was almost a mystery to him how she'd gotten pregnant, or when. There were still times when he blamed himself bitterly, but he knew it served no purpose and marriage would have been a serious mistake.

He leaned on the fence and the wind died and there was not a firefly in sight. What he liked about Charlotte was the way she took chances. Even when she was afraid she risked herself. Coming to the beach to find him and reach for him and speak her heart. What power she had held that day, and she had no inkling. And destroying that piano. What a terrible thing to do, so selfish, but it was daring. And it worked. No, you could never call Charlotte meek. He liked her storms and her extremes and her ability to endure pain. He was afraid of pain. Maybe that was the cause of his limp, routine life of virtue. An old story, avoidance of pain. Not Charlotte. She wanted fire in her life. And so, thought Brian, do I. No more dry pages and imagined lives. Easy to say, he thought.

Sunday morning he went for a drive to the beach and was surprised to find the beach deserted. Where were the mothers and children? He swam out, back and forth between the cliffs, and then lay on his towel for an hour. Not a soul appeared. And when he got up to go back home, he was disappointed—first that no one was there and secondly, that he rather liked it that way. But driving slowly back, there ahead of him, standing under the silver willows, was Charlotte, barefoot, bending over a little blond boy and buckling his sandals. He stopped the car.

"Hi, Charlotte."

She looked up, startled. "Mr. Parton!"

"Still Mr. Parton?"

"Brian . . . "

"I thought you'd gone home," he said.

"No. I have a baby-sitting job till Sunday."

"Is that a little Macready?" He was surprised at her scowl.

"No. A little Ramsey. A neighbor of Mrs. Chase's." She felt cool air lifting her blouse in the back and she let it distract her from the shaking in her heart.

"Are you still living with Mrs. Chase?" he asked.

"No, she went to her daughter's graduation at Oberlin." She had the sudden impulse to grab the little boy by his arm and fling him into the woods.

"But I thought you were back in Boston," she said.

"My tenant doesn't leave till the fifteenth." The car was idling and he glanced around. "This place sure clears out in a hurry."

She said, "People go to Nantucket this weekend to open their summer houses. I think I wish you were gone, too."

"Oh?" said Brian and searched her face.

She fell silent, annoyed with herself.

"Want a ride?" he said.

"Okay." She picked up the little boy, straddled him on her hip, and walked around the car. Brian reached over and opened the door.

"My feet are full of sand," she said.

"It's okay."

She got in but Brian didn't move the car, and she settled the little boy in her lap.

"Where do the Ramseys live?" asked Brian.

"Right there." She pointed to the house on the left. Brian glanced over, amused, and pulled the car away from the house. He thought about what she'd said.

"If it makes any difference," he said quietly, "I'd prefer that you weren't still on the Point, either."

Charlotte looked up. "Really? Why?"

"For the same reason, I imagine."

"Don't tease me," she said, suddenly cross.

"I'm not," he said.

Charlotte turned to him and stared. He pulled the car over to the side of the road again. With the little boy falling asleep against her, she was still, unblinking, and didn't smile. Neither did he. If she had, he would have quit right there and closed it off, but she was grave and said, "What are you saying to me?"

Brian made the leap. "You said you wanted to be in my pocket. Well, you are." He turned off the motor and there was a long quiet. He saw her confusion, maybe irritation too.

"You said men wanted women in their bed," she said coldly. It was ice cubes dropping on stone.

"I know."

"Are you suggesting that I get out of your pocket and into your bed?" she snapped.

He stared at her. She was so unpredictable. A breeze came in off the water through the open window and a big cricket landed on the windshield and slid down the glass. Brian watched the cricket scrambling around and he was aware of how intently Charlotte looked at him. He turned to her and said in a voice he didn't mean to sound so uncertain, "Would you . . . if you could?"

Charlotte looked down the road watching the salt grass bend in the soft June wind. How could this be? She'd walked away with her head high, resigned herself, accepted fate. She'd told herself, I can do it alone. I have an unbending center that has finally learned to bend—to accept what life deals me. And now sitting two feet from her, the man who made her crazy, the man who kept her sane, who for months had filled her with hope and emptied her with despair, the man she loved, who had suddenly, unexpectedly, impossibly extended his hand. Did he want to make love? Did the rules still apply? She was afraid to move, afraid he'd know she was trembling inside, and when she finally looked at him, his eyes, which were always so opaque, were clear and close, like small blue flames, and she fell right in. She was taken and held. "Yes," she said a little tightly, "I would."

"No, you wouldn't," he said, caught off guard again, but she sounded like she meant it.

And Charlotte's voice slid out with a resigned cadence. "You know, you said I was grown-up and I am. I'm ready to go back to the desert where I came from. I know how to live there. I'm like a cactus. I can go for weeks without water because I have no choice. And when school ended, I even came to terms with the notion that what I wanted most to do was what I most didn't want."

"What was that?"

"To give up the idea of you."

"You're still going to have to give that up." She turned to him and her hurt was not hidden. He hadn't meant to sound so harsh. "I'm sorry, Charlotte, what I said about you in my pocket. I overstepped."

"No, you didn't."

"Yes, it was inexcusable," he muttered.

"How can you overstep when there is no boundary?" And she whispered, "Not anymore." To her surprise, he didn't contradict. She said, "I'm sorry—I was pretty rude before."

"You don't think I overstepped and I don't think you were rude so we're even." And now neither one of them knew what to say. The silence of inner thoughts they couldn't speak—forward, backward, a silence both patient and impatient was all there was. For endless minutes they sat there together and Brian, wishing for some distraction, wanted to get out of the car and walk to the marsh with her. He noticed the wispy hair around her forehead had turned the same blond color as the little boy's in her lap. Damn kid. Brian asked, "Do you get any time off from this job?"

"After supper."

"I've been packing my books. I was going to take them to the school library tomorrow. Would you like to stop by later and see if you want any?"

She looked up happily. "Oh, I *would*. Are you sure?"

"Of course," he said and felt her warmth pour forth, the way it had when she hugged him on the sofa.

"I could come around seven-thirty. Is that good?"

"That's fine."

He started the engine and drove her back to the Ramseys' while she woke up the little boy.

When Brian got back to his apartment, he started straightening up. He pulled down books and piled them in a carton, stacked others on the floor. He didn't pay attention to what went where, except for putting aside a couple of anthologies for Charlotte to examine. When he opened a can of corned beef hash and watched it fry to a dark crust, he was hungry, but when he sat down he couldn't eat. He was full. He pulled up the blankets on the bed and threw more books around on it. Excited and nervous, he felt like a fool, but when he went outside and sat on his terrace steps, the sound of bees in the mountain laurel by his door was calming and he sat and watched their busy work for a long time, pulling out a scrap of paper to jot down his thoughts.

Charlotte wasn't nervous about Brian in the least—not yet. It was Mrs. Ramsey she was nervous about. Mrs. Ramsey was the opposite of Mrs. Macready, whose vague way of not noticing what Charlotte was doing until it was already done gave Charlotte freedom. Mrs. Ramsey watched Charlotte every minute, it seemed, as if she thought Charlotte was about to break the china and run away—even though her time off had been clearly stated.

After supper she took a bath and brushed her hair. Her skin was hot and full of color from the day at the beach. She was thinking maybe, finally, he'd kiss her good-bye. He almost had before, she was sure of it. A steamer trunk with her summer clothes had been sent to her father's apartment the day before, so she had nothing to wear but Bermuda shorts and a camp shirt, but that was good. Mrs. Ramsey wouldn't notice a thing. Charlotte wanted to run to his apartment because this time she was invited and her whole body was smiling—not just her face, but her arms and knees and even her very toes.

Mrs. Ramsey was prickly when Charlotte said she was going to the beach. "Very well, I heard you have a penchant for walking," she said.

Charlotte hurried under the great white pines behind the house. The day's heat was gone with the disappearing sun and the wind was up. Barn swallows swooped around her, skimming the air back and forth, up and down catching gnats and making nests. She noticed how at dusk they put on a great air show, as if like children they didn't want to go to sleep. Me either, she thought. Ahead of her was the long curved driveway of the Armbruster house, that sat like a calm, old Tudor eminence at rest on a low hill. Because of the hill, you couldn't see the beach behind the house, only the water glistening. The pillared and arched causeway that reached like a welcoming arm toward the side terrace led to Brian's apartment as well, and Charlotte thought she saw someone standing under an archway. She walked a little faster.

The door was open and she knocked and walked in. All the windows were open, too, and Brian stood with books in his hands. "Hi, have a seat. There's a couple of books on the table there." She sat down and looked around. So much for falling into each other's arms, she thought. Outside, the sun slid down and the daylight in his apartment turned the pale amber color that comes before the summer solstice, when summer is pressing in and spring is singing faintly. Before she'd noticed plaster coming loose on one wall, but now she noticed how nice the apartment was, with crown moldings over every door and casement windows that cranked open, an Oriental rug and glassed-in bookshelves. Brian moved restlessly back and forth in front of a wall of books, pulling them out, a little roughly, she thought. Suddenly she realized she was scared to death. Maybe he was, too. She got up and joined him at the books. So many beckoning titles: *The Letters of Abelard and Héloïse, The Oxford*

Companion to English Literature, and something called *The Greeks and the Irrational* sounded interesting.

Brian said, "You can take it. It's perfect for a Bryn Mawr student." At one point, when she was standing still, reading titles, he walked over, stood behind her, reached to pull a small volume down, and dropped his arm over her shoulder to put the book in her hand. He was so close if she turned around, she'd be in his arms. "Here, I have two of this. *Eight Harvard Poets.* You can have one." But when she turned to thank him, he stepped back. She'd never seen him so nervous. Where were his graceful pacing steps, his swivels on little beads, the confidence he always exuded? She was touched. Maybe he really liked her.

But Brian's hopes were drowning in guilt at the moment. *It would be so easy . . . she's waiting . . . just move, reach. Shut up, it's wrong . . . it's not fair, let her go . . . you'll live. . . .* And he picked up a used carton and started taping the bottom with great vigor. Charlotte didn't know what to do so she got up to go, and taking the books with her she said good-bye cheerfully, but she was numb and confused and no longer smiling. She walked down the long drive deep in thought and then stopped, annoyed. Why had he asked her to come if he was just going to let her leave in such an unfriendly way? This wasn't fair, damn him. She put the books on the grass and turned to run back to the apartment. To her surprise, Brian had come up silently right behind her. She jumped. "What?" She hadn't heard a sound.

"Charlotte . . . Don't go yet. I want to talk to you." He took her hand and she followed him quickly back up the terrace steps. He walked to the sofa. "Come, let's resume where we left off."

"Resume?"

"Hugging."

Charlotte thought her knees would buckle. "What are you doing . . . " she muttered, and she sat, but not too close this time.

"Charlotte, you said you'd . . . you meant it, didn't you?"

"Yes, I did."

"Then come—on Monday. Stay for a few days."

"Oh, Brian, don't play with me. I thought I'd never see you again and now you appear and ask me to come and stay with you and . . . overnight. What should I believe? How can it be right?" He didn't answer. Where was the Brian she knew? The silent Brian, inscrutable, closed, distant, hinting at starvation? *That* Brian she could give up. But this was different. "For how long?" she said.

"All week if you can. Where would you tell your mother you are?"

"Not my mother—my father. I'm supposed to spend the summer with him. He says he got me a job on Wall Street."

"Your father? But your father—he's trouble."

"No, he's not. I can handle him. How will I get to your house?"

Brian thought. Nothing furtive. "What was the plan before?"

"I was going to take the noon train Monday. Mrs. Ramsey is dropping me off. My trunk was shipped yesterday."

"Will you have any clothes?"

The thought of kissing him was in the front of her thoughts and she leaned over. "Will I need any?"

He barely managed not to laugh and said, "Get serious."

"I am," she said. "I have been for months."

"I could pick you up at the station if Mrs. Ramsey doesn't wait."

"All right," said Charlotte.

He hadn't expected her to say yes so fast. "Charlotte, between now and Monday you can change your mind, you know."

"So can you."

"We may be found out. We may pay a terrible price." She kept her eyes down. "We may feel nothing," he added.

"Not possible." She was barely breathing over the visceral feelings of desire, too powerful not to give in to, no matter how disappointed Miss Haddam might be with their decision.

"We may be consumed with guilt," he said quietly.

Now she looked at him, and, lowering her voice, unused to him talking so much, said, "Why? You said yourself these things are on the knees of the gods. I think they picked us up and we're in their hands."

"It was just a sentimental quote, nothing true."

She thought it over. "It can't be anything else. Brian, listen to the things we're saying. Maybe we're in another place, some place free."

"Keep telling me that," he said.

"It's true. I didn't plan this. Neither did you, did you?"

"No. It's ironic, you know, Charlotte, you reassuring me when I should be reassuring you."

"My turn will come later."

He smiled and shook his head. "How can you be so honest?"

"It's part of having a 'healthy naivete.' "

"You *saw* what I wrote in your reports?"

"Yes, we snuck into the office last winter."

"So much for the honor code," he said, and Charlotte nodded. "Let's say I'll be at the station at eleven-thirty on Monday."

"Okay . . . But, Brian, what if you change your mind?"

"I won't." He paused. "What will you do if I only have number-three pencils?"

At last she smiled and looked down. "I don't expect to do much writing."

"Charlotte, if either of us changes his mind, we'll still be there Monday—no matter what. No *Casablanca*. We won't just not show up."

She looked back at him, sealing it with a nod and no smile.

He got up and looked out the window. "It's not dark yet. I don't think I should walk you back."

"I'll be okay."

Charlotte waited to call her father until Mrs. Ramsey was out watering her peonies in the dark. "Dad, when is the interview at Kidder, Peabody?"

"Tuesday morning, but it's just a formality, you know. You'll be here Monday, right?"

"Well, that's why I'm calling. Mrs. Ramsey asked me to stay an extra day and—"

"Charlotte, the firm is doing me a favor. You don't change a courtesy interview for a summer job. Jobs are scarce as hens' teeth down here, you know."

"She needs me. And I have to go to Washington for a couple of days. I haven't been home since Christmas. Can't you just say my other job was extended a few days? That doesn't sound so bad."

There was a pause. "Charlotte, what's going on? Let me talk to Mrs. Ramsey."

"She's out for the evening."

"Never mind. I think I can change it to Friday, but it's not nice."

"Okay. Thanks, Dad," Charlotte said eagerly.

"I thought you couldn't wait to start working in the city."

"Yes, but it's only a few days."

"Leave me the Ramsey number in case Friday isn't feasible." Charlotte froze. "Charlotte?"

"She doesn't like me to get calls. I'll call you from Washington," but she gave him Mrs. Ramsey's number. He'd never call. He hadn't once all year.

Monday

SHE WAS DROPPED off at the station Monday morning, and from the car Mrs. Ramsey said, "If you want to work all summer, Charlotte, I can use you."

"I have a job in the city, thanks. Mrs. Ramsey, if my father calls, I'm going home for a couple of days, but he tends to forget things. Just remind him, if you don't mind."

"Very well."

"You don't need to wait with me. I'll be fine. Thanks for everything."

She looked around for Brian and saw his blue Buick parked behind a row of cars. He was leaning against the hood. He looked different in jeans. She went into the station and out another door.

"You're here," she said.

"We promised." There was an awkward silence. "Have you changed your mind?"

"No," said Charlotte. "Have you?"

He shook his head and they got in the car. "Charlotte—"

"What?"

"What time does the train come?"

"Twenty minutes."

Brian hesitated. "I've been thinking."

"So have I. I think maybe I should get on the train."

He looked at her. "Maybe you're right."

"Isn't that what *you* were thinking?" she said.

"Well, no," he said in a quiet voice.

"Oh."

"I was wondering what you think about what we're doing."

"We haven't done anything yet."

"Yes, we have."

Charlotte realized he was as nervous as she was. "I have the courage of my convictions. Don't you?"

"Yes, and I want you to stay," he said, "but I don't want you to feel that I expect anything." Her features softened into something wistful and she put her hand on his.

"I'm excited, aren't you?" It was almost a whisper.

"I don't know if I'd use those words, exactly," he said.

"What, then?"

He didn't say anything and then, "I need your love."

All she could do was look at him as if she'd never seen him before. On the way to Flanders Point she said, "Thank you for saying that. I've been shaking for two days." And doing a most un-Brian-like thing, he reached over calmly and touched her cheek with the back of his hand. When they approached his apartment he drove right past. "Where are you going?" she asked.

"See the workers behind us?"

"I sure do. Where'd *they* come from?"

"They showed up a few days ago."

"No one's built a house here in twenty years. People like it untamed."

"A big estate is going up."

"That must be what Mrs. Macready was talking about."

"What?"

"There was a big fight about a buyer who wanted to build a big showplace. We won't have much privacy."

"We can go down to the beach without them seeing us."

"How?"

"Through the Armbrusters' house," said Brian. "They're not here. They leave me the keys." And he drove up at last and parked in front of the garage. When they went in, Brian hugged Charlotte. "I'm so glad you came," he said, and, "Here's a drawer for your things."

They spent the afternoon on the Armbrusters' beach, where they sat on a blanket reading and talking about school. It was odd and awkward. Charlotte waited. Maybe she'd misunderstood his intent, but probably most people made love at night. It wasn't night. The afternoon crept by. Brian swam a mile while she sat on the blanket, popping seaweed bulbs and watching. Farther out, black cormorants were feeding, diving under the waves, their thin necks appearing and reappearing like little black periscopes. When he came back up, she sat down next to him and said, "Brian, let's go back in." He didn't answer. With his index finger he wrote in the wet sand, THE HEART MISGIVES.

Charlotte paused, surprised. She reached down and smoothed away the first three letters so the big letters read, THE HEART GIVES.

She was puzzled. He seemed to step back, not forward. She remembered Dana saying, "Once they have you, they don't want you." It was nonsense but she said, "Don't you need me anymore?"

And he heard a fragile twinge in her voice that seemed to come from the troubled, doubting soul of a girl wanting to grow up and wanting to say, "I won't let you down," but not knowing how. Fearless Charlotte, who said she could handle anything, but he was being pulled apart by her wavers, made whole by her fierce convictions, and then rendered wordless by her need. Need for whom, for what—occupant, father, teacher, brother, lover, or maybe—him? Struck by her shy, hopeful look he took her hand and said, "Let's go in." They were starving and he said, "I'll make us grilled cheese sandwiches," and Brian looked aghast when she covered hers with salt but then he smiled.

"Why are you smiling?" she asked.

"Just glad you're here."

"Hmmm. I guess we'll just be friends," she said cheerfully.

"I guess," he said.

It was a small world, Brian's apartment. Trips to the bathroom were embarrassing and delayed. With every hour that passed Charlotte was more uncertain. She thought it would have happened by now. She wanted to feel his hands on her and the desire excited her. Surely he didn't expect her to approach him. What was he waiting for?

At nine she said, "I didn't see a shower in the bathroom . . . "

"Just a tub," said Brian. "Test the water, though; it's scalding." He worked at his partners desk.

Charlotte soaked in his tub and imagined Brian scrubbing himself in the spot where she sat. When she got out of the tub, put on her plaid pajamas, and saw herself in the mirror door, she was disappointed. Faded pajamas weren't sexy. She took down her hair and fluffed it around to counter the pajamas. Not sure where to sleep, the only thing to do was walk to the old brass bed and get in it. She wasn't going to stand around like a ninny.

"I'm sorry about these pajamas. You're going to think you have a Boy Scout in your bed." The double doors into the living room were folded open, making one big room. When would something happen? "Is this where I should sleep?" she asked.

"That's fine."

"Are you going to sleep here, too?" This was weird. Of course he was, but she wasn't going to try to be seductive, not in Max's pajamas.

"I thought I would," he said in his most refined voice. She almost laughed.

"When?"

"I'm kidding. I'll sleep on the sofa tonight. I'm not finished with what I'm doing."

She stared at him. "And what are you doing that's so important?"

"I'm thinking."

"What makes you think I can go to sleep?"

"Friends can."

Charlotte turned on her side. She couldn't keep up this brave front, trading quips like Dana. She'd misjudged and it wasn't fair. When the thatch cottage suddenly appeared in her thoughts she sat up. "Brian. I'm sort of . . . nervous."

He saw her distress. "I know. It's hard to forget who we are."

"That's not what I'm nervous about. It's worse."

"What do you mean?"

"Could you come over here?" she said. He went over and sat on the bed. "Closer. I have to tell you something."

She was so serious. "What? Tell me."

She threw off the covers and climbed into his arms and they lay back together and he started to kiss her. He'd waited so long—not another minute—and he muttered, "You certainly had me fooled. I thought something was wrong. What an imp you are, following me around all year with those dark eyes of yours," and he kissed her on the neck and started to unbutton her pajamas.

"No, wait." She grabbed his hand. "I'm *not* an imp, I wasn't fooling. Listen . . . oh, I can't talk." She turned over and slid back against him, pulling his arm around her chest and holding on.

"There's entirely too much talking going on here," he said and climbed around and slowly kissed her twice, his fingers light on her collarbone and her cheek. She was assured at such a sweet, soft invitation because he acted like a perfectly normal thing had just happened. But all Charlotte could think of was it was the first time he'd kissed her mouth, and how intimate it was. She wanted more.

While he smoothed her hair on the pillow and thought a minute, he said, "Don't you want to take this off?" She nodded, anxious for more kissing. He unbuttoned her pajama top and removed it, looking at her with a mysterious smile. As he took off his shirt and unzipped his pants, it was hard not to rush. Things that he'd never thought of before seemed a little crude with her. "Are you nervous now?"

"No . . ."

"Good," he said.

But when Charlotte felt the intensity of his embrace under the covers, other images flooded in and she stiffened and pulled away, and she heard herself cry, "Wait . . . wait . . ."

"Charlotte, what is it?" Her eyes were full of the fear he'd seen hovering at the edges sometimes and it rushed out, a storm pouring through, cracking against his desire. "Talk to me."

She was motionless. "I don't know . . . nothing, nothing."

"It's not nothing—it's something but this is not written in stone." He pulled her into his arms as if they were on the sofa again. "Try to sleep." She was numb, humiliated, shredded. They didn't talk. They weren't asleep, but they weren't awake either. They were lost and adrift in a strange and troubled reverie. And then Brian got up, pulled on his robe, and sat on the sofa, watching her.

What door had she slipped through? All weekend while he told himself she'd never come, he cleaned his apartment, shopped for groceries, changed the sheets. Maybe this was what Eben had meant about the perversity of the heart. Brian had thought about what they could do, what was safe, what was not, the sleeping arrangements, but all he could think of now was making love and how to approach. This hadn't happened to him since he was a teenager. Bridget, for all her refusals and protests, once she got to a certain point, which wasn't often, there was no stopping her.

But something else was burning small and hot in the back of his mind. Something beneath the passion. He turned to it. Anger. Charlotte had won, injected herself into his life, and now he was caught and ready to do something against his principles, and he could hardly wait—and she made him wait. He'd never trusted the world and now he didn't trust himself. He lay down on the sofa and pulled the spare blanket over himself. It was a night he wouldn't forget—a night of searching questions, of inconsistent guilt, of false denial, of creeping anxiety. *You're sleeping with a student, you're reaching for what you need, you're sleeping with a student, there's a girl who loves you, you're sleeping with a student, what will happen, does she mean it? I know I mean it—but why do I feel no guilt? The only thing I feel guilty about is that I don't feel guilty. What is that? Does it mean this is natural? Destined? It can't be. . . .* Back and forth he went.

He went outside and looked up. Stars that might have suggested with vast indifference what little consequence this had were lost in a cloud cover. This girl so dear to him, lying in his bed was immediate, real, and of the greatest consequence. It was close to dawn and he felt as if his heart had been pulled through the eye of a needle, everything extraneous stripped away except a taut, invisible filament that pulled him toward her. Faintly, through the scrim of his memory and into his mind's ear, the ancient voice of Ovid suggested he wait "for the kind of light that woods tend to have—or when night has gone but the sun not yet risen. That is the light to offer to shy girls, in which their timid modesty may hope to find a hiding place."

His quandary was nothing new, it seemed. He took off his shorts and got under the covers, closing his eyes though he wasn't asleep.

Charlotte wasn't asleep, either. It was a dark but graying five o'clock, the silent break of day. She turned and listened to his breathing and loved that he was bold enough to climb into bed with her. She felt safe. The blanket draped over him so smoothly, she realized with a start that he wasn't wearing anything. The shock of it hit her under the sheets, and she pressed her hand hard on her breastbone, not daring to move. Last night she'd lain alone, unkissed; now a naked man was next to her. Why such extremes? Her family from rich to poor in one day when she was nine, her body from short to tall and flat to full in a few months at seventeen, her virtue from untouched to violated in nine seconds last winter. Why was she never gradual? And listening for the birds in the still morning, she heard a different sound, a faint and hidden hum, like a quiver in the earth's rotation, and with the vibration something in her heart started, swift and loose and licking. The ache of loving him spread through her. Like a brushfire hidden low in the grass, heat crept across her porous skin, up through her stomach, and down her legs in a warm shower of sparks. Motionless and soundless, she was awed at the power of her body to overwhelm her this way. And although she didn't want to wake him, she had to see and carefully, she raised the covers to look.

It was all Brian could do to remain still, because inside his heart was laughing with joy. Not yet, he thought. Hold off, let her be a few minutes older. But then Charlotte put her hand on his shoulder and he said, "Charlotte?"

"What?" she whispered.

He pulled her hand to his chest. "I thought I'd wake up and find you gone."

"Where would I go?"

"I don't know," he said.

"Why are we whispering?"

"Shhh. Stop asking questions," he said, his voice hoarse. He propped his head on his elbow and she smiled at his rumpled hair. "It's so early."

"I've been lying here for an hour. We're awake before the birds."

"You and your birds," he said. And he approached her slowly. Her pajamas were back on and he asked, "Will you take these off? They're for sleeping." And carefully, sweetly, persuasively, he began to make love. She was more analytical than he might have wished, but he understood, and even though he said, "Charlotte, are you with me?" and she said, "I'm with you," he knew she wasn't. There was a small noise in her throat as she pressed closer. He smoothed and touched and searched her body as if he'd never seen a woman before, and he kissed her and kissed her, all different kinds of kisses that would have embarrassed her beyond words just a few weeks ago.

Making love had a sound, she noticed, of skin brushing like the meadow grass that rubbed in the marsh. She always thought nature never repeated itself, not a leaf, not a cloud, not a snowflake. But it was a myth. To her surprise he was smiling when he aligned himself over her, and this time she didn't pull away. She was as ready as she could be, but she stepped outside herself at that moment. And though she found pleasure in his silent pleasure, she was sure he was disappointed. They lay next to each other under the covers. He must have been reading her mind, because he moved close and said in her ear, "Stop worrying. It's just the beginning. I know what I'm doing." Her inchoate attempt to respond had touched him deeply because he knew something was making her anxious. As consummations went, this had rather missed the mark, but he'd have to wait and see.

When the first of the sun slipped over the edge of his bedroom window, Charlotte got up to pull the shades and got back in bed, loving the way Brian pulled her into him without even opening his eyes, as if her being in his bed was the most natural thing in the world. She had to believe and they slept lightly through the morning, although so powerful and erotic and forbidden were their feelings, that for each the opening presence of the other transcended all else and they found only the thin sleep of people who have come together after denying and pretending and waiting. The scent of each other's skin, the warmth underneath, and the curious areas of cool when they shifted positions—the touch of a shoulder, the slide of a calf—was enough to wake them. They slept, woke, slept, woke, reassuring each other that each was there and would not leave and this was more than a dream.

A Hint of Trouble

TUESDAY AFTERNOON BRIAN went to Gristede's to get English muffins and milk for Charlotte, and at the checkout he saw a woman he'd seen at Haddam on a tour with Margaret Chase. To his surprise, the woman started to talk.

"Aren't you the English teacher at Haddam?"

"Yes."

"My daughter's starting the seventh grade this fall. Her name is Linda Ramsey. Will you be her teacher?"

"I teach the upper school."

She looked at him oddly and asked, "Don't you live on Flanders Point?"

"Yes."

"Did you have Charlotte Delafield in your class?"

"I did." Brian felt an unpleasant adrenaline rush.

"What a small world. She was looking after my children just two days ago." Mrs. Ramsey was piling cans of dog food on the counter. "You don't know where she is, do you?"

"She has a job in the city, I think."

"Yes, but it seems she's not there," she said, rather pointedly, he thought.

"Oh?" said Brian.

"She never showed up. Her father called last night. I reminded him she was in Washington. But he called me back half an hour later and said she wasn't there either."

"Really . . . " said Brian.

"I feel terrible. So does Margaret Chase. And I didn't actually see Charlotte get on the train."

Brian felt as if the floor was suddenly moving. "I thought Margaret Chase was in Ohio."

"She's back. I gather Charlotte's disappeared before."

"Well, she'll turn up, I'm sure. Those seniors are independent. Nice to meet you," he said, picking up his groceries and acting busy. Hadn't Charlotte made some sort of excuse to her father? Surely she wouldn't be so cavalier. Brian knew he should tell Charlotte right away, even though she'd never feel free with him if she had to start worrying about her father breathing down her neck.

And the first thing Brian said when he got back was, "I saw Mrs. Ramsey at the store. I think your father is looking for you."

"I've taken care of it, so let's not think about that now."

"But he . . . "

She put her fingers on his lips. "I don't want *you* to think about it either."

"But he knows you're missing."

"I told him I was going home. He thinks I'm there. He told me once nothing would ever be important enough to make him speak to my mother and he *never* calls our house. He writes nasty notes and if he writes, by the time she gets it, I'll be in New York with him. He's expecting me Thursday."

Brian looked at her, more than a little concerned but he said no more.

The Most Natural Thing

WHEN CHARLOTTE HAD called her father to postpone the interview he was put out, but then when he called the Ramseys' and she was gone he was angry and suspicious. Before he called Charlotte's mother, he called Boston information and got the phone number for Brian Parton. He hesitated for a minute, but the thought that they'd lived a mile from each other all year urged him on. He dialed the number and said, "Mr. Parton, please," and the male voice on the other end said, "He won't be back for another week. You might reach him at his place in Connecticut. Do you want the number?"

Jack wrote it down and sat thinking, That son of a bitch, if he's shacking up with my daughter, I'll kill him. But he called Washington to be sure. Charlotte's mother answered and Jack didn't bother to say hello. He was already blaming her. "Is Charlotte home?"

"I thought she was in New York with you."

"No."

"Then where is she?"

"I'm surprised you ask, but I have a pretty good idea. If I'm right, I'll let you know. If you'd taken the time to come to graduation," said Jack with a sneer, "you'd know the trouble she was headed for. Of course, you'd probably think it was wonderful—just like the movies."

"What are you talking about?"

"Use your limited imagination, and perhaps you'll figure it out." He said no more.

· · ·

Charlotte got up while Brian was at the store. She sat out on the terrace steps in her pajamas and waited for him while she studied the construction. There was a huge steam shovel now. On the roof of the old house that was being torn down were three tall, fair-faired men who looked like Vikings. When the sun was high they stripped off their shirts and tied them around their hips. Bending at the waist, their odd, lug-soled shoes gripped the shingles and their hands in leather gloves used crowbars. They removed the old shingles with a muscular rhythm, prying, ripping, pulling, tossing and never looking up as the sound of the sliding shingles slapped onto a growing pile on the ground. They spoke another language. Brian said it was Polish. New groups of men came and stood and stared and pointed and walked the site in their ties and shirt-sleeves. Charlotte called them pod-men because they seemed to hatch like different species of insects—contractors, carpenters, phone men, stonemasons, foremen, and probably the owners, too. But the intrusion was noisy, nerve-wracking, and infuriating. Charlotte wanted to roam the Point and now they couldn't.

They had an early supper on the Armbrusters' beach and the cove wind died and Flanders Point lay soporific as a sleepy cow, the spring tide creeping in. Charlotte and Brian went in and returned to the sofa. Brian had noted the curious way they measured their time by their change of locations in the tiny piece of space they shared, and they'd both felt an immediate and sentimental attachment to his sofa, as if it were their mooring. Brian thought he should try again to tell her that her father had called Mrs. Ramsey, but he put if off because Charlotte put on one of his T-shirts, lay down on top of him, her head under his chin, and said sweetly, "We're joined now. You're my rock and my tree and your roots are in me," and with a happy smile she fell asleep on him. No woman had ever fallen asleep on top of him, and for the first time he felt how different the very bones of a woman were. Her bones just didn't feel as if they were meant for battle. They were meant for love, and he lay in silence, enjoying the weight of her limbs. She must have slept for twenty minutes before she woke up and slid off him, embarrassed. "I'm not bored, I promise," she said.

"Don't worry. I love it."

She got up and looked out the back windows. The water reflected the hot, white, burning clouds and crackled light filled the air. She asked, "Do you remember that day I did that bit with the cherries during the play?"

"I think it was the day I started to love you, though I didn't know it."

"But you were so mean that day."

"I was fending you off."

"Was I so close?"

"It wasn't that." And he thought a minute and said, "You revealed myself to me. That I was a good teacher. That maybe I was worth loving and there was a breath of possibility."

"Possibility with me?"

"Well, no, not then. I had no idea of that yet. You know, Charlotte, we should talk about what's ahead."

"Tomorrow." She opened the windows wide and they lay on the bed and listened to the contractors' trucks driving away. It was after four. They talked quietly and Brian told her about his mother and how she'd died and the carnelian ring. Charlotte touched him with light fingers while she listened and he touched her while he talked, as if both of them understood their hands knew another language. Soon. Any minute, he would make love to Charlotte the way he wanted. His way. Not sticking to basics. He turned to her. "What are we going to do if I fall in love with you?" he said.

"Now who's fending who off?" she muttered and turned her back on him, hurt and stunned.

"I'm not," he said. There was an awkward pause. "But I don't know if my feelings can meet your expectations."

"Expectations? What makes you think the class valedictorian has any expectations?"

He grabbed her shoulder and pulled her around to face him. "Stop it. I didn't mean it the way it sounded."

"A man who has as much to do with words as you do knows how things are going to sound," and she sat straight up. He reached up to pull her back but she tossed his arms away as if she was flinging off wet, dirty clothes and walked into the living room.

"You're such a hothead. Let me explain," he said.

She put her hand out and her voice broke. "If you say another word I'll walk out the door."

He didn't have the heart for this. He sat at his desk. The air outside rattled and clicked with small disturbances, and the evening drifted down in a sudden spring chill. The apartment was full of long sighs, footsteps, books opening and closing. Somewhere far off Brian heard a voice calling, maybe a mother calling in her children—maybe Mrs. Ramsey. "Charlotte, the apartment's too small for two people who aren't speaking." She didn't answer.

Brian kept looking over at her as if nothing was wrong and she went into the kitchen to get away. There was a loaf of French bread and green apples and a dark green bottle of wine, which she picked up and tried to open. Brian's chair scraped backward, and he came in without a word, took the bottle, used some small instrument to pull out the cork, poured a glass, and handed it to her. He poured himself some wine, too, tore off a piece of bread, and went back to his desk. Charlotte stood alone in the kitchen. She didn't like wine but the glass felt good on her lips and the wine was white and cool with a soft green fruity taste. She drank it down and went into the bathroom and filled the tub, soaking until she itched. But nothing helped. Then in her pajamas, she returned to the sofa and lay with her back to Brian, still trapped in the small prison she'd locked herself in.

"If you're trying to get my attention, you have it," he said, almost at the point of laughter. He knew something was happening that had little to do with him. He was not the extremist—she was. So he got up and lay across his bed on his stomach and listened for the night sounds. He loved the way Charlotte knew nature. She could tell how hard the wind was blowing in the lonely marshes by how deeply it bent the cord-grass. Whitecaps in the cove appeared at thirteen knots. Rabbits could scream. In the wild meadows trees with odd trunks were strangled by their roots.

Just then, the dry lightning of an impotent storm flicked the sky. He was patient; he felt as if she was calling him and his passion grew.

There were small thrashing sounds from the sofa, then steps, and suddenly she was at the bed looking down at him.

"Will you stop wearing those darn pajamas?" he said and pulled her down next to him on the bed. And with this she hid her face in his chest and said, "Brian, what am I doing? Why do I hurt so much when I'm happy . . . even here, now, with you? Oh, God, Brian, help me." And she started to cry without a sound. He loved the way she said his name again and again, even though he was right next to her. He couldn't remember anyone calling his name with such desire and such pain. Why did he so like the sound of her pain? He held on to her and watched the hands on the clock. She cried so long. Except for once, he'd never cried for more than thirty seconds. When she stopped at last, sniffing, spent, she said, "The last thing I expected to do was cry in your arms."

"I can handle it."

"Why would you want to?"

"I don't know, but I do."

"I'm so tired. It must be the wine," she said. "Will you think I'm fending you off if we just go to sleep?"

"No, no. Lord, I never should have used the words . . . but still, no sleeping in pajamas."

She took them off and got under the covers quickly, feeling shy for the first time. He paused, pulling hard to get out the next sentence. "I'm sorry if I hurt you. We're both too sensitive," and he was free. "You can sleep but I'm going to kiss you in your sleep."

"Okay." She sighed. He began to kiss her shoulders with light, careful kisses, and he knew she wasn't going to fall asleep, not with the new direction he was taking. When she understood his intent and where his lips were going, her startled breath rushed deep, and she tried to draw him back up but he didn't think she meant it. He pulled her hands away so he could go where he wanted, and then her hands were on his hair, and he could hear her breathing as she moved with him and he felt something had broken in her, something that had to break, something that had owned her and held her too hard. This time he wouldn't leave her behind and, later, when they were making love, and she seemed to be with him in a way that Ovid would approve of, but she still held off, he fell back on what he knew best. He whispered words.

"Let go, Charlotte, let go. It's a kind of surrender."

"To what, to who?" and she started to move away.

"To yourself, to yourself and to me," he said as he held her, "to me, to me." He felt a shock in his heart as she held him hard, trusting with a soft, falling sound that reminded him a little of her owl. Listening to her, he made no sound of his own because he was overwhelmed. When they breathed quietly again he was surprised to find his eyes were wet, and he dropped his arm over his face so she wouldn't see.

Another minute passed and she whispered, "Brian, I don't know what to say. That was amazing."

"Yes, it was."

"I never knew about that. I had no idea."

"I know."

"I felt as if you loved me."

All he could manage was a small nod.

"You shouldn't," she said. "I'm not good."

"Yes, you are."

"I kick dogs in the face."

"So do I."

"I had a passion for my brother."

Her brother, too, he thought to himself. "So?"

"I'm pigeon-toed and my sister says I have winter in my heart."

"We all have winter for our siblings sometimes, so quit the negatives." He turned and pulled her into him. She pressed her back against his chest, and he put his arm around her. At last, he thought. She started to giggle.

"What is it?" he said, glad the tears were over.

"I don't want you to think I'm weird."

"I already think it. So what now?"

"I can't sleep this way. I feel these little pings. I think it's your chest hairs pinging on my back." He started to laugh. "No, really. Every time you breathe your chest hairs move and they ping me."

All smiles, he turned on his back. "Are you always this much trouble?" She laughed and he said, "Why don't you arrange us to your liking?" She sat up and turned him on his side, running her hand down his spine. "You have a wonderful back. It tugs at the seams of your jackets, you know." She lay behind him, glued herself, bonding, and said, "That's better, and now good night."

Like a silk cloak over his skin, like summer water spilling over him, warm and liquid she pressed close, her legs bent into the hollow behind his knees. "Are you sure it's better?" he asked.

"Yes . . ."

"Then go to sleep," he said, then turned: "Wait. Let's get this right. I want to hold you. Here, slide back to me. Put the sheet over your back so you won't get pinged." Quiet returned to the room and Brian was at peace, but Charlotte was overcome. He wanted to hold her. He said the very words.

Suddenly he asked, "Charlotte, why did you smash the piano?"

"Because I couldn't stand the humiliation."

"That's what I thought."

"Sshhh," she said. The night was cool and dry, and if they hadn't been so absorbed in each other they would have seen the moon rise such a bright orange it seemed a sister of the sun. More important, they would have heard the murmuring sound of a car turning into the driveway and backing out again, not once, but twice.

At one point, Brian woke up. All he heard was Charlotte breathing next to him and he felt a peace that he couldn't recall feeling before. Not with anyone. Not ever. This relationship, moral or immoral, exploitation, sexploitation, it was none of these no matter what anyone claimed. It was love, ontologically pure, free of guilt, devoid of shame, and, at that moment at least, Charlotte felt like the answer. But Brian was not one to be caught in the thrall of emotion for very long, and before even a few minutes passed, he understood that this love, these hours, so out of time, so disconnected from their daily context were connected to everything, the webwork beyond the bedroom. They could never survive this way, out of their context. The question remained if they could survive in it, if their separate lives could ever adhere. The idyll was overdue for interruption, maybe more than one.

Blasting at the Site

CHARLOTTE WOKE UP early Wednesday ready to put on "Susie Q" and dance the jitterbug with him, but before she could do either they heard an immense blast outside. The venetian blinds rattled and the floor shook. It reminded Brian of the shelling he used to hear in the war. Charlotte ran to the window. There were loud shouts and two men running across the road.

"Brian, something's wrong."

He hurried over and saw one of the stocky stonemasons running up the driveway.

"Charlotte, get dressed quick. There must have been an accident."

He pulled on his shirt and pants and grabbed the Armbrusters' keys. "Stay here." He started down the steps. When the worker reached Brian he said, "A man is hurt . . . his leg is crushed very bad under a rock."

Brian said, "Follow me." He rushed into the Armbrusters' kitchen and called the police, then he and the workman ran back to the site. There were jagged pieces of rock everywhere and Brian asked, "Is the foreman here, an engineer, anyone?"

"Not yet."

The man's leg was under a large piece of boulder that had split off from an even larger one. "How did this happen?"

"I don't know. We covered the charge."

The injured man was propped on his elbow, shivering. He fell back. "C'mon," said Brian, "let's move the damn rock." All four men took positions and carefully lifted and rotated it aside. When Brian saw the leg he took a deep breath. The man had been working in shorts. The knee was crushed and the lower leg looked like red and white jam. There were pieces of bone in the flesh. Blood was pumping out. "Where's your first aid?"

One of the men said, "I don't know."

"Go look. You . . . do you have a small rope?" Rope for a tourniquet. This was desperate, he thought. He leaned over the man. "What's your name?"

"Roman."

"Roman, we have to stop the bleeding. There's an ambulance on the way. You'll be all right." He turned to the man who'd gone to get rope. "Hurry it up!" And the man reappeared with thick hemp rope. "Jesus! This is no good." Brian took off his shirt and twisted it into a cloth coil. "Roman, I'm going to have to move the leg a little. It's going to hurt like hell. Get a grip." When he lifted the leg the man screamed and passed out. Brian reached slowly around the uninjured part of the leg, and with his other hand pulled his shirt under and tied it tightly. The other three men were transfixed. "Want to get me a blanket, please?" said Brian.

They looked at each other. "No blanket here."

"What kind of an outfit is this?" said Brian. "Stay here. I'll go get one." He ran back to the apartment, where Charlotte was waiting. "What happened?" she said.

"One of the men has a crushed leg. Stay here, okay?"

"But—"

"Look, if you're there when the ambulance comes, your name will end up in the report."

He took a blanket off the bed and ran back down. Charlotte followed.

He covered the man and said to the workers, "I don't know how long the ambulance will be, but every few minutes we have to release the tourniquet or he'll lose the leg." Brian didn't think this leg could be saved, but he kept his thoughts to himself. He'd seen miracles before. When he looked up there was a couple hurrying down the road toward them and, behind them, a black sedan. Suddenly he noticed Charlotte, cold and white as the sky, staring at the blanket where it covered the man's leg. "Excuse me a second," he said to the workmen.

He took her by the arm and walked her quickly away. "Charlotte, have you lost your senses? What are you doing down here?"

"I'm sorry. I'm good in a crisis. I want to help."

He walked across the road with her, looking over his shoulder in the direction where the ambulance would come from. There was a man in the black sedan that had moved up next to the fence on Nathan Hale Road. Brian was about to signal to the driver when it backed slowly away. "Well, thanks for the help," he muttered and turned back to Charlotte. "Look, there's nothing you can do. Someone may know who you are and all hell will break loose. Go back in. I won't be long."

"Okay, okay." She ran back to the house.

But when the ambulance arrived, to Brian's annoyance they asked him to come to the hospital to help them fill out a detailed report.

The phone was ringing when Charlotte walked in, but she ran to the bathroom and threw up in one heave. She'd never seen anything like that man's leg. How could any doctor repair it? Putting on her bathing suit she ran down to the Armbrusters' beach. She'd swim laps in the icy water the way Brian did, but as she swam back and forth thinking the exertion would warm her, instead she found the cold sapped her strength. Growing stiff and weaker she pulled in toward the shore and walked up the beach, out of breath and shivering. She took a warm bath, and her thoughts turned back to Mr. Macready in the thatch cottage. Since she'd arrived at Brian's she'd felt the nine seconds pushing around inside with a kind of dark, insistent re-presence. When the dynamite shook the earth it was as if the secret dislodged, and now it heaved up again, bigger than before. Maybe she should tell Brian. He seemed to take everything in stride. But this was no small thing. No, she decided. Now is not the time. Maybe never. He doesn't have to know everything. It's enough to love him.

Things Have to Be Told

WHEN BRIAN GOT back, to his surprise Charlotte was asleep on the sofa. She'd forgotten to let the water out of the tub, so he soaked in the cold water and went over the event. None of the workmen had said a word about her. Neither had the couple. Why would anyone think anything? Certain they were still safe, he slept the rest of the morning away, the first deep sleep since Charlotte had come. It was noon when he woke. He pulled the cotton blanket off his bed and went over to cover Charlotte. She was wearing one of his T-shirts and it looked better on her than it did on him. He watched her a minute. One of the things he loved was the way she loved him, and he wasn't sure this was fair. Her eyes opened. "Keep sleeping," he said.

"I don't want to miss anything."

"You won't," and he arranged the blanket around her neck.

She smiled. "Are you tucking me in?"

"If you're like me, you'll nap better with a cover." Her eyes suddenly took on a look of distant purpose and she looked down at the blanket. "What is it?" he asked.

"I just remembered something," she said slowly. "Brian—pull the blanket down to my hips, really slow."

He did and she sat up. "That's it. I knew there was something else."

"What are you talking about?"

With her voice so low he could hardly hear, she said, "I need your help with something."

"What?"

She got up and paced around, restless, anxious. He was so open to her now. Would he close off if he knew?

"Charlotte, what is it?"

"I'm afraid of what you'll think. Let's talk in the Armbrusters' library."

Brian got his keys and they walked over to the empty mansion, and while she sat on an oversize leather sofa in the library, he stood. "What?"

"Do you remember when I came to your house last winter and why?"

"Yes."

"And do you remember when I was out of school for ten days?" He nodded. "Something had happened to me."

Now he started to pace. "I knew it, I just knew it."

"What did you know?"

"That something was wrong and you weren't telling."

"I'm telling now." He stopped pacing and she said quietly, "There was a rape. Mr. Macready assaulted me."

His expression of vindication vanished. "Hol-y Christ," he whispered. "That bastard. I'll kill him. I'll kill him with my bare hands." Brian could see his thumbs on the man's windpipe, pressing, and his anger spit about inside like a wire short-circuiting, but as his thoughts sprayed about he was also amazed, just amazed that she could have come to his bed so soon. "You didn't tell anyone?"

"The doctor who treated me. I couldn't fool him and I know he told Mrs. Chase."

"What did she do?"

"Nothing."

"Nothing! This woman is no friend."

"But think of the scandal—the shame, you know."

"No, I don't know," he said. "What's the matter with her?" He started to get up.

"Don't you see?" She grabbed his arm. "Listen to me, Brian. I didn't want to tell. It was my decision. It's no one's business. When it happened, Mr. Macready told me I was asking for it. I guess I believed him."

"Bull." Brian found her attitude shocking. "I should think you'd want revenge. If not revenge—justice, if there's any difference." But she said nothing. "How many times?"

"God, only once! He found me asleep in that cottage." She sat back and Brian shook his head. "What are you thinking?"

"It explains a lot," he said.

"What does it explain?"

But he didn't answer. Finally he said, "Charlotte, this is not a thing to swallow alone. It's poison."

"I know, but you were my antidote. In the pages of your E. E. Cummings—the poems you marked, you came and talked to me. I'm here. Look at me. It was your . . . " she couldn't say *love* " . . . your caring."

"If that's what you subsisted on it's very little," he scoffed. "I don't understand why you didn't at least tell Mrs. Macready. There's no need to martyr yourself."

"But it didn't happen when I lived there, and anyway, I did tell her—later. Don't you see. When I left, I told Mrs. Macready about the way he abused Peter. She must have told her husband what I said. Maybe this was his sick justice on me. His punishment. But I didn't provoke him. He trespassed before *anything*, before I ever saw Peter's bruises."

"Wait, I don't follow you. What's the thing you remembered?"

"Last fall, after you brought me in from the fog, I was in bed asleep and Mr. Macready was in my room. He pulled down the covers. He was looking at me. I'd forgotten." Charlotte noticed Brian blush, something he hadn't done since she'd gotten there. "As long as I thought it was my fault, how could I tell you? But it wasn't, not even a little." Charlotte wondered why Brian looked at her with such pleasure.

Maybe this was all an eighteen-year-old could do, he thought, and he said, "And you didn't tell your mother because she would have gone to court?"

"Yes. But Mrs. Macready—how can a woman stay with a man knowing such a thing?"

"I don't know, but it never fails to amaze me what people are capable of."

"I guess you're right." But Charlotte saw something else. Nothing earth-shattering, but—how much little things count. The power of seemingly small acts of no significance, like the thoughtful way Brian had brought her a cover on the sofa. A simple act of taking care, but it was no small thing. It carried the weight of love, and that love had called out her secret.

Phone Calls and Lies

T HEY WALKED BACK to Brian's and she said, "What are you thinking?"

"Don't you think we should deal with your father knowing you're missing? I keep thinking about him calling Mrs. Ramsey and being told that you'd gone home."

"That's what I asked her to say. But I told you, he never calls home."

"He did this time according to Mrs. Ramsey."

"What? Why didn't you tell me?"

Brian stopped and turned to her. "I tried, but you said he'd never do that."

"Oh God—then I really am 'missing' as you say. Damn, if he starts to fixate, we could have a problem. Come on. I'm going to call my mother at work right away. She trusts me. She'll be at lunch but I'll leave the number and say I'm at Theo's."

"I don't get it. What's the point now?"

"You'll see, but I'm going to have to lie in front of you."

"I hope so."

She called Washington and left the number with her mother's secretary. "Please tell her to call me as soon as she gets back from lunch. Tell her I'm at my friend Theo's." Charlotte turned to Brian. "When my mother calls here and talks to me, I'll be 'found,' *and* we'll be safe. She doesn't even know Theo's last name. But I should answer the phone."

"I sure hope this works," said Brian. "I'm glad now I never got around to listing my number." They had a half an hour to wait for

Charlotte's mother to call. Charlotte was confident, Brian uneasy, and he said, "I can't stand this waiting. I have to sort my socks."

"Where's the Plato? I'll read some more *Symposium,*" said Charlotte, amused, and Brian busied himself rearranging his top bureau drawer. Charlotte kept looking over at him. Plato's discourse on love couldn't compete with Brian sorting his socks. He looked about eighteen years old, shirtless, with wrinkled chinos and bare feet as he examined every pair of socks for holes, rolled them up, arranged the sock balls by color, and put them back as if he were doing a jigsaw puzzle. It was a wonder to Charlotte and she was not reading a word of Plato. "Should I help you clean up?"

"After we get this settled."

Then he went to the closet and took out two pairs of brown shoes, two black leather moccasins, white bucks, tan loafers, black dress shoes like her father's, and lined them up on the coffee table. He dumped shoe polish, rags, brushes, and saddle soap on the floor in front of him. Charlotte watched him put polish on all the shoes, line them up again like a drill sergeant, and start brushing back and forth with great vigor, shoe after shoe, oblivious to the world. A man polishing his shoes struck her as a very sweet thing. She'd never seen such a performance.

The phone rang at two-thirty. Always late, thought Charlotte and picked up the phone. "Hi, Mom." Then she froze. "Just a minute." She recognized the voice of Margaret Chase and she handed the phone to Brian with a look of horror.

She listened to him saying calmly, as if he lied every day, "My niece from Boston." There was a pause and Brian looked over at Charlotte. "She's thirteen, why?" There was another pause and, "Well, some thirteen-year-olds look eighteen. . . . No, there was an accident across the road." Charlotte covered her face. Then he said, "Yes, I heard she was AWOL from a woman in the grocery store but I haven't any idea." Then he added an impatient "Very well," and hung up. They stared at each other. "Did it sound believable?" said Brian.

"I don't know. Do you think she recognized my voice?"

"No, she's suspicious, but you'd never be expecting a call from 'Mom.'"

The phone rang and they looked at each other in a panic. "It's got to be my mother!" And it was. Charlotte told her mother she was going to her father's Thursday and her mother reminded her to always call and let her know where she was. Charlotte was full of apologies. It was fine.

But Brian said, "This is not good. I keep thinking what you told me about your father. Do you think it's wise to move in with him?"

"Of course. I like New York and I'll be able to come see you on weekends."

"How? You told me he'd kill us both."

"He only threatens to kill people. He never does."

And the phone rang again. "What the hell . . . " said Brian. They didn't answer. Then it rang again. "Damn," said Brian and picked up the phone. "Hello . . . " and he stiffened and mouthed the words "your father" to Charlotte.

"Why on earth have you called *me*?" said Brian. And then, "How dare you say such a thing," and he hung up.

"What did he say?" said Charlotte.

"He said, 'Who are you shacking up with . . . my pretty daughter?' "

"What?" Charlotte shrieked and jumped up. "He's just guessing. My father has a foul mouth." She was abject, and fearful for Brian. "But no one's going to understand, are they?"

"No."

"He knows where you live."

"He does?"

Charlotte grimaced. "We had lunch after graduation and we were talking about Flanders Point. I mentioned the Armbrusters. He used to know them. How could I have known?"

"He also said he'd been waiting for a chance to load his German pistol."

"Him and his famous German pistol. I don't think he even has one anymore," muttered Charlotte, but she was uneasy just the same.

Brian sat at his desk, worried. "Maybe you shouldn't take the job on Wall Street. I think you should go home tomorrow morning, first thing, I can even drive you—and stay away from him. A job is just a job. I think a man who could say what he did to me is out of control." Charlotte sat like a lump. "I wonder if it's even safe for you to stay here tonight. What if he shows up?"

"He doesn't have a car, but . . . " She didn't tell him he drove a friend's car at graduation.

Brian said, "What?"

"I'm thinking," she said. "He has certain habits. His work *always* comes first. He spent too many years out of work to jeopardize his career for anyone, least of all me. He'll go home and have a couple of drinks before supper, and then he'll probably forget and fall asleep. God, this is like a stupid soap opera. Indignant father comes to save innocent daughter . . . "

"From cradle robber," muttered Brian.

"Don't you dare say that. I'm responsible for myself."

"Yes, but you can't trust this world, Charlotte. We're up for question. We've broken powerful rules that are hard in place and we may fall."

"The only place we're falling is in love, I hope," she said. "Isn't this destiny?"

"No, this is a breakout."

"Destiny is always a breakout." But suddenly scared she said, "I'm surprised at you. You're always so sure of everything. But I'm sorry, the outside world has no veto power over us."

He sighed and slumped behind his desk. "I'm an imperfect believer."

"What does that mean?"

"There's going to be big problems."

"But at least the problems are worthy of us."

He looked up, hinting at a smile. "Yes. But we won't sleep here tonight."

"Where then?"

"We'll sleep in one of the Armbrusters' guest rooms," he said.

She was shaking her head in disagreement. "It's *your* bed I love."

He smiled in spite of himself. "Come here." She walked over and he put her on his lap. He loved it when she started to kiss him tenderly, and touch his face, but he said, "Charlotte, stop. Listen to me. This is serious. You're eighteen. You were my student. That may not mean much or it may mean a great deal. Lord knows I never expected you and you may be the best thing that's ever happened to me, but there's a big difference. I'm the *only* thing that's ever happened to you."

"Can't the first be right? Don't we fit really well?"

"We have to have time. We have to let our feelings grow, accept separations, endure the tests that lie ahead."

"I know," she said. She loved it when he talked to her this way. She wanted his words as much as his kisses. Men's words, so important but so seldom coming—her silent brother, her silent father, her silent lover, who was no longer silent. "I know," she repeated. She put her hand over Brian's heart and then she climbed off his lap and knelt next to him so she could put her ear against his chest. She listened quietly to the sound of her lover's heart beating—Brian's heart.

Brian's Fantasy

After the confusions, it seemed as if, to comfort Brian and Charlotte, the late afternoon turned slow and sleepy on Flanders Point. Deceptively so. The wind died and birds left the open air. Monarch butterflies sought a spot of shade, woodchucks slept in their tunnels, bees returned to the hive, ducks drifted aimlessly on the sound; even the starlings were silent, and only a few errant cicadas hummed in the trees. But Brian was churning. The night that approached stretched ahead, cool and clear, perfect for lovers, idyllic. But how could he make love to her now, knowing what Mr. Macready had done? He would have preferred not to know so soon, not to know the man, nor the place—easier to shut out the awful scene that haunted his imagination. Would he be impotent? "I'm going for a walk," he said to Charlotte.

"Okay." He knew she understood and he set out. Trouble seemed to follow her around. He knew that wasn't fair, but he hadn't counted on an irate father and now this. The violence of rape and the power of love could hardly occupy the same space, but suddenly they intersected and the odd result was new guilt. What if someone accused him of the same? He walked over to the site and a rat appeared, ran along the new foundation, and disappeared. Charlotte would see a white heron; what did he get? A rat. Well, walking was Charlotte's thing—it didn't work for Brian. He had to enter his own healing place, and when he got back he said, "Let's go swimming before the day is gone. We have to make every minute count." They went down to the beach but the water was still too cold for Charlotte and she sat on the blanket, noticing that he swam faster, harder than usual. What could she do to clear away the images that must be lodged in his mind? That she had put there. Poetry couldn't help her now. When Brian came back up he said, "Charlotte, you never swim."

"It's too cold. Besides, I like to watch you."

"How boring."

"No. Swimmers need joints that line up perfectly. Yours do. It's classic."

He took her hand. "Come on. Swim with me." She got up.

With his usual crazy sprint he was submerged in three seconds. Charlotte walked in slowly, tortured herself, with her arms held oddly above the water. He came over. "Let's do laps. C'mon, it'll warm you up."

"Okay. No race, though," she said.

"No, but serious swimming." They each swam at their own pace between the jetties and she forgot the cold. Brian saw that she was a strong swimmer, who switched strokes every lap. They passed back and forth, and suddenly she said, "Brian, here!" and he laughed. She'd just tossed him her bathing suit. Turning fast, he caught hold of her foot and pulled her back. "This is your element, too, I see," he said, taking his suit off, too. He could see her treading water under the surface, trying to stay warm. "That's a very nice sight." He stood in shoulder-high water and she put her arms around his chest and her legs around his hips as if he were a lamppost. "Let's go in," he said, with a broad smile.

"Have you got my suit?" she asked.

"I'll take it up with me."

She smiled. "Oh no, you don't. It's going right back on."

And forgetting himself, he said, "No, wait, wait—ever since you came I've had this image in my mind. That I'd be waiting on the beach, and you'd come out of the water—with nothing on—and walk toward me, like some long-lost daughter of Aphrodite or something. I've thought of it a lot."

"Constantly and instantly?" she said with a smile.

"What?"

"Never mind . . . "

"Will you do it?" he said, encouraged by the smile.

"Brian, I can't believe you want me to do these rude things . . . "

"Oh, but what's rude in public is usually wonderful in private," he said.

She faltered, looking around, not sure if she was touched or insulted. "What if someone saw? I'd be so ashamed."

"The Greeks believed that if no one sees, there is no shame. No one's here."

"I don't know," she said, "an imagined viewer is just as bad."

Surprised he said, "I thought women liked to be looked at."

"All done up, not all undone." But his request was seeping through her modesty like water flowing under a door, seeping in, spreading everywhere.

"Charlotte," he said. "Let me see you. Let me watch you. I don't think you have any idea how beautiful . . . how a man wants to look at a woman—freely, completely, slowly, not in a furtive rush, not concealing his pleasure, not only in bed. Can you give me that?"

She didn't answer and Brian thought she was being coy, but he'd taken her breath away and she couldn't speak. Finally she said, "The real you is much better than the person I invented." Her father was devious when he looked at women and it hardly seemed to give him pleasure. And here was Brian asking so earnestly. Men were *not* all alike, as Dana used to say. What a sad, impoverished view. A man could be open. A man could be romantic. A man could be honest with his need. Brian reminded her of her brother standing up in the bathtub, asking her to look at him that night when she hadn't had the courage to look.

Brian drifted and watched her. Squeezing water out of her hair with a twist, she said, "Yes, I can give you that." He smiled, a slow smile of understanding between them, and she didn't think she would ever forget the achievement of that smile. Carrying their suits, he started up the beach. "Brian . . . " He turned back and she said, "Actually, I kind of like the idea."

"I know."

"You better get back to that blanket or I'm going to lose my nerve." She watched him, thinking, What a wonderful thing, the body of a man . . . he's like a tree walking. . . . All year she'd been in love with loving him, and now she understood that it was sort of like loving herself. Now it was him she loved and there was nothing lonely in her ache anymore. It could be answered.

While he sat on the blanket, she swam laps to slow the thoughts that came like a meteor shower, a tumult of fragments too fast for her to catch. She didn't want the moment to end, and she also needed a little extra nerve to get herself up out of the water. The Macreadys' pictures in the linen closet were lewd—pleasantly lewd, but lewd nevertheless. But this wasn't lewd, and as she swam one more lap she thought of the lovemaking the night before, how no part of her had not been kissed. She turned to the beach.

Brian watched her come out of the water, shading his eyes from the sea's reflection so he could see clearly the sheer edges of water as her steps pushed ruffled swells ahead of her, and the water fell lower and lower like silk slipping down. With deep pleasure he saw that Ovid was wrong. Charlotte made no shy attempt to cover herself. She was unashamed. She even took her time—as if it gave her pleasure to please him. He wished the stretch of sand between them was a mile wide and he started to edge back farther. She saw him and smiled, and streams of water ran down her body, catching glints of light. When a cloud covered the sun, the sparkles of water vanished from her skin, the sea turned steel gray behind her, and light came from Charlotte, not the sun. She walked up the sand, and the water sheen shifted and moved over her body, drying in the wind, until the wind dropped abruptly as if startled into watching. And Brian stood and shook out the blanket, ignoring the sand flying around, reluctantly holding it out for her, intent on his vision, missing nothing. Charlotte looked down, surprised this could arouse her so, and when she looked back up, every muscle in his face was still, as if he was spellbound. Did he think she was giving him something? Didn't he realize what he had just given her? He'd reinvented her, as if she was a found treasure. But she kept it to herself. The power of his look was how unconscious he was of its power—a moment of male innocence is how she saw it, and it gave her new understanding. A small voice in the back of her mind remembered that Max used to say, "You're terminally naive about this stuff, Char . . . ," but she shut it off. She needed to find her own way, and she was entitled to it. She said to him lightly, "Do you know how I did that?"

He fussed with the blanket, embarrassed at his show of pleasure and mumbled, "Did I recognize Titania?"

"You see right through me, don't you?"

He didn't answer, but his mysterious smile was better than words. "Do you want to spread out the blanket," he asked, "and lie in the sun before we go up?"

Knowing he wanted to do the same thing she did, but unwilling to go that far on the beach, she shook her head.

"Okay," he said, and she clutched the blanket around her shoulders, ignoring the itchy wool. Coming to the beach crest not far from the house, they stepped into a fresh draft of wind and Brian wrapped his towel around his waist, and reached inside the blanket to hold her hand. Charlotte never expected these smaller gestures, more revealing, more loving, than sex.

If Charlotte had her way, this is where she would end the telling of her love story, where she could choose her ending, a simple ending with no hint of pain to come. But walking back up the beach Brian heard something that sounded like crumbling newspaper and he realized it was tires creeping slowly over the bluestone and then he heard the low growl of a motor and saw a black sedan inching up the driveway.

"Christ," he muttered. "We have company, Charlotte," and he almost fell over putting on his trunks.

"Should I disappear?" she said.

"Yes, into the Armbrusters'—quick!" They ran up the back terrace steps, and he opened the French doors. "Stay upstairs. Find some clothes." He tossed her bathing suit and warned, "Wait for me to come get you, even if it seems long. Don't answer the door no matter what." He went back out and said over his shoulder, "Does your father have a black sedan?"

She stopped, nervous. "He hasn't had a car for years." She disappeared.

But Brian had seen the car before, and he had a sinking feeling who was at the wheel—and he was right. It was Charlotte's father. Brian walked around the side of the Armbrusters', slipping the house keys into the pocket of his trunks. In his state of undress it was hard to have confidence. A hand grenade in his pocket would have been reassuring. He crossed the front terrace, and Mr. Delafield was standing in the causeway with his back to the house, staring at the construction site. He was wearing a gray seersucker suit and a straw boater. When he turned to Brian, his bow tie made it seem as if he'd come to pay a social call. He was striking, although his innocuous rimless glasses made his eyes look small and gleamy behind the thick lenses. Brian had noticed how nearsighted he was at graduation, but how could he have missed the deep vertical scar that appeared to bisect his forehead, as if he was a man with two minds? "Mr. Delafield?"

Charlotte's father looked at Brian as if Brian were an intruder. "Is Charlotte around?"

Brian stopped a few feet from him. "Charlotte?"

"That's what I said."

Brian offered a baffled, "No."

"Well, I spoke to her last night," said her father.

"Not here . . . "

"Yes, here."

Brian squinted, trying to size up the man. "If she said she was here it's not a very funny joke . . . so excuse me, Mr. Delafield, but your daughter is elsewhere." He turned and strode toward his apartment. To his surprise, Charlotte's father followed him—a bit unsteadily. Brian paused, turning. "Are you all right?"

"I'll just wait, if you don't mind." He was acting as if he thought the invitation was implied. It seemed an odd misreading to Brian.

Brian said pointedly, "Would you care for some coffee?" Mr. Delafield stared at him, momentarily confused, and Brian said, "What makes you think she's here?"

Again no answer. He just kept staring. "I'm sure you know, your daughter lived with the headmistress, Margaret Chase. She's probably there. It's the last Tudor house before the beach."

"I spoke with the headmistress yesterday. *Other* suggestions?"

Brian was curt. "No. If you'll excuse me." He expected the next move to be a fist swung in his direction, but Mr. Delafield said, "May I use your phone?"

Brian was stunned at Mr. Delafield's capitulation. His whole voice had changed. This man wasn't out of control, just obsessed. And rather sad.

"Why don't you just drive over? Mrs. Chase is there. It's two minutes."

"I'll call first if you can manage that," he said, now with pointed venom.

With Mr. Delafield a shaky step behind, Brian walked in praying there was nothing of Charlotte's lying around. There was. Her pajamas were on the unmade bed, her book bag was on the desk. Christ, he thought, it's all over. But Mr. Delafield went over to the phone, looked around confused, without noticing anything, and then he never even picked up the phone. He turned to leave. Outside the door Brian froze when he saw him head for the Armbrusters' front door and knock loudly.

Brian muttered in his head, "Don't move, Charlotte, don't move. It isn't me . . . just stay where you are."

But Mr. Delafield was so impatient that he didn't wait long enough for anyone to get to the door. Instead he turned and came back toward Brian. He said, "Let me tell you something . . . you. I'm good with a carving knife, very good, and I saw the way you looked at her. She's a sick and disturbed girl. No longer having a father and never having had a mother, she needs help. But not the kind of help you're giving her, my perverted friend."

Any distraction . . . "What do you mean, 'never having had a mother'?"

"Good lawyers make lousy mothers. Charlotte grew up like a weed on a roadside."

"Why didn't *you* take care of her?"

"It's *you* I'm going to take care of," he said. "I think she's been here, and you know where she is. She probably thinks this is romantic, just like her mother, just like in a grade-B movie. I, however, do not. If you get her in a jam, if you knock her up, or if I even catch you anywhere near her, I won't kill you—there's a fifty-dollar fine for that in this town, and I need my fifties. I have something nicer for you. As good as I am with my Sabatier, I'm even better with a razor. When I get finished, your face will be the bloodiest mess a plastic surgeon has ever tried to unscramble. And if they do unscramble it, I might just do it again. Your teaching days are over."

Neither frightened nor surprised, but amazed that the man's confusion still led him to the truth, Brian straightened and said, "I think you better leave."

Mr. Delafield stood straighter too, raised his chin to look down on someone taller, and said, "Nuts to you." He turned and went out the door.

Brian almost laughed in his face. "Nuts?" he said out loud. "Nuts?" But he was fascinated, and he stood at the door and watched Charlotte's father get in his car, start the motor, and back the car around fast. The motor let out a painful screech, as if perhaps he'd turned the ignition key again, forgetting the motor was already running. The car swerved and sped down the driveway kicking up bluestone dust, skidding a bit, hitting the rocks on one side. At the bottom, where the last two rocks were larger and higher, he seemed to deliberately drive over one. Sparks came from under the car as it careened dangerously, heaved up, and thumped down, hitting the second rock as well. A hubcap popped high into the air and landed in slow motion with a sharp clank and rolled down the road after the car, disappearing into the saltgrass. Brian's head dropped back, and he sighed. Talk about a scene from a grade-B movie . . . but even so, Brian's neck was tight as a drawn bow, and his skin was taut and damp. As he went to get Charlotte, she opened the Armbrusters' front door.

"I know what you said but I thought you were locked out."

Brian stepped inside with a disapproving look and closed the door. "Your father was here."

"I saw. What did he say?"

"He's on his way to Margaret Chase's."

"What for?"

"I think he was here the day the dynamite blew up that rock. I saw a black car down the road. I think he saw you."

"Oh no." Now Charlotte looked alarmed. "What should we do?"

"First, spend the night in this house, not mine. Just in case. Then get up early and make the trip to Washington."

"I think I should take the train."

"We'll see. I also think I should go over to Margaret Chase's by myself."

"While he's there?" she gasped.

"No. Later."

"Why?"

"To find out who knows what."

"I'm going to call home and see if I get any hints from my mother."

"Be careful."

"Don't worry. My mother is used to my father's paranoia. If he called her with angry accusations, she'd take it with a grain of salt." She paused. "Are you angry?" Brian didn't answer. "Do you regret what we've done?"

He studied her and felt a heavy sorrow approach that he knew would be with him for a long, long time. He put his arms around her. "Oh, Charlotte, I wish we'd thought it through better. This is my fault."

"Oh no, we're in this together." They went in.

Brian Outwits Margaret

Later, the Point lost its quiet and seemingly deserted state, and a vigorous wind swept in, bringing the threat of a line squall. Brian and Charlotte moved her few things to the Armbrusters', and after supper he drove to see Margaret Chase. He had no plan. He hadn't wanted to worry Charlotte, but Margaret had asked him to come. When he got there she was in her living room rushing to close the casement windows. She looked rumpled, as if she'd just gotten out of bed.

"When the rain drives in from the south," she said, "it always soaks the floor over here." He helped her crank the windows shut. And she twisted a towel and lay it along the sill. "This one leaks even when it's closed," she said sheepishly, but he felt how tense she was. Well, so was he.

"Sit down," she said. "There's a serious matter."

He sat on the edge of a deep leather chair, knowing his proclivity toward the taciturn was about to be tested sorely.

"It seems," she said, "my tenure as headmistress is about to crack wide open, and the school, my career and yours, may fall right into the abyss—something I'll prevent at any cost," she added and stopped again, expecting a query from him. There was none. "Charlotte's father was here this afternoon. He's still furious about Radcliffe's rejection, and by an unfortunate fluke of fate, when he asked them why Charlotte was turned down, some untrained staff member sent her entire admissions folder to him."

"Why unfortunate? We were all for her."

"Yes, but my recommendation included three words about Charlotte that in hindsight should have been taken out."

"What words?"

" 'At times inconsistent.' "

Brian winced. It could hardly have been an oversight. "So he's blaming you?"

"Well, yes, and for that, perhaps, we owe him," she said.

"We?"

"The school. But there's something more devastating." In the long, suspended pause that followed, Brian had time to wonder what words she'd choose, ready to react. "He says you've seduced his daughter."

"What! When?"

"Just. Did you?"

"How can you even ask? Of course not."

"He said he saw you with her."

"Where?"

"On Nathan Hale Road."

"He's lying. Or hallucinating."

"Why would he lie?" she snapped.

"To get back at you," he snapped right back. "Is that all?"

"Isn't that enough?"

"I mean, what else did he say?"

"He said if you aren't removed from the staff, he'll drag us into court for God knows what."

Brian ignored this and stood up, coolly putting his hands in his pockets as if he were in total control. "He came to my apartment this morning, you know. In fact, I sent him over here. He seemed rather disoriented to me. What did you tell him?"

"I said if it was true, you'd be out," but this new information rattled her.

"And?"

"Well, it seems to be his word against yours at the moment, but there's a real question about where Charlotte's been."

Brian stood up. "Why doesn't someone ask Charlotte where she was?"

"Is . . . She still hasn't turned up."

"Oh." Brian walked to the window and looked out. Should he admit it? He couldn't think of one good reason. But he could think of a way to save himself and maybe Haddam too, if he could handle it in just the right way. "I'm sorry, but I won't leave Haddam because of the canard of an unstable mind."

"I have the school to think about. I think you should resign."

And at that, Brian sat down and looked at Mrs. Chase in a way that made her want to shrivel from sight. Her prized English teacher looked like he knew something.

And Brian knew the weapon in his pocket was like a loaded gun but it didn't need bullets because he'd never have to use it. All he had to do was point it at Margaret Chase and she'd cave in. "What about the Haddam student who was raped when she was in your care, Margaret?" She sat up. "Charlotte was assaulted by her employer, Mr. Macready, your friend, I'm told. When you were told, you didn't do a thing."

"Did Charlotte tell you that?"

"It's not important, but how long have *you* known?"

Margaret said, "I thought it best to keep still to protect her. You would have done the same."

"Don't insult me. You, Margaret, have covered up a criminal offense. That's obstruction of justice. *You* put her in that house. Maybe that could even be construed as conspiracy or accessory, I don't know. I'm not a lawyer but Charlotte's mother certainly is," he said. "You let it pass to protect yourself because you know as well as I do that if it got out, even now, it would destroy Haddam quicker than any gossip about me."

Margaret knew she was trapped by this obscene confluence of events, but damnit, so was he, this man she felt such ardor for, and instead of fear at his revelation, she was angry. Now she couldn't fire him and he had the power. Minutes passed. Brian was amazed at how long she took. But he offered not one word. "Either way, then, the school is finished," she said with sly melodrama, "unless I can find a way to placate Mr. Delafield. Your denial won't mean a thing. He's convinced and he's out for your throat. Are you aware that Charlotte's father is the man who brought in John Colter's endowment?"

Brian was startled. "No, I wasn't."

"So you see, even if we don't think we owe him, it's understandable that *he* thinks we do."

Brian felt his edge dull a little. Finally he said, "There's a solution, you know, Margaret."

"What?"

"I'll get out of town, as they say—teach in England for a year at the school in Devon. Mr. Delafield doesn't know about Devon, does he?"

Margaret didn't answer.

He said, "A year will pass and it'll blow over."

She eyed him, savoring the fact that he'd be out of touch with Charlotte. That obscenity would blow over too. She said, "Done. I'll arrange it."

She didn't tell him that the teacher in Devon had been pleading for an exchange for two years. She wanted Brian to owe her because she equated what she'd done, ignoring the assault and botching Radcliffe, with what she suspected Brian of doing. And even better, Brian was showing no interest in "saving" Charlotte any more than she had.

Brian said, "I think you should know I've corresponded with the Devon teacher. Hazel Pierce gave me the address. The woman's very anxious to come here so don't think this evens the score." Margaret was silent. "There's one more thing. I want a house for the entire year, not just the school year."

"That is not a problem."

"And I want to bring a friend over during the vacations at Haddam's expense."

"Are you crazy?"

"Are you forgetting your position?" She turned away, furious. Brian hoped it looked like he was trying to save his job. He suspected that Margaret Chase knew about Charlotte but he also knew that Margaret's malice toward Charlotte and his love would never equate.

So it was decided. Now all he had to do was explain to Charlotte and get her off the Point and home safely before her father showed up again. *If* he showed up again. And before Margaret Chase saw her. Although as for that, he almost thought at this point he'd relish it. She couldn't touch him now.

One Last Night

B RIAN AND CHARLOTTE spent the night in one of the Armbrusters'
bedrooms, one with a double bed. They whispered in the dark and made
love. At every strange sound, Brian got up, went to the window, pulled
aside the cretonne curtains to look out and listen for cars. Their idyll
was shattered, but Charlotte's father's fury had drawn them closer and
they created a new one. By sleeping an hour, then waking up, talking
and dreaming, then going back to sleep again, tangled together and
drifting apart, they'd wake with a start, the inadvertent separation of
their bodies intolerable, and they'd embrace again. They seemed to
gain control of time, expanding it outward in a manner that seemed
otherworldly, as if they were spending many days and nights together
in that one night. At one point Charlotte said, "Brian, do you think a lot
of people who are married sleep together with nothing on?"

"Maybe."

"Every night?"

"Sure."

"I don't think so."

"Well, you're an innocent."

"Not anymore, but I'm glad if you think so." She loved the way he
squeezed her when she said it. "You like me, don't you?" she said.

"I surely do."

"Brian, I think sleeping in the same bed for a whole night—
undressing, lying down on soft pillows, getting under the covers, touching, feeling warm skin, sleeping, breathing, turning, snuggling, waking

with the one you love—is so intimate, so private, it's sexier than sex."

He smiled. "Just like a woman."

"You don't think so?"

"Sshhh. What's that?" They listened a minute. It was unmistakable—bluestone grinding under the wheels of a car. Brian jumped up and edged toward the window. "I don't believe it. It's him again!"

"You're kidding." She got up and tiptoed up behind him. "This is pathetic. Does he know we're in here?"

"How? Everything's dark, locked, and looks deserted. He can't know."

"But every other house is dark, locked, and looks deserted. That's how houses look at two in the morning."

"Hmmmm, good point."

"Your car—"

"He doesn't know my car. It's in the garage with the others." They saw a bobbing flashlight and stood back a little farther, not moving. They heard no footsteps, but did hear small tapping noises, the bell, then one bold, loud knock, doors being tried, windows too. Then it seemed a long time passed with no sound at all, until her father reappeared and Brian saw Mr. Delafield walk to the garage, shine the light into the garage door windows, pause, look around, passing his eyes over every window in the Armbruster house. He was searching and when his face turned up to the window where Brian and Charlotte watched, Brian had the eerie, heart-stopping feeling that Mr. Delafield knew exactly where in the house they were. Then Mr. Delafield lit a match and started to smoke as if he had all the time in the world. Brian stared at the shadowy outline of the man taking his time, his cigarette a moving bead of red. But even so, Brian half expected a bullet to come flying through the window.

Charlotte whispered, "I think he's enjoying every minute of this." Brian never moved and when Mr. Delafield finally drove slowly away, Brian collapsed on the bed and said, "I think you're right. He won't be back, though."

Brian reached over and drew her back to bed. "Charlotte, I was surprised about something. Your father doesn't seem dangerous. He's sort of sad."

"I never said he was dangerous . . . just a problem."

"I got the feeling that you were frightened of him."

"Not me. That's my mother. I could see the fear in her eyes and hear it in her breathing when he was drinking. And the nights when he came to get her out of my bed, she was terrified. My mother is not a submissive woman, but she was submissive then. I don't know. It's not important now."

"I think maybe it is important."

"What do you mean?"

"Nothing."

"Really, he doesn't scare me. You know what I did when I was thirteen? My brother and I were arguing in the house. And my father always got pissed off when we fought, and he heard my brother swearing at me and he went over and punched my brother in the stomach right in front of me. In the stomach! My brother ran upstairs, and you know what I did? I ran at my father and started hitting him and beating him. My mother had to pull me off. I kept screaming, 'You bastard, I hate you, I hate you.' "

"What did your father do?"

"Nothing. He just stood there and took it. Didn't say a word. Didn't even lift his arm to block my fists. But oh God, Brian, the vision of my brother bent over, stumbling up the stairs, his hands climbing ahead of his feet . . . Max was sobbing. Max. I'll never forget it. Every time I think of it I want to pound my father's face."

Brian believed she was sincere but he remained unconvinced: Charlotte could deny it, but she *was* afraid of her father and Brian saw that she hadn't learned her fear from anything her father did. She learned it from watching her mother, her mother's eyes and hands—from her mother's fear. But this was more than Charlotte understood. Watching her mother, year after year, she'd imagined the answers to this mystery of her mother's fear. How could Charlotte have known that these wrong ideas she invented were swallowed by her soul, where they took on life in her unconscious, more subtle, more hidden, more dangerous, and far more powerful because Charlotte didn't see them or understand them? She couldn't know these misshapen ideas weren't real because she didn't even know they were there.

Suddenly without warning, Charlotte said to Brian in a way that frightened him, "Please don't let me go, Brian. Don't leave me."

"Charlotte, we can't live our lives glued to each other."

"But you're all I want." He seemed so calm it scared her.

He kissed her fingers and said, "Charlotte, forgive me if I sound harsh or didactic but you must never say such a thing. I can't be your life. No one can."

"But I can't let you go now. Will I ever see you?"

"Charlotte, listen. Someone once said, 'For it is great to give up one's desire, but it is greater still to hold fast to it after having given it up.'"

"Who said that?"

"Kierkegaard. He wrote it."

"Who's Kierkegaard?"

"A Danish philosopher."

"But what has he got to do with us?"

"Well, when men write their thoughts, their hearts, it has to do with all of us."

"But it doesn't make any sense."

"I know. Sometimes what's true doesn't make sense. But if you think on it, read his book, wait, maybe it will."

"Where did he write it?"

"In *Fear and Trembling.*"

"Oh, Brian, if you leave me—"

"I'm going to leave you."

"But not forever . . ."

"No, not forever," he said. "For a year."

"What?"

"I'll be in England and if things work out, and if you want to, you'll come and stay with me at Christmas and Easter."

"Devon—the other school?"

"Yes." Charlotte fell quiet for a long time. She knew what trouble her father could make. "Brian, listen. If you leave, when you leave, I'll kiss you a hundred times a day in my mind, from my heart. Anywhere you let me put my lips, or anywhere I can think of putting them—and I know your body now and where you like to be kissed—there I'll kiss you. Anywhere you are, anywhere you go, Haddam, English class, the drive home, swimming in the cove, England; if you think of me I'll be kissing some part of you. And at night, oh, at night, you can be *sure*. I'll listen for my owl. Even if he isn't there, I'll hear him and he'll carry my kisses all the way across the sky, over the sea, through the clouds, down through the distant branches of the trees and leaves in Devon, and in your window. You must always leave your window open for my kisses and believe in me."

"You've got to believe in me, too. I didn't come to this school looking for love and certainly not for the love of a student. I'm stunned and frightened, sometimes, and . . . "

"And what?"

"I was going to say guilty, and yes, maybe a little guilty, but I don't feel ashamed."

"You can't be ashamed of what's authentic, Brian."

"I know." And she started kissing him again in the dark, warm, blue light from the moon. She was kissing him where she hadn't before, and he mumbled in delight, "What are you doing?"

"What you do," she whispered and said no more, but moved over him, her limbs twisting and rubbing against him. He noticed new things about her, how supple she was, how thin her wrists were, and how heavy and warm her hair on his skin. They drifted back and forth on the strange bed like the last small waves of high tide, and Brian and Charlotte both knew these were leaving kisses, full of hunger, kisses of remembering and reassuring. These kisses hurt. Even the little ones.

A little before dawn, Charlotte and Brian were awake, wrapped in each other's arms and whispering thoughts, when Charlotte said, "Shhhh . . . listen. A screech owl."

Brian was quiet and heard the high whistle of the owl's quivered call. Charlotte jumped up and went to the window and pushed it open slowly. Signaling him to come, she said, "Listen . . . it's not one, it's two. They're talking to each other. This is amazing." They stood together for long minutes, motionless. Then there was a third sound, different, in between the screech owls. Charlotte recognized the low, mournful hoot drifting in from some far distant tree and she felt goose bumps on the back of her neck. "Brian, that's a great horned owl. He's joining in the conversation. I've never heard anything like this. Three owls. What could they be saying?"

Brian didn't answer but looked at her and felt for a minute that she wasn't even aware that he was there. "Maybe they're saying good-bye to you, Charlotte. You *are* their very good friend."

She looked up at him, "What a nice thing to say."

"What a nice thing to be."

"It's like a little gift, isn't it? And they don't even know." And they got back under the covers and listened until it was quiet again and light started to overcome the dark.

Charlotte said, "Brian, I have a present for you."

"A present?"

"I found a poem."

He sat up. "Where?"

"E. E. Cummings."

"I mean where is it?"

She pulled him back down. "It's in my head."

He smiled a smile of such pleasure that it seared and healed her heart at the same time. "May I have it?"

"Yes, lie back. I'm going to cover you like a blanket so I can tell if you laugh."

"I won't. This isn't funny."

She aligned herself on top of him as she had before, and crossed her arms on his chest. "I think it's a sonnet." She put her hand over her eyes, saying it in her head one more time, and thought to herself, God, let me get through this without forgetting. And she looked up at him:

> *it is so long since my heart has been with yours*
>
> *shut by our mingling arms through*
> *a darkness where new lights begin and*
> *increase,*
> *since your mind has walked into*
> *my kiss as a stranger*
> *into the streets and colours of a town—*
> *that i have perhaps forgotten*
> *how, always(from*
> *these hurrying crudities*

of blood and flesh)Love
coins His most gradual gesture

and whittles life to eternity

—after which our separating selves become museums
filled with skilfully stuffed memories

He opened his eyes. "Thank you . . . but it's a little troubling."

"I know . . . fear and trembling. I like the line about your mind walking 'into my kiss as a stranger.' That's our story. That's how it started."

"Let's sleep a little more," he said.

In the morning, as they had planned, Brian took Charlotte to the early train that went to New York, then she'd take a cab to Penn Station and get the train to Washington. They'd decided it wasn't wise for him to drive her. Charlotte looked younger than usual with her hair down and a barrette holding her bangs back, but there was a quiet dignity in her attitude of acceptance. Brian was sorrowful and silent. The train came in slowly, as if it was in no hurry to go anywhere. They'd said their good-byes already. "Write me letters," she said. "You know how much I love your words."

"I will," and with her head down, she turned and walked away. Conductors stood around in the sun, bored with the routine, and the train expelled squirts of air from under the cars, as if it was catching its breath. Suddenly, Charlotte turned and rushed back to Brian, holding onto his arm.

"Brian, you said that night you weren't at all sure I was in your destiny. Have you made up your mind?"

As he looked at her images flooded his mind, going all the way back to her lying on the stone wall in the fog. They had a story now, even if it was not resolved, and no one could take it away. "I've made up my mind."

"And?" she said, breathless.

"I'll write you."

The conductor took his cap off, mussed his hair, and called "All aboard . . . "

Charlotte kissed Brian, her lips as light as a moth wing, but she said with her old fierceness, "I'm coming to Boston before Bryn Mawr. I love you, I need you, and somehow I'll find a way."

He smiled. "I know."

"Wait for me," she whispered, and she hurried to the train and disappeared up the steps. Brian watched the conductor step up, lean back with his hands on the rails, look to the left, look to the right, look at Brian as if he knew him from somewhere, and disappear. The train moved, gathering speed, and Brian couldn't turn away until it was out of sight.

When Brian got back to his apartment, he stared out the window at the construction site. The workers had arrived. He walked out and watched for a minute but he didn't care. It was nothing to him. And the Point seemed different, as if with Charlotte's leaving, everything had changed. The land seemed to lie now under a dense air mass that left the still reeds along the roadside drenched in fever. The leaves on the trees seemed limp and sweating and the water flat as if suddenly prostrate under a summer heat that burned off the cooling wind. He went back in, returned to his bookshelves, and started packing books into a cardboard box. Nothing fit but he had to trust. He pulled down his book of Eliot's poems and opened it. Perhaps the *Four Quartets* would offer comfort. But when he sat down at his desk, the pages fell open elsewhere—on a poem he was thoroughly conversant with. As he read what was on the page in front of him, his face was somber, his jaw slack, his spine curved oddly, like a monk reading an ancient codex after a long day, and he saw lines he didn't remember seeing before in this poem he knew so well and they spoke to him.

> *My friend, blood shaking my heart*
> *The awful daring of a moment's surrender*
> *Which an age of prudence can never retract*
> *By this, and this only, we have existed*

He closed the book, crossed his arms over it, and put his head down on his arms. He sat that way a long time. Then without looking up, he reached over, pushed the book of poems aside, and closed it. Words.

Epilogue

On Saturday morning, just outside the empty gatehouse to Flanders Point, under a white and windy sky, a car pulled over onto the grass and a man got out. He walked along the road toward the beach club with strong but oddly stiff, unsteady steps. He wore a blue and white seersucker suit and a straw boater tilted back, and he walked purposefully as if he lived there. When he reached Margaret Chase's house, he knocked and was let in. An hour later he reappeared, with his boater now set straight and low; he walked more slowly and with difficulty, as if he were under the weight of a hundred feet of ancient blue ice. Along the road that bordered the salt marsh, he paused and stared across the cove at Dovecote and the boathouse. There was a red pram tied up at the dock, tugging at its mooring. And there was man with one arm standing on the boathouse roof. In the cove, motionless as decoys, mallards floated with the tide and with the always wind. He turned off Nathan Hale Road onto Sarah Potkin Path, which took him in the opposite direction from the beach club. The path came out near the construction site, and when he saw it he abruptly stopped and stared. Red markers were painted on the trunks of a dozen towering maples with odd trunks. Criminal to take these down, he thought.

Now Charlotte's father put his hands in his pockets and stood for long minute. He took a step or two into the muddy rubble, saw the foundation was full of water, and retreated. Behind him was the Armbrusters' house. He turned and walked heavily up the steps to Brian's apartment. The driveway was empty and the venetian blinds closed. He paused a minute and didn't knock on the door. Instead he rang the Armbrusters' bell, but no one answered. After waiting, he picked his way through the narrow grassy path to the beach and stood in the sand a long time, staring out over the water or looking down at his feet like a man retracing his steps to find what he had lost. The tide was moving out. Before he left the beach he picked up a handful of smooth, speckled gray stones, and turned back to Nathan Hale. He walked slowly along, one foot in front of the other, his shoulders curved, his arms drooped. He came to the split-rail fence. He stopped and climbed through into the orchard. The apple trees had finished blooming, and brown-edged pedals drifted onto the grass. He heard the aspirant whistle of a hawk overhead, but he kept his eyes down, failing to notice the swift dark slide of the hawk's shadow across the grass ahead of him.

Making one more stop, he ducked back through the fence and walked to Windshore Road to his old house on the hill. He stood and looked at the house a long time, not moving until he looked at his watch, took off his boater, rubbed his neck, and wiped his forehead with his sleeve. The wind picked up his thinning hair and he smoothed it down, replacing his hat. He unbuttoned his shirt collar and walked back to the empty gatehouse with his head down. His gait seemed even less steady than before, as if he might sink down. Every now and then he reached into his pants pocket and absently dropped one of the small gray stones onto the sandy tarmac. Then he turned and threw the last stone as hard and far as he could, and it vanished deep in the meadow grass that grew along the road. An egret flew.

On this unknown finger of land, unspoiled, private, privileged, Jack had lost Charlotte's mother, the only woman he really loved. Charlotte, too, had lost her mother here. But for Charlotte it was different. Here, so much later, in the very same place, she found the one she loved.

And Flanders Point remains the same. The great estate across from Brian's apartment was never finished. The foundation was filled in and a damp meadow grew again and woodchucks and muskrats took up residence. Venus has touched the moon again since Charlotte and Brian were there and the Point can be found to this day untouched, unchanged, as beautiful and wild as ever. The wind brings nothing with it but the wind.